THE EMPTY THRONE

BOOK TWO
OF
THE BLACKWATER CHRONICLES

PAUL HEWER

Also by Paul Hewer

THE BLACKWATER CHRONICLES
The Wooden Crown

Published: 2025 by The Book Reality Experience,
Leschenault, Western Australia

ISBN: 978-1-923454-22-4 - Paperback
ISBN: 978-1-923454-28-6 - E-Book

Cover Design by Brittany Wilson | Brittwilsonart.com

For Linda

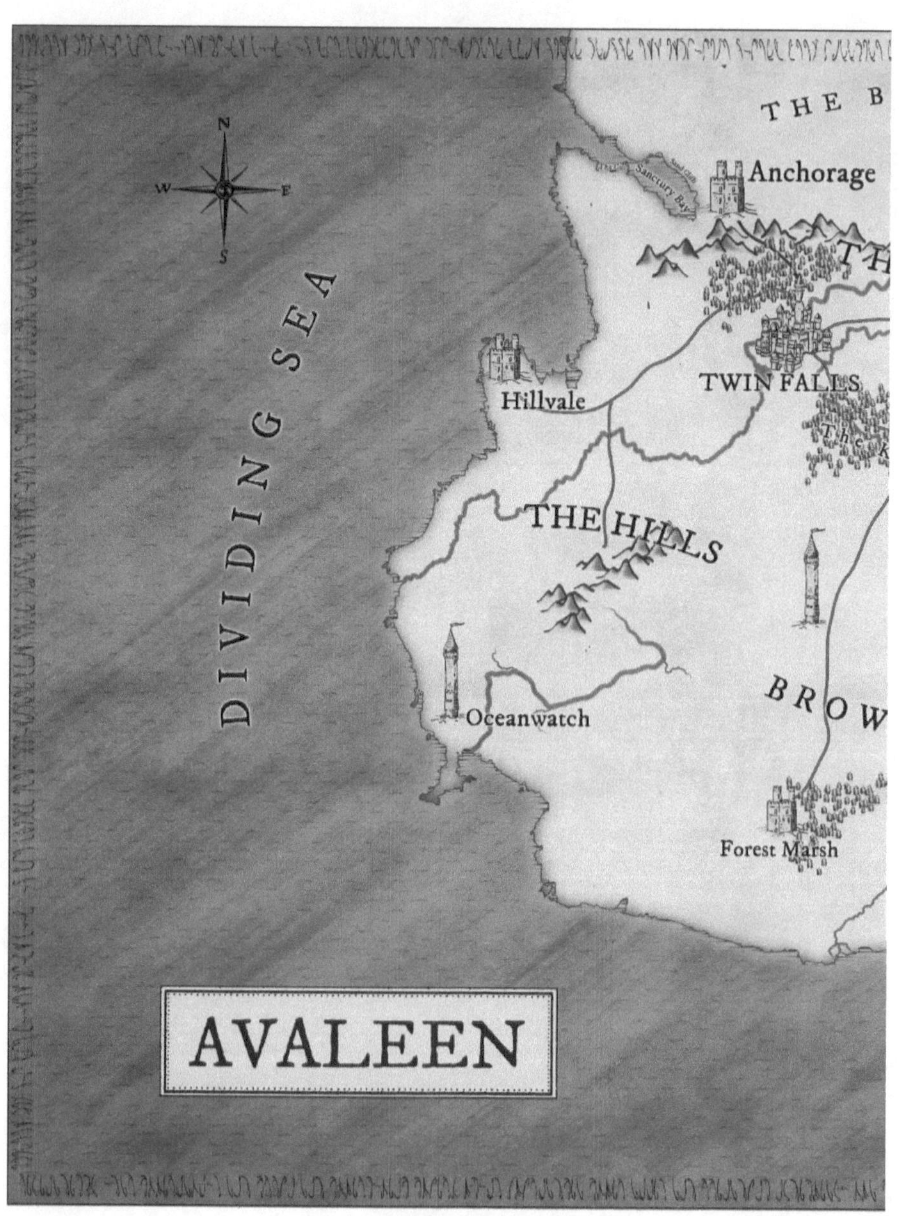
AVALEEN
DIVIDING SEA
N
S
E
W
Anchorage
Sanctuary Bay
Hillvale
TWIN FALLS
THE HILLS
Oceanwatch
Forest Marsh

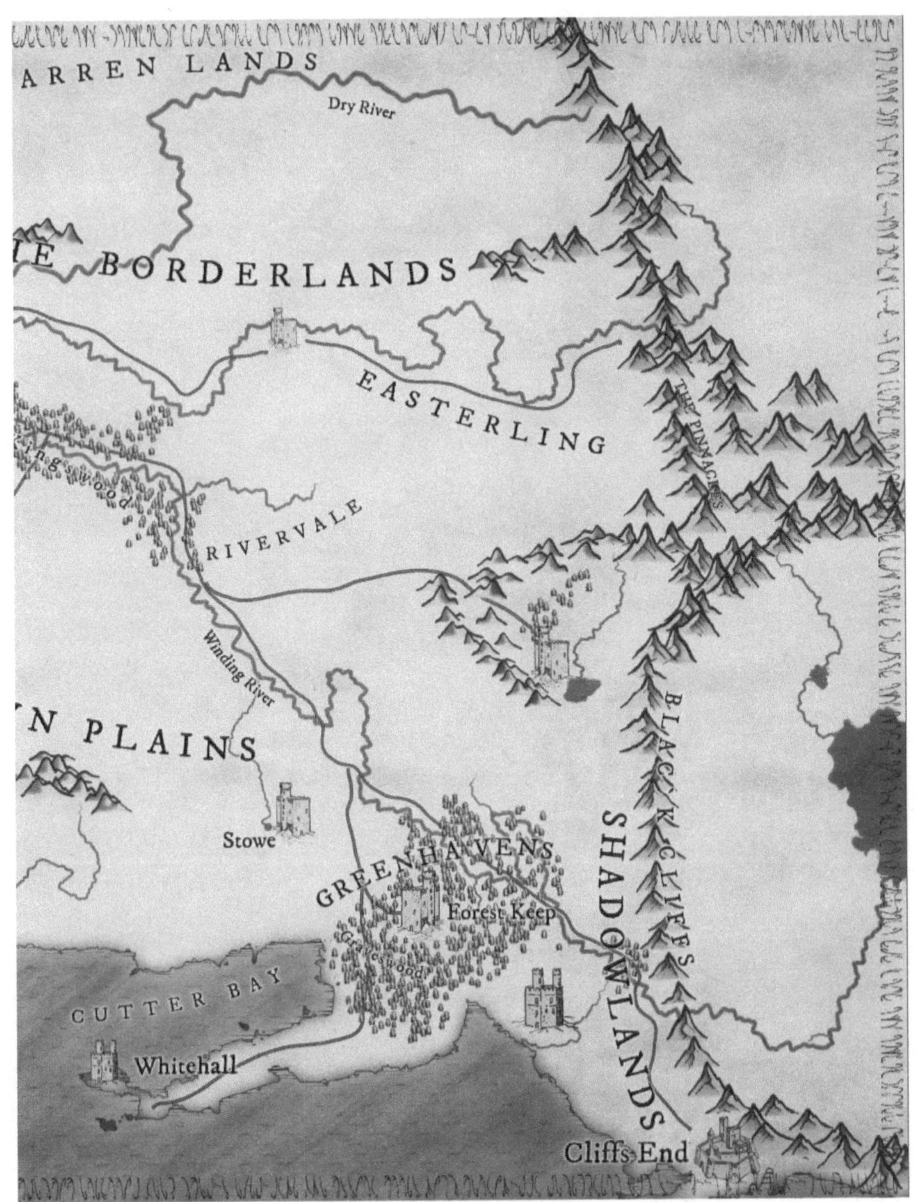
ARREN LANDS
Dry River
BORDERLANDS
EASTERLING
THE PINNACLES
RIVERVALE
Winding River
N PLAINS
Stowe
GREENHAVENS
Forest Keep
Gracewood
CUTTER BAY
Whitehall
BLACK CLIFFS
SHADOWLANDS
Cliffs End

THE GREAT HOUSES OF AVALEEN

BLACKWATER

(The Royal House)

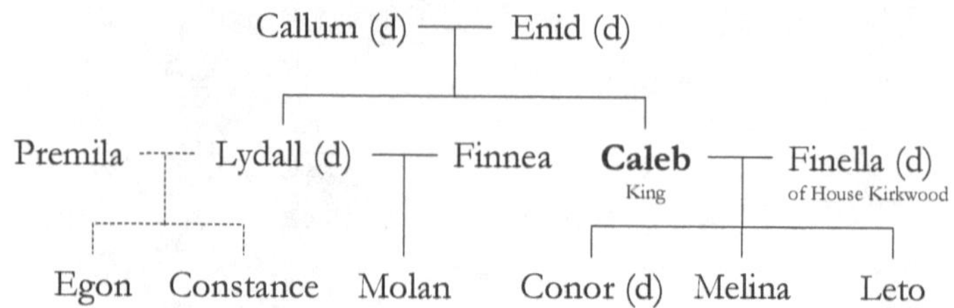

Fergus Trotter
Noble Guard

Peyton Holmguard
Knight Commander of the Noble Guard

Jacob Rivers
Companion of Leto

KIRKWOOD

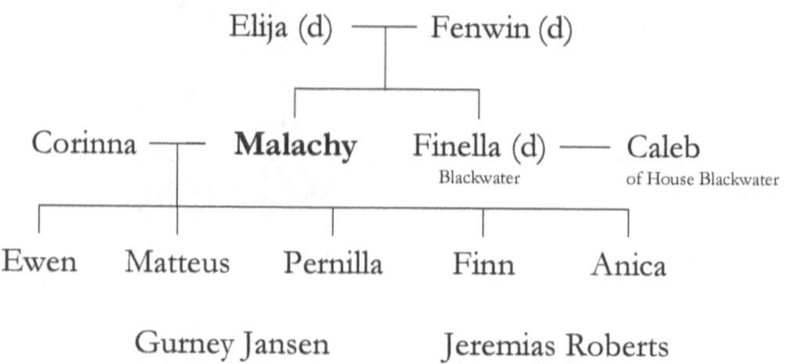

Gurney Jansen
Commander

Jeremias Roberts
Advisor

REDSTONE

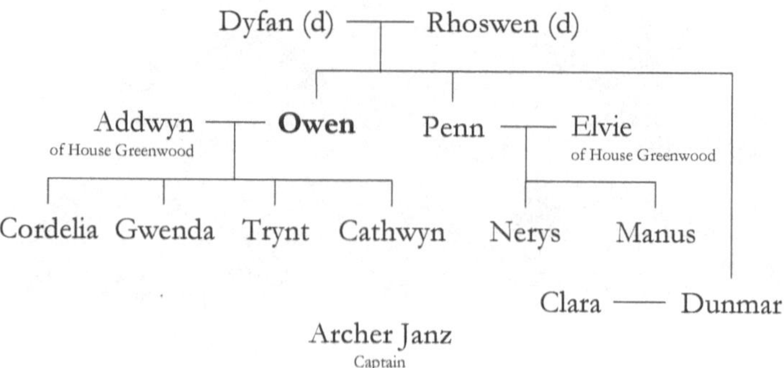

Archer Janz
Captain

The Great Houses of Avaleen

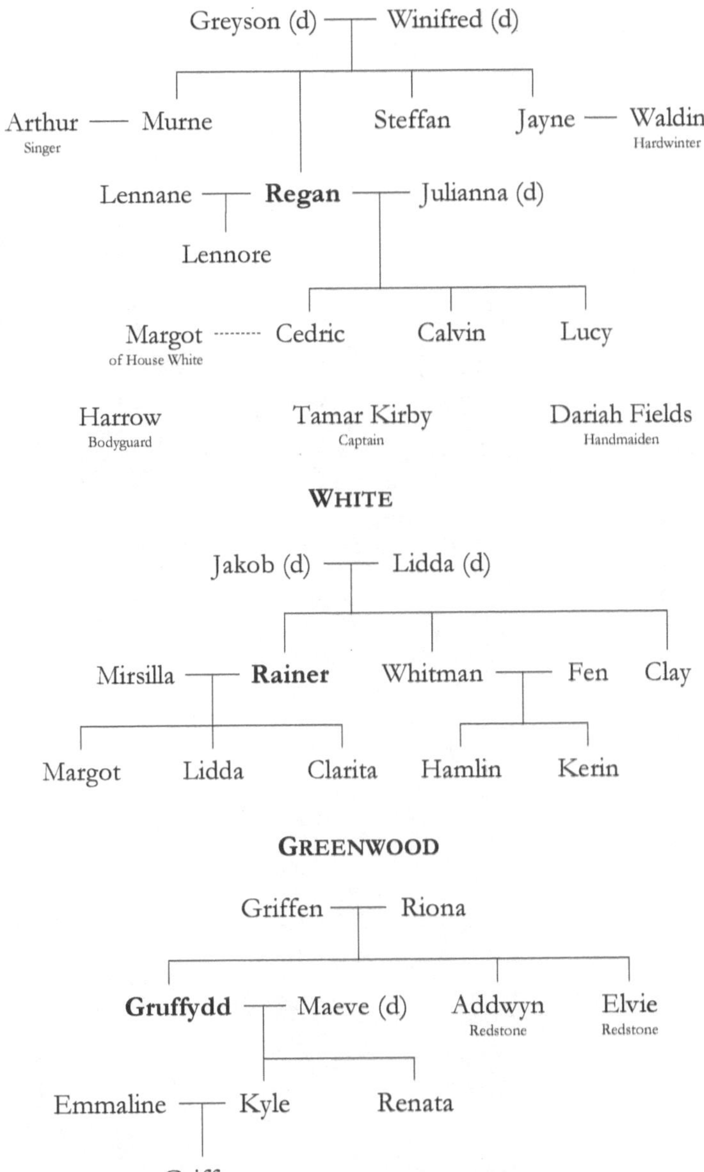

1

CONSTANCE

The flight from Sisters End had taken them from Whitehall, down the Narrows and east into the Greenhavens. For nearly two days, Sir Kyle Greenwood had led them through the Graveswood, rarely stopping except to camp or water the horses. Their progress slowed as Melina's condition worsened. On the third morning, Sir Fergus insisted they find somewhere to stay until the princess could recover.

'We should continue to Hampstead Heath,' Sir Kyle had said. 'We'll be there in two more days, three at the most.'

'No!' the Noble Guard insisted. 'Her Highness needs somewhere to rest, out of the cold.'

'She'll have her own quarters with a fire and everything she needs at Forest Keep, and we have a maester who can treat her sickness.'

'None of that will help if she dies before we get there.'

'She won't die.'

'Maybe, maybe not,' Sir Fergus said, 'but I'm not willing to take the chance, so either lead us to a suitable place, or we'll find one ourselves.'

Constance trusted Sir Fergus with her life, but the idea of them wandering about Avaleen in unfamiliar territory made her anxious.

'Please,' Constance said to the young knight. 'Her Highness hasn't been well for many weeks, and I fear for her health. We need your help.'

'I am trying to help!'

Sir Kyle glanced from Constance to the Noble Guard, who gave him a stony look. Duncan, his lieutenant, just shrugged.

The young knight threw up his arms in defeat. 'Fine! I should know better than to argue with a bloody Noble Guard.'

'Thank you,' Constance said.

Sir Kyle acknowledged her with a slight bow of his head.

'There's a place about ten miles east of here, just south of the main road,' he said. 'It's not the closest, but I know the people there. We can trust them.'

Sir Fergus nodded his agreement.

They arrived at the small village of Willow Creek, around midday. There seemed to be no tavern or inn, but before long, Sir Kyle had arranged a room for the princess in the home of one of the residents. The small room had a proper bed and a fireplace, and within an hour of their arrival, a fire had been lit, and the princess had fallen into a fitful slumber.

Constance spent most of her time watching over the princess, who slept for the rest of the day and all through the night. A tired Constance began to think they should never have left Whitehall.

'You should get some rest yourself, Lady Constance,' said Sir Fergus. 'She'll wake when she wakes, and your hovering around won't make it happen any quicker.'

'I'm trying,' she said, unable to stifle a yawn.

Constance lay on the makeshift bed on the floor and closed her eyes, but still sleep evaded her. Something always entered her mind, real or imagined, that stopped her from drifting off. When she did manage to sleep, she often woke with a start. As a result, Constance barely managed to get a few hours' sleep at night and even less during the day. Thankfully, by the third day, Melina felt well enough to take short walks, and Sir Fergus and Constance accompanied her along the edge of the small but picturesque lake.

'When are we leaving?' Melina asked.

'When you're well enough to ride, Highness,' Sir Fergus said. 'A few more days, perhaps.'

'I'm well enough now,' Melina said, her voice soft but resolute. 'Are we not still in danger?'

'Sir Kyle assures me that we're perfectly safe here.'

'If I ask Sir Kyle the same question, will he give me the same answer?' the princess asked the Noble Guard.

Constance agreed with Sir Fergus but didn't want to defy the princess's wishes. 'Just one more day. One more, then we'll be off to Hampstead Heath.'

'Yes, one more day,' the Noble Guard agreed. 'I'll advise Sir Kyle that we'll leave tomorrow morning.'

Melina glanced at them both. 'I feel I'm being conspired against, but I will accede to your recommendation.'

The princess's words contained no venom, and that she acquiesced so quickly proved to Constance that she had still not fully recovered.

Constance smiled. 'Only because we love you, Mellie. Isn't that right, Sir Fergus?'

'Err … yes,' he said.

Constance had always seen him as the strong protector who would die before allowing any harm to come to the princess or herself. She never considered that the mention of love could cause him discomfort.

'In your case, Sir Fergus, maybe it's love as one would feel for a granddaughter?' she said.

It took a few moments, but his confidence reasserted itself.

'Like a grandfather, is it? Yes, I can live with that.'

This brought a smile to Melina's face, one of the few since her father's death.

'It's good to see you smiling, Highness,' Sir Fergus added. 'Even if it is to remind me of my advanced age.'

The Noble Guard broke into a slight grin, a rare occurrence. He bowed, turned, and left the girls near the edge of the pretty lake.

'Thank you, Connie,' Melina said, 'for looking after me.'

'You've been pushing yourself too much,' said Constance, less afraid to speak her mind privately to the princess.

'I know I can be stubborn at times,' Melina said.

'You're a princess of the realm. One would argue it's your right to be stubborn.'

Both girls managed a restrained laugh.

'It is good to see you smile again,' Constance added. 'I know there isn't a whole lot to be thankful for at the moment.'

The princess grabbed Constance's hand.

'If the situation we're in has taught me anything, it's that I should appreciate what I do have because it can be taken away all too easily.'

Constance gave the princess's hand a gentle squeeze.

'We may even get Sir Fergus to smile again,' the princess added.

The approach of the Noble Guard and the young Greenhavens knight interrupted their conversation.

'We have a minor problem, Highness,' Sir Fergus said.

'What now?' the princess's smile disappeared.

'I'll let Sir Kyle explain,' the Noble Guard said, stepping back to give the young knight room.

'Highness,' the young knight bowed his head, a worried look on his face.

'I sent some men ahead to Forest Keep to inform my father of our delay. They returned at first light.'

'And?' Melina said.

'They reported at least half a dozen patrols along the main road alone. They were not from the Greenhavens.'

'Whitehall?'

Sir Kyle shook his head.

'I've had men watching the main road from Sisters End. It looks as though they're staying their side of the Steppes.'

'So, who are they?'

'We don't know.'

'What do you propose?' Sir Fergus said. 'That's the only road to Hampstead Heath, is it not?'

Constance shared the Noble Guard's concern. If they couldn't get to Forest Keep, where would they go?

'For those unfamiliar with the Greenhavens, that may be the case, but I've been travelling these lands since I was born,' said the young knight.

'We can go through the Deep Wood and avoid the roads altogether. It'll be slower, but there'll be no chance of us being seen.'

'These men patrolling your roads, how do we know there aren't more of them waiting for us when we get there?' asked Sir Fergus.

Sir Kyle did not answer at once.

'We should head southeast, straight for Millars Landing,' Sir Fergus continued. 'We can travel to Cliffs End from there. We cannot risk the princess falling into the hands of the Whites or their allies.'

'That would take ten days, if not more,' Sir Kyle said, 'and even though Her Highness is well enough to make it to Forest Keep, travelling to Millars Landing could kill her.'

'*Now* you're concerned for her well-being?' Sir Fergus said to the young knight.

Sir Kyle seemed offended. 'The safety and well-being of the princess has always been my top priority, sir.'

'I don't think –' the Noble Guard began, but Melina interrupted the argument.

'Sir Fergus, Sir Kyle,' she said. 'If we were to approach Hampstead Heath through the forest, would it be possible to ascertain if it would be safe to enter Forest Keep without making ourselves known?'

'We could stand twenty yards from the forest edge and not be seen,' Sir Kyle said. 'The advantage would be with us, Highness.'

Constance just wanted somewhere safe and warm, free from pursuit and worry, where Melina could recover properly and get strong again.

The princess glanced at her before looking up at Sir Fergus. 'We'll head to Forest Keep as Sir Kyle has suggested.'

The Noble Guard seemed about to protest, but a raised hand from Melina silenced him.

'If there's any sign of danger,' she said, 'or Sir Fergus believes we cannot safely enter the keep, then we will make for the Shadowlands.'

'As you wish, Highness,' Sir Kyle nodded. 'I'll prepare for our departure.'

They set out mid-morning the following day, led by Sir Kyle and his two scouts, with Constance, Melina and Sir Fergus following. Three more soldiers guarded the rear. They entered the Deep Wood, where the thick forest canopy cast a perpetual shadow on everything. Constance had started out riding beside the princess, but the closeness of the trees and the dense undergrowth that covered their path eventually forced them to ride in single file. Constance often turned in her saddle to check on Melina, relieved that she seemed to be holding up. Being restricted to a walking pace certainly helped.

That night, they camped on the forest floor. Thankfully, the forest ceiling that hid the sunlight during the day also kept out some of the chills of the night. Exhausted, Constance hoped that Forest Keep would be their final destination.

'This is the longest I've been away from my little boy since he was born,' Sir Kyle lamented as they sat around the campfire.

'What's his name?' asked Constance.

'Griffen, after his great-grandfather,' he said proudly. 'He's a smart boy, already wielding his toy sword like he was born to it.'

'And terrorising the servants like his father did, from what I hear,' Sergeant Hudson added.

Sergeant Elias Hudson sat opposite Constance. She liked the old scout. He told stories and joked with everyone, including Constance and Melina. However, he avoided any verbal sparring with Sir Fergus.

Elias held his hand three feet above the ground. 'When he was small, he used to stick the servants with his toy sword, including my mother.'

'It was just wood,' Sir Kyle protested with a smile, 'and quite blunt.'

'My mother used to come home with scratches all up and down her legs,' Elias continued with his story. 'Sir Kyle was quite the horrid child when you think about it.'

Constance and Melina laughed.

'That's a bit harsh, Eli.'

'Thankfully, he grew out of it,' Elias gestured towards Sir Kyle, 'and is now the fine young knight you see before you today.'

'Yes, well, Emmaline is managing to keep Griffen under some semblance of control. Apparently, I give him too much leeway,' the young Greenhavens knight shrugged.

'My father did the same thing with Leto,' the princess said. 'He was quite the troublesome child, especially when he and Jacob got together. I'm certain you were an angel compared to him, Sir Kyle.'

For a few moments, no-one spoke after Melina mentioned both her father and her missing brother. Aside from a tinge of sadness in her voice, there weren't any overt signs of distress.

'You are most kind, Highness,' Sir Kyle said, breaking the silence, 'though I'm sure the Sergeant is overstating my horridness.'

For the next two days, they trudged through the forest on foot, leading their horses through the green maze, vines, fallen branches, and ever-thicker undergrowth impeding their progress. At times, Constance had the impression the guides had become lost, but they finally came across a small watercourse. It led to a log cabin where they set up camp in the neighbouring clearing.

'I apologise for the rather erratic path,' Sir Kyle said. 'Even the best trackers have trouble navigating the Deep Wood. Eli has been walking these forests for nearly thirty years and still gets lost occasionally.'

'How far to Hampstead Heath?' Sir Fergus enquired.

'We use this as a base for hunting in these parts,' Sergeant Hudson said, pointing to the nearby brook. 'Just follow the stream, and you'll be at Forest Keep in no time.'

'We'll be there by mid-morning,' said Lieutenant Foster.

'You may sleep in the cabin, Highness,' Sir Kyle said. 'But there's no hearth, so it may be warmer out here by the fire.'

Constance liked the idea of the cabin, away from the forest creatures, large and small, but she would sleep wherever the princess decided.

'This is your territory, Sir Kyle. Whatever you think is best,' Melina said, yawning.

They slept by the campfire again. It could have been fatigue or the relief at the possibility of their journey being nearly over, but Constance slept deeply that night, having to be woken by Sir Fergus long after dawn. As a result, there was a delay in getting Melina ready to travel.

It wasn't long before they arrived at their destination. As they neared the forest edge, Sir Kyle sent some of his men to scout ahead. They left the horses in a small clearing half a mile downstream and proceeded on foot, following the waterway to the forest's edge.

Constance could now see the castle through the trees. It sat atop a hill in a large clearing, its outer walls only a hundred yards from where they hid.

'Look, Mellie. We're here,' Constance whispered, and looked up to Sir Fergus, who stared out at the castle. 'How long before we can go in?'

'When Sir Kyle's men return, and I'm satisfied that it's safe,' the Noble Guard said, and turned to the young Greenhavens knight who also surveyed the keep. 'The scouts have not yet returned. Why?'

'I don't know,' Sir Kyle said, peering out of the woods. 'Everything seems fine from here, but this is the back of the castle. We should move around to the northern side. We'll see more from there.'

'What about your scouts?' Sir Fergus repeated.

'They'll return soon.'

They followed the knight and the rest of his men back into the forest fifty yards before they turned and made their way around to the northern side of the keep. This time, they got closer to the edge of the woods, finding a fallen tree with a trunk so wide that they could all stand behind it and remain hidden.

Constance moved a few yards to the left and peered out. She could only see the northern wall and the beginnings of the town of Hampstead Heath to the west.

'Sir Kyle?' the Noble Guard tried to get the young knight's attention.

Sir Fergus stepped closer, and Sir Kyle pointed east.

'What's wrong?' Melina said. 'I can't see a thing.'

Constance gazed in the direction that Sir Kyle had pointed. Beyond Hampstead Heath, at the bottom of the valley, they could see a cluster of tents, men and horses. Flags flew, but she couldn't make them out.

'Who are they?' Sir Fergus said, but the young knight ignored him again.

Constance stifled a scream as two Greenhavens soldiers appeared out of the forest like wraiths. Sergeant Elias had one of the scouts sent out earlier that day with him. The scout sounded out of breath.

'My lord,' the Sergeant said. 'Villy has returned.'

That got Sir Kyle's attention, and he turned towards the two men. 'Report!'

'They have control of the keep, my lord,' Villy said.

'Who's they?'

'I saw banners for House Greythorpe and … … ' the scout paused.

'And who?'

Villy looked confused. 'I saw banners of the King, but I thought the King was dead?'

'He is,' Sir Fergus said. 'They're most likely banners of the Steward.'

'It's bad enough the Greythorpes are here,' said Sir Kyle, 'but why take over the keep if they're on the Steward's business?'

'I'm sure we all know why they're here, and the Greythorpes have never been a friend of Lord Owen or his allies,' Sir Fergus said grimly.

The Greenhavens knight glanced at Melina, who had been listening to the exchange. 'My father won't give us up, not even to the Steward.'

'But to take control of the keep, it doesn't make sense,' Sir Fergus said. 'That's very provocative, not like Lord Regan at all.'

'What do we do now?' Melina said.

'Whatever the actual situation is in Forest Keep, it's not safe.'

'I can't argue with you there,' Sir Kyle agreed.

'We should go before they learn of our whereabouts,' Sir Fergus urged.

'They may already know,' Villy said.

All eyes turned to the scout.

'Villy, speak quickly!' Sir Kyle commanded.

'They … they have Otto, my lord.'

Villy's gaze dropped to the forest floor.

Sir Kyle rubbed his temple for a few moments. 'Otto's a tough nut. He wouldn't have given away our plans, not yet anyway.'

'They'll still know we're close, so we should go now,' Sir Fergus said. 'That's what you agreed, Sir Kyle.'

'Yes … yes, you're right,' the young knight said.

Duncan came running over. 'My lord! Something's happening.'

Sir Kyle turned back towards the castle.

'The northeast tower,' the Lieutenant said.

'What the … ' Sir Kyle's voice trailed off.

'What is it?' Constance moved forward and tried to focus on the closest tower.

'No … no, no,' the young knight murmured. 'No … don't!'

A man stood at the top of the tower right at the edge of the battlements. Constance gasped as someone shoved the man from the tower. He fell in silence, the only sound being a faint thump as his body hit the ground two hundred feet below.

'No!' Sir Kyle whimpered.

The nearby soldiers cursed as Constance stared at the place where the body had landed.

'Who … who was that?' Melina asked.

'That … was Lord Gruffydd,' Sergeant Elias replied, his face grim.

Sir Kyle leaned against a tree, his head bowed.

'He was killed because of me?' The princess's voice expressed her anxiety.

'The reason for this heinous act is immaterial,' Sir Fergus said.

'Of course, it's about her!' Duncan said, his face red with anger.

The Noble Guard turned on the Lieutenant. 'Silence that mouth of yours!'

Duncan stood his ground. 'I don't answer to you! The Lord of Forest Keep gives me orders, and now he's dead.'

The Noble Guard pointed at Sir Kyle, who remained slumped against the tree. 'Your lord is now here. Sir Kyle is now responsible for everyone in the Greenhavens, not just your band of merry men.'

'Do you think we give a shit about what happens to her?' the Lieutenant spat. 'The capitol is over four hundred miles away. They can fight amongst themselves and kill each other for all I care. I say we hand her over to the Greythorpes and be done with it.'

Constance heard murmurs of agreement from some nearby soldiers.

'You speak treason, Lieutenant,' Sir Fergus placed his hand on the pommel of his sword. 'I'd advise you to choose your next words carefully.'

Constance stood protectively in front of the princess. 'You will not give Her Highness to them.'

'I'll do whatever my Lord commands, girl,' Duncan growled.

Lieutenant Foster had been quite amiable with Constance and Melina during their journey from Sisters End. Now, he wanted to hand the princess to their enemies without a second thought.

'Coward!' Constance said, the insult flying off her tongue before she knew what happened, but she wouldn't back down. 'You'll have to kill me before I'll let you touch her.'

Duncan could easily brush her aside if he wanted, but she had to try and protect the princess as best she could.

'You little bitch,' Duncan only made one step towards her before Sir Fergus had whipped out his sword and held it to his neck.

'I thought you were smarter than that,' the Noble Guard said.

'Lieutenant!'

Everyone except Duncan and Sir Fergus turned at Sir Kyle's voice.

'Duncan, stand back.'

'But my –' Duncan started, but Sir Kyle silenced him.

'We'll not squabble amongst ourselves,' the young lord said.

The Lieutenant stepped back, away from the blade of the Noble Guard. 'I apologise, my lord. I only want what's best for us.'

'I know,' Kyle said as he approached Duncan and Sir Fergus.

Sir Fergus sheathed his sword and faced the young knight, now Lord of the Greenhavens. 'You have my condolences, but we must leave now.'

'We can't just leave –'

'Duncan! I understand that –' Sir Kyle cut short Lieutenant Foster's protest but was interrupted.

'My lord!' Sergeant Hudson called out and pointed towards the keep.

Constance and everyone else looked back at the tower where a woman had now appeared, pushed forward by her captors.

'The absolute bastards!' Lieutenant Foster exclaimed.

'Be silent!' Sir Kyle commanded.

'– out there somewhere,' a gruff voice from the keep could be heard. 'The death of your father is on his head. He was a stubborn fool.' The voice was raised now, carrying across the space from the keep.

Constance didn't recognise the voice that continued to taunt the young knight.

'However, any harm to your wife will be on yours if you don't produce the princess.'

The Lady Emmaline teetered on the edge of the battlements.

'You cannot accede to their demands,' Sir Fergus said. 'Your father died for his beliefs. Don't let his death be for naught.'

'Do not lecture me about what my father did or did not believe!' Sir Kyle said, unable to hide his torment.

'I will not allow you to give Her Highness to these animals,' Sir Fergus steeled himself.

'I'm not a patient man, Sir Kyle,' the voice from the keep warned. 'Or should I say, Lord Kyle?'

Constance thought she heard faint laughter coming from the battlements. Sir Fergus stepped back and leaned close to her.

'Be ready to run,' he said, his voice low. 'Our alliance with House Greenwood may be at an end.'

Constance glanced at Sir Fergus, her face a mask of worry, but she nodded.

The Noble Guard moved and faced Sir Kyle and the Greenhavens soldiers, with Constance and Melina now at his back. Constance moved closer to the princess. 'Can you run, Mellie?' she whispered.

Constance doubted Melina's ability to run for any distance, but they may not have a choice. The princess had tears in her eyes, but she nodded her readiness. Constance gave her an encouraging smile and squeezed her hand.

Sir Fergus would defend the princess with his life, but Constance hoped the new Lord of Forest Keep would see sense.

'Don't give in, my love,' Lady Emmaline shouted from the tower.

Constance could hear the defiance in her voice.

'Em … ' Sir Kyle muttered.

There was a collective gasp as someone pushed the young woman from the tower, her dress fluttering in the breeze as she fell. Constance turned away, but the sickening dull thud as the woman's body hit the ground still reached them. The young knight sunk to his knees and whimpered.

'It's time for us to go,' Sir Fergus said, not bothering to hide his intentions.

Most of the remaining soldiers turned towards him, some drawing their weapons.

'You'll stay here until the Lord of these lands gives you leave,' Duncan stepped forward, keeping a respectful distance from the Noble Guard.

'You forget yourself, Lieutenant,' Sir Fergus again drew his sword against Lieutenant Foster. 'Her Highness will go where she pleases.'

For a few moments, no-one moved, but Sir Kyle stood and turned towards them, his face wet with tears. Constance bit her lip in anticipation.

'Put away your blades,' he said.

Still, not a soul moved.

'Now!' his tone hardened.

Sir Fergus slid his weapon back into its scabbard only after the Greenhavens soldiers had done the same.

'There'll be no fighting between us,' Sir Kyle said.

Constance realised she had been holding her breath and slowly let it out.

'Then let's leave before we're discovered,' Sir Fergus pleaded.

'You may leave,' Sir Kyle said, 'but I won't be going with you.'

Constance didn't understand.

'Two of my men will accompany you to the Shadowlands to act as guides through the Deep Wood,' Sir Kyle turned to his men, who had gathered in a small group. 'Eli, Villy, you will escort Her Highness and her companions to Millars Landing.'

'My lord, I humbly request you send someone else,' Sergeant Hudson said. 'My place is by your side, as it has been since you came of age.'

'Your place is where I want it to be,' Sir Kyle snapped.

His harsh tone surprised Elias. 'Err … yes, my lord.'

'I need someone I can trust to carry the message of our plight to my uncle and to request assistance,' the young lord's voice softened.

Eli accepted his new orders with a nod and turned to the scout. 'Villy, get ready to move out.'

'You should come with us,' Melina said, approaching Sir Kyle.

'No, Your Highness. As Sir Fergus pointed out, I am now the Lord of the Greenhavens. I will not desert my people.'

'What will you do?'

'I don't know. I just know I cannot abandon them –' Sir Kyle stopped as the gruff voice again penetrated the forest's edge.

'I'm impressed, young lord.'

Everyone turned towards the voice. A man had climbed onto the battlements where Lord Gruffydd and Lady Emmaline had previously stood. However, this time, the man who had been taunting them stepped up to the edge of the wall.

'Let's see how strong your resolve is now.'

Constance felt sick when she finally recognised what Sir Kyle's tormentor now held. He held a tiny infant by the leg, its cries easily carried to where Constance hid.

'Please,' Sir Kyle stepped closer to the edge of the trees. 'Not my boy. No … no … no!'

Sir Fergus reached for the young knight but he burst out of the trees and raced towards the keep, pleading for his son's life.

'Shit!' Duncan shouted and surged out of the trees after him, along with most of the other Greenhaven's soldiers.

'Damn!' Sir Fergus said, whirling to Constance and Melina. 'Back to the horses, now!'

Constance didn't question the Noble Guard and fled into the forest. The princess had already started running, but she quickly caught up to her and slowed.

'Keep going!' Sir Fergus yelled.

Constance obeyed and bolted, running as fast as her legs would allow. She glanced back and saw the Noble Guard scoop the princess up in his arms without slowing.

They eventually reached the small clearing near the stream where they'd left the horses. Sir Fergus lifted the princess onto one of them and helped Constance onto hers. The rustling of trees and breaking twigs alerted them to someone approaching fast through the trees behind them. Sir Fergus stepped away from the horses and drew his sword. Elias and Villy spilled out of the forest into the clearing.

'He's dead. The bastards shot him as he … ' the Sergeant's voice broke. 'They … they shot him with a dozen arrows … he tried to catch Master Griffen! The fucking animals!'

'The gods help us,' Sir Fergus groaned. 'And the others?'

'I don't know,' Elias said. 'Once Lord Kyle fell, I grabbed Villy, and we ran. They're probably dead, too.'

'Were you followed?'

'Just before we ran, a bunch of riders came out of the main gate and headed this way,' Villy said.

'Then mount up before they figure out where we are,' Sir Fergus said and reached for the reins of his horse.

Villy stared upstream for a few moments. 'It's too late. I can hear them.'

'How many?' Elias said.

'A dozen or more,' the scout said.

'Villy, take Her Highness and Lady Constance to the cabin,' Sir Fergus said. 'But stay hidden in the woods until one of us gets there.'

A surprised Villy glanced at Elias for confirmation.

'Go,' the Sergeant said, and the scout hauled himself onto his horse.

'What are you going to do?' Melina said.

'Whatever we can, Highness,' Sir Fergus climbed into the saddle but turned his horse towards the keep. 'We'll see you both soon.'

Constance wanted to say something to the Noble Guard but couldn't find the words. He sounded confident they would prevail, but she understood nothing could be certain, not anymore.

'Lady Constance, you go first,' Villy said. 'I'll guard the rear.'

She tugged on her reins and kicked the horse with her heels. Melina couldn't handle a gallop, so Constance urged her horse to a slow canter. She turned her head as she followed the bend in the waterway and glimpsed Sir Fergus and Sergeant Hudson riding upstream, weapons out. Constance felt a lump rise in her throat. She may never see him again. He had always treated her like a lady.

They arrived at the cabin, but Villy led them to a place fifty yards further on amongst the trees. They dismounted and settled down to wait for Sir Fergus and Elias. Constance and Melina sat on an old stump while Villy climbed a nearby tree and perched on a low-hanging branch.

'I can see more from up here,' he explained.

After a while, he climbed down. 'I'm just going to take a look around.'

'Is it safe?' Constance said. 'Sir Fergus said to stay in the woods.'

'I'm a scout. It's what I do.'

'Of course,' she said, feeling foolish.

'Don't worry, I won't be long.'

Villy disappeared into the forest, leaving Constance and Melina with the horses. They waited in silence.

An hour passed, and the scout had not yet returned.

'He promised he wouldn't be long,' Melina eventually said.

'He'll return soon,' Constance said, trying to sound optimistic.

The light began to fade, and Constance began to feel the cold. She glanced at Melina, who sat, hugging her knees to her chest, shivering.

'We should go to the cabin,' Constance said.

The princess looked up. 'Sir Fergus hasn't come.'

No, he hadn't, and neither had Sergeant Hudson. Villy had not returned either. They had to look out for themselves now.

'We'll freeze if we stay out here,' Constance said. 'I … I don't think Sir Fergus is coming.'

'But he said he would,' Melina said and began to cry.

Constance shuffled across to the princess, embraced her, and fought back tears of her own. She had to be strong.

'Let's get you inside.'

Melina offered no resistance as Constance helped her up and led her towards the clearing.

'I think I remember Elias saying there were some blankets in one of the chests, and I'll build a fire.'

It had been a long while since Constance had needed to light a fire outside of a hearth, but it shouldn't be too difficult. She glanced around as they approached the rear of the cabin. Only the sound of running water and the forest could be heard. Constance decided to settle the princess inside the cabin before retrieving the horses.

Constance and Melina entered the clearing and froze. Panic rose in her as she stared at Villy. He lay on the ground near the remnants of last night's campfire. Arrows protruded from his chest and neck.

'So predictable.'

Constance and Melina squealed as a man stepped out of the trees at the opposite edge of the clearing. He held a small crossbow in one hand, pointed at Constance, and a long dagger in the other.

He approached them with a swagger. 'Don't try to run, or you'll end up like him.'

Even from this distance, Constance could see the revolting scar across his face. Her heart raced. Terrified, she knew she needed to do something now, but what?

The man with the scar got closer.

'How dare you point that thing at me!' she blurted out with as much bravado as she could muster. 'Don't you know who I am? I'm a princess of the realm, and you have no right to –'

'Don't get all high and mighty with me,' the man cut her off and kept walking towards them. 'I've had enough of lords and ladies trying to tell me what to do.'

'But I –,' Melina began, but Constance turned on her.

'Be silent!'

She didn't know what this man had planned for the princess, but it would not be good. Constance turned back to the grizzled soldier who stood only a few steps away.

'Leave us be and … and I'll forget this ever happened.'

'Don't make this harder on yourself.'

His gruff voice frightened her.

Constance seemed to have convinced him she was the princess, a small victory, as long as Melina kept quiet.

'Hurry up and get it over with then,' Constance said with false bravado. 'Kill me, or are you going to rape me first?'

'I've never had a princess before,' he said, ogling her for a moment. 'But the Steward has plans for you, and he wants you taken back to the capitol, unspoiled.'

Her heart still pounded in her chest despite the relief that they didn't want Melina dead. Constance would endure the journey back to Twin Falls, but she didn't want to contemplate what would happen once they discovered her deception. For now, at least, she wouldn't be killed or molested.

'Hold out your hands,' he ordered.

She complied. He hung the crossbow on his belt and retrieved some twine.

'Don't try anything smart, or I'll cut you,' he waved the dagger inches from her face.

She nodded, and he bound her wrists together. She let out a whimper when he pulled it tight. He chuckled and cut off the excess twine.

'Turn around.'

She did as ordered and glanced at Melina, who again had tears rolling down her face. This time, she wasn't crying for herself, but for the sacrifice Constance had made. She could see it in Melina's eyes.

'It'll be alright,' she said and gave Melina a weak smile as her captor bound her ankles, managing not to yelp as he tightened the binding.

He spun her around and shook his head in disgust. 'You look like a fucking slum rat.'

Neither of them had bathed since before they had left Sisters End, and Constance knew she didn't look very presentable in the clothes she wore and everything they'd been through.

The man looked across to Melina. 'And what's wrong with you?'

'My handmaiden has not been well of late,' Constance said.

'I'm not carting a sick girl to the capitol,' he said.

Constance thanked the gods, sure the princess could survive long enough out here until help arrived.

An instant later, he flashed his dagger across Melina's neck.

Constance opened her mouth to scream, but nothing came out. Her captor picked her up, slung her over his shoulder, and started across the clearing.

She could hardly breathe.

Melina stood still. Her pale, gaunt features had turned a sickly shade of white. She reached out towards Constance as the thin red line across her throat widened. The trickle of blood turned into a flood, her eyes rolled back into her head, and she collapsed onto the forest floor.

Constance's captor carted her into the woods and hoisted her over the back of a horse. The horse began to move under her, but she didn't even try to hold on, not caring if she fell. She closed her eyes and cried slow, deep sobs.

Constance had only wanted to protect Melina from harm. Why had she pretended to be the princess? She had reconciled herself with the sacrifice she made, but it turned out all for nothing. Melina, her cousin, her best friend, her beautiful princess, was dead. It should have been her.

'Well, look at this,' her captor said with mild surprise.

Constance only realised the horse had come to a halt when the soldier pulled her from the horse and unceremoniously dumped her on the ground, burying her face in the wet dirt that skirted the edge of the stream.

'I'll be taking Her Highness with me now,' a familiar voice said.

Constance rolled over in the mud and looked upstream. Sir Fergus! He stood there, tall and fearsome, his sword at the ready.

'I don't think so,' her captor said, seemingly unconcerned that he faced a Noble Guard.

'I know you,' the Noble Guard said. 'You're Steffan Greythorpe's dog, nothing but a thug and an assassin.'

'I'm on the Steward's business now,' the scarred soldier replied. 'So, get the fuck out of my way.'

'I don't think so,' the Noble Guard echoed the soldier's words as he approached.

He sported a slight limp.

'Good,' the man snorted. 'I've already killed three lords and a lady today. A Noble Guard will top it off just nicely.'

'He killed … ' Constance lay on her side in the mud and tried to shout. 'He killed her!'

'Lady Constance?' he said with a flicker of surprise.

‘I tried to protect her. I did … ’ her voice faded as she again descended into uncontrolled sobbing.

Melina’s murderer glanced back at Constance and laughed. ‘Lady, huh? Well, that little trick backfired, didn’t it?’

‘You have nothing to take back to your master,’ the Noble Guard said, ‘so leave.’

‘It looks like we’ve both failed our duties today, old man,’ the soldier said, drawing his sword. ‘Only you won’t live to regret it.’

Constance tried to stand but slipped in the mud as the men circled each other, each taking stock of their opponent.

‘No-one will know of my failure, but everyone will know of yours,’ he taunted. ‘I’ll make sure of that.’

She picked at the ties around her ankles without success.

‘The final failure of the last Noble Guard,’ her captor continued to goad Sir Fergus.

Sir Fergus drew his dagger. Blood dribbled down his side from under his arm. He tossed the blade towards her. It landed a few yards away.

‘Cut yourself free,’ he said, not taking his eyes from his opponent, ‘then hide in the trees and don’t come out.’

The soldier lunged at the Noble Guard, but he blocked the attack, retreating a few steps. Constance scrambled to the dagger and picked it up with her bound hands. She began to cut at the binding on her ankles. She grimaced as she sliced the skin of her leg but didn’t stop hacking at the bindings. Her lower legs had become slick with blood, but Constance kept cutting. The dagger too became slippery, but eventually, the bindings broke apart, and she scrambled to her feet.

Constance glanced up at the two men fighting not twenty yards from her. Sir Fergus remained on the defensive, his movements stymied by his injuries. She jammed the dagger's hilt between her knees and started to cut the bonds around her wrists. She rubbed the twine binding her wrists up and down the upturned blade, but the dagger kept slipping from between her knees. She righted it and clamped her knees together even harder. Constance rubbed her bonds against the blade again. This time, the bonds began to fray. She kept at it, up and down, and suddenly, the twine parted and fell into the mud.

Constance grabbed the dagger and stood. 'Sir Fergus!'

She wanted to help.

'Run!' he called out as he blocked another savage attack.

Constance just stood there. What could she do?

'Run!' Sir Fergus yelled again.

It pained her that she could do nothing to help him, but she turned and fled into the forest, leaving the injured Noble Guard at the mercy of that vicious killer. She entered the trees and stumbled through the foliage. Branches scratched her arms and face, but she kept moving, not knowing which direction she headed. She caught her foot in a vine and tripped. Sprawled face down on the damp forest floor, she continued to sob.

She rolled over onto her back, dirt and leaves sticking to her face, with the overhanging greenery a blur through her tears. She could no longer hear shouting, no skirmish cries or clashing of swords, just the sounds of the forest and the thumping of her heart. Had Sir Fergus been victorious? Surely, he would be calling for her if he had. Constance sat up and leaned against a nearby tree. Maybe she'd run too far away and couldn't hear him. She hugged her knees to her chest.

She would wait.

2

CEDRIC

Smoke rose from what was left of the town of Hampstead Heath, and Cedric turned to Captain Kirby, his face grim.

'Gather a half-dozen men and follow me,' Cedric ordered. 'Lieutenant Huttert, get the rest of them settled back into the camp and ready my tent.'

Cedric had returned to the Greenhavens, hoping to salvage some pride by returning the princess to the capitol, but the scene he now gazed at filled him with dread.

The captain and six other riders followed Cedric, who had urged his mount to a canter. They had to slow to a walk as they passed through the remains of the main gate. Wisps of smoke still emanated from its charred edges.

'What the hell happened here?' Captain Kirby said.

Cedric asked himself the same thing as he viewed the devastation. Not one of the buildings had escaped untouched. Some sustained only minor damage, while others had been razed to the ground, smoke rising from the charred remains. Amongst the ruins, he glimpsed only a few of the townsfolk. Those who acknowledged his presence did so with a look of pure hatred or utter despair. Where had the rest of them gone?

The gate to Forest Keep had been left wide open, with no guards to be seen.

'A trap?' Tamar wondered out loud.

'Maybe,' Cedric replied but urged his horse forward anyway.

His escort followed him under the barbican and into the bailey of Forest Keep. He'd been disturbed by the town's devastation, but what he saw in the courtyard staggered him. Cedric had assumed many of the townsfolk had hidden or fled from whoever had wrought the damage to the town. He couldn't have been more wrong.

A hundred or more bodies had been piled up in the centre of the courtyard, with the mass of corpses over six feet high. Some belonged to Greenhavens soldiers, but most had been simple townsfolk. The four pikes that projected out of the sickening pile, each topped with a severed head, completed the ghoulish scene.

Cedric barely recognised the first two, Lord Gruffydd and his son Kyle. He suspected the third head had been a woman's due to the long black hair, now matted in dirt and dried blood. The last one, smaller than the others, didn't even resemble a head anymore, looking like a little ball of bloody flesh. Cedric heaved, his stomach churning.

'I think I want to puke,' Tamar said.

Cedric sympathised with his captain. They'd seen dead bodies before, but this … this was pure butchery.

No-one came out to meet them. The keep seemed deserted.

'Anyone here?' Captain Kirby's voice echoed around the bailey.

No answer.

'Captain, search the keep,' Cedric said. 'Question anyone you find. We need to know what the fuck happened here and who was responsible.'

'I have a fair idea,' Tamar said.

Cedric knew precisely to whom the captain referred. 'If you find him, bring him to me.'

'Unharmed?'

Cedric shrugged. 'I don't care. And remove those pikes. I'm returning to camp.'

'Yes, my lord.'

Cedric pulled his mount's head around and headed out of the keep.

He passed back through the castle gate alone and kicked his horse to a canter, only slowing when he approached the camp. He walked his mount along the makeshift path towards the command tent, noticing the subdued mood around the camp. The soldiers spoke in whispers or not at all.

Lieutenant Huttert and Sergeant Mason Tolas stood when Cedric approached the campfire near his command tent. He'd left the Sergeant behind to hold the keep. Maybe now he'd get some answers.

'My lord,' the Lieutenant said. 'Your tent isn't quite ready, but Mason has told me some of what happened while we were gone. You may want to hear it for yourself.'

'I'd certainly like to know why the fuck there is a pile of dead bodies in the middle of the keep,' Cedric said.

He wanted to shout at the man but thought better of it.

'Willem, fetch some food and wine. I have a feeling we'll be here a while,' Cedric ordered.

The Lieutenant rushed off, and Cedric sat on one of the logs encircling the fire. Sergeant Tolas remained standing.

'Sit,' Cedric said.

The Sergeant settled back down on the log across from Cedric.

'Mason, what the fuck happened?'

'He made us do it,' the soldier stammered. 'Threatened us if we didn't.'

Like his Captain, Cedric suspected who was behind this colossal screw-up, but he wanted to hear his name.

'Who did?'

'It … it was Harrow, my lord.'

'Why?'

Cedric knew that Harrow had a vicious streak, but this – it couldn't be called anything else – this *massacre* defied belief.

'The villagers attacked us.'

'With weapons?'

Even an unskilled person with a blade could do damage if the attack is unexpected.

'No,' Sergeant Tolas said, embarrassed. 'They threw things … vegetables.'

'Are you fucking kidding me?'

'I'm sorry, my lord,' the Sergeant said. 'Harrow wanted to make an example of a few of those who had attacked us, but then more and more of them started throwing things, and it just got out of hand. Before long, he ordered the town put to the torch.'

'Are you telling me that a hundred people are dead and a town burned to the ground because someone threw a fucking potato at you?'

'He was out of control. There was nothing we could do.'

Cedric battled to keep his anger in check.

'Fuck, Mason,' Cedric said, looking back at the soldier. 'Civilians don't attack fully armed soldiers without provocation.'

'He ordered us to put the heads of Lord Gruffydd and his family on pikes in the middle of the bailey,' the distressed Sergeant paused.

'Go on.'

'A mob had gathered as we began to put up the pikes. We put Lord Gruffydd's head on the first one and then his son's, but … but when he ordered the head of the Lord's grandson to be put up as well … that's when we were attacked.'

Cedric rubbed his temple. No wonder the townsfolk revolted. He felt sick at the image of that small head on a pike.

'I refused,' the Sergeant said. 'I thought he would kill me, but there was no way I was going to do it. So, he did it himself, then everything went to shit.'

Cedric sat there in complete disbelief. He didn't have a problem with killing, but what had occurred here would turn the stomach of the most hardened soldier. Harrow … the animal … a rabid dog that needed to be put down.

'Where is he now?'

'No idea, my lord,' Mason said. 'I haven't seen him since last night.'

Lieutenant Huttert returned with food and drink, poured some wine and handed the cups to Cedric and Mason. Cedric drained his and helped himself to another. He gestured to the Lieutenant to sit as well. He sat next to the Sergeant, who just stared into his cup.

'And the princess, what of her?' Cedric dreaded asking this but hoped something good might come out of this mess.

The Sergeant dropped his chin and shook his head. Cedric groaned. His father would not be pleased.

'Okay … okay … tell me everything that happened after I left.'

It took over an hour. By the end of it, Cedric's blood was boiling, and to add to his fury, Captain Kirby returned at sunset with no real news.

'We found the Chamberlain in one of the cells, along with some servants, but that's about it,' the captain said. 'We let them out.'

'Harrow?'

'Not at the keep. I think he's gone.'

'Deserted?' Cedric said. 'As if we need another reason to hang the bastard.'

After failing to capture the prince, Cedric hadn't hurried back to the Greenhavens, a decision he now regretted. Things could have been different if he had arrived back at Hampstead Heath even one day earlier.

'Captain, we'll be leaving at first light.'

He didn't see the point of staying in the area any longer.

3

REGAN

Regan stood in the centre of his solar in the Governor's tower, trembling with fury. The fools, the absolute imbeciles!

Moments before, the contents of his desk had been in ordered piles. They were now strewn around the desk and covering the floor. Regan prided himself on his ability to manage his emotions, but recently, he'd begun to lose control more often. The door burst open, and into the room rushed two guards.

'My lord?' one of them said. 'Are you –'

'Get … out!' Regan said through gritted teeth, and they promptly retreated into the corridor, closing the door behind them.

He tried to compose himself and glanced down at his left hand. In his rage he had torn the tiny scroll in two. He flattened out the pieces of parchment on the hard top of the desk.

He held them together and reread the message from his son. Both dead. How could he be so incompetent? Regan's plans catered for one being killed, but not both. He slammed the note back onto the desk and one of the pieces flew off, floating to the floor.

It would be war unless he could get rid of Redstone some other way. Without him, the southern lords would quickly fall into line. His brothers were of no concern. Fortunately, he already had a plan in motion to complete this task. He would use professionals this time; the expense would be well worth it.

Thinking of that helped settle his mood. Ridding Avaleen of Owen Redstone would simplify things, especially now that his moronic son had all but destroyed his original plans. Regan would deal with him when he returned, but in the meantime, he needed to make new arrangements.

As superior as his army was, Regan didn't want it caught in the harsh winter of the Shadowlands, so any war wouldn't happen until the beginning of summer. This gave him plenty of time.

He picked up some blank parchment from the floor and a new inkpot from the sideboard and sat at his desk. With the semblance of a new plan in his mind, his anger receded. He began writing, compiling a list of those he wanted at his war council. Regan perused the list. It wasn't complete, but it would do for now. He began to write letters to each person on the list, summoning them to the capitol. He wouldn't mention anything about the war but made the point that decisions about an occasion of great importance required their presence.

Regan finished, put aside the quill and placed the final letter on top of the sizable stack of messages. Redstone didn't have a chance.

The following morning, Regan dispatched riders with strict instructions to personally hand the letter they carried to the nominated recipient, and they were to wait only a day before returning even if a reply had not been drafted. This would also give Regan an indication of his allies' level of loyalty.

With that task out of the way, Regan looked to the next. He had delayed a decision on how to deal with his deceitful wife. Lennane's collaborator had been quietly thrown into the dungeon, and over the past weeks, Regan had been having fun with her. She hadn't dared complain outright about his rougher treatment of her, and her screams and tears just spurred him on. He hadn't been so active in the bed chamber for years.

It also seemed that the little bitch his wife had taken to her bed had aided the prince's escape. It couldn't have been a coincidence that she'd disappeared the same night. It had briefly entered his mind that the handmaiden had lied to him about his wife, but Regan would know soon enough.

He now had to prepare himself for the forthcoming Ruling Council meeting where he'd reveal the death of the Blackwater children. They would be shocked, but since most of them were Greythorpe allies, it wouldn't have any detrimental effect on his position. The only one from whom he'd expect a strong reaction would be the monk, but Regan considered him of no consequence.

The council met that afternoon. Regan didn't want any distractions, so planned to wait until the end of the meeting to reveal the fate of the King's children. After two hours, some of the council members had begun losing interest. Arturo Exley seemed to be the only one paying attention. Always alert and scrutinising the possible cost of everything that came up before allowing it to a vote, the High Chamberlain seemed in his element.

'Before we bring this meeting to a close,' Regan said, 'I have some tragic news to impart.'

That got their attention. They usually listened when Regan spoke, but tragic news meant drama, and most preferred a bit of drama to the dry accounts and processes they had been hearing.

'It is my sad duty to inform you that Prince Leto and Princess Melina are dead,' Regan said, and paused momentarily to let the council members digest the revelation.

Surprised murmurs began to emanate from most council members, but they weren't as shocked by the news as Regan expected. However, the monk looked shattered, as if his life had suddenly lost all meaning.

Regan smiled to himself and continued. 'I don't have any details at this point. My son will soon be returning to the capitol. I'll learn more then, and I'll inform the council.'

'I guess that's the end of the Blackwater line,' Clay White said without emotion. 'Who'll assume the crown now?'

'There are more Blackwaters,' Arturo pointed out. 'Sir Lydall's line.'

'Bah!' Clay White snorted. 'I wouldn't trust his widow to run my kitchen, and I'm sure we all agree we can't have his idiot son as King. And don't even get me started on his bastards.'

Then, everyone started talking over one another. Some agreed with Sir Clay, and some did not. Regan let it go for a while and glanced up the other end of the table at the monk. He had his head bowed like a broken man. Hopefully, this meant he would be even less trouble.

'Gentlemen,' Regan raised his voice. 'Gentlemen!'

The chatter ceased.

'Who will or will not succeed King Caleb is a discussion for another time,' Regan continued. 'The question I put to you now is, what do we do about Lord Owen?'

'What do you mean?' Bertram Taverner said.

'He was … is the Blackwater's staunchest ally,' Regan said. 'I fear he may place blame where it isn't warranted.'

'Will it be war?' the Merchant Guildmaster said.

'I sincerely hope not, but we would be remiss if we didn't prepare for such an eventuality.'

'It's never too early to prepare for war,' Marion Holm said.

As Master of the Iron Guild, he had the most to gain from a war. He would have a hand in assigning lucrative war contracts. Regan had no doubt he'd take his cut, making him even richer.

'I think it's premature to speak of war,' the High Chamberlain said.

'Yes, yes,' the Abbot raised his head. 'Let's not be too hasty. We should first send someone to Cliffs End to learn Lord Owen's intentions, should we not?'

'I thought you would know already,' Clay White said, his disdain for the monk barely hidden. 'Are you not friends with the esteemed Lord of the Shadowlands.'

'I do count Lord Owen as a friend,' Abbot Alwen said, glowering at Clay White. 'But since he was harangued out of the city, I have not heard from him.'

Regan couldn't remember the last time the monk had expressed annoyance or disgust, but Sir Clay's comment had him worked up enough to cast aside his usual amiable disposition.

'He left the city of his own free will and with the prince,' Sir Baltair said, 'He should be charged with treason.'

'Don't blame others for your incompetence, Sir Baltair,' the Abbot shot back.

'I resent that assertion,' Sir Baltair rejoined.

'That's twice now you've misplaced the prince, is it not?' Walker Seabourne said, his lips forming a faint smile.

Laughter came from the other members of the council. Regan had hoped Sir Baltair would have learned to keep his mouth shut. The Commander of the Capitol Guard had lost a lot of people's respect, even that of Regan's closest allies. Something would have to be done about him, but it would have to wait until after the situation with Redstone had been resolved.

'Abbot Alwen is correct,' Regan interjected before Sir Baltair could speak again. 'We should send an envoy to Cliffs End to garner Lord Owen's intentions. Bring your suggestions to the next meeting. Any objections?'

Mutterings and nods of agreement greeted Regan's question; as no-one objected, Regan closed the meeting. Whether anyone was ever sent to treat with Lord Owen didn't bother Regan. Redstone had made himself the enemy and would be defeated.

Night had well and truly fallen by the time Regan returned to his solar. He poured himself a cup of wine and settled back into one of the chairs by the hearth. He gazed into the fire and contemplated the events of the past few days. Despite the fact he had to radically change his plans to accommodate the ineptitude of those around him, the new arrangements had come together easily and would deliver the same result. With the crown under Regan's control, House Greythorpe would be invulnerable.

Regan finished his wine, stood and reached for the jug but stopped. He already felt quite relaxed and didn't need another, and he always slept poorly if he consumed too much wine. Instead, he made for the door.

'Don't leave just yet, my lord.'

Regan stopped at the unexpected voice from behind him.

'I've only just arrived.'

His mind raced. How did anyone get past his guards and into his solar undetected? Regan turned near the balcony. In the darkness, the outline of a man could barely be seen.

'Who are you?'

'A friend.'

'Friends don't lurk in the shadows. Come into the light where I can see you?'

'That's not the way we do things.'

'You may skulk around in the darkness if you wish, but I'll be leaving.'

The shadow laughed.

'You hide your fear well, Lord Regan.'

'What makes you think I fear you?'

'Smart men fear the unknown. It's how they handle the fear, that sets them apart. But don't worry, I'm not here to kill you. If I was, you'd be dead already.'

Regan realised the stranger spoke the truth; it reassured him his life wasn't in imminent danger.

'Then show yourself.'

'If you insist, my lord.'

The shadow moved towards him. The torchlight revealed a slightly built man of average height, dressed all in black, but the hood of his cloak still sheltered his face from view.

'Is this better?'

The man seemed open to negotiation, so Regan pushed a little more. 'Now remove the hood and identify yourself.'

'Don't mistake my polite tone for weakness,' the man said, no less conciliatory.

'Do you wish to talk?'

'That is why I'm here.'

'Then show yourself,' Regan repeated.

Regan waited for an answer. The man stood silent for a few moments, not moving. He had skills, so Regan didn't want to anger him unnecessarily, but talking to someone he couldn't see made him uncomfortable.

‘The stories are true,’ the intruder broke the silence. ‘You're a hard man to refuse.’ He took another step forward, pushed back his hood and bowed his head.

‘I am Nestor Alvaro, pleased to make your acquaintance.’

Nestor Alvaro had a nondescript face, dark hair to his shoulders and a short-cropped beard. Other than that, he didn’t have any particularly distinguishing features.

‘Now that we've been properly introduced,’ Regan said, ‘tell me why you’ve entered my home without an invitation.’

‘Yes, let's get down to business.’

Nestor seemed less threatening now he had a face and a name, though Regan stayed on guard. He returned to the sideboard and seized the jug of wine. Now he needed another drink. He filled his cup, sat back in the chair beside the hearth, and drained half of it in one go.

‘Now, Mister Alvaro, what do you wish to discuss?’

Nestor approached the hearth and gazed at the flames, his back partially to Regan.

‘I understand that you attempted to enlist my employer to complete a task,’ the intruder said. ‘A rather unpleasant and difficult task.’

The man was an assassin.

‘And you're here to deliver a message?’

‘Of sorts.’

He had decided weeks ago that Lord Owen would continue to be an inconvenience just by his mere presence. Regan had sent one of his trusted lieutenants to contract Grim's Shadows, the most lethal band of assassins in Avaleen, to kill Owen Redstone.

‘Of sorts?’

‘I am not here at Master Grim's request,’ Nestor said.

Interesting.

‘So why are you here?’

‘In three days, you will receive a visit from a member of Grim's Shadows. He will most likely reveal himself in the same manner as I have done.’

Regan frowned.

‘Do not be concerned,’ the assassin continued. ‘He won’t be here to kill you either, but to return the gold you sent as a down payment for the service which will now not be carried out.’

‘Isn’t my money good enough?’

‘No, no. It's not that. It is because your money is not better than that of … ’ the assassin paused, ‘Lord Owen Redstone.’

The mention of Redstone in this context disturbed Regan.

‘Stop speaking in riddles.’

‘I apologise if I have caused you confusion,’ the assassin said. ‘I still cannot believe it myself. Allow me to explain.’

‘Please do,’ Regan said through gritted teeth.

Nestor’s smile changed to a look of disgust.

‘Master Grim originally assigned me to carry out your request, and as you're aware, Grim's Shadows have never refused a request … until now.’

Regan knew of the Shadow’s creed. They accepted all contracts, with only the level of payment to be negotiated.

‘Before I left the enclave to carry out my mission, Master Grim advised me that the contract had been cancelled.’

‘I never cancelled it!’

‘Nevertheless,’ Nestor shrugged. ‘My orders were rescinded.’

‘Preposterous,’ Regan snorted. ‘A contract is a contract.’

‘I said the same thing, my lord,’ Nestor said. ‘It was outrageous, unprecedented. I pushed him for a reason. Apparently, Lord Redstone had placed a request as well … ’

The assassin left the sentence unfinished.

So, the high and mighty Lord Owen Redstone wasn't beneath using assassins to do his dirty work either. Regan had underestimated him, yet again.

‘Master Grim was in a quandary,’ Nestor continued. ‘He could carry out both contracts and have two of the most powerful men in Avaleen killed or decide which one to fulfil. He chose neither.’

Regan thought for a moment. The fact he wasn't dead tempered his initial anger at his contract not being honoured. The appearance of this assassin proved that even someone in his position could be murdered if someone had enough money, which Redstone did.

'I understand,' Regan said. 'But Mr Alvaro, if I'm to be officially informed in three days, why are you here?'

'I am glad you asked,' Nestor's smile returned. 'It's simple, really. I will carry out your request anyway.'

'You?'

The assassin nodded.

'And what of your employer?'

'On acceptance of my proposal, you would be my new employer, my lord.'

Other groups could kill Redstone for him, but as far as Regan knew, Grim's Shadows had never failed. This Nestor Alvaro had been one of them, which made him one of the deadliest men in Avaleen.

'How do I know you're one of the Shadows and you can carry out the required task?'

Nestor sneered.

'I may be an assassin, but I'm not a liar.'

'Why have you gone against the wishes of your current employer? Should you not be grateful to him?'

'A valid question given the circumstances,' the assassin said. 'I'm grateful for the time and effort Master Grim put into my training, but he's getting old and beginning to lose his mind. The cancelling of your contract is a prime example.'

'I'd be dead if he did not.'

'True, but he used to take great pride in the work. Now he's playing politics. That's not what I have always believed Grim's Shadows to be about.'

'A man of principle?' Regan didn't think the man lied but suspected that he had told only part of the story. 'How much would you expect to be paid for this service?'

'Half of your original fee.'

Regan had discovered the assassin's primary motivation; greed.

'I don't doubt your skills, Mr Alvaro, but that sounds excessive. I was buying the experience and resources of Grim's Shadows as a whole. You are but one man.'

Nestor's smile returned.

'You're a shrewd businessman. It's a skill I lack, but let me make this offer: I will perform this task, and you will pay me.'

That sounded fair. 'Half?'

Nestor bowed his head. 'Half.'

Having his very own trained assassin could be a boon. Regan already had Harrow, but he lacked finesse, being more of a hammer. This Nestor Alvaro would be like a fine blade, able to remove an irritation without affecting its surroundings.

'If you succeed, I may have more tasks for you,' Regan said.

'You are most generous. I foresee a bright future for us, my lord.'

Excellent, he'd be rid of Owen Redstone at half the cost, and avoid an expensive war into the bargain.

4

LETO

Forty-two graves.

They stretched for a hundred yards down the riverbank, their locations marked by a pile of stones or a mound of dirt with a stick. The forest had begun to claim the older ones, now overgrown with moss, debris, and creeping vines.

The old man's weathered face was creased, his grey hair thinning. He gestured towards the ragged line of graves.

'Most end up here,' he said. 'You should count yourself lucky.'

Leto had a few scrapes, cuts, bruises, and a sore head, but he didn't feel lucky. He felt foolish.

He'd stopped at the Red Pass against Lord Owen's advice. But instead of crossing over to the south side as suggested, he rode straight past and watered his horse down near the waterfall, away from the rest of the group. That had been his first mistake. When Greythorpe's men had attacked, he'd jumped onto his horse and made for the bridge, only to be thrown into the river when one of the attackers collided with him at a full gallop. Not thinking, Leto began to swim to the opposite bank instead of returning to the north bank, his second mistake. He had glanced back towards the bridge where Lord Owen and his soldiers were gesticulating towards him, then he had been swept over the falls.

He had plunged into an icy pool fifty feet below. He fought to the surface and struggled to keep himself afloat as the strong current dragged him into the pitch dark of the Dragon's Throat.

The darkness was absolute, and he lost all sense of direction and time. One moment he floated along, able to catch his breath; the next, he was sucked underwater and tumbled over and over, not knowing which way to the surface. He must have been knocked unconscious because he could only recall a vague memory of someone carrying him, and a young woman looking down at him when he woke. Leto had tried to rise, but his head swam in dizziness and pain.

'Stay down,' she had said in a soft voice.

Good advice, he thought and lay back down. The woman had delicate features, with unkempt dark hair to her shoulders. She introduced herself as Darcy, the daughter of the old man, Mathius. She and her mother had tended his wounds, and it would be another full day before the pain retreated to a dull throb and he could stand without falling.

A single torch lit the hut, and he couldn't see his armour and garments anywhere, but a neat bundle of clothes had been placed near the sleeping mat. He ached all over, but managed to slip on the simple hose and shirt, and shuffle outside.

Leto spied a helm hooked over a piece of wood stuck in the freshly dug plot. He bristled at the House Greythorpe sigil. He must have been part of the group that attacked him.

He glanced across at the old man. 'Why did you bury him? He was my enemy. He should've been thrown back into the river.'

'Everyone's the same once they've journeyed through the Dragon's Throat,' Mathius said, his voice calm.

Leto reached for the helm, intending to throw it into the water, but a gentle hand on his shoulder stopped him.

'You have no enemies here,' Mathius said. 'Besides, the man is dead. What harm can he do you now?'

Leto paused for a moment and stepped back from the grave.

'None, I suppose.'

'Even if he'd lived, he wouldn't have been your enemy. Avaleen doesn't exist here, and there's no going back.'

Leto turned to the old man. 'What?'

The old man shook his head.

'But … surely there has to be a way?'

Leto had thought once he'd recovered, he would thank Mathius and his family for rescuing him and journey back to Avaleen.

'I've been here over thirty years, and I don't know of one.'

This revelation hurt more than any of his wounds.

'I'm sure you'll like it here,' Mathius added.

Leto had heard the stories of the Dragon's Throat since he was a child. And despite never hearing of anyone returning from the land beyond the cliffs, he couldn't accept being unable to return home,

He wandered to the river's edge and looked upstream towards the dark crack in the cliff, the height of the waterfall, and the fast current into the rocky pool below. Leto couldn't believe he had survived.

'I don't remember much at all,' Leto said as the old man came up beside him. 'Where did you find me?'

'You were found at the top of the falls hanging by your belt,' Mathius said. 'As I said before, you're a lucky man.'

Leto's hand went to his hip, but his sword belt wasn't there.

'My sword, did you recover it?'

Mathius shook his head, and Leto sighed.

'How did you get me down?'

The old man could not have made that climb. Leto, a skilled climber, doubted even he could have done it, and while carrying a body as well … impossible.

'Oh no,' Mathius said, chuckling. 'Even in my younger days, I wouldn't have attempted it.'

'Then who was it?'

'I think it's time you met your saviour,' Mathius said, heading towards the cliffs.

Leto didn't argue and followed the old man, whose slight limp didn't seem to slow him down. They made their way along the shore, followed a well-trodden dirt path into the tangle of forest, and climbed up to a small outcropping at the base of the cliffs. A cave disappeared into its side. The place seemed deserted, and only a large campfire with a large elk carcass cooking on a spit indicated any habitation.

'How many live here?'

'Just one,' Mathius said with a smile.

Leto was about to ask another question, but the old man interrupted him, his smile disappearing.

'Don't act surprised when you first see him,' he warned. 'He's … different to you and me.'

That sounded ominous, but Leto nodded anyway. How different could he be?

'Stay here,' the old man said, disappearing into the cave.

While Leto waited, he took in the view. Low-hanging clouds obscured the top of the cliff, but he could still see where it curved gently towards the east. This side of the cliffs had a gentler slope than on the Avaleen side.

'Leto, this is Rogar.'

Leto turned and prepared to greet the man who had saved his life, but the words caught in his throat. He stood there, mouth agape.

The man … the creature … his saviour, stood beside Mathius, and Leto stared at him in awe.

He looked like an ordinary man, but he was … huge, a true giant. Stories about them had always been used to scare children. At over twelve feet tall, he made Mathius look like a small child beside him. He had light brown skin, a short, scruffy beard and long, unkempt hair a few shades darker. A normal-looking man, only three times the size.

The giant hadn't threatened him in any way, so he pushed down his initial instinct to flee. He just stood there looking at Leto, waiting.

'Is there something wrong with him?' the giant said to Mathius in a deep, gravelly voice.

Leto came to his senses when the giant spoke. He stopped staring and stepped forward.

'My apologies, Lord Rogar,' Leto gave the giant a short bow. 'I'm honoured to meet you and have the opportunity to thank you for saving my life.'

'Lord?' the giant laughed. 'Far from it, but I'm pleased to see you up and around. Most of those I drag from the river aren't so lucky.'

'I am in your debt,' Leto said as the image of the graves flashed in Leto's mind.

The giant's squint eyes widened in surprise.

'Hmmm. Are you now? Then I'll have to think of something for you to do for me.'

'Err … yes,' Leto said.

He wasn't going to disagree with this huge man.

'Come back tomorrow,' the giant said, and looked down at the old man. 'Is there anything left of that deer?'

Mathius nodded.

'Morn's making a stew. Leto can bring it with him when he returns.'

'Good, good. It's always good to see you, Mathius,' Rogar said, 'And I'll see you tomorrow, Leto.'

'I'm looking forward to it,' Leto said, unsure if he spoke the truth.

Rogar trudged back towards his cave.

'Is that it?' Leto said when Rogar had disappeared into the cave.

'What did you expect?' Mathius said as he started back down the rocky slope.

Leto followed the old man.

'But he hardly said anything.'

'You should be flattered he spoke to you at all. His kind isn't usually so talkative, especially with us small folk,' Mathius said as they reached the edge of the trees. 'He must like you.'

'Why do you say that?'

'He invited you back. He hasn't done that with a stranger in a very long time.'

'Are there any more like him?'

'There's a village about two days walk north-east of here. About fifty of them when I last visited ten years ago. There may be more now.'

'Are they friendly, like Rogar?'

'They aren't war-like if that's what you mean,' Mathius said. 'They generally keep to themselves. We occasionally see a party heading south across the river to hunt.'

'They'd be hard to miss.'

'You'd be surprised. They may be big, but they can move very quietly.'

Leto had been in awe of just one giant. To see a whole lot of them would be a remarkable sight.

In the village, Leto sat on a well-worn log near the campfire and took in his surroundings. Four huts, barely a village at all. He'd been told other survivors had built huts nearby, and they treated Mathius, who had been here the longest, as a leader of sorts, their Elder.

The sun rose late in the valley, so Leto found himself trudging along the river's edge in the morning shadows. He carried a large pot of stew that Morn had prepared the previous evening. He had to stop and rest several times, and it was mid-morning when he at last managed to haul the pot up to the giant's cave. He lowered the pot to the ground near the fire, careful not to spill any of its contents, and sat beside it, catching his breath.

'Good, you're here,' a deep voice sounded behind him.

Leto quickly stood as Rogar approached from the cave entrance. 'And I see you've brought something with you.'

He nodded as the giant picked up the stew pot in one hand. Sparks flew as he placed it in the centre of the coals.

'I didn't expect you to come,' Rogar said, stirring the contents with a stick.

'I said I would.'

Rogar nodded his approval. 'A man of his word.'

'My father often said that no matter who you are, you're nothing if you don't keep your word.'

'A wise man, your father.'

'Yes, he is … was,' Leto said.

Rogar glanced at Leto, his brow furrowed.

'He was killed not three moons ago.'

'I am truly sorry to hear that,' the giant said solemnly.

Leto nodded his agreement but changed the subject.

'Have you decided what task I am to perform to repay my debt?' he said.

Rogar stirred the stew again and sniffed it.

'You came back, and you brought me a tasty meal. That's enough for me.'

'I'll now take my leave, Rogar. Thank you again.'

Leto turned to go.

'Do you have somewhere else to be?'

'Err … no,' Leto said.

'Then stay,' Rogar said, gesturing at the pot. 'Share a meal with me.'

Leto hesitated. He had nowhere to go or anything particular to do, and the giant no longer seemed as intimidating as he had the day before.

Leto sat on a log while the giant lowered himself to the ground and sat cross-legged. According to Mathius, Rogar's people considered him average in size but even seated on the ground, Leto still had to crane his head to look the giant in the eye. The giant must have noticed Leto craning his neck.

'My father was this much taller than I am now,' Rogar said, lifting his hand about three feet above his head. 'He always teased me about it when I was young. You'll be as big as me one day, he used to say.'

As a child, Leto recalled his father telling him a similar thing. It seemed all fathers had the same idea, wanting their sons to grow tall and strong.

'But I never did rise to his lofty height. I was quite disappointed, but discovering you little people made me feel big again.'

Rogar laughed and stirred the stew again. The giant's amusement brought a smile to Leto's face.

'How did you come to live here?' Leto asked. 'Mathius says there's a village of your people two days' walk from here.'

Rogar stopped stirring, and his smile faltered. Leto tensed. He didn't want to make the giant angry. Rogar stared stony-faced at the pot for a few moments.

'I'm sorry if I've offended you,' Leto said.

'You haven't offended me,' Rogar said, eventually. 'You've just reminded me that not all people are good.'

'I'm here because bad people killed my father and others that I loved,' Leto said, 'and then tried to kill me.'

'That is sad. My people pride ourselves on honesty and the ability to compromise.'

'I don't understand.'

'We disagree,' Rogar said. 'We even shout and curse each other but rarely come to blows. And once a compromise has been reached, everyone moves on, and that's that. We haven't had a civil war in over three thousand years.'

Leto thought about all the civil wars fought in Avaleen's brief history. The Northern Wars had raged for twenty-five years; and the War of Colours, Red Rivers, and the Silver Rebellion. They engulfed practically all the great houses at one time or another.

'Sounds most civilised.'

'We think so, but a few of us carry the resentment from an argument lost.'

'So why did you leave?'

Rogar shrugged.

'I didn't want to fight them, so I conceded this particular issue and left. I didn't like it there anyway.'

Leto hesitated to ask, but he wanted to know. 'Do you know how to fight?'

'We don't like fighting, but we can and will defend ourselves and our friends,' Rogar said, his face grim.

Who would be stupid enough to attack a giant? Leto tried to envisage facing an army of charging giants. It sent a chill down his spine.

'Remind me not to make you angry.'

Rogar's smile returned.

'I'm sure you won't. Now let's eat.'

The sun had begun its descent when Leto finally took his leave, carrying an enormous portion of the cooked elk across his shoulders. He came away from the experience feeling good, and he found himself grinning as he made his way down to the forest floor.

He had made a friend, and he was a giant.

5

CONSTANCE

She huddled behind a fallen tree. Covered in dirt and wet leaves, she pulled her knees up to her chest and hugged them, trying to make herself as small as possible. Her heart thudded so loudly, she thought he might hear it. If that happened, it would be the end of her.

'You may as well come out,' he snarled through the trees. 'I'll find you eventually.'

Constance had stumbled through the forest for hours, but he had kept coming, always seeming to know where she'd gone. He must be tracking her, but she had no idea how to cover her trail.

'Your heroic Noble Guard is dead,' her pursuer's voice sounded close. 'So now there's no-one to protect your lying arse.'

She choked back a sob and bit down on her fist, knowing she had to stay quiet. Constance had tried to protect the princess, but she had failed, and he had killed Melina, slitting her throat as if she was an animal. Now, Sir Fergus had met his end protecting her. They were both dead because of her. Her eyes burned, but she squeezed them shut.

She tasted blood and found she had broken the skin on her fist where she had bitten down on it. A loud whimper escaped her lips as she let her hand drop.

'No need to cry. I'll make it quick and painless,' he growled, much nearer now.

Her head snapped left, and she peered into the trees. She couldn't see anything, unable to focus through the tears. She wiped her eyes with her sleeve, but it did no good; her dress was already damp from the rain and covered in dirt and blood.

A guttural laugh echoed around her. She flinched, and this time, she jumped to her feet and ran. She dashed through the forest, but the dense undergrowth hampered her flight. She came upon the trunk of a fallen tree. Scrambling onto it, she jumped off the other side and landed badly. Collapsing to her knees, she screamed as a bolt of pain ran up her right leg. She struggled to her feet, but her leg gave way, and she crumpled into the undergrowth in a sea of agony.

'Too easy,' came the dreaded voice from right behind her.

Constance rolled over and shrieked in terror. He stood there, sword in hand. He'd found her! She scrambled back on her elbows, dragging her injured leg through the grime and dirt of the forest floor. She glanced at her knee and saw a six-inch shard of bloody wood sticking out from under her kneecap.

'Told you I'd find you,' he said, giving her a crooked smile, made worse by the scar that seemed to crawl across his face as he spoke.

The killer moved towards her, slow and steady. The sword he held still had blood on it, the blood of Sir Fergus! Her shoulders hit a tree, and she could move back no further. She started crying as Sir Fergus and Melina's killer stopped three feet from her. She shook her head and held her hand out as if to stop him.

She then remembered the dagger. The one Sir Fergus had thrown to her with which she had cut her bonds. She reached for her hip as he lifted his sword, ready to strike. It wasn't there. Had she dropped it? She twisted and reached further around. The cool steel of the dagger brushed her grasping fingers. Relieved, she yanked it out of her belt and held it up towards her assailant. Her hand shook, unable to keep it steady.

'Get back,' she yelled at him between sobs.

The dagger seemed puny and useless against the sword that now pointed directly at her. He just laughed, his crooked smile now an awful grin, as if he enjoyed it.

'Pathetic,' he said, unmoved by the appearance of her tiny blade.

He batted aside the dagger with a flick of his sword, and she cried out as hot agony erupted in her hand and her weapon flew into the undergrowth. Glancing at her hand, Constance blinked in confusion. Blood poured down her hand and forearm from the three bloody stumps where her fingers had been.

Her assailant laughed, and she looked up at him as he brought his sword down onto her neck, giving her no time to scream.

Constance jolted awake in the makeshift cot, her eyes wide and her breath quick and shallow.

'Bad dream?' a kind voice enquired.

The dream had felt so real, but she wasn't dead, killed by a slash from the scarred soldier that had hunted her. Her eyes flicked around in the half-light, her gaze settling on the woman who approached, a bowl in her hands.

'You should try and eat something,' she said, offering the bowl to Constance.

'Thank you.' Constance accepted the proffered bowl of what she recognised as some kind of soup.

She lifted the warm bowl to her mouth with both hands and sipped the liquid. It was hot, but not unbearably so, warming her throat as she swallowed. Despite the lack of flavour, the hunger she had pushed aside came back with a vengeance. Without stopping, she gulped the rest down and chewed the few remaining lumps of vegetables.

Constance returned the bowl to the woman, swapping it for a small chunk of hard bread, which she took and shoved into her mouth, making short work of it.

'Where am I?' she asked, looking around the unfamiliar room.

She regarded the woman, whom she did not recognise. However, she had a kindly look, and Constance didn't feel threatened or afraid, unlike before; the memory of her flight through the trees flashed through her mind.

'I am Lena,' the woman said with a gentleness that surprised her, 'and this is my home.'

'How did I get here?'

Constance remembered arriving at the town but nothing after that.

'You fainted in the middle of the road to the keep. My sister and I brought you here,' Lena explained.

The other thing she remembered before collapsing made her wary.

'What happened here … to the town?'

She remembered the burned-out buildings and smoke rising from some of them, but mostly the charred black ruins stuck in her memory.

'You were Princess Melina's lady-in-waiting?' Lena asked.

Constance grimaced slightly at the mention of Melina, but she nodded. She wasn't about to correct the woman. How Lena knew that she had served Melina also played on her mind. Had she told the woman and then forgotten?

'Then you should go to the keep,' Lena said. 'You should talk to the Chamberlain.'

She noted the pain and despair in Lena's eyes as she spoke.

'What happened?' Constance repeated.

'It's not for me to say,' Lena said and went to the door.

Constance could see that this woman wouldn't answer her question, either because she didn't want to, or couldn't. She understood, recalling the devastation that had been wrought on the town.

'Right,' she said and, with careful, slow movements, swung her legs off the cot and stood, swaying ever so slightly.

Constance knew she wouldn't get any more information from Lena, so she stepped towards the door the woman had opened for her.

'Thank you … for helping me,' she said and attempted a weak smile.

The woman's face betrayed no hint of a smile in return, only nodding in acknowledgement.

'You are part of the royal court,' she said as if that explained everything, and Constance walked out into the daylight.

She squinted at the brightness of the day and briefly wondered in which direction the keep lay. Once her eyes adjusted, she glanced around. She stood in a narrow dirt lane. Directly ahead of her lay the ruin of what may have been a dwelling or a shop; wisps of smoke still rose from parts of the charred timber. Behind it towered the high stone wall of Forest Keep. Constance looked back to Lena but found the door had already been closed.

She surveyed her surroundings, seeing no-one amongst the burned buildings. Her nose wrinkled at a faint, unsavoury odour, but she couldn't work out from where it came. Aside from finding someone who could help her, Constance needed to know what had happened to the town. During their trek through the Graveswood, Sir Kyle had mentioned the town held over two hundred people and was growing. He had been quite proud of the fact. He would have been distraught to see it now.

She turned right and began walking. After about thirty yards, the lane spilled out to what looked like the main road through the town, with the gate of Forest Keep fifty yards up a slight incline. She spied a few villagers amongst the ruins, but most either hid or avoided her gaze as she approached the keep.

Oddly, no-one guarded the gate. Only a lone boy stood at the edge of the road just outside. He just stared into the keep, unmoving. His clothes, just rags, were covered in dirt and soot. She stopped short of him, remaining out of arms reach. He looked younger than Constance.

'Are you alright?' she asked.

He didn't respond, not acknowledging her presence, and his blank stare remained unchanged. What had happened to this poor child?

'Where are your parents?' she said, stepping closer and touching his shoulder. Aside from a slight flinch, he didn't react to her presence and continued to gaze into the keep. Promising herself to come and check on him after seeing the Chamberlain, she started through the gate.

'There are ghosts in there now,' the boy said so quietly that Constance barely heard the words, but she stopped and faced him again.

'Ghosts?'

Constance waited and watched the boy for a long moment, but he remained silent, staring. She turned back into the keep.

The faint odour she had smelled within the town now assaulted her senses as she entered the bailey of Forest Keep. Her face screwed up in disgust, and she reflexively lifted her hand to cover her nose and mouth. The pungent smell reminded her of rotting meat. She wondered what could produce such a rank odour inside a keep. She blanched when she saw it, and a short, high-pitched gasp escaped her lips.

In the centre of the courtyard, lay scores of dead bodies, carelessly piled up higher than Constance was tall. Flies buzzed about, and several carrion birds perched atop the mass, pecking at the eyes of the dead.

She fought back the bile that rose in her throat and turned away from the grotesque sight. By the gods, who had done this? She began to sway but righted herself. She had to find the Chamberlain.

Averting her eyes from the horror, she skirted the courtyard and pushed open one of the double doors of what she hoped would be the main hall. The stench lessened as she closed the door behind her and moved further into the hall, but it never entirely disappeared.

Removing her hand from her mouth, she glanced around. A few scattered torches barely lit the space, but from what she could see, it did look like the main hall. However, the silence made the hair on her arms stand on end.

'Hello?' she said, her voice echoing around the empty space.

Upturned benches and chairs littered the floor and several tapestries hung askew or lay crumpled on the stone floor.

'Chamberlain?'

Constance halted as a squelch emanated from her foot. She glanced down and saw she'd stepped in a large dark patch. It glistened a dark, deep red, even in the dim light. She jumped back, realising she had stepped into a pool of blood.

Constance shuddered, stomping her foot several times on a dry patch of the floor. The sound, louder than expected, filled the hall. Giving her foot one last flick, she stepped around the drying blood and, keeping an eye out for more, approached the long table at the far end. Half a dozen large chairs lined the opposite side of the table, though some had been pushed over, leaning awkwardly against the table.

'Hello,' she said a bit louder. 'Chamberlain?'

She whirled at the clang of metal on stone. A faint sliver of light surrounded the edge of a closed door halfway down the side wall. Constance took a deep breath and approached the door.

'Hello?' she said and knocked, the faint pressure causing the door to open a crack.

She pushed it wider and heard a man grumbling over the sound of the creaking door. Poking her head through the doorway, Constance spied a lantern on a table. The room, tiny compared to the hall behind her, also contained shelves that lined two of the four walls, cluttered with jars, papers, books and bottles.

Her nose wrinkled at the smell of ale and wine as she entered the room and headed for the table. Near the lantern, a goblet lay on its side, spilled wine splashed across the table's polished surface. She turned up the lantern, hoping to see better. The light bloomed and filled the room.

'Urrrgghh,' a voice moaned. 'Too bright.'

Her gaze flicked to the corner of the room beyond the table. An old man sat on the floor, propped against the wall and a wooden barrel. He held up a hand, shielding his eyes from the lantern.

'Off … turn it off,' he pleaded, his words slurred.

Constance turned the lantern down a bit.

'Are you the Chamberlain?' she asked, trying to keep the disgust from her voice as she noted the empty tankard in his lap.

He lowered his hand to reveal a gaunt, white-bearded face. Squinting, he peered back at her but said nothing.

'Are you the Chamberlain of Forest Keep?'

He snorted.

'Chamberlain of nothing,' he slurred.

Despite the stains and rumpled appearance, his clothes seemed of fine quality. It must be him, she thought. He didn't look dangerous, so she skirted the table and knelt a few yards away.

'What happened? Where is everyone?'

The old man grumbled something unintelligible but didn't try to move. Constance saw that no helpful information would be forthcoming, not in his current state. She needed to tell someone about Melina, someone who could do something and advise her what to do next. Unfortunately, this drunken old man seemed to be the only one who could possibly help her.

The Chamberlain hiccupped and groaned. She needed him sober. She needed someone else to learn what happened to the princess and … and she needed to be told it wasn't her fault. She kept playing it through her mind and always came to the same conclusion; she was to blame.

She left the Chamberlain on the floor and started exploring, hoping to find food or someone else who could help. Compared to Whitehall or Riverview, Forest Keep was relatively small. Consequently, her search for the kitchen didn't take long. She smelled something cooking even before entering; she remained wary of who might be here, not knowing how they might react to her.

'Anyone here?' she said as she stepped into the kitchen, her voice tentative.

'What do you want?'

A skinny boy with a shock of short, mousy brown hair stood near one of the cooking hearths where a large pot hung above the glowing coals. Constance guessed him to be twelve or thirteen, and he held a cleaver in one hand and a knife in the other.

'Who are you?' he added, a hint of fear in his voice.

Her eyes flicked left and right but saw nothing that could be used as a weapon, not that she knew how to wield one.

'I'm the lady-in-waiting to the Princess Melina,' she said, standing a bit straighter, hoping to appear confident and believable. 'The Chamberlain requires a meal, so here I am.'

She hadn't lied to the boy, but he didn't move, his hands clenching the kitchen blades he held.

'My name is Constance,' she added, her tone softer. 'May I ask your name?'

Her conciliatory manner seemed to relax the boy, his face no longer sporting an untrusting stare.

'I'm Tomaz,' he eventually said. 'I'm the cook.'

Constance doubted his claim but didn't voice it, but then the boy's chin dropped, and his shoulders sagged.

'Well, I am now … since Suro and Maitlen are dead,' he added.

'Well then, Head Cook Tomaz,' she said, resisting the urge to ask the boy what had happened, 'what can you give me for the Chamberlain?'

The boy's face switched from sadness to disdain.

'That old fool?' he said with a vehemence that surprised Constance. 'All he does now is get drunk on the Lord's ale! No use to anyone.'

'He's decided to stop drinking and help the town get back on its feet,' she lied, desperately wanting him sober to help her, but maybe he'd decide to help the town if he wasn't always drunk. 'Is there someone else of rank that I can talk to?'

Misery returned to the boy's face.

'Err … no … the Lord's family were all killed. So were the guards, and old Lord Griffen is at Cliffs End.'

Constance remembered now that Lord Gruffydd's father was Lord Griffen, and his sister had wed Lord Owen Redstone.

'Then you better come up with some food for the Chamberlain. You wouldn't want him to tell Lord Griffen that his head cook can't cook.'

The boy's eyes widened.

'No … no. Of course, I can cook,' he said, gesturing to the pot in the hearth. 'I made this stew.'

'Then bring some of that stew and some bread to the main hall,' she ordered.

'Err … yes, ma'am.'

'Good boy,' she said and nodded once.

Constance left the kitchen and returned to the hall, sure the boy wouldn't be too far behind. On entering the Chamberlain's room, she found the old man snoring in the corner where she had left him. Grabbing the lantern, she returned to the hall, letting him sleep it off. She righted one of the chairs and dragged it to a nearby table. Exhausted, she sat and waited for the boy.

Still no closer to discovering what kind of tragedy had struck the town, she had the fleeting thought of simply leaving. However, with Tomaz and that young man at the gate at the forefront of her mind, Constance realised she couldn't. Melina would have stayed and done something to help. But what could she do? Nothing at the moment, not with the Chamberlain in a drunken slumber.

Tomaz entered the hall, tray in hand, and Constance called him over.

'I found some cheese as well,' he said, placing the tray on the table.

Constance looked at the tray and then set her gaze on the boy. He looked at her expectantly, his tentative smile slowly disappearing.

'You've done a great job. Keep it up.'

'Thank you, ma'am,' he said, his smile returning. 'Do you need anything else?'

She almost said no, but realised how parched her throat felt.

'Just a pitcher of water.'

No wine until the Chamberlain has sobered up, she thought as the boy nodded and rushed out of the hall. Constance sniffed at the bowl. The stew seemed edible, so she had a taste. She swallowed the first spoonful and stared at the bowl. It wasn't what she expected. Spooning more into her mouth, she found herself nodding. The boy could cook. It was just a stew, but … she shovelled in another spoonful, and then another.

Before she knew it, the spoon came up empty. Whether or not it tasted good only because of her hunger, she didn't know, but Constance would undoubtedly be singing Tomaz's praises to the Chamberlain, whenever the old man woke up. She tore a chunk from the small loaf of bread, scraped the remnants from the bowl, and shoved it into her mouth.

The Chamberlain snored his way through the night and woke just after dawn. Constance, who had fallen asleep at the table, woke to a loud clattering and the creak of the door to the Chamberlain's room. She rubbed her eyes, then rose and approached the old man who stood in the doorway, staring quizzically at her.

'Who are you?' he said, massaging his temple.

'I'm Constance, Princess Melina's lady-in-waiting,' she said, thinking there was no way he'd know she was only a handmaiden, or a bastard.

He attempted to stand up straighter at the mention of the princess.

'The princess is here?' he asked, glancing around the hall.

'No, she's dead,' she said, fighting to keep her voice steady.

His brows pinched together.

'Dead?'

She nodded.

The Chamberlain dropped his gaze and shook his head.

'So,' he said, pointing towards the main doors. 'that was all for nothing?'

Constance ignored his comment.

'We must talk,' she said, keeping her voice even, hopefully projecting a confidence she did not feel and an air of importance she did not have.

She knew Melina would have had both the confidence and the importance. The old man looked at Constance as if deciding whether to pay her any further attention.

'Sit down,' she said, gesturing at the table, 'and I'll get you some food.'

He placed a hand on his stomach. For a few moments, he just stared at the table. Eventually, he nodded.

She found Tomaz asleep on a mat near the cooking hearth. She gave him a nudge, and he sprang up, his fright receding when he saw who had woken him.

'Mornin', ma'am,' the boy half stifled a yawn.

'Good morning, Tomaz,' she said with a gentle smile. 'Any of that stew left?'

His eyes flicked to the pot hanging in the hearth.

'Yes, yes,' he said, nodding vigorously.

'Do you have barley tea?'

'I … err … I'll have a look. They took a lot of our supplies.'

Constance could guess to whom he referred, but didn't question the boy.

'Bring some hot tea and two bowls of stew to the main hall as soon as you can.'

'Yes, ma'am.'

'Good boy,' she said and returned to the Chamberlain, now seated in the chair Constance had slept in.

She pulled up another chair and set it across from the old man. He seemed more awake now and studied her with an intensity that almost made her uncomfortable.

'How did you get here?'

She gave him a brief explanation of what happened, their escape from Whitehall, the rescue by Sir Kyle and their witnessing the death of Lord Gruffydd and his family. She halted when she got to the part about how the princess had died.

'A man with a scar pursued us into the forest,' she said. 'He killed the princess and Sir Fergus.'

His brows rose.

'A scar, you say?'

'You know who he is?'

Constance needed to know his name. She couldn't have Melina murdered by a nameless assassin.

'Harrow's his name,' he said, nodding. 'Cedric Greythorpe left him in charge while he went off somewhere, but really, he's Lord Greythorpe's dog.'

She could see him reliving the horror in his mind; his pained expression exuding despair and sadness. She pondered this information as she waited for the old man to continue.

'That animal was also responsible for what you see out there in the bailey; him and his soldiers,' the Chamberlain continued, his face hardening. 'All because they wanted the princess, and Lord Gruffydd wouldn't give her up.'

'What will you do?' she said, ignoring the accusation. 'Have you sent word to anyone?'

He snorted.

'What is there to do?' he said, shaking his head. 'There's no-one left.'

Of course, there were people left. She had seen some of them.

'But –'

'The town is dead,' he said, cutting her off, 'and this keep will become a haven for ghosts.'

Constance felt hot anger rising inside her, both from him laying fault at her feet and also for his lack of courage.

'So, you're just going to give up, is that it?' she said, trying to suppress her fury. 'Drink yourself into the grave?'

He spread his hands in surrender.

'May as well. There's nothing for me here.'

She jumped to her feet.

'You should be ashamed of yourself,' she said even louder. 'By the gods, you're the Chamberlain. Don't you represent your Lord when he is not here?'

'Weren't you listening, girl?' he said. 'That filthy murderer killed the Lord of this keep, his son and his grandson. There is no Lord for me to represent.'

'When Lord Griffen hears of this, he'll be back quicker than you can scoff another skin of wine. Of that, I'm sure.'

The Chamberlain looked at her, unable to hide the despair that wrought his face.

'There's nothing to come back to,' he said and slumped back in the chair, his chin dropping to his chest. 'Leave me be.'

'Well, if you aren't willing to do anything, maybe I will!'

He glanced up.

'You?' he said, shaking his head.

Constance opened her mouth to give him another spray but stopped. He wouldn't listen.

'You disgust me,' she spat and strode from the hall.

She almost ran into Tomaz, who, despite his small size, held a tray laden with two bowls of stew, a pitcher of tea and some bread. She grabbed one of the bowls and a spoon.

'Take the rest to the Chamberlain,' she said, probably more curtly than she should have, and continued on her way.

Once in the kitchen, she sat on the bench nearest the hearth and began to eat the stew. She wanted to scream, not understanding why the Chamberlain had given up. Leaders, whether they be a king, a lord, or a chamberlain, were supposed to help those less fortunate than themselves.

Constance had once heard King Caleb tell Melina that leading when things are good is easy, but it's when things are bad that good leaders shine. Things couldn't possibly be any worse, and that stupid old man had lain down and refused to help. He wasn't even helping himself, except to the wine and ale.

This place had been attacked only because the Greythorpes wanted the princess, and the honour of House Greenwood forbade it to give her up. They had all died for it, but the manner of Lord Gruffydd's death and that of his family and the resultant massacre – Constance didn't have the words to describe the viciousness of it all. How evil does one have to be to burn and murder the innocent and then present it like a trophy?

The Chamberlain's words returned to her after she'd told him of the princess's fate. Had he been right after all? Melina had died anyway, and all the honour in the world didn't save her. Had Sir Kyle, his family and the people of Hampstead Heath really died for nothing?

'Are you alright, ma'am?'

Constance raised her head, only then realising she'd been crying. She wiped her sleeve across her eyes and looked at the boy. Genuine concern afflicted his young face.

'I'm fine,' she lied. 'I'm just tired.'

'You can take a nap in Chef Suro's room if you want,' he said, pointing towards the other end of the kitchen. 'It's up the end on the right.'

She didn't know how long she'd slept at Lena's. She couldn't even remember when she got there; morning or afternoon? Nightmares plagued what sleep she did have, including last night, slumped in the chair onto the table. It couldn't hurt to have a short nap.

'Thank you, Tomaz,' she said, yawning.

He beamed at the thanks.

At the end of the hall, an open door led to a small room with a cot on one wall and a timber chest on the other. She pulled back the blanket on the cot. Relieved to see a mattress, she sat on the edge of the bed, removed her boots, and slid under the blanket. The mattress felt very thin, but at least it wasn't straw on a wooden pallet. Before long, her eyes fluttered and closed, and she slept.

She woke to someone shaking her.

'Constance, ma'am,' he whispered, giving her shoulder another light shove. 'Someone wants to see you.'

'Okay,' she murmured and sat up. 'How long was I asleep?'

'Nearly the whole day.'

She'd only meant to have a short nap, maybe a couple of hours.

'Did the Chamberlain say what he wanted?'

The boy shook his head.

'No, it's not the Chamberlain. Soldiers have come.'

The revelation caused the sleep fog to quickly dissipate. She pulled on her boots and motioned the boy to lead the way. She followed him through the kitchen, towards the meeting hall.

'Tomaz, wait,' she said, coming to an abrupt stop. 'Who are these soldiers? How many are there?'

Constance didn't want to walk into a trap, not after avoiding that awful Harrow. Her body tensed at the thought.

'I don't know, but the Chamberlain seemed happy to see them.'

He may be a drunk, but she was sure he'd be cautious, especially after recent events. She nodded, and Tomaz continued towards the hall, with Constance a few steps behind.

Constance and Tomaz entered the hall. Someone must have gone to the trouble of lighting all the torches because she could now see into every corner. The benches and chairs had all been righted, and a fire burned in the hearth. She also noticed that two soldiers guarded the closed main doors.

The boy led her towards the hearth, where the Chamberlain conversed with a soldier. Both men turned as they approached. The old man seemed to have cleaned himself up; he was wearing clean clothes and showed few signs of his earlier inebriation, even smiling when he caught sight of her. She hoped this could be counted as a good omen. The soldier towered above the old man, a full head taller, with broad shoulders, close-cropped dark hair and a short, neat beard. His demeanour gave her no clue as to his mood.

'Ah, here she is,' the Chamberlain said as if happy to see her, which surprised her, given what she'd said the last time they spoke. 'Tomaz, fetch wine and some food for our guests.'

He shooed the boy off and returned his attention to the soldier.

'This is the young lady I was telling you about,' the Chamberlain said.

Had he been talking about her to this stranger? He's just a soldier, she thought. Nevertheless, she straightened and held herself like she and the princess had been taught. The soldier studied her momentarily and gave her a weak smile, bowing his head.

'Lady Constance.'

His voice surprised her, deep but not rough as she had expected. Nothing in his manner caused her concern, but she knew things were not always as they seemed. She noticed the sigil on his uniform, a black prancing horse on a red background. Constance recognised that sigil and relaxed, letting out her pent-up breath.

'You have me at a disadvantage, sir,' she said, noting he addressed her in the same way that Sir Fergus had, even though she was far from being a lady. 'I don't know your name.'

'Lieutenant Cailen Oates,' he said and nodded again.

'Are you here because of what happened, Lieutenant?'

The soldier shook his head.

'We were returning home from Twin Falls and thought we should visit and pay our respects to Lord Gruffydd,' he said, his face tensing as he glanced towards the main doors. 'But it seems that won't happen now.'

Constance lowered her gaze. She tried not to think about the atrocity that lay just outside in the courtyard.

'And the Chamberlain has told me some of what happened to Princess Melina.'

She winced at his words. Of course, he would have told him. She shouldn't have expected otherwise. She lifted her gaze to the soldier, ignoring the burning in her eyes.

'I will tell you what happened if you wish it,' she offered, knowing full well she'd have to tell someone, sooner or later.

Despite needing to tell someone, she didn't relish saying it out loud.

'If you could,' he nodded. 'And then I'll need you to take me to where she was killed.'

No … no. She didn't want to go back into that forest. She couldn't, she couldn't. Her chest tightened.

'I … I can't,' she stammered, again lowering her gaze.

The lieutenant's eyes flicked to the Chamberlain, questioning, and back to her.

'I'm sorry, Lady Constance,' he said, 'but I'll have to insist.'

She looked up at him, almost pleading.

'Why? I can tell you where she is. I can do that. You … you don't need me.'

'We aren't familiar with the terrain, and you are the only one who witnessed her death.'

Constance didn't understand. The only reason she could think of why he would …

'You don't believe me?'

'We believe you,' the Chamberlain said. 'I have vouched for your honesty and integrity.'

The soldier dipped his head in agreement.

'But what we believe doesn't matter. Lord Owen will ask questions, and I want to have as many answers as possible,' he said and hesitated. 'As the only witness, he'll want to question you as well.'

What?

'Lord Owen's coming here?'

'No, you'll be coming with me to Cliffs End. We'll depart immediately after you have taken us to the princess.'

'But I don't want to go,' she implored, looking at the Chamberlain. 'I want to stay here. They need help.'

'I am sure once Lord Owen hears of this, help will be despatched.'

'You have been a huge help already,' the old man said with an encouraging smile. 'We'll be fine.'

She didn't want to go anywhere. Melina would have wanted her to stay and help. Constance felt responsible, not for the horrific massacre, but she hadn't protected the princess – and all the people out there in the courtyard had died for no reason.

‘I don’t want to,’ she pleaded, the tears threatening to flow. ‘I don’t want to see her … ’

‘I’m afraid you don’t have a choice,’ he said, his tone now more of an order than a request.

Constance put a hand to her face and turned away, hiding her tears.

6

CEDRIC

Cedric squinted as he exited the Kingswood. With Twin Falls in the distance, he knew he couldn't avoid facing his father much longer.

He had failed, and he had no-one to fault but himself. However, he laid the blame for the death of the princess squarely at the feet of that murderous bastard, Harrow. The thought of his father's enforcer filled him with anger and dread.

Cedric's trepidation increased as the day wore on. He passed through the southernmost gate of the city and thought of putting it all off until tomorrow, but his return would already be known.

'Captain, release the men,' Cedric said. 'I'm going to see my father.'

'Do you need an escort, my lord?'

Cedric didn't want anyone else to be a witness to his humiliation. 'No. Get some rest.'

'As you wish,' the captain said. 'Some of us will be at the Swinging Pig if you wish to join us later.'

Cedric nodded and urged his mount towards the royal stables.

He entered the Governor's Tower and climbed the stairs. The guards came to attention as he approached.

'Is my father in?'

Without a word, one of the guards turned and opened the door, and Cedric strode into the room with a confidence he didn't particularly feel. As usual, his father sat behind the large oak desk.

'Father,' Cedric said as he stopped before the desk.

He remained standing, not daring to sit. His father continued writing, so Cedric waited. Eventually, he put down the quill, lifted the parchment, and gently blew on it to dry the ink. He put the letter aside and finally looked up at Cedric.

'You didn't follow my instructions,' he said. 'Why?'

He would have hardly called the vague message delivered by the Thorne boy, instructions, Cedric thought.

'Because if you had,' his father continued, 'you'd be standing there about to tell me you have one or both Blackwater children in custody, not that they are both dead!'

'I take full responsibility for Prince Leto,' Cedric said, knowing he couldn't dodge the blame for that. 'The manner of his death was unexpected, but the fault was mine.'

'Yes, it was.'

'But the princess was killed on Harrow's watch, not mine, and what he did to the townsfolk was … the man's an animal.'

Regan leaned back in his chair. 'We'll get to him soon, but first, we need to talk about you.'

Cedric knew he had failed, but the contempt in his father's voice filled him with anxiety. 'Yes, sir.'

'I'll ask again. Why didn't you follow my instructions?'

'I don't understand,' Cedric said. 'I tried to do what you asked, but I failed.'

'No! You did not do as I asked. I said finding the prince was the top priority, yet you left half of your force behind.'

How could he know that? Even if one of Cedric's men had been a spy, he knew none had ridden ahead to the capitol. Cedric also doubted anyone left alive in the Greenhavens would have the knowledge and the means to send a message to his father.

'I did make it my top priority,' Cedric said. 'Seventy men was more than enough and would move much faster than a hundred and fifty, and since I already held Forest Keep, I thought –'

'But that's not what I wanted!'

'Your orders weren't clear. They said nothing about how to perform the task.'

His father glowered at Cedric, a look that made most men cringe.

'What happened at Hampstead Heath?'

Finally, he could tell his side of the story and divert the attention from himself.

'I ordered Harrow to hold the keep until I returned. I said he could question Lord Gruffydd but told him not to kill anyone. But on my return, I found the entire Greenwood family dead, the town burned to the ground, and the bodies … '

His father looked at Cedric in silence.

'And the story goes that the princess was mauled by wolves in the forest,' Cedric continued. 'But Harrow and a group of men pursued her into the woods, and he was the only one who returned. That sadistic prick probably killed her himself.'

Confused at the lack of response from his father, Cedric kept talking.

'And now he's nowhere to be found, so when I find him, I'm going to hang the bastard for desertion from the highest place I can find.'

'You left him in charge,' his father finally said. 'Therefore, whatever happened there is ultimately your responsibility.'

'What?'

'If you'd followed my orders, I doubt we'd be having this conversation, but you chose to split your force and leave Harrow in charge … '

'You're defending him?' Cedric said, his frustration beginning to show.

'No, but because of your decision, a princess, a lord and a hundred people are dead.'

Why would his father make such an accusation?

'In that case, this mess is all your fault!' Cedric blurted out. 'You put me in charge, so you're accountable for my failings.'

'True, but I don't answer to anyone but myself.'

Cedric no longer felt dread or nervousness, just anger and frustration.

'Fine. Punish me or not, I don't care. But if that murderous bastard Harrow ever shows his face in the city again, I will kill him.'

'No, you won't,' his father said.

'I may be responsible for his actions, but he disobeyed my orders, massacred innocent people and then deserted his post.'

'I am fully aware of what you think he did,' his father said.

Cedric hadn't told his father the whole sorry story yet.

'How could you know unless … he's here?'

His father stood and went to pour himself a drink.

'Two days ago.'

'Where is he?' Cedric demanded. 'I'll cut his fucking head off and put it on a pike myself.'

'You'll do no such thing!'

'He's a fucking murderer! Why are you siding with him?' Cedric said. 'I'm your son.'

'You'll find that sometimes we have to work with people we despise,' his father said. 'And besides, he's currently performing a task more suited to his talents.'

'You don't give a shit about me at all, do you?' Cedric pointed at his father. 'You never have.'

'Now listen here –'

'No, you listen!'

Cedric had once interrupted his father as a boy and received a cuff across the head. Now he didn't give a shit.

'I'm your eldest son. I'm your heir, but you treat me like a common soldier!'

'I've given you important work, so stop complaining.'

'But you never advise me on how to do any of it. You assume I'll somehow know what to do just because I'm your son.'

'I always tell you what to do.'

'You tell, but don't show me how or why,' Cedric said. 'How am I to succeed if you don't teach me?'

'Don't be so dramatic,' his father said and sat back down at his desk.

'You don't care, so why should I?'

He turned and headed towards the door.

‘Cedric!’ his father raised his voice. ‘You will remain until I’ve given you leave.’

He stopped and turned.

‘You’re a pathetic excuse for a father. I’m surprised you even remember my name.’

Cedric pulled the door open and left with his father’s voice fading at his back as he hurried down the corridor. He half expected the guards to try and stop him as he descended the stairs to the foyer. He exited the tower into the open air, broke into a run, and didn’t stop until he had reached the stables.

His heart raced, and he felt sick, but at the same time, it felt like an enormous weight had been lifted from his shoulders. He should have confronted his father ages ago. He mounted his horse and made his way out of Riverview into the city. Maybe he’d travel to Oldtown, visit young Rosie at The Grey Stag again, and on to Anchorage. He could get passage on a ship away from his father and family. He could be his own man. The idea sounded better and better the more he thought about it.

He’d leave Avaleen behind for good. Fuck them all!

7

LETO

Mathius met Leto as he returned from visiting Rogar.

'It went well?'

'Yes,' Leto said but didn't elaborate.

The old man went to tend the cooking fire as Morn led Leto to a large chopping block at the rear of one of the huts, onto which he flopped the elk meat, the gift from Rogar. Leto stepped away from the block, relieved of the load.

'Thank you,' Morn said.

'Is there anything else I can do?'

Until a few days ago, he had felt too weak and sore to do anything except sleep. They had cared for and nursed him back to health, and they hadn't done it because of his position as heir to the throne. He had been careful not to reveal his true identity.

'Darcy will be checking the fish traps soon,' Morn said, chopping at the elk meat with a small axe. 'I'm sure she could use some help.'

He doubted the young woman needed help, but he nodded and returned to the campfire, where Darcy had just picked up a large reed basket.

'Your mother says you may need help with the fish traps,' Leto said.

She smiled at him and nodded. Darcy seemed to have taken a shine to Leto in the brief time he had been here and tried to converse with him any chance she got. Part of him enjoyed the attention. Darcy had a lithe body and pretty face but wasn't nearly as beautiful as Cordelia or Dariah. However, she would still attract a lot of attention at court. He frowned at the thought. She would never be seen in the royal court, and now neither would Leto.

'Lead the way,' he said, following her towards the river.

He had never handled live fish before, and it showed. He tried to retrieve the contents of the first trap but failed. He just couldn't get a grip. They just kept slipping out of his hand back into the trap.

'Never been fishing before?' she said, laughing.

Being a prince meant you never had to catch your own meals. He'd been hunting, of course, but he'd only shot at the game, never having to skin or prepare the animals he'd killed.

'Is it that obvious?'

'Here, let me show you.'

Darcy handed him the reed basket and easily pulled the fish out of the trap. Leto tried again at the next trap but failed. Darcy seemed to find his ineptness amusing. At least he didn't drop any fish back into the river. After they had checked all the traps, Leto carried the half-full basket back to the village. Thankfully, Darcy didn't push him further on his lack of fishing skills.

That's how it went for the next few days. Leto helped Mathius, Darcy and even Morn with their chores, with varying degrees of success. When collecting and chopping wood, his ability with a blade came to the fore. He also managed to kill a couple of rabbits with the old bow Mathius had. It kept him occupied, but in his moments of solitude, his mind always wandered back to home, which began to darken his spirit.

He had enjoyed helping around the village, but Leto soon avoided them wherever possible, even eating alone occasionally. When he did join them for a meal, he ate in near silence, barely speaking. He started taking long walks by himself, usually up and down the river's edge. Darcy offered to go with him several times, which he politely rebuffed.

During one of these solitary walks, Leto went downriver further than he'd ever gone before. The trees grew to the river's edge, forcing him to step from rock to rock along the shore, not paying attention. He brought himself to a sudden halt, finding himself at the top of another enormous waterfall. Leto glanced down, but a cloud of mist blanketed the pool over a hundred feet below. With no obvious way around, Leto glanced behind, wondering whether he should start back to the village, but he didn't feel like returning.

Leto stared out over the edge again. He would have been killed for sure if he'd fallen. However, it would have solved all his problems. He'd no longer have this constant sick feeling in the pit of his stomach. He'd only felt this twice before; once when his father was murdered and again when he'd returned to Riverview after Jacob had been killed. He'd been balancing on the balustrade outside his bedchamber contemplating one last step, but a knock on the door had stopped him. Dariah had then come into his life and given him hope. She'd facilitated contact with Lord Owen, listened to him, and possibly even loved him. When thinking of home, he had found his thoughts wandering to her much more than Cordelia, his supposed betrothed. She wasn't noble born or educated but … he missed her.

Despite his regret at leaving Dariah behind when he escaped Riverview with Lord Owen, Leto had begun to believe everything might work out. But now, through his own stupidity, he couldn't help his sister, he wouldn't see Dariah again, he could never go home, and he wouldn't be King.

Again, Leto considered taking that last step, but he couldn't. He didn't know why. It would simplify things for everyone, and all his problems would disappear in an instant, but as he had back at Riverview, he turned away from the edge.

He returned to the village. To Leto's surprise, he found Rogar had paid them a visit. He and Mathius stopped their conversation and turned towards him as he approached.

'Here he is,' Mathius said with a wide smile.

'Greetings, young Leto. It's good to see you again,' Rogar said.

The giant seemed to be in good cheer.

'Likewise, Rogar,' Leto replied.

He didn't feel in danger around the giant anymore, but it didn't hurt to be polite despite not feeling very sociable.

'Are you ready then?' Rogar said.

Leto had kept to himself the past few days and couldn't recall organising anything with the giant.

'Ready for what?' he said.

Rogar looked back to Mathius, his huge brow furrowed. 'You didn't tell him?'

'I apologise, my friend,' the old man said. 'He's been rather distant of late.'

The giant turned back to Leto.

'Yes, I can see it in his eyes.'

Leto didn't care what they thought or saw.

'Ready for what?' he repeated.

'We're going on a journey,' Rogar said. 'A short one, but I'm sure it'll be worth it.'

Leto sighed.

'Thank you for thinking of me, but I don't feel like going anywhere right now.'

Rogar shook his head. 'That's a shame. I guess that means you don't want this.'

The giant lifted his other hand, which held something about four feet in length, wrapped in a cloth.

'I was going to give it to you when we reached our destination, but Mathius was right. You need cheering up,' the giant continued.

Rogar extended the cloth-covered item towards Leto.

He certainly hadn't done anything to warrant a gift. Back in Avaleen, Leto received many gifts. He considered very few of them true gifts, as most were intended simply to curry royal favour.

He contemplated refusing the gift but hesitated. He looked at the cloth again and up at Rogar, who nodded his head in encouragement.

Leto stepped forward and took the item from the giant's hand. Mathius watched on anxiously as Leto carefully unwrapped the cloth, exposing a scabbard. He assumed it might be a sword that Mathius had saved from one of the many unfortunates who had not survived Dragon's Throat. But as he examined the scabbard, he realised this wasn't just any sword. It was his.

He'd thought it lost forever, sunk to the bottom of the river, never to be seen again. Any sword with a sharp edge can kill just as easily as an ancient weapon with a name and a long history. His father had given him the sword on his fifteenth name day, and now it provided Leto with his only tangible link to his father and Avaleen.

'I … I don't know what to say,' Leto said, caressing the scabbard. 'How … where … where did you find it?'

'You were hanging by your belt when I found you,' Rogar said. 'The simplest way to get you down was to cut the belt. Mathius said you had asked about it, so I went back and climbed up to where I found you. Sure enough, it was still there, wedged between some rocks.'

'It saved your life,' Mathius said.

Leto nodded as he drew the sword from the scabbard. He ran his eye over the weapon. He could see no damage to the blade.

'I repaired the belt as best as I could,' Rogar said as Leto sheathed the blade. 'I hope it still fits.'

The leather of the scabbard and belt wasn't as soft as before, probably from being submerged in the water for so long, but it didn't matter.

Leto looked up at the giant. 'Thank you Rogar, very much.'

'You're most welcome,' he said. 'May we leave now?'

Leave? Leto had been so overwhelmed with the return of his sword and the memories it conjured he had forgotten about the journey Rogar had spoken of only a few moments earlier. His dark mood had lightened somewhat, but he still wanted to be alone. However, the giant's expectant look and the effort he had gone to in retrieving the sword swayed Leto.

'Where are we going?' he asked.

Rogar's smile broadened. 'It's a surprise, but if you insist on knowing …'

Leto managed a brief smile. 'No, that's fine.'

He went to put the sword belt around his waist but stopped. He still wore the simple trousers and shirt he'd been given after his rescue. His armour and own clothes had been cleaned and placed near his bed, but he hadn't wanted to wear them. But now, with his sword back in his possession, it seemed like the right thing to do.

'How long will we be gone?'

'Three days, maybe four,' Rogar said.

'I'll be right back,' Leto said and hurried to his hut.

He entered the small shelter that had been his home for the past weeks. He stripped off the simple garb, pulled on his breeches and tunic, and decided to wear his leather breastplate. He strapped the belt around his waist, his sword now hanging comfortably at his side. It felt good, he thought as he exited the hut.

Darcy and Morn had appeared. The young girl had a satchel strapped to her back and another in her arms.

'There's enough food for five days,' Darcy said to her father.

'You're joining us?' Leto said, not realising Darcy would be going with them.

'Of course,' she said, handing him the other satchel, which he tossed over his shoulder.

It didn't matter; he enjoyed her company. She had dispensed with the usual shapeless dress and now wore trousers and a long shirt tied at the waist with a thin piece of leather. The outfit accentuated her womanly curves, and Leto caught himself staring.

'Let's go, then,' Leto said, averting his gaze.

Now the decision had been made, his mood lightened further. He actually looked forward to getting away from the village and seeing somewhere new. At worst, it would distract him from the recent dark thoughts plaguing his mind.

'Be careful,' Mathius said as he and Morn kissed Darcy's cheek.

'Yes, Father,' she said.

They finished their goodbyes and walked out of the village, Rogar in the lead, followed by Darcy, and Leto bringing up the rear. The giant took long, slow strides, but his steps equalled five or six of Leto's, so he and Darcy had to set a brisk pace to keep up.

Rogar led them back to the river, up towards the falls, and back along a familiar path into the jungle again. Leto thought Rogar would turn to the left and lead them up the rocky slope towards his cave, but the giant stopped and reached up to the top of an enormous boulder. He pulled down a huge sack which he slung over one shoulder with ease. Without a word of explanation, he started off again, following the smaller path underneath the rocky overhang to the right, that headed north. Leto and Darcy hurried after him.

They made their way along the edge of the jungle in the shadow of the cliffs. Thankfully, Rogar seemed aware of the limitations of the small folk following him and regularly stopped to allow them to rest.

The sun had long since dropped behind the cliffs when Rogar finally suggested making camp for the night. Leto slid the satchel from his back with an exhausted groan. Before he could rest, the giant asked him to help gather fire wood. When they returned, Darcy had unpacked the bedrolls and set out a circle of small rocks for the fire. Before long, the fire had been lit, and Darcy gave Leto some food, simple fare of bread and a piece of the elk Rogar had given them the day before. Leto had worked up an appetite and ate like a starved beggar, wolfing the food down in no time.

'How far until we get to wherever we're going?' Leto asked in between mouthfuls.

He had yet to see anything new, only the cliffs to the left and the jungle to the right.

'Mid-afternoon tomorrow, I expect,' Rogar said, chewing on a large chunk of meat the size of Leto's arm. 'If you can keep up.'

Darcy chuckled. She didn't look tired either. She'd probably worked hard every day of her life, so he shouldn't have been surprised. Leto remembered when he could walk and ride all day and well into the night without getting out of breath. However, the past couple of moons had taken its toll, and his physical condition had deteriorated.

'I'll keep up,' he said, yawning.

'Turn in,' Darcy said. 'I'll clean up.'

'Thank you,' Leto nodded.

He removed his armour and lay on the blanket, using his pack as a pillow. Night had only just fallen, but sleep came quickly.

He woke to Darcy's cheery face.

'Sorry to wake you,' she apologised.

He pushed himself up into a sitting position and rubbed his eyes. He couldn't see the giant anywhere.

'Rogar wants to leave soon,' she said by way of explanation.

He stood, wandered down to the trees at the edge of the jungle out of sight of Dariah, and relieved himself. When he arrived back at the campsite, Rogar had returned, and Darcy had already packed everything, ready to continue their journey. Leto picked up the satchel and tossed it over his shoulder.

'Sleep well?' Rogar asked, almost as cheerful as Darcy.

He had slept well, but weariness still dogged him.

'Yes,' Leto said.

'Good, good,' the giant said. 'Then we should go.'

'Which way?' Leto looked to the north, the way they had been heading yesterday.

Rogar grinned and turned towards the cliff. 'Up.'

Leto craned his neck. The dark rock shone in the early morning light. Low-hanging clouds obscured the top of the cliffs.

'Up there?'

Rogar laughed and started up the escarpment as Darcy handed Leto some bread and meat.

'We'll have to eat and walk.'

At first, the slope was gentle, and Leto kept up easily, but within a couple of hours, he could feel himself beginning to tire. They stopped to rest several times, Leto lagging as the slope increased, and the terrain became more rugged. If he'd known this much effort would be required, he may not have come.

The clouds had dissipated, and he could now see the top of the cliff he'd been climbing, perhaps a thousand feet or more. He turned and gazed out over the valley below.

The Black Cliffs bordering the jungle canopy acted like a wall that curved slightly to the southeast as far as the eye could see. About fifteen miles to the east, beyond the trees, a shimmering haze emanated from what looked to be a vast body of water. To the north, the dark rock also bent to the east but disappeared into a mountain range with peaks far higher than the cliff he had begun scaling.

'Leto!' Rogar called out and stepped down from a ledge six feet above and came towards him. 'Are you alright?'

'I'm fine,' Leto said, breathing deeply as he stood. 'I didn't expect to do so much climbing.'

He hadn't thought he'd be doing any at all.

'Would you like me to carry you?' Rogar said.

I'm not a child!

'What? No, I'll be fine,' he said. 'How much farther?'

'We should be there before sunset at our current pace,' Rogar said.

'To the top?'

Rogar nodded and stepped up, passing Darcy.

Leto momentarily contemplated the giant's offer of assistance. He may have accepted with minimal humiliation if it had only been himself and Rogar. However, with Darcy here, he couldn't bring himself to do it, especially since she hadn't stumbled, complained or fallen behind.

Leto struggled up the ever-increasing incline. It got so steep in places that even Rogar had to climb, though he did it without difficulty. Where Leto and Darcy couldn't climb, the giant lifted each of them as if they were small children, and carefully placed them on the level above.

The warmth of the afternoon sun disappeared behind the cliff. Leto knew he'd slowed them down. It'd be dark soon, and they would be stuck on the side of the cliff. Not the safest place to spend the night, Leto thought. He started to use the last of his energy in an extra effort to reach the top when the giant's voice broke him out of his concentration.

'We're here,' Rogar said.

To the east was a slight incline of black rock and a few hardy shrubs that had somehow grown in this inhospitable place.

'Is this it?' Leto said.

'Yes,' Rogar said, looking out over the Valley and spreading his arms wide. 'Isn't it magnificent?'

He couldn't argue. Even in the fading light, the view of the Valley impressed Leto, but he did think it looked just as good from halfway up the cliffs.

'Err … yes,' Leto said, struggling to hide his disappointment.

'It's wonderful, Rogar,' Darcy said with genuine excitement. 'Thank you for allowing me to come along.'

For a few moments, no-one spoke, and Leto's disappointment turned to irritation. He turned to the giant, about to voice his displeasure, but Rogar sported a wide grin and burst into a deep, cheerful laugh. What did he find so damn amusing? Leto's annoyance grew.

'No need to be anxious, young Leto,' the giant motioned towards the Valley below. 'This was for Darcy, but for you … '

Rogar gestured in the opposite direction, up the rocky slope. With reluctance, Leto ascended the gentle incline. He reached the top and once again felt the sun's warmth on his face. His heart skipped a beat, and he sucked in a breath.

'Does this satisfy you?' Rogar said, but Leto hardly heard him.

He now stood at the very top of the Black Cliffs with Avaleen spread out below him. From the Highlands in the north down to Bitter Bay in the south, his eyes darted about, not knowing where to look next. He could even see over the Burned Range towards the Greenhavens.

According to Lord Owen, his sister, Melina, should be there by now, possibly on her way to Cliffs End. She'd be heir to the throne and eminently more sensible than Leto. He probably wouldn't be in this situation if he'd been as astute as his sister. She would make a good Queen. The thought gave him solace.

His anger had quickly dissipated, but his heart still felt divided by joy at seeing his homeland and by heartache, knowing that he'd never again set foot in it. As the tears welled, he slumped to the ground ten yards from the edge. He was so close.

After a time, he felt a gentle hand on his shoulder.

'May I sit with you?' Darcy said.

Leto nodded but didn't say anything. He gazed out over the Shadowlands and beyond as she settled beside him. A thunderstorm had rolled in from the southeast across the bay, but it didn't yet obstruct his view of the sunset.

'It's beautiful,' Darcy said.

Leto agreed but stayed silent as tears trickled down his cheeks.

'It's so much better than my father described.'

They watched the burnt orange sun burnish the misty water of the Dividing Sea. Leto wiped the tears with his sleeve and faced the young woman.

'You've never seen a sunset?'

'It's the first time I've seen the sea.'

Leto shouldn't have been surprised. This valley contained no sea. He turned back just as the sun disappeared below the horizon.

Unless he made the trek up here again, this would be the last time he would see the sea or Avaleen. He stood and strode back down the slope to where Rogar had started a campfire.

'Why did you bring me here?' Leto's challenged.

Rogar gave Leto a puzzled look.

'Mathius told me you were feeling dispirited and missed your home. Did this not make you feel better?'

'Yes, but,' Leto held back the tears. 'No!'

'I don't understand. I haven't been to my homeland in over fifty years. I would love to see it again, even just a glimpse.'

Leto recalled the giant explaining that his homeland lay over two thousand miles to the north, over the mountains through the wastelands and across the sea.

'But if you wanted, you could make the journey back,' Leto said, more a statement than a question.

'True, but it's a long, dangerous journey, and there's nothing for me there now.'

'But you could if you chose to.'

'I suppose I could.'

'I have a sister, I am betrothed, I have … ' Leto's voice cracked, 'but … I can't go back.'

'Why not?' Rogar said as Darcy came up behind Leto.

Didn't he understand?

'Because there's no way back home for me!' Leto cried. 'I'm stuck here. The only way home for me is to jump off the edge.'

There was silence, and Leto shivered as he felt the wind increase.

'But you'd be dead,' Darcy said, frowning.

'At least I'd be home.'

Leto began to walk over to the satchel he'd left near the eastern edge of the cliff top.

'There is a way,' Rogar said, 'that will not result in your death.'

Leto turned and faced the giant.

'What?'

'There is a way you can return,' Rogar said.

'Mathius said there was no way back.'

'There is, but it can be quite dangerous,' Rogar said.

'Are … are you saying I can go home?'

Rogar nodded, and Leto tried to speak, but nothing came out. The revelation left him reeling.

'Would you like me to take you?' the giant said.

Leto could only nod.

'Good. Can we eat now?'

Leto didn't hear the giant's last comments. He rushed back up the slope and again looked out over Avaleen. Dusk had given way to night, and there wasn't much to see, but he didn't care.

He could go home.

8

OWEN

Owen woke with a start, his heart pumping and breath rapid, the images still sharp in his mind. Damn, would it never end?

He lay still for a few moments, calming himself.

The dreams had begun soon after arriving home, and they all ended the same way, with Owen failing to rescue the prince from the rushing waters of a river. Sometimes, he dreamed about the Winding River at the Red Pass and, at other times, a bridge near a strange waterfall or a river with no falls at all. No matter how hard Owen tried, he could never save Leto. There had been a difference this time, however; he'd managed to grab one of Leto's hands, but then they had both been washed over the falls and plunged into blackness.

At least he hadn't screamed out. The panic of the nightmare gradually receded even though the imagery did not. He glanced across to his wife, thankful he hadn't woken her. He couldn't see her face, but he knew exactly how it would look … peaceful … beautiful. He loved her very much. A dutiful wife and an excellent mother to their children, Addwyn wouldn't hesitate to challenge him if she thought he stepped out of line.

Since returning from the capitol without Leto, he had been content to stay hidden away in his solar, envisioning what he could have done differently. Addwyn had eventually had enough and confronted him.

'It wasn't your fault,' she had said. 'Stop beating yourself up about it.'

Owen gulped down another goblet of wine. 'But you weren't there!'

'He was young and foolish,' Addwyn continued. 'He should have known better, after all he'd been through.'

If Addwyn had been there, she would have admonished the prince and told him to stop being an irresponsible child and grow up. Owen had pandered to the boy. He did advise Leto they shouldn't stop until they'd at least crossed the bridge. Owen hadn't wanted to stop at all.

'I should have insisted.'

'You did,' Addwyn said.

He supposed he had, though he didn't want to bully the young prince. Leto had endured so much, and besides, they had made good time, with at least a day or more head start on any pursuit from the capitol. That someone had dared to follow them so deep into the Shadowlands still surprised Owen.

'I should have been firmer with him,' he had said.

'What's done is done,' Addwyn retorted. 'You have to look to the future now.'

Owen had contemplated his fate many times since his return to Darkmoor, and it wasn't pleasant, no matter how he looked at it. Greythorpe had yet to play his hand.

'What future?'

'You said it yourself; there's a war coming,' she'd said. 'We have to prepare.'

Let them come. Owen didn't care. No matter what he did, it wouldn't go well for him and his allies.

'Prepare then. You don't need me for that,' he'd said.

And for the first time, Addwyn had actually shouted at him.

'You are the Lord of this land!' she'd said, pointing a furious finger at him. 'Not me, you! Your people need you, and all you can do is hide and hope it all goes away! Well, it's not going anywhere.'

Owen couldn't meet her eye. He finished off the last of the wine in the cup.

'And what of your family, your children … of me? Don't you care anymore?'

Her anger and frustration had finally penetrated his melancholy, and he relented. Even though Penn had begun preparing since his return to the Shadowlands, Owen had, at last, formally ordered his commanders to begin preparations for war.

Smiling, he carefully pushed the blankets aside, slid his legs over the edge of the bed and yawned. The palest of dawn light forced its way around the edges of the shutters from the nearby window. Still tired, he knew he couldn't go back to sleep, so he slipped off the bed, deciding to dress and head to his solar. His servants had first-hand experience of his recent moodiness, so Owen knew he would remain undisturbed, for a while at least.

He crossed to the sideboard, but a casual glance at the hearth made him wary. Flames flickered where there should only be coals. The servants wouldn't enter his sleeping chambers without invitation, even to tend the fire. If they had, he would have heard them. He approached the hearth.

'Good morning, my lord,' a deep voice said.

Owen spun towards the voice, reaching for the sword he did not have. A man dressed all in black sat in one of the high-backed chairs facing the hearth. An older man of slim build with a narrow, lined face and long, greying hair. He also sported a short dark beard shot through with grey.

'Who the hell are you?' Owen said, keeping his voice at a firm whisper.

His heart began racing again, and his eyes flicked briefly to the bed. He didn't want Addwyn to wake to a stranger in their bed chamber.

'How did you get in here?' Owen growled.

At least a dozen guards had been assigned to the rooms that made up the Lord's apartments, not to mention the scores patrolling the rest of Darkmoor castle.

'It's fortunate you woke early today,' the man said.

As well as the intruder's conversational tone, it irritated Owen that the man was completely ignoring his questions.

'I took the liberty of tending your fire,' the stranger continued. 'I feel the cold much more than I used to. The joys of aging, I suppose.'

'Answer me!' Owen said through gritted teeth.

He stepped towards the seated figure, but the man raised his hand.

'No closer,' he warned, an edge to his voice. 'It would be most unfortunate if your guards were alerted.'

The man had penetrated Darkmoor's very tight defences. Still, Owen could barely contain his fury as the man glanced towards at the bed.

'You bastard!'

'I'm only warning you of the possible consequences if I find myself in danger,' the man said. 'I have no desire to harm you or your wife. Quite the opposite.'

The man gestured towards the chair opposite and waited.

'I'm here to help.'

Owen bristled. With reluctance, he sat.

'What help would I need from you?'

'More than you realise, though I am forced to admit I'm partly responsible for the danger in which you currently find yourself.'

'Me, in danger? Tell me something I don't know.'

He had been a Lord of Avaleen for decades, and you didn't stay in such a powerful position without making enemies, and if anything, being a close advisor and friend of the King had made it worse.

'This is different,' the intruder said.

'Why? And tell me why you needed to sneak into my bed chamber to warn me of this danger?'

'Someone in my line of work cannot just walk into your Great Hall and petition a lord like a commoner.'

Owen glared at the man, who had reverted to that irritating conversational tone.

'What makes you so special?'

The man indicated the surrounding room with a wave of his hand. 'I'm here in your bedchamber in the early hours of the morning, speaking directly to you, the Lord of the Shadowlands. Doesn't that show I am a serious man?'

'I don't take skulking thieves seriously.'

'I'm hardly a thief.'

'Just tell me who you are and what you want and then get out and leave us be.'

The man grimaced and took a deep breath.

'If you insist on being so boorish, I'll be more direct,' he said. 'You recently paid me a great sum of money to have someone killed. That someone also paid me a considerable amount to have you killed.'

Owen's astonishment at this revelation quickly abated. It should have come as no surprise. He began to speak, but the man raised his hand to quieten him.

'Please allow me to finish,' he continued. 'I don't generally get involved in politics. Who wants who dead and why, is not my business. Killing is my business, and I am very efficient at it.'

Owen scowled but stayed silent, now knowing the identity of the intruder. He hadn't heard of anyone who had ever met Grim Baldonado, the head of the cadre of assassins, Grim's Shadows. Something must be very wrong for him to be here.

'Is Greythorpe dead?' Owen said without thinking.

Grim Baldonado raised a finger to urge Owen to be silent. He bit back a retort.

'But there is politics, and there is business,' the assassin said. 'If I carry out both contracts, there would be chaos in Avaleen. You may think chaos would benefit my business, but it does not. Stability means people have more money and are inclined to pay more for my services. Therefore, I am declining your request, and your money will be returned in full.'

'But we had a deal.'

'This is a good thing for you, my lord,' Grim Baldonado said as if explaining something as obvious as the nose on his face.

'How so?'

'They are connected in such a way I either decline or accept them both. If I accept your request, then I must accept the other, and you would already be dead.'

Owen sat up straighter in the chair.

'You bastard!'

'It's not a threat, just the reality of the situation.'

Owen's anger continued to simmer, but he recognised that all manner of protection didn't mean a thing with Grim Baldonado and his ilk, hence the costly price of such a contract. He slumped back into his chair but straightened up again as he remembered the main reason for the assassin's visit.

'If you've cancelled the contracts, why am I still in danger?'

'It's something about which I am quite embarrassed,' Grim Baldonado said, spreading his hands in resignation. 'I rescinded the order, but unfortunately, the member of my organisation assigned to carry out the contract against you has instead decided to approach the client directly to offer his services.'

'So, I'm still a target for one of your assassins?'

'I am afraid so.'

'When?'

'Who knows? Soon, most likely, but trust that we will find him before any harm comes to you or your family. You have my solemn promise.'

'Trust you?' Owen almost laughed at the incredulous situation. 'Who's to say you can stop him?'

'I trained him,' Grim Baldonado said. 'I know everything he knows. You will be safe. Of course, there will also be compensation for your inconvenience. It's the least I can do since this situation was partially of my making.'

Owen had had enough.

'Partially? You're supposed to be the best, but one of your trusted assassins has gone rogue? Maybe you're getting too old for your chosen profession.'

The assassin stood, setting a stony glare at Owen.

'Most who see my face, it is the last thing they ever see. I have placed great trust in you, my lord.'

'Don't threaten me, old man.'

'I will leave now before you say something you'll truly regret.'

Owen stood and returned the old man's glare.

'Good. Don't come back.'

'You will not see me again, that is certain. And because I am an honourable man, I will fulfil my promise of protection and, in a way of apology, the offer of a further service.'

'I don't need your protection.'

'You do.'

‘Get out.’

Owen turned, strode towards the bed, and observed his sleeping wife. Addwyn wasn’t shy with her opinions, and no doubt she would have complicated matters if she had awoken. Not only that, but he had yet to tell her of his plan to have Greythorpe assassinated.

Owen took a few deep breaths to calm himself. Making an enemy of an assassin wasn’t a wise move. He turned back towards the hearth, but Grim Baldonado had gone. Owen glanced towards the window nearest the hearth and noticed the shutter wasn’t completely closed. Maybe he had been too disrespectful.

He sighed. He had screwed up yet again, feeling that he had made too many mistakes lately, some proving costly.

Maybe he was the one getting too old.

9

LETO

Leto raised his voice even more.

'Why?'

He had been energised by the news that he could return to Avaleen. As a result, the sluggishness he'd felt on the way up to the cliff top had disappeared, and he had no problem keeping up with Rogar and Darcy on the return journey. During the trek back to the village, his elation had been moderated by a nagging irritation. The old man had lied, saying he couldn't return to Avaleen. The resentment grew to anger the closer they got to the village. He questioned an embarrassed Darcy.

'He hardly ever spoke of it,' she said. 'I still don't know anything about him before he came to the Valley. "It's not important, it's all in the past," was all he would say.'

Leto found her explanation difficult to believe, but he couldn't see why she would lie.

'I'm sorry my father has kept this from you. I truly am.'

They approached the village late in the day. Leto ran ahead, glancing around, searching for Mathius. Not seeing him anywhere, he went straight to the old man's hut. Mathius appeared in the doorway at Leto's approach.

'Good, you're back safely,' the old man said.

'Why, dammit?' Leto said.

'Leto, what's wrong?' Mathius said, his face a picture of surprise and confusion.

'Why didn't you tell me there was a way home?' Leto said.

He now stood directly in front of the old man.

'I don't know what you mean,' Mathius said and threw a questioning look at Darcy, who had appeared with the giant right on her heels.

'Rogar said he can take me back to Avaleen.'

'He did?' Mathius questioned.

The old man stepped around Leto and went to the campfire, this time glancing up at Rogar. The giant nodded but said nothing.

'Why did you lie to me?' Leto demanded.

'I didn't lie,' Mathius said.

'Why didn't you say anything?' Darcy said. 'As much as I want Leto to stay, I wouldn't deny him the opportunity to return to his home. You didn't raise me that way. He should have a choice, if there is one.'

The old man's shoulders visibly rose and lowered with his deep sigh.

'Please, everyone, sit,' he said.

Morn came from the direction of the chopping block. 'What's going on?'

Mathius glanced at his wife. 'It's time to tell them my secret, my dear.'

'You don't need to tell them anything,' she said, a flicker of alarm crossing her face.

'I do now,' Mathius said, seating himself on one of the logs around the fire. 'Leto, Rogar, daughter, please.'

Leto and Darcy removed their packs and sat together on the opposite side of the fire. Rogar settled onto the ground beside them.

'Are you sure?' Morn asked quietly as she sat beside her husband.

Mathius nodded.

'Father?' Darcy's voice was a mix of apprehension and confusion.

'I haven't spoken of this in many years,' Mathius said. 'I rarely even think about it anymore. I have a life here, a loving wife and a beautiful daughter. What more could a man want?'

Leto glared at the old man, not even trying to hide his irritation.

Mathius looked Leto in the eye. 'I didn't lie to you. I honestly don't know if returning to Avaleen is possible.'

'How could you not?' Leto said. 'You've been here so long.'

'That's true. Thirty-two years since I came through the Dragon's Throat, and like you, Rogar saved me,' Mathius said.

Leto glanced at the giant, who nodded, confirming the old man's story.

'I survived and, aside from my leg, made a full recovery,' Mathius said, rubbing his thigh absently. 'I soon knew I didn't want to return home, so I never asked.'

'Not in all this time?' Leto said, sceptical.

The old man shook his head, and Leto turned to face the giant again.

'If you knew there was a way back to Avaleen, why didn't you at least offer it to him, like you did me?'

The giant seemed surprised at the question, and a few moments passed in silence.

'When I first knew Mathius, I didn't know such a path existed,' Rogar said. 'He only told me he never wanted to return, so when I became aware of a way into the Lowlands, I didn't see the point. I would have told him if he'd asked, but he did not.'

Leto still couldn't believe it, but he didn't want to get into an argument with the giant.

'What happened to make you choose to stay?' asked Leto, turning back to the old man. 'Who are … who were you? Is your name even Mathius?'

'Let me answer your second question first,' Mathius said.

The old man took a deep breath and began.

'Yes, my name is Mathius. Mathius Greenwood, Knight Eldar of Avaleen and youngest son of Noah Greenwood, Lord of the Greenhavens. I had two brothers, Griffen and Pieter, and a sister, Eliane. They were all older than I was. My mother was Darcy, after whom I named my daughter.'

Leto glanced at Darcy, now watching her father with rapt attention. But it was odd; Mathius referred to his family in the past tense.

'Griffen is still alive,' Leto said. 'But his son Gruffydd is now the Lord, and I was – am – betrothed to his niece, Cordelia.'

Leto's anger waned as he thought of Lord Owen's daughter. His heart knotted as memories of Dariah and their time together again flooded his mind. He shouldn't have left her there, surrounded by the Greythorpes.

'Gruffydd was always a good boy,' Mathius said, a faint smile crossing his lips. 'I always thought he'd make a fine Lord.'

A hint of chagrin returned as Leto remembered that the old man had nearly denied him the chance of ever seeing home again.

'Why didn't you want to go back?' Leto asked again, his voice harsher than he'd intended.

'You're too young to remember the War of Colours,' Mathius said.

'Yes, but my father told me about it. House Greenwood was one of his allies.'

'House Greenwood may have been, but I was not,' Mathius said. 'I was very young and idealistic. My father and I rarely saw eye to eye. I won't go into details, but we had a major disagreement, and I ended up fighting with House Brown.'

'Brown?' Leto said, thinking back to his father's stories and history lessons. The Browns had been a significant house in Avaleen for hundreds of years, controlling most of the southeastern lands north of the Winding River.

'Weren't they wiped out?' Leto asked Mathius.

'They were?' the old man's eyes widened at Leto's words. 'Then I certainly picked the wrong side.'

The old man sighed again.

'My father would never have forgiven me. I wouldn't have been welcome anywhere in Avaleen, so I resigned myself to making a life here.'

He clasped his wife's hand and smiled, glancing at his daughter.

'I have no regrets.'

Despite Mathius's admission that he had fought against his father, any bitterness Leto felt towards the old man receded, replaced by a sense of pity. Thirty years was a long time. Leto had been in the Valley for less than thirty days and had already begun descending into despair. Admittedly, Leto had reasons to go back to Avaleen.

'Now, may I ask why you wish to return?' Mathius said.

'Tell us who you are,' Morn challenged Leto, clearly bothered by his demands on her husband. 'Is your name even Leto?'

Now, everyone's eyes were on him. Leto hadn't wanted to divulge his true identity to anyone. Mathius had fought against his family in the War of Colours. If the old man had told the truth, the relationship with his father had been the reason for his change of allegiance, not any hatred towards the Blackwaters. And, as Leto wouldn't be staying, he didn't see the harm.

'My name is Leto,' he said, directing his words at Morn. 'Like your husband, I did not lie. I had no idea where I was or who was here, so I kept my identity to myself.'

Even though he had decided to tell them the truth, Leto felt a flutter of nerves, but he continued. 'I am Leto of House Blackwater, the last living son of Caleb.'

Depending on what Mathius had shared with his wife, he would be the only one to understand the significance of his family name. Moments later, the realisation appeared on Mathius's face, and he sat up a little straighter.

'Blackwater?' the old man said.

Morn leaned close to her husband, and they conversed briefly in whispers. The old man eventually nodded.

Morn faced Leto. 'I … apologise for my attitude. I didn't know who you –'

'Don't apologise,' Leto interrupted her. 'As Mathius said when I first arrived, there is no Avaleen here. I'm just a man.'

'But –,' Morn stopped as Leto raised his hand and shook his head.

'What's going on?' Darcy asked.

She shot her father a confused look. Mathius threw Leto a questioning glance, seeking permission to speak. Leto nodded his assent.

'We have a prince of Avaleen in our midst,' Mathius said.

'A prince?' Darcy said, now staring at Leto in bafflement.

'House Blackwater has been the royal house for as long as I can remember,' Mathius said. 'Callum was King during the war. Is he still alive?'

'He died when I was a small boy,' Leto said, his voice quiet.

'Therefore, Caleb Blackwater, Leto's father, is the King,' Mathius said.

'What does that mean?' Darcy said.

How could she not know, Leto thought, but he reasoned that Darcy was a child of the Valley. She had led a very sheltered life, not exposed to stories of kings and princes, especially with her father's reluctance to speak of his previous life.

'Leto could be next in line to the throne,' Mathius said. 'He will rule Avaleen after his father.'

Rogar cleared his throat. 'I don't like to bring this up, but did you not tell me that your father had been killed?'

Leto dropped his gaze to the flames and nodded.

'You have my condolences,' Mathius said. 'But that means you are the King?'

'Not yet,' Leto said, not looking up. 'And even when I return, I'm unsure what will happen.'

'Why not?' Mathius said, leaning forward.

Leto told them about his father's murder, his eventual escape from the capitol, and the attack at the Red Pass. No-one said a word as Leto spoke. Darkness had fallen by the time he finished.

'I now understand why you wish to return,' Mathius said. 'I met Regan Greythorpe many years ago, before the war. He'd accompanied his father on a visit to the Greenhavens. Lord Greyson tried to convince my father to ally himself with House Greythorpe. Sir Regan was only a knight then, and as cold and distant as his father.'

Leto found this piece of information interesting. House Greythorpe had fought on the same side as the King in the War of Colours. They had entered the war late, but when Lord Greyson and his army joined the fight, it tipped the scales heavily in favour of the King and his allies.

'If I have my way, he'll lose his head at the earliest opportunity,' Leto said.

Darcy expelled an audible gasp.

'You would kill this man?' she said.

Compared to people in Vale, Darcy, Morn, and even to a certain extent Rogar, did not understand how people acted in the real world. No laws applied here, and Darcy had been insulated from violence and death. Leto had said it without thought, and he regretted shocking her. He thought about his comments and came to an uncomfortable conclusion. Yes, he did want Regan Greythorpe dead, and he wanted Cedric Greythorpe dead as well. Not because they had broken the law. He wanted revenge, pure and simple.

'I watched him kill my father, with my own eyes,' Leto said. 'His son killed my best friend right in front of me. He has broken the law, and he should be punished. Without law, there is chaos, and no-one is safe.'

Darcy got up and walked out of the village towards the river. Leto felt guilty he had offended her but mostly felt shame for the burning desire for revenge on those who had destroyed his family. He rose to follow her.

'Let her be. She'll be alright,' Mathius said. 'She's young and doesn't know the way of the world outside this valley.'

'I don't like killing, but as King, sometimes hard decisions must be made for the greater good. That's what my father used to say,' Leto said, 'I won't apologise for that.'

'Then don't,' Mathius said. 'Kings should never apologise.'

Leto returned to his seat and gazed at the flames.

'I've never rescued a King before,' Rogar smiled.

Leto gave the giant a weak smile of his own.

'What do I call you now? Your Majesty … Your Royal Highness … ?' Rogar said, his smile widening into a grin.

'Just Leto,' he said. 'I'm no King here, and I'm amongst friends, I hope.'

Mathius nodded.

'That you are, young Leto,' Rogar said. 'That you are.'

Despite his concern for Darcy, Leto felt more relaxed than ever.

Weary from the trek back to the village and the long night's conversation, Leto slept well that night, better than he had since his arrival in the Valley. He woke well after dawn and stumbled out of his hut. He found Mathius seated near the fire in nearly the same position he had left him the previous evening.

'Where's Rogar?' Leto asked, glancing around.

'He'll be back in a few days,' Mathius answered. 'He has things to do before you depart.'

Anxious to begin his journey home, Leto had assumed he'd be leaving today, but it made sense. Rogar lived here and couldn't be expected to just up and go at a moment's notice, so he nodded in understanding.

'Before you go, I have something to ask of you,' Mathius said.

The old man looked haggard, like he hadn't slept. Leto sat down near the fire.

'Take Darcy with you.'

'What?' Leto said.

He had expected the old man to give him a message for his long-lost brother or ask him to complete some chores before he left this valley.

'I'm old,' Mathius said. 'I might last another ten years, maybe more, possibly less. Who knows what the gods have in store for me? Darcy can look after herself, but I want more for her than this solitary life. She has missed out on a normal childhood, stuck here with just her mother and me. A few others are around but aren't much younger than I am. I want her to have friends, fall in love, have children. She'll never have that here.'

'Are you sure?' Leto said.

Mathius nodded, letting the tears flow freely down his lined cheeks.

'She deserves better,' Mathius said, his voice cracking. 'Morn and I discussed this at length last night, and as much as it pains us, we've decided it's the best for Darcy.'

'Why don't you all come with us?' Leto suggested.

Not to ever see your parents again, he knew the heart-wrenching feeling, but he had never been given a choice. Sickness had claimed his mother, and Greythorpe had murdered his father. Why would Mathius send his daughter away, most likely never to see her again, when he had the choice to accompany her?

Mathius shook his head.

'If you're worried about your family, about how they'd react because you fought for the wrong side in a war that –'

Mathius raised his hand and shook his head again.

'Even though I know I can, I still have no desire to return,' Mathius said. 'Morn was born and raised here. She's too old to learn another way to live and doesn't want to leave.'

'Does Darcy know about this yet?' Leto said.

'Not yet. I wanted to know first if you'd be willing to take her.'

The old man looked expectantly at Leto.

‘Of course,’ Leto said, not hesitating. ‘But she must agree to it. I understand why you want her to go, but she shouldn’t be forced into something like this, even if you think it’s for the best.’

‘Thank you.’ The old man was visibly relieved. ‘She’s a headstrong girl and knows her mind, like her mother, but if she agrees to go, it’ll be her decision.’

Leto liked Darcy and would do as Mathius asked, but the journey would be long, and he didn’t want an unwilling travelling companion.

That afternoon, Mathius and Morn took Darcy to their hut to inform her of their plan. Leto sat near the campfire and couldn’t help but overhear the family’s conversation. As expected, emotions ran high, and Darcy burst into tears before her father could fully explain the reasons.

‘You want to send me away?’ she wept. ‘Don’t you love me anymore?’

‘Of course, we love you,’ Mathius said.

‘Then, why?’

Mathius again tried to give his reasons, but Darcy continued sobbing.

‘No! I won’t go. This is my home,’ she said.

Leto started feeling uncomfortable listening to Darcy’s anguish and her father and mother’s desperate attempts to console her, so he walked out of the village until he heard only the sounds of the jungle.

Leto kept walking until he came to the river. He approached the line of graves and stared at the nearest plot that belonged to the Greythorpe soldier. That could easily have been me, he thought, but the gods had smiled on him, and now he would be returning home. He no longer felt hatred towards his buried enemy. Leto directed his anger squarely at Regan Greythorpe and his moronic son, Cedric.

Leto blinked in surprise as it dawned on him that he had no idea what to do when he arrived back in Avaleen. How would he regain the crown? Should he find Lord Owen first, or his Uncle Malachy? Could he have the Greythorpes punished for what they had done? He sat on a dry patch near the water and considered these questions.

The sound of someone running through the jungle interrupted his quiet contemplation. He glanced over in time to see Darcy burst out of the trees and stop twenty feet from him at the river’s edge. She glanced at him as he stood. Her reddened eyes and pained look betrayed the decision she'd made.

'Are you sure you want this?' Leto said to the young woman after yet another bout of crying.

'Yes,' she said. 'I will miss them terribly, but I want to go.'

'I'll make sure you are looked after,' he said and embraced her.

She leaned her head on his shoulder and sobbed.

On the morning of the second day, Rogar returned to the village.

'Look after my little girl,' Morn said, sobbing.

'We'll keep her safe,' Rogar assured them.

Mathius and Morn nodded their acknowledgement as Darcy embraced her parents for the last time.

'She will have a good life in Avaleen,' Leto said. 'You have my word.'

'Thank you,' Mathius said as he hugged his daughter again.

Leto wanted the journey to begin immediately, but he wasn't about to hurry the soon-to-be-parted family, so he waited. Eventually, they departed from the small village with Rogar leading the way, Darcy behind him, and Leto bringing up the rear. After a brief stop at Rogar's cave to pick up some supplies – two large sacks the giant carried with ease – they made their way along the jungle's edge.

For the first couple of nights, camped in the shadow of the cliffs, Leto heard Darcy's quiet sobs as he lay on his bedroll. By the third day, she had stopped crying; by the fourth, she'd even begun to smile on occasion.

Despite being exhausted at the end of each day, Leto always woke ready to go. He needed no urging from the others. On the fifth day, they followed Rogar away from the cliffs into the jungle. Mathius had said it took about two days to get to the giant village, but all Leto had seen were rocks and trees since they started out.

'Rogar,' Leto said, 'I thought we were going to your village.'

'No,' Rogar said, his tone flat. 'There's another village of my kin at the base of the mountains. We'll be more … welcome there.'

Would we be more welcome, or would *he* be more welcome, Leto wondered as they trudged through the half-light of the jungle. No-one spoke for the rest of the day.

After making camp and lighting a small fire, Leto, Rogar and Darcy sat on the forest floor to eat their evening meal. They didn't need the fire for warmth, but rather to discourage wildlife from encroaching while they slept.

'Where are we going?' Darcy asked.

'The village is called Kresor, after its first chieftain,' Rogar said. 'The current chieftain is Stein, a good leader. The last time I was there, it was home to over a hundred of my kin.'

Leto had only just begun to feel comfortable around one giant, but a hundred?

'Are they all as friendly as you?' Darcy quizzed.

'Don't fret, Miss Darcy,' Rogar said. 'You'll be most welcome, I promise.'

Leto found Rogar's words reassuring, but his apprehension grew. One hundred giants!

'When will we get there?' Darcy said, echoing Leto's thoughts.

'Sometime tomorrow,' Rogar replied.

They'd been walking for over a week, and his initial enthusiasm about heading home that had given Leto extra energy, had started to wane.

Soon after dawn the next day, the steamy jungle began to thin out as they headed up into the mountains, which now loomed large over them. Before the sun had reached its zenith, they arrived at Kresor.

Before long, dozens of giants surrounded them. Some shot questions at Rogar, but most just gawped at the two tiny people who followed him. Darcy clutched Leto's arm as Rogar led them through the village.

They stopped in front of an enormous hut that stood five times as high and at least ten times as wide as the hut where Leto had been living. Rogar disappeared into it, and the crowd of giants around them grew until Leto couldn't see anything else.

'Make way, make way,' a deep voice ordered.

Leto turned towards the voice. The crowd parted to reveal Rogar and an older giant who looked down at Leto.

'Leto, this is Stein, the chieftain of Kresor,' Rogar explained.

Stein stood a few inches taller than Rogar but had a more powerful build. With his long, grey-flecked beard and completely bald head, the village chieftain had a presence unlike any Leto had encountered and he caught himself staring blankly up at the man.

'Rogar said you are a King?' Stein said.

'Err … yes,' Leto said. 'Well, I will be when I return home, but since my father's death, I'm … umm … I'm not crowned yet, but when I return, I'll be … '

Leto dropped his gaze from the giant chieftain. He hadn't openly talked of his father with anyone for weeks, and the act of saying it out loud again brought the feelings of loss and grief seething to the surface. He took a moment, pushed the feelings aside, and stood straighter.

'I'm sorry,' Leto looked back up at Stein. 'My father's loss is still fresh in my memory.'

'No apology necessary,' the chieftain said, waving his hand dismissively. 'Rogar has told me some of your situation. A tragedy.'

Leto bowed his head in acknowledgment.

'That would never happen among our people,' Stein added, his face impassive.

Leto glanced around as the nearby giants murmured their agreement, unsure whether or not the giant chieftain had delivered a rebuke.

'Rogar has told me something of your people,' Leto said, 'and I hope to bring the same level of peace and tolerance to my own … when I'm King, of course.'

That brought a smile to the chieftain's face.

'He says you are a good, kind man and that I should help you return to your home to reclaim your crown.'

Leto glanced up at Rogar, who smiled and shrugged.

'His opinion of me is most generous,' Leto said, meeting Stein's gaze again. 'Though any assistance you can provide would be most appreciated.'

'Hah!' Stein turned to Rogar. 'You didn't tell me he was also a diplomat.'

Rogar's smile widened.

'A true King, yes?' Rogar said.

Stein's smile disappeared, but his tone remained friendly.

'I know you wish to return to your homeland as soon as possible, but I'll need some time to think about it,' the Chieftain said.

Leto hoped to get an answer immediately, but he nodded his assent.

'Take as long as you wish, my lord,' he said.

They spent the rest of the day in the village, Darcy not leaving his side for most of the afternoon. They both followed Rogar as he visited various friends and acquaintances. After the sun had set, they sat around a fire with Arve and Wulftan, a pair of giants visiting from Rogar's home village. Arve began telling stories of Rogar as a younger man, with Wulftan, the more guarded of the two, interjecting occasionally, correcting Arve or adding to the story being told. The mood soured when the subject of Bor, the current chieftain of Rogar's home village, came up.

'We have missed you, but it was wise you did not return,' Arve said. 'Bor has been in a bad mood lately. He would not have helped you as I am sure Stein will.'

Wulftan nodded his agreement.

Rogar frowned. 'How bad is it?'

'There's been talk that the elders think he's too unstable and no longer want him as our chieftain,' Arve said.

'Some are threatening to leave,' Wulftan added.

'Leave?' Rogar said.

Both Arve and Wulftan nodded.

'That's not good,' Rogar said. 'Not good at all.'

'Bor has always been touchy, but he's been getting worse ever since you left,' Arve said.

Rogar grimaced.

'You embarrassed him,' Arve said. 'Everyone knows that wasn't your intent, and most of us admire you for what you did.'

'He shouldn't have pushed so,' Wulftan said.

'He was always a hard negotiator,' Rogar agreed.

'But labelling you a coward for conceding was a low act,' Arve said.

'The man's an arse,' Wulftan said, 'just like his father.'

'He lost a lot of respect that day, and he's done nothing since to change anyone's opinion,' Arve said.

Rogar had touched on why he had left his home village to live a solitary life in the cave. Still, it seemed to Leto that his story had just scratched the surface. This wasn't a simple disagreement. The story had some history behind it, and there were ramifications.

'My father warned me, but I didn't listen,' Rogar said. 'A new land, new attitudes, I thought.'

'He's always been an arse. A change of scenery wasn't going to change that,' Wulftan said.

Arve's cheeky smile returned. 'Anyway, what's done is done. Enough of this serious talk. I have plenty more stories about Rogar if you'd like to hear them?'

Rogar rolled his eyes in mock exasperation as Leto and Darcy nodded, grinning.

Leto relaxed a little more as Arve told his stories. To him, giants were the stuff of legends. No-one from Avaleen had ever seen a giant, and stories always painted them as lumbering, stupid creatures. That couldn't be farther from the truth. They were just like his own people, only bigger and from what he had been told, smarter. A race that could be at relative peace and not fight amongst themselves for over a thousand years must be intelligent.

Arve and Wulftan kept Leto and Darcy amused well into the night, taking turns telling stories, often to the embarrassment of Rogar.

'Don't listen to them,' Rogar said after a particularly awkward story. 'They exaggerate.'

The following morning, Stein led Leto, Darcy and Rogar towards the village's northern edge.

'The council elders have agreed to an escort for you, Prince Leto,' the Chieftain said.

'Thank you.'

'But I wasn't going to order any of my people to perform this task, so I asked for volunteers.'

That suited Leto. He didn't need any escort who wasn't happy to be there, especially when they were five times his size. They entered a large clearing surrounded by rocks and a few trees. Five giants stood in the centre, three men and two women.

'It seems escorting a prince back to his homeland to reclaim his crown was too good an opportunity to let pass. Half of the village wanted to go,' Stein said, somewhat bemused. 'I ended up making the decision myself anyway and picked those that would be most suitable.'

Leto had expected either one or two at most, but five? And he wondered what Stein meant by most suitable. The waiting giants stopped talking and moved into a loose line as Stein, Leto, Darcy and Rogar approached. They all acknowledged the Chieftain with a respectful nod. A couple of them glanced across to Rogar and did the same.

'Let me introduce you to this lot then,' Stein said.

The Chieftain indicated the woman on the far left.

'This is Sunni. You'll never get lost while she's with you. She could find her way out of a dense jungle in the dark, with her eyes closed.'

The same height as Rogar, she had an athletic build, long dark hair that hung in a braid down past the middle of her back; she wore a stern look.

Stein moved to the next giant. 'Big Gil. He's good in a fight. He'll keep you safe.'

Big Gil was definitely big, lean and muscled, and a foot taller than Sunni. His shaggy, light-brown hair came to his shoulders, the same colour and length as his unkempt beard.

Stein took a few more steps.

'This vagabond is Little Gil.'

Leto thought he'd misheard. The man could not be considered little, half a head taller than his namesake and with significantly broader shoulders. However, they did share the same dishevelled look. He would have been terrifying, but for the huge grin that emanated from his bearded face.

'He's here for two reasons,' Stein said. 'One, he's a pain in my arse, so I'll be glad to see the back of him, and two, I couldn't keep him and Big Gil apart anyway. Just don't let him drink too much ale.'

Stein and the others laughed, and the Chieftain of Kresor moved to the next giant in the line and sighed. The youthful woman looked tiny compared to the others, but still stood about ten feet tall. Her size aside, she could have been the same age as Leto's sister.

'This is Leila,' Stein said as he stopped before her. 'If I didn't let her go, I'd never hear the end of it. She's as stubborn as her mother but more beautiful. She has the voice of an angel, and I will miss it.'

Stein's voice had softened, his affection for the young woman obvious.

'Thank you, Uncle,' she said with a smile.

There was one more left to introduce, and Leto gazed up in awe at the enormous creature towering over Leila. He had long dark hair and a short-cropped beard. Except for a slight scowl, his face revealed nothing.

'This rather large lad is Viggo. He's here to keep this lot in line.'

Stein turned to Leto and waved his huge hand at the other members of the group.

'If you have a problem with any of them, tell Viggo, and he'll sort them out,' Stein said.

The massive man nodded dispassionately. He held an enormous wooden club at his side, six feet long and at least a foot wide at its end. Leto shuddered to think of the damage that could be done with that simple weapon.

'There you go,' Stein said. 'I hope you find them satisfactory.'

Satisfactory? Leto could barely hide his surprise, looking back to the Chieftain. He thought he'd be getting the miscreants and troublemakers Stein didn't want around. It seemed the giants held Leto in much higher esteem than he'd expected, and it appeared his escort consisted of highly skilled people.

'You honour me with this fine escort,' Leto said.

'Good, good,' Stein smiled. 'You'll leave first thing in the morning.'

That evening, Leto sat near the fire across from the Chieftain. Stein had invited him to share a meal, which Leto readily accepted. They ate well and drank ale, and Leto answered Stein's many questions about his family and the situation in his homeland.

'Why are you helping me?' Leto asked, eventually. 'You have no reason to. Our people have never met. We had no idea you even existed.'

'I will admit,' Stein said, 'when Rogar came to me with this request, I was in two minds. We haven't had any real dealings with the little people for many years. The number of your kind I have met in my lifetime I could count on my two hands.'

The giant held out his huge fists, extending his fingers.

'None impressed me much, but Rogar insisted you were different. I have known him a long time and I respect his judgement.'

'He's a good man,' Leto said. 'I wish more of my people were like him.'

The Chieftain shrugged.

'You are who you are,' Stein said. 'It is said that people are shaped by their leaders. Bad leaders, bad people, simple.'

'My father was a good man,' Leto said. 'Unfortunately, a few close to him weren't.'

The talk of his father brought the dark feelings to the surface again.

'It only takes a few,' Stein said.

'I'm going to fight like hell to lead my people just like he did,' Leto said, resolute. 'Maybe in time, my people will become more like yours.'

The big Chieftain smiled.

'Rogar is a gentle soul, and if everyone was like him, there would be no arguments, ever,' Stein said. 'But I fear he may have given you an overly flattering view of us. Generally, we are a peaceful people, but we do fight amongst ourselves, even coming to blows.'

'I don't know how long it will take, but once I have gained my crown, I'd like to return to Kresor,' Leto said. 'I'm sure there'd be something we could do that would be mutually beneficial.'

'A lowly village chieftain such as I, receiving a King,' Stein said. 'That would be a great honour.'

Leto surprised himself with the offer he had just made. Three moons ago, he would tell anyone who would listen he never wanted to be King. Now, here he was telling a giant chieftain he would take back his crown and open negotiations.

Dawn saw the entire village turn out to see them off; even the children, most of whom also towered above Leto. He had nearly become used to being amongst the enormous creatures in the village. Even Darcy wasn't quite so nervous, but she still left Leto's side only when necessary. However, with so many massive bodies in the relatively small area, he felt a little overwhelmed again as Stein and Rogar led him and Darcy to the clearing. The chatter died down when the chieftain stopped in front of the mammoth Viggo and the other members of the escort near the centre of the throng.

'Look after our new friends,' Stein said. 'And bring our kin back safe.'

Viggo nodded.

'Especially young Leila,' he added. 'If anything happens to her, Gaila will have my balls.'

'You got that right,' a female voice shouted from the crowd.

The uproar of laughter from the crowd was such that Leto had to cover his ears. He glanced at Darcy, who grimaced and did the same. Stein raised his arms for silence. After a few moments, the laughter died down, and the Chieftain looked down at Leto.

'Good luck,' Stein said. 'I hope you're successful in your quest and that you return someday soon.'

Leto bowed his head in deference to the giant.

'Thank you,' Leto said. 'And I look forward to seeing you and your people again.'

Leto estimated it took almost two hours before they even started to leave. It appeared every single villager had to personally wish the travelling company good luck and encouragement.

'Are all goodbyes like this?' Darcy whispered to Rogar.

'Usually, this would take half a day at least,' Rogar chuckled. 'But Stein has let it be known that farewells are to be kept brief today.'

By mid-morning, the goodbyes were over, and Viggo led the procession out of the clearing into the sparse tree line at a slow walk. He didn't look back. Sunni trailed a few steps behind, and like Viggo, her gaze remained ahead. Leila, the Chieftain's niece, followed, still waving goodbyes and shouting farewells. Leto and Darcy followed at a brisk pace, with Rogar and Little Gil close behind. Big Gil anchored the rear.

It wasn't long before they had left the trees behind and began ascending the mountain in earnest. There wasn't a defined path or track that Leto could see, but Viggo seemed to know where to go.

They stopped for brief rests, but the giants didn't look the least bit weary. Just as the sun disappeared beyond the cliff, Viggo stopped the day's trek and ordered the others to make camp. Despite the scarcity of wood, before long, a sizable campfire had been built up. At this point, the giants became more vocal, talking amongst themselves and to Leto and Darcy; Little Gil and Leila prepared the evening meal. All except Viggo, who remained silent.

They ate well. A hot stew of meat and vegetables and large crusts of bread.

'This is good,' Darcy said.

She glanced at Leto, who simply nodded and took another bite of his bread.

Little Gil laughed. 'Don't get used to it. The first couple of days of a journey, we always spoil ourselves a bit, but after that, it's always dried meat and whatever else –'

Little Gil stopped mid-sentence; Viggo, Sunni and Big Gil jumped to their feet as one and stared towards the southern edge of the makeshift camp. Everyone, including Leto and Darcy, looked in the same direction.

No-one spoke or moved.

Muffled voices could be heard from beyond the rocks. Viggo grabbed his mammoth club and strode to the edge of the camp. He stood in silence as the voices became louder. Leto could now make out what the voices said.

' … aren't stopping until we've caught them up.'

'I'm tired. We should stop and wait until morning.'

'You shouldn't have drunk so much then. Now, unless they're carrying the small folk, they won't be too –'

The voice stopped as two more giants appeared from behind a large pile of rocks near where Viggo stood. He raised his club and rested the head of the mammoth weapon in his other hand. Leto recognised them at once, the two from Rogar's home village, Arve and Wulftan.

'See,' Arve said. 'I told you we'd catch up to them today.'

Everyone visibly relaxed, except Viggo, who continued to glare at the newcomers.

'What are you doing here?' Viggo said.

'We've come to join your little expedition,' Arve replied.

'On whose authority?' Viggo challenged.

'Our own, of course,' Arve said.

'I'm sure Bor would disagree,' Viggo said.

Arve and Wulftan approached and stopped a respectful distance from Viggo.

'I don't care what Bor thinks,' Wulftan said. 'Just let us by, Viggo.'

Leto could feel the tension of the group rise once more. He remembered his conversation with Stein the previous evening, but would they come to blows over such a small matter?

'Let them pass,' Little Gil said. 'They're harmless.'

'Stein never consented to anyone but us to accompany the King of the Lowlands,' Viggo said.

'Are you serious?' Arve said, exasperated.

Viggo nodded slowly, lifted the head of his club slightly and let it drop back into his open palm with a smack. Rogar stood and moved to the side of the tall giant.

'Viggo,' Rogar said. 'I'll vouch for them.'

Viggo seemed not to have heard and continued to scowl at the newcomers. Leto couldn't see a reason not to allow them to stay at their camp, or join them on the trek. Leto liked Rogar's kinsmen, so he took a deep breath, stood, and faced Viggo and the newcomers.

'Viggo,' Leto's voice quavered ever so slightly. 'Let them stay with us.'

The enormous man turned to face Leto.

'Stein has not given his permission,' Viggo said.

'I'm giving my permission,' Leto said.

Viggo's face remained impassive. The giants owed Leto no allegiance, so he hoped he hadn't gone too far. Everyone awaited Viggo's response to what could easily be seen as an order from Leto.

Moments passed.

Eventually, Viggo lowered the club to his side. 'As you wish.'

Leto let out the breath he'd been holding as the stony-faced Viggo returned to his place around the campfire.

Arve's smile returned.

'Thank you,' Wulftan said.

The newcomers joined Rogar, who led them back towards the campfire.

'Arve, Wolf,' Leto said. 'I'm pleased to see you, but understand that Viggo is in charge of this expedition.'

'Sure, sure,' Arve said.

Leto looked expectantly at Wulftan.

'Certainly,' Wulftan said.

Leto cast a questioning look at Viggo. The giant stared at him, his face expressionless, and eventually nodded his agreement. The last thing Leto needed was a sixteen-foot giant upset with him.

The others made room for Arve and Wulftan around the fire, and the mood lightened. Leto took his seat and looked around at the members of his giant escort. Even if he stood, he still had to look up at Leila, the smallest member of the entourage, even when she was seated. However, it didn't bother him any longer.

The conversation flowed freely into the night, including Leto and Darcy on occasion. Leto excused himself as he began to yawn continuously. Darcy had the same problem and excused herself as well.

'I'm not surprised,' Big Gil said, 'You would have taken five times as many steps as we normal-sized folk.'

Everyone laughed at his joke and bid Leto and Darcy good night.

Leto lay down and pulled the blanket over his chest. Darcy did the same, her bedroll close to his own. He thought she had placed it rather close, but before he could think much about it, he fell into an exhausted sleep.

Over the next few days, the troupe ascended ever higher into the mountains, through rocky gorges and deep crevasses. As with the ascent to the cliff top, some sections proved too high for Leto and Darcy to climb, so the giants carefully lifted them to the next level. At the end of each day, Leto retired to his bedroll soon after the evening meal and fell into a dreamless slumber.

Around mid-morning on the fourth day, they came to a fast-flowing river running through the narrow gorge they'd just entered. Sunni led them downstream, easily stepping along the water's edge from boulder to boulder. With the incident at the Red Pass forefront in his mind, Leto trod carefully, but still lost his footing and nearly slipped into the water several times. Both Rogar and Big Gil offered to carry him, but he refused.

Darcy had no qualms and allowed Little Gil to carry her. She seemed to enjoy it, and Leto could hear her laughing as she conversed with the gentle giant. He smiled at the thought of Little Gil trying to charm the young woman. It seemed to be the giant's natural demeanour, but the question crossed his mind: what if a giant and a woman Darcy's size fell in love? It couldn't possibly work. He pushed the thought aside and concentrated on not falling into the river.

After several hours, they headed away from the water and descended through a broad crack in the cliffs. Aside from one twenty-foot drop, Leto made the descent under his own power.

To his surprise, Leto jumped down from the last ledge of the day and landed on dirt. Some moss covered the ground; it wasn't the hard, unforgiving rock of the past few days. Had they reached the bottom of the mountain? Viggo called a halt to the day's trek, and Leto sighed and slumped to the ground. He didn't think he could manage much more of this.

They didn't light a campfire that night, so after a plain but filling meal, Leto wrapped himself in his cloak and blanket and drifted off to sleep.

The following morning, Rogar woke him, the giant giving him a gentle nudge.

'Already?' Leto said as he yawned.

'Up you get,' Rogar said cheerfully. 'Another fine day.'

His tired limbs protested as he got to his feet. Darcy already had a plate of food ready for him. As usual, she brimmed with energy, bright-eyed and set for the day. However, she had expended hardly any energy, having spent most of the previous two days either in Little Gil's arms or perched on his broad shoulders.

Soon, Leto was again following in the footsteps of Leila, head down, placing one foot in front of the other. His legs ached, and Leto suspected he had slowed everyone down. He wanted to return to Avaleen as quickly as possible, but wouldn't ask for help. He thought it would be unkingly, especially given the flat ground on which they now travelled.

He nearly collided with Big Gil. Everyone had come to a halt and faced Leto.

'So, King of the Lowlands,' Viggo said. 'Where to now?'

Leto didn't understand and gave Viggo a blank look.

'How do I know? I thought you knew the way?' Leto's tiredness gave way to mild annoyance as he stifled a yawn. 'Are we lost?'

Viggo's puzzled expression mirrored his own.

'I've completed the first of my tasks,' Viggo said. 'We are in the Lowlands.'

Leto blinked, wondering whether he'd heard correctly.

'This is Avaleen, here?'

Viggo nodded impatiently.

Leto rubbed his eyes and took a proper look around. A flat plain spread out before him with a forest of trees several miles distant. The mountain range disappeared over the horizon to his left. Off to his right, a towering waterfall spewed out of a crack in the cliff face, which Leto surmised must be the source of the Winding River. They had come out in the northeast, but it was Avaleen.

Leto sank to his knees and bent forward until his forehead touched the ground. He scratched at the earth with his hands, feeling the dirt between his fingers. He stayed that way for a few moments, and raised his head, his arms slack at his sides. The tears welled in his eyes.

Darcy appeared at his side. 'Are you hurt?'

Leto glanced up at her and smiled. He shook his head. The relief overwhelmed him.

He was home.

10

REGAN

The little upstart!

Regan was livid when Cedric stormed out of his solar, barely able to believe he'd been spoken to like that.

'Should we retrieve him, my lord?' one of the guards asked, but Regan declined with a dismissive wave.

He had to quaff two cups of wine in quick succession before the shaking abated. He sat in front of the hearth with a third cup and considered the actions of his belligerent son. As he did so, Cedric's words echoed in his mind. He'd never been particularly close to any of his children. He'd left their upbringing to their mother. Even after her death, he still hadn't felt the need to overly involve himself. The children's governess had been more than capable of performing the child-rearing duties. He couldn't be bothered with children who weren't old enough to contribute to the success of House Greythorpe.

Regan's own father hadn't treated him any differently than he treated his own children. His younger son, Calvin, much brighter than Cedric, had turned into a fine administrator, but he didn't have the backbone required to lead. He had to admit that Cedric did have that trait. He just didn't know how to use it.

Consequently, Regan found himself dismounting from his horse outside a tavern in the East Quarter of the city. His escort of six Capitol Guards also dismounted. Two stayed with the horses while the other four took up their positions, two in front of Regan and two behind. He glanced up at the battered wooden sign hanging above the doorway, The Swinging Pig, the words above a crude image of a pig hanging by a noose.

'Are you sure he's here?' Regan said.

'Yes, my lord,' Captain Armin Penna said. 'He took a room for the night.'

Captain Penna led the way, and Regan entered the tavern, accompanied by his guards. The large room contained only a dozen customers at most. Regan scanned the space but couldn't see his son. A woman swept the floor, and a young boy scrubbed intently at something on one of the tables. Captain Penna approached the bar and spoke to the man behind it. This tavern had no redeeming features, as far as Regan could see.

'My lord,' Captain Penna returned and motioned towards the left of the bar.

Regan followed him towards the back of the room, where a burly man guarded another door. He hesitated, almost surprised at having to perform his duty so early in the day but quickly stepped aside when he sighted the Governor.

They entered the back room. Regan stopped inside and spied his son sitting at a table in the far corner.

'I want to be alone with my son,' Regan told Captain Penna.

The captain barked orders to the other two soldiers, who began herding the other patrons out of the room. One of them protested and required some rough handling, but within a short time, only Regan and Cedric remained, with Captain Penna guarding the door. Cedric glanced up at the commotion but returned to picking at his plate of food, shaking his head in resignation.

Regan crossed the room to Cedric's table.

'May I sit?'

Cedric waved his right hand casually without looking up, shoving a chunk of meat into his mouth with the other. Regan sat and waited while his son finished his mouthful, picked up the tankard near his plate and took a large gulp of its contents.

'Ale?'

Cedric looked like he'd just risen from his slumber, his red hair unkempt and still wearing the clothes he'd had on the previous evening.

'Milk,' Cedric said. 'Would you like some?'

Regan scowled at his son.

'Suit yourself,' Cedric said.

He stabbed his knife at another piece of meat, looked at it, but put it back on the plate and pushed it away a few inches.

'For some reason, I've lost my appetite,' Cedric said.

He looked up as Regan started to speak.

'Emiel!' Cedric yelled. 'Emiel, get your fat arse out here!'

It took all his control to resist voicing his displeasure at his son's disrespect.

Cedric gestured to a short, dark-skinned man wearing a dirty apron. He'd been stopped from entering the room by Captain Penna.

'Let him through. He's harmless,' Cedric said.

Regan signalled his permission, Captain Penna stepped back, and Emiel waddled towards the table.

'How may I serve you, my lord?'

The man had an unexpectedly soft voice for a man so large.

'Some ale, it's a celebration,' Cedric said. 'My father's come to visit.'

Emiel seemed nervous when he turned to Regan. 'And for you, my lord?'

'Nothing.'

'As you wish,' Emiel said.

The innkeeper cleared the table, except for Cedric's tankard of milk, and waddled off. Cedric leaned back in his chair and shrugged, glancing at Captain Penna.

'Are you going to have me dragged back to the castle and tell me not to be such a naughty boy again?'

'Don't be flippant with me,' Regan said, trying to keep calm.

'I suppose if you were going to do that, you wouldn't have come yourself.'

'Precisely,' Regan said. 'So, you should take my being here more seriously and cease the smart comments.'

Emiel returned and placed a tankard of ale in front of Cedric. They both waited in silence until the fat man had left the room. Cedric took a swig from the newly delivered tankard.

'Okay then, let's be serious,' Cedric said.

Regan bit back a retort as an odd feeling crept up on him. He usually gave orders, and people obeyed. Aside from the now-dead King, he never had to tiptoe around anyone's feelings. Regan had well-developed diplomatic skills but navigating this personal conversation with Cedric was proving entirely foreign to him.

'I want you to come back,' Regan said.

'Why the hell would I want to do that after the way you've treated me?'

'I may have underestimated you.'

He spoke the truth. Regan never suspected Cedric would dare to defy him as he'd done.

'Yes, you did,' Cedric said. 'But what's in it for me other than further ridicule and embarrassment? I think I've had quite enough for one lifetime.'

'Your brother is intelligent, but too soft,' Regan said. 'You're much stronger than he is, but you're rough. You have no idea how to conduct yourself or lead a powerful house like ours.'

Cedric took a swig of his ale. 'I get it. I'm the best of a bad bunch.'

'Let me finish,' Regan said through gritted teeth.

Cedric raised his hands in mock surrender.

'I was remiss in this part of your education. I made assumptions where I shouldn't have and wish to correct the oversight. You need to know what is required to lead a great house.'

Cedric leaned forward. 'You're serious.'

It wasn't a question, but Regan nodded.

Cedric rubbed his chin thoughtfully. 'What would this mean if I accepted this … offer?'

'I'd expect you to attend me nearly every waking hour,' Regan said. 'You would watch and listen. You'll take note of my opinions, my decisions, and the reasoning for those decisions. If you pay attention, eventually, you will know everything that I know.'

Cedric leaned forward, placed his elbows on the table and clasped his hands. Regan seemed to have piqued his son's interest, at least.

'I'd be your right hand?'

'To begin with, you'll just observe,' Regan said, 'but in time, if you learn, you'll be second only to me.'

'And you won't keep anything from me?'

'To understand how to rule, you'll need to know everything I know.'

'No secrets?'

Regan shook his head, knowing there'd always be things he'd never share. Cedric leaned back in his chair again, seemingly contemplating Regan's offer.

'Can I think about it for a few days?'

Inwardly, Regan seethed. What's to think about? I'm offering you Avaleen, you idiot.

Aloud, Regan said, 'Two days. If you don't present yourself by then, I'll assume you aren't interested, and I'll send for your brother.'

'Fair enough,' Cedric said. 'Two days.'

'Good.'

Now I can get out of this wretched place, he thought. Regan honestly couldn't see the appeal.

On the morning of the second day, Cedric turned up at Regan's solar. Thankfully, he'd cleaned himself up. His hair and beard were trimmed, and he wore decent clothes. He almost looked the part, not like that dirty, bedraggled mess Regan had seen at the tavern.

'So, what's first?'

'Just be quiet, watch and learn.'

'Even if it's just you and me?'

'No, but work still needs to get done, so don't ask too many questions.'

'How will I know how many is too many?'

'I'll let you know.'

Cedric accepted Regan's comment with a nod. 'Okay. I'll try, but most of it will be new to me.'

Instructing you is also new to me, Regan thought, but at least Cedric seemed to be taking this seriously. 'Sit.'

He thought about the next task. Regan needed Cedric to understand what he had planned. Lennane would be arriving soon, so he gave Cedric the salient points about her betrayal.

'The bitch! I've always detested her, but I never thought her capable of this.'

'We don't know for certain,' Regan said. 'This is all on the word of a servant, but Harrow's been working on the hedge knight for the last few days.'

His son stiffened at the mention of the bodyguard's name. Someone knocked on the door; Regan ignored it.

'I'm aware of your feelings towards him,' Regan said, 'but for the time being, he's needed, so you'll be quiet and put up with him, understand?'

Cedric averted his eyes but nodded.

'Good.'

Regan rose from his chair and headed towards the door but stopped and looked back, where Cedric remained seated. He recognised the look on his son's face, and Regan thought maybe this wasn't the best way to begin his apprenticeship.

'You can stay here if you wish.' Regan couldn't have Cedric lose his temper around two of the people he most despised.

Cedric looked up, snapping out of his fuming reverie at Regan's words.

'No, no,' Cedric said and stood. 'I want to come.'

'Then keep your feelings in check. Self-control is one of the most important traits required to rule successfully. Don't let others know what you're thinking.'

The boy had a lot to learn.

'Yes, sir.'

Regan continued towards the door, this time with Cedric in tow. He opened the door himself and entered the wide corridor outside his solar. There she stood, looking beautiful as ever in a subdued lavender gown, her hair down past her shoulders. Lennane had been dressing more demurely these past weeks, usually with long sleeves and higher necklines. She gave Cedric a fleeting look and turned her attention to Regan.

'Good morning, my love,' she said.

Regan only nodded.

'Good morning, Mother,' Cedric said with a grin.

Lennane ignored him.

'Follow me,' Regan said and kept walking.

She obediently fell into step behind him as he continued down the stone steps into the marble-floored foyer. Instead of exiting through the main doors, Regan strode towards a short corridor to the left of the large staircase. He didn't look back as he descended half a dozen steps into a much longer passage, lit by sconced torches. Regan heard Lennane's quick steps on the stone floor behind him. She struggled to keep up, but he continued his brisk pace along the passage, down a narrow stairwell and into another corridor. Even fewer torches lined the walls down here, just enough to light the way.

'Where are you taking me?' Lennane's voice sounded slightly strained.

Regan suppressed a smile. Consider yourself lucky I didn't just throw you into the dungeon and ask questions later.

They turned a corner, and ten yards ahead stood Harrow, a lighted torch in hand. At Regan's appearance, his bodyguard turned to the heavy oak door. It creaked as he pushed it open and entered. Regan stopped just outside the opening. He glanced back at Lennane and Cedric. She hid her unease well, and his son's face held a stony grimace.

Regan gestured towards the door. A slight furrow appeared on Lennane's otherwise perfect brow, but she entered the room. Regan and Cedric followed. She stopped a few steps into the room. Regan stood to her right, while Cedric stayed near the doorway.

The room was gloomy despite the torch that Harrow held. The clink of iron and a low moan permeated the shadows. At Regan's signal, Harrow stepped into the darkness and lit a three-foot-high brazier near the centre of the room.

'What's this?' Lennane shot a glance at Regan.

Harrow lit a second brazier to the right of the first and left the torch there, stepping back into the shadows. It took a few moments for the braziers to fully catch, but they suddenly flared and pushed back the darkness.

'What is the … who's that?' Lennane's voice quivered.

The man's clothes had been removed, his arms pulled up above his head, his wrists shackled with iron. The chain connecting his fettered wrists looped through a large metal hook suspended from the ceiling. The man hung there, head flopped forward, his feet six inches above the stone floor. Dirt and dried blood covered the man's body from head to toe. Regan could smell him from twenty feet away. Thankfully, the prisoner had been brought to this room from the chamber where he had been interrogated. The man's wounds indeed showed Harrow's penchant for the blade. Regan stayed silent. He expected her to try and run out in horror or vomit where she stood, as others would have when confronted with such a sight, but she did not.

'Who is it?' she repeated.

'A friend of yours, I believe.'

She looked at Regan. 'It's … difficult to tell,'

'Sir Masten Checker.'

Lennane stiffened but said nothing.

'He says he knows you,' Regan continued.

'Yes, yes, I know him,' she said. 'What has he done to incur your wrath?'

'Plotting against the crown, conspiracy to murder.'

And coveting my wife, thinking I wouldn't find out.

'If that's true, why hasn't he been executed?' she said.

'A mere hedge knight wouldn't even contemplate a crime of this magnitude without support or the promise of a substantial reward.'

'Anything's possible, but what's it to do with me?'

Regan had expected her to plead ignorance.

'Sir Masten claims you are his benefactor. The architect of the conspiracy.'

'What conspiracy?'

'You know,' Cedric chimed in. 'Arranging the death of the Princess Melina.'

Regan glowered at his son.

'Ridiculous,' she said, outraged. 'Why would I do that?'

'I asked myself the same question.'

'You should know by now that I only want what you want.'

'So why would he implicate you?'

Lennane stared at Regan for a few moments.

'Look at him. He'd say anything after having your … dog work on him,' she said, flicking a hand towards Harrow, who continued to stand silent in the semi-darkness, a sneer on his face. 'Hardly a reliable story.'

'By itself, yes, you'd be correct,' Regan said. 'But he's not the only one who's implicated you.'

'Who? Another one of his victims?' she scoffed, pointing again at Harrow.

'Your former handmaiden.'

'That little cow?' she said. 'Wait, did you have her spying on me?'

'She came to me of her own volition.'

Lennane laughed derisively. This wasn't what Regan had expected. She should be begging for forgiveness by now.

Lennane shook her head. 'You don't see it, do you?'

'See what?' Cedric said.

She ignored him and continued to look at Regan.

'She wasn't spying on me for you. Lord Owen or one of his allies probably sent her into your household to gather information and sow discontent in our family.'

'Preposterous,' Regan said, but her words gave him pause.

That Lennane could betray him like this had become more credible as time passed. This is what happened when things weren't dealt with promptly.

'Dariah wasn't the sweet, innocent girl she led us to believe,' Lennane's voice rose slightly. 'She opened her legs for the prince and then disappeared when he did. She had us all fooled. She probably helped him escape.'

Regan's mind raced. Could she be telling the truth? He had his sources of information in most of the major houses in Avaleen, but for Redstone to have one in his house so close to him was of grave concern. He'd have the girl found and question her himself.

'I see it now. You've had reservations about my loyalty these past weeks,' Lennane continued, her voice softening.

Regan noted the reference to his rough treatment of her in the bedchamber, but he didn't care. She needed to learn her place, whether she had betrayed him or not. However, her reaction to this accusation troubled him. By now, he had fully expected to have Harrow dragging her directly from this room to the dungeons.

'What do I have to do to prove it once and for all?' she pleaded.

'Don't believe her,' Cedric said. 'She's always been a lying, conniving bitch.'

'Be quiet,' Regan snapped.

'But you –'

'Silence!'

Regan had been taken aback at the accusations made against his wife. He had always suspected she ran her own agenda, but he felt betrayed by her conspiring against him in such a way. Without him, she would be nothing.

'I'll do whatever you command,' she said, eyes lowered.

Everyone is mine to command, Regan hovered over the thought.

He gestured to the bloodied man hanging between the braziers. 'What do you propose we do with him?'

She raised her head and glanced at the hedge knight. 'You can't let him go.'

'If what he says is false and he's only incriminated you due to his interrogation, why not release him?' Regan said.

'Look at him,' Lennane said. 'He'll never be the same man. He'll just end up a beggar on the city streets, blubbering lies about our family because he doesn't know any better.'

After being questioned by Harrow, no-one would ever be the same.

'Should I leave him to rot in the cells?' Regan said.

'Executing him would be kinder,' she said.

Regan paused for a moment.

'You're probably right,' he said.

She nodded her agreement. 'May we leave now?'

'Oh, no,' Regan said. 'I require one more thing from you before we put this distasteful episode behind us.'

'Anything, my love,' she said.

'Sir Masten's execution,' he said.

'Can it wait until I leave?' she said.

'You misunderstand me,' Regan sneered. 'You are going to execute him.'

She couldn't hide the shock as her head snapped up. 'Me?'

'Show your compassion. Put him out of his misery,' Regan said.

'But –'

'You wanted to prove your loyalty,' Regan said, returning her stunned look with a stony gaze. 'And it was your idea.'

Cedric smiled.

'Now?' she whispered, her voice suddenly hoarse.

He nodded at his wife and glanced at Harrow, who drew a long dagger from his belt. Lennane's breasts heaved under her bodice as she took a few deep breaths. He gestured in the direction of the prisoner. Lennane eventually bowed her head in assent and moved towards the bloodied man suspended between the braziers.

Harrow offered her the dagger, hilt first. She hesitated but took it, holding it at her side. Sir Masten groaned as Harrow stepped behind him and grabbed his hair. He yanked the helpless hedge knight's head back, exposing his throat.

Lennane stood directly in front of the suspended man. She glanced back at Regan, his pitiless look affirming his command. She faced the prisoner again, his body swinging slightly despite Harrow's grip. Eventually, she reached up and placed the point of the blade in the hollow of the man's throat.

Her hand trembled, and the blade pricked the skin. A small rivulet of blood began to flow, barely visible on his already dirty blood-covered neck. She held the pose for a few moments. Lennane placed her other hand behind the dagger's hilt before she made an audible intake of breath and pushed.

The hedge knight's body began to writhe as the blade pierced his neck barely an inch. Harrow quickly steadied the suspended knight, and Lennane pushed again, this time with a short, high-pitched wail. The dagger slid into Sir Masten's throat up to the hilt. The dying knight's body convulsed again.

Lennane yanked the dagger out, and a spray of blood followed. She jumped back and dropped the blade, which clattered on the stone floor. She stood there and watched the life disappear from the hedge knight, fresh blood pouring from his throat down his damaged body. The knight ceased struggling, and Harrow let go of the lifeless body and let it sway.

Lennane spun and strode towards the door, but Cedric blocked her way. She scowled at him. The spray of blood had stained the lavender dress across her heaving chest and over her shoulder. Regan nodded, and his son moved aside. She marched out of the room and disappeared up the dimly lit corridor.

'I didn't think she'd do it,' Cedric said.

Ordering her to kill the hedge knight had been a spur-of-the-moment decision. His wife had a ruthless streak, condemning the man to death without a second thought. That she performed the deed herself, even at his command, surprised him. Regan took one last look at the corpse of the hedge knight and walked out of the room.

Cedric followed. 'What now? Is she off the hook?'

She had proved her loyalty.

'For now.'

'So, she'll be visiting us more often again.' Cedric said, disappointed.

'Maybe,' Regan said. 'But I'll be sending her away on an errand soon.'

'What errand?' Cedric said.

'Malachy Kirkwood is one of the Blackwaters' staunchest allies, but he's isolated.'

'What can she do?'

'I'd prefer not to have to worry about an attack from behind when we march on the Shadowlands, no matter how small,' Regan said. 'On my behalf, she'll demand the Kirkwoods remain neutral, keep the port open and trade going, and in return, he won't meet the same fate as Redstone.'

'Do you think he'll accept?' Cedric asked.

'I'm sure the Lord of Ships will see he doesn't have much choice, and besides, my wife has many faults, but she does have a gift for negotiation.'

'I still don't trust her.'

'She won't be going alone.'

'Not me, I hope.'

Regan's original plan had been to send Cedric, but recent events caused him to amend is plans. 'No, you won't learn anything by delivering more messages.'

'Good.'

'Though I'm sure you'll be pleased with my choice of escort,' Regan said. 'I'm sending Harrow.'

Cedric laughed as they exited the long passage and entered the foyer of the Governor's tower. 'I couldn't think of anyone more deserving of her company than him.'

Regan considered his son's comment. Harrow is loyal, but the incident at Forest Keep showed he can easily get out of control.

With war coming, he needed as few worries as possible. Once Harrow and Lennane returned from Anchorage, he would decide what to do with him. His son could be right, and Harrow needed to be put down before he did any real damage.

11

OWEN

Owen scowled at the back of the merchant being escorted out of the Great Hall by the Door Warden, Captain Botas Argall.

'Wasn't that a little harsh, my dear?' Addwyn said.

Owen had been in a morose mood ever since the prince's death, and with the assassin's visit still fresh in his mind, he didn't hide his reluctance to perform his lordly duties. The arrival of an envoy from the Ruling Council hadn't helped either. He'd sent the Greythorpe lackey packing without an answer.

He glanced across at his wife, who was watching him, eyebrows raised.

'I gave him what he wanted, didn't I?'

'You didn't have to scare the man half to death.'

'I merely reminded him not to return until summer has been and gone.'

'Or you'll toss him into the bay.'

'Some try to take advantage of my generous nature,' he said, turning back to see the large oak and iron door close behind the merchant. 'I should've threatened to confiscate his wares. That would have hit the greedy bastard where it hurt the most.'

It was Addwyn's turn to snort.

'Really?'

He indicated the expanse of the hall with a wave of his arm.

'If you aren't happy with my performance, maybe you should attend to the people instead. You did such an excellent job while I was away.'

Her eyes narrowed. 'Oh, no! You aren't getting out of it that easily.'

He hadn't expected her to agree.

'Should I bring in the next petitioner, my lord,' the Steward inquired.

Owen glanced at his wife, who gave him a gentle smile. He nodded, and Soren signalled for the next supplicant to be admitted.

'Happy?' Owen said to Addwyn.

'It'll take time, my love. But at least pretend you're in a good mood.'

Owen still had not told her about the rogue assassin. He would have to soon, but he knew she wouldn't be pleased.

The next petitioner was another well-to-do merchant vaguely familiar to him, though he couldn't recall his name. In his younger days, he remembered a name and face after a single meeting. Nowadays, unless Owen saw someone regularly or they made a particularly memorable impression, he sometimes struggled to recall names.

The Door Warden led the merchant to the dais and stepped aside. The merchant performed a perfunctory bow. Owen may not stand on ceremony, but he earned a more respectful acknowledgment than this fat merchant had just provided, and he was in just the right mood to admonish the smug bastard.

'My lord,' Soren said. 'May I present the –'

The Steward was interrupted by the creak of the hall doors opening again. Everyone looked towards the entrance as one of the guards entered and hurried up the aisle. Captain Argall met the man halfway, and they spoke briefly. The Door Warden nodded and hurried back towards Owen.

'Captain?' Owen raised his eyebrows.

Captain Argall stepped in front of the merchant, who was clearly unimpressed at having his introduction interrupted.

'Lieutenant Oates has arrived, my lord,' the Door Warden said.

This was good news.

'Is Coen with him?'

'I believe so.'

Good. Owen missed his valet. The man could be aggravatingly straightforward at times, but Owen valued his opinion and always knew what he needed, usually before he did himself.

'He has requested an urgent audience,' the Door Warden continued.

This request for an audience irked him a little, but at least it gave him an excuse not to deal with another greedy merchant.

'Show him in,' Owen ordered. 'And find Archer.'

Captain Argall bowed and signalled to the guard near the entrance. The merchant opened his mouth to say something, but Owen raised his hand to silence him.

'We'll have to do this another time,' he said, keeping his tone as polite as possible.

The merchant looked as though he was about to protest but gave Owen and Addwyn a short bow and allowed himself to be ushered out by the Door Warden.

Usually, Lieutenant Oates should have reported to Captain Archer Janz upon arrival, who would have passed on any relevant information to Owen. A sense of foreboding replaced his initial annoyance. Good news rarely required immediate attention.

'I'll see no more today, Soren.'

'Yes, my lord,' the Steward said and hurried out of the hall, papers in hand.

A short time later, the doors to the Great Hall reopened, admitting Soren Vierra, freshly returned from delivering the bad news to the unseen claimants. Close behind him were Captain Archer, Lieutenant Oates and Coen Boon. They hurried to the dais. Soren took up his usual position to Owen's left. The two soldiers and his valet bowed.

'Lieutenant,' Owen said, his gaze settling on his soldier. 'It's good to see you've finally made it back.'

'It's good to be home, my lord.'

He didn't look that pleased, and neither did the others.

'What took you so long?' Owen said.

Addwyn lay her hand on his own and gave it a gentle squeeze, but he ignored the intention behind it.

'You should have been here a week ago.'

'We were delayed,' said the Lieutenant, his gaze flicking between Addwyn and Owen. 'You haven't heard?'

'Heard what?' Owen said.

The Lieutenant started to speak but stopped.

'Archer,' Owen was beginning to get impatient. 'Do you know what's going on?'

'Just what the Lieutenant told me on the way here,' the captain said. 'It's not good.'

'Out with it, then,' Owen said.

Captain Janz stood a little straighter. 'There was an incident, my lord … at Hampstead Heath.'

The captain's eyes settled on Addwyn, and Owen felt his wife's grip tighten on his hand.

'What are you on about, man?' Owen said. 'Explain yourself.'

'It was a massacre,' Archer said. 'They're dead.'

'Who, Captain?' Addwyn said.

'All of them, my lady,' Archer said. 'Over a hundred villagers … and Lord Gruffydd, Sir Kyle, Lady Emmaline and … young Master Griffen.'

Addwyn gasped and released Owen's hand. He looked at his wife. She had dropped back in her seat, a hand over her mouth. He was stunned beyond belief.

Owen had thought the news might be that one of his soldiers had been killed in a skirmish with some bandits or that the chest of gold, meant as payment to Grim's Shadows, had been stolen, but not this. Owen considered an attack on the House Greenwood as an attack on House Redstone. They were family, after all.

'So many,' Soren murmured.

So, who had perpetrated this monstrous slaughter? A mere bunch of bandits wouldn't have attacked Forest Keep. Owen's eyes settled on the Lieutenant.

'Tell me exactly what you saw.'

Lieutenant Oates nodded and gave a full report from the moment they had arrived at Hampstead Heath, describing the smouldering ruins of the town, the stinking pile of bodies in the courtyard of Forest Keep, and the pikes. He also relayed the stories of some survivors, in particular the

Chamberlain of Forest Keep, Elbert Tanke, who personally witnessed the deaths of Lord Gruffydd and his family.

By the end of the report, Owen was livid. Again, he looked at his wife. Tears flowed down her cheeks, but she wasn't sobbing. At least Gruffydd's family weren't completely wiped out. His daughter Renata had been here at Darkmoor visiting Addwyn and her grandparents, Lord Griffen and Lady Riona. She had been meant to return several weeks ago but, at her father's request, had stayed on to try and convince her grandparents to come back to Forest Keep for the winter and see their newest great-grandchild. They would now return, but not under the circumstances they would have wanted.

Owen's mind raced, and he quickly surmised that this tragedy in the Greenhavens had occurred around the same time as his encounter at the Red Pass, where Prince Leto was lost. Regan's son had led that detachment of Greythorpe soldiers, Owen had recognised Cedric at the bridge, even from a distance. At the time, Owen had been confident he and his men had enough of a start ahead of any pursuit from the capitol, but now it made sense. You couldn't outrun a raven. Cedric must have come from Hampstead Heath, not the capitol!

His thoughts turned to Princess Melina. Owen's message must have reached the Noble Guard at Whitehall, and the princess had escaped, but what had happened after that? Did Greythorpe now have the King's only surviving child?

'Where is this Chamberlain?' Owen inquired, his voice grim.

He wanted to question the man himself.

'He refused to come with us,' the Lieutenant said. 'He insisted on cleaning up in preparation for the return of Lord Griffin.'

'Did Greythorpe's men find the princess?' Owen asked. 'Was she taken back to the capitol?'

Lieutenant Oates' already sombre face turned ashen and shook his head.

'The princess is dead.'

Another collective gasp sounded from everyone within earshot. The massacre of his wife's family was a heinous tragedy that would not go unanswered, but this revelation hit Owen like a club. He slumped back in his seat, and silence descended on the Great Hall. Everyone looked to Owen, who, for a few moments, could not speak. He glanced at his valet, who confirmed the news with a solemn nod. He looked back to the Lieutenant.

'Are you certain?' Owen said.

The soldier nodded, stepped aside, and indicated the young woman behind him. She looked vaguely familiar.

'This is Constance Penti,' he said. 'Princess Melina's lady-in-waiting.'

Now her name had been spoken, the recognition was complete. Owen beckoned her closer. She moved to the base of the steps and curtsied. Her face was pale, but she held her head high.

'Constance,' Owen said. 'You were the last one to see the princess alive?'

After a few moments, the girl nodded, her face a mask of sadness.

'Did you see her killed?' he said.

'My lord, we saw –' Coen began before Owen raised his hand, cutting him off.

It wasn't that he didn't believe what he'd been told, but he wanted to know from someone who had seen it with their own eyes.

'I want to hear it from her.'

He looked at the girl, who again nodded.

'Speak, girl.'

'Y … Yes, my lord,' Constance said.

'You witnessed the death of Princess Melina?'

Constance nodded again, and her chin began to quiver. Owen was about to demand the girl speak again but felt a hand on his arm. Addwyn leaned towards him, tears still in her eyes.

'Not here,' she said, her voice raspy.

Owen glanced at the sniffling girl and back to Addwyn. He patted his wife's hand and faced the Steward.

'Soren, ensure Miss Penti is refreshed and brought to my solar in one hour.'

'Yes, my lord,' Soren said.

'Lieutenant Oates, Archer and Coen as well,' he said.

They bowed and exited the Great Hall.

Owen and his wife had barely reached their own chambers before Addwyn broke down and wept. Gruffydd was her only brother, and she had adored him. He had always looked out for her, giving Owen a hard time during their courtship.

'He's just testing you,' Addwyn had said with a smile. 'Wants to ensure you're good enough for his little sister.'

She was a strong woman, but to be told her brother and his entire family had been killed in such a barbaric way was just too much.

Owen held his wife tightly as deep sobs racked her body. A black fury filled Owen's heart as he vowed the Greythorpes would pay for these cowardly murders. After a while, he managed to get Addwyn to the bed, where she sat on the edge, her head bowed.

'Lie down. You should rest,' Owen said. 'I'll get the Maester to prepare a sleeping draught.'

Addwyn lifted her head.

'You'll do no such thing,' her voice was firm even through the tears. 'I'm not a fragile woman of the court. I'll be there when you question the girl.'

She certainly wasn't fragile, that Owen had to agree.

'It can wait until tomorrow.'

'No,' she wiped her eyes with a kerchief. 'I'll be fine.'

'Right, but I'll go and tell Lord Griffen,' Owen said. 'I don't want him hearing it from a servant.'

'No,' she said and stood. 'I should do it.'

Owen resisted the temptation to argue, knowing he couldn't dissuade her.

Later, with the shutters closed and a roaring fire in the hearth, Owen and Addwyn sat together on a settee in his solar. He placed his free hand on hers. Opposite, on an identical settee, sat the girl. Behind her stood Archer Janz, Lieutenant Oates and Coen.

'Constance,' Owen said. 'I know this is difficult, but we must know exactly what happened to the princess.'

'Yes, my lord,' she said.

'It's alright, dear,' Addwyn said. 'You're amongst friends.'

Despite her grief, his wife projected a calm that Owen could never have attained. The girl hesitated and nodded.

'I don't know where to start,' Constance said.

Her voice was soft, barely audible above the crackling of the fire.

'How about telling us how you got out of Whitehall?' Owen said.

Thankfully, she began to speak a little louder and told them about their escape from Whitehall, and they listened without interruption. She only broke down when recounting the death of the princess in the woods in the Greenhavens.

'This man with the scar,' Owen said. 'He killed Sir Fergus as well?'

She nodded.

'But Sir Fergus was already hurt. He and Sergeant Hudson faced a dozen soldiers so that the princess and I could get away,' Constance said, biting her lip. 'He was very brave.'

'And after that?' Owen said.

'I don't remember much,' she lowered her head again. 'Except that I managed to get to Forest Keep.'

'The Chamberlain spoke highly of Lady Constance and how she helped him deal with the tragedy,' Lieutenant Oates added.

'And what of Her Highness?' Owen said.

The girl blanched at the mention of the princess.

Owen had spoken briefly with Coen before this gathering, and he had also related the Chamberlain's good impression of the girl.

'The Chamberlain admitted to me he had not taken the death of Lord Gruffydd and his family well, but she helped him see the error of his ways,' Coen had said. 'And she initially refused to return to the site of the princess's murder, and after seeing it all for myself, I couldn't blame her.'

'But she did go?' Owen had enquired, and his valet had nodded.

The girl's actions impressed Owen. She had tried to sacrifice herself to save the princess, and even though the attempt failed, her bravery was not in doubt. He thought she had suffered enough and didn't want to cause her further anguish, so he looked to Lieutenant Oates.

'We decided that finding Her Highness was more important than anything else, so we headed into the forest. We came across the body of Sir Fergus first,' the soldier said and paused. 'It wasn't pleasant.'

'Who would do such a thing?' Addwyn said.

Owen had a fair idea but urged the Lieutenant to continue.

'We found the princess right where Lady Constance said she'd be. We didn't have the expertise or materials to preserve her body, and it was too wet to build a pyre, so we buried her in the middle of the clearing. I hope we did the right thing, my lord.'

Owen nodded. Her bones could be retrieved later, and the young princess could finally be laid to rest with her family in the crypt at Riverview.

'The Chamberlain asks that we send reinforcements and supplies,' the soldier added.

'How many survivors?'

'About three score villagers and a dozen or so from the keep, including the Chamberlain and some servants.'

'No guards or soldiers?'

The Lieutenant shook his head.

If Hampstead Heath wasn't of such strategic importance, he'd just evacuate everyone and leave it for the forest to claim. It would have hardly seemed worth sending anything with so few survivors, especially without protection. But he couldn't sit by and do nothing. Aside from the fact that his wife would curse him if he refused, old Lord Griffen had already insisted on returning to his ancestral home no matter how few remained.

'Coen, was it all as Lieutenant Oates described?' Owen said.

'Yes, my lord,' his valet said.

'It's all my fault!' Constance interjected. 'If it wasn't for me, she'd be alive, and Lord Gruffydd and Sir Kyle wouldn't be…'

Her voice trailed off.

'You can't blame yourself,' Addwyn said.

'I should be the one lying in the middle of that clearing, not Mellie!'

'Some things are beyond your control, no matter what you do,' Owen said, as images of Leto being washed over the falls flashed through his mind.

Addwyn moved across to the other settee and sat beside the girl, resting a hand on her back.

'You aren't responsible for her death or anyone else's,' Addwyn said, her voice soft.

'The animal that murdered her is the one who's to blame, no-one else,' Owen said.

He looked up at a knock on the door. It opened, and a guard stepped inside.

'A message arrived for you by raven, my lord,' the guard said, holding up a tiny bound scroll.

Owen beckoned to the guard, but Archer intercepted him and took the message, glancing at it.

'It's from Abbot Alwen,' he said, handing the scroll to Owen.

He'd heard enough. It left no doubt where the responsibility lay for this massacre.

'You may all go. Archer, bring Commander Holt in an hour to discuss support for the Greenhavens. Soren, take Lady Constance back to her room and send word to my brothers. I want them here post-haste.'

After their departure, Owen removed the ribbon from the small scroll and broke the seal. He unfurled it and began reading. He always appreciated missives from the Abbot, having received several since his return to Cliffs End. It was a relatively short message written in the Abbot's impeccable small lettering. As expected, it contained updates on the situation in the capitol, none of which boded well for Owen. He read the last few lines, and his face fell.

'What is it?' Addwyn said.

He reread the message., then looked up at his wife. 'That girl who helped Leto contact me in the capitol … '

She nodded. 'Dariah … has something happened to her?'

'You could say that.'

'Well?' Addwyn urged.

'She's with child.'

12

LETO

The Grateful Crow tavern held barely a dozen customers. Leto had hoped to learn about what was happening in Avaleen. Had Lord Regan taken the crown for himself, or was he controlling his sister like he'd tried to control Leto? Had Lord Owen escaped the Red Pass unharmed? He needed answers and could not wait until he made it to Anchorage for them to be answered.

Everyone in Avaleen must think him dead, and he ached at the thought that Melina, Cordelia and even Dariah would be mourning him. His future father-by-law had risked his life and the future of his own family to help Leto escape the clutches of Lord Regan, and all he had done was repay him with ignorance and foolishness. Leto vowed never to make that mistake again.

He felt a tug on his arm.

'Can we leave?' Darcy said.

He glanced at the young woman and thought bringing her along may have been a mistake. Aside from the village of the giants, this was the first town of any size she had visited and certainly the first tavern she had ever entered.

Viggo had not been pleased when Leto had informed him of his intentions. The giant had ordered Leila and Big Gil to go with him into the nearby town, but Leto refused.

'I want to be inconspicuous,' he had said. 'Having someone of your … size … would attract attention we don't need.'

'I don't want you going off alone,' Viggo said.

Viggo eventually relented, but with the condition that Leto take Darcy with him. He agreed, and the next morning he and Darcy entered the town while his giant escort hid in the nearby forest.

'We'll be fine,' he said and lowered his hand to the pommel of his sword. 'Just stay near me.'

They had not been welcome. Not even the grey-haired woman behind the bar seemed happy to see them, so he understood Darcy's anxiety.

'They're looking at us,' she said. 'Please, can we go?'

Leto surveyed the main room of the tavern again. He noticed men at one of the tables staring at them. He had hoped to find a busy tavern and hang around and overhear something … anything. It wasn't much of a plan, but it was all he had.

Looking at the near-empty tavern, Leto soon realised he'd come at the wrong time of the day. He should have known better. He felt another tug at his sleeve and decided there was no point in staying. He wouldn't learn anything without attracting attention, so he turned to leave. Darcy hurried outside, and he went to follow.

'Hey, stranger!'

Leto glanced back and froze.

'Leaving already? Come and join us.'

The man who spoke was seated and had turned in his chair. Leto recognised the man instantly. It was Cross, the bandit who had captured him and Jacob after they'd fled the capitol. He rubbed his jaw as the memory of the beating jumped into his mind. Another man at the table had also turned, a skinny bald man with a huge scar across his face.

Leto turned and followed Darcy out of the tavern, hoping he hadn't been recognised. Outside, he grabbed her arm just above the elbow and propelled her forward.

'Let's get back to the camp,' he said.

She glanced down at his hand, gripping her arm.

'What's wrong?' she said.

'Nothing, but Viggo was right. This was a bad idea.'

Leto surveyed the buildings as they hurried down the town's main street. He directed Darcy towards a gap between two nearby buildings.

'Hey!' Cross's voice came from behind them. 'Stop right there.'

Leto ignored it and kept walking.

'What's he want?' Darcy said.

'Nothing,' Leto said. 'Just keep moving.'

'Scar,' Cross said. 'If they don't stop, put a bolt in his back.'

Damn it! Leto pulled Darcy to a stop.

'Stay behind me,' he said.

'What's going on?'

He could hear the panic rising in her voice but ignored her question.

'Just be ready to run,' Leto said, his voice low.

He turned to face Cross and his men. They had approached within ten yards. Flanked by Scar on his left, who had his crossbow raised, and a tall, thin man on his right, the bandit leader took another step forward.

'There's nothing to fear,' Cross said, smiling. 'We're harmless.'

'Then leave us be,' Leto said. 'We have no quarrel with you.'

'But I have one with you.'

Leto's heart skipped a beat. It had been over three moons since their earlier encounter, and Leto's hair had grown. A short beard covered his face as well, more than enough of a change to hopefully conceal his identity.

'You're a rude little bastard,' the bandit leader said. 'Nobody walks away from me and gets away with it.'

He hadn't recognised Leto, but had selected him and Darcy as their next potential victims.

'We have nothing,' Leto said. 'Let us be on our way.'

Cross gestured towards Darcy with a leering smile.

'I wouldn't say that. I'm sure she has something to offer. Whether it's of any value, I'll tell you afterwards.'

The other two bandits chuckled.

'What does he mean by that?' she said.

‘So, you’re not a murderer, only a rapist?’ Leto said to Cross, ignoring Darcy.

‘Who’s to say she won’t offer herself willingly?’ Cross said. ‘I can be quite charming.’

Cross and the tall bandit laughed, but Scar did not.

‘I say,’ Leto said, his growing anger pushing back the fear.

Leto felt Scar staring at him quizzically. He leaned in towards Cross and spoke. Leto couldn’t hear the conversation, but both men glanced at him. Eventually, Scar raised his weapon and held it with more determination. Now Cross stared at Leto, taking in his features more carefully. The anger Leto had felt dissipated, replaced with dread.

‘You!’ Cross said. ‘It is you!’

He’d been recognised.

‘I told you it was,’ Scar said. ‘Let’s kill him now and be done with it.’

Cross ignored him and strode towards Leto, drawing his sword.

‘You bastard!’ he said.

Leto unsheathed his weapon and readied himself.

‘You got my band killed,’ Cross said, his voice taking on a savage tone. ‘I’m going to gut you, then have some fun with your woman.’

He glanced at Darcy. She looked back in horror.

‘Run!’ he said.

She didn’t move, so he pushed her away with his free hand.

‘Go! Find Viggo.’

Leto turned back to see Cross now only a few yards away, his face full of anger.

‘Stringer, go after the girl and bring her back,’ Cross said.

‘Yes, boss,’ the tall bandit said and ran off, giving Leto a wide berth.

He prayed Darcy could find her way back to the giants before the bandit caught her.

The bandit leader wasn’t a huge man, but he was taller than Leto, had a longer reach, and used both to his advantage as he struck. Leto jumped back, the point of the sword missing his chest by an inch.

‘I’m going to make you hurt,’ Cross said.

He was quick, too. Leto deflected the second blow, which came in hard and fast. Again, he retreated under Cross’s advance, unable to go on the offensive. The man was angry. Usually, that would have tipped the scales in Leto's favour, but Cross's anger seemed measured. It wasn't affecting his judgement, as Leto had hoped. Again and again, he barely fended off Cross's blade. He was out of practice.

He tried to take advantage of a small opening, but the bandit leader parried his attempt with ease. Leto stumbled and felt a sting. A line of blood began seeping through his sleeve.

'There's more where that came from,' Cross said. 'You'll be begging me to kill you. I promise you that, little man.'

Leto continued to give ground under Cross's renewed assault and realised he couldn't win this fight. Even if he could defeat Cross, Scar was waiting off to Leto's left, ready to skewer him with an iron-tipped bolt. He was tiring already and wouldn't last much longer. An idea began to form.

'Little man?' Leto said. 'You aren't so big yourself.'

He shuffled to his right, trying to get Cross between himself and Scar.

'Big enough to cleave you in two.'

Leto used this slight distraction to launch a quick counterattack. He didn't pierce Cross's defence, but it did force him to stop his forward movement.

'You can fight after all,' Cross said.

He shuffled around a little more.

'I'm full of surprises,' Leto said.

Scar was now out of Leto's field of view. He retreated a few steps and crouched low. With his free hand, he scooped up dirt from the dusty street and flung it at his assailant's face. It wasn't a good throw, but it was enough.

'Aaarrrgghh!' Cross bellowed.

The bandit leader stumbled back and rubbed at his eyes. It was the opening he needed. Leto turned and ran. He ignored the shouts from behind and cut into a gap between two nearby buildings. Leto sprinted down the shaded alley, came out into the morning sunlight. There was no cover between the buildings and the forest, fifty yards away, but he kept running, changing direction occasionally, hoping to disrupt Scar's aim.

'Stop, you prick, or you'll be sorry!' Cross yelled.

Leto was already sorry. Sorry he hadn't listened to Viggo, sorry he had dragged Darcy into this mess and sorry he'd been so stupid as to get himself into such a situation. He had promised to listen to those who knew better, and he had ignored Viggo's advice. What an idiot. He couldn't even keep promises to himself, he thought, as he sped towards safety.

Thirty yards to go …

… twenty yards … ten … five …

Leto dashed into the forest. He had made it!

A crossbow bolt whistled past and thudded into the tree just to his left. He flinched and stepped to the right, caught his foot on a concealed tree root and fell face-first to the forest floor.

He scrambled to his knees. His sword lay a few feet away and he scrambled on all fours towards it. He had nearly reached it when white-hot agony sliced through his shoulder. Leto screamed and fell to the ground again. He tried pushing himself up, but his left arm wouldn't obey.

'Viggo!'

Six inches of a crossbow bolt protruded from his shoulder, but he managed to get to his knees and grab his sword. Cross had already entered the trees, with Scar a dozen paces back.

'Gil! Rogar!'

He hoped his new friends weren't too far away.

'You're a dead man!' Cross shouted after him.

Leto struggled to his feet and turned. Cross was now only fifteen feet away and had slowed to a walk. Leto felt the dirt clinging to his face and neck as he raised his sword and pointed it at the approaching bandit.

'Good try,' Cross said. 'But you aren't escaping me this time.'

Scar came to a halt beside Cross, his crossbow directed at Leto.

'We should kill him now,' Scar said. 'He's caused us too much trouble already.'

Cross glared at Leto and dropped his sword arm to his side. Leto did the same. He suspected the bandit leader would grant Scar's wish, but he had one more play to save his life.

'Ransom me,' Leto said, finding it difficult to breathe. 'I'm worth a lot.'

'Is that so?' Cross said.

'He's nothin' but trouble,' Scar said. 'Let me kill him.'

Cross smiled. It wasn't a happy smile, and at that point, Leto knew his final gambit had failed.

'You're right,' Cross said. 'Kill him.'

Leto dropped his sword and fell to his knees. He was a dead man.

'About bloody time!' Scar said.

Leto sighed as the bandit took careful aim. He wouldn't miss this time. He hoped Darcy was alright. Leto looked up at his killer, resigned to his fate.

Suddenly, there was a roar to Leto's left and one of the giants burst out of the trees. He felt a breeze as a massive club swung past his face. Before Scar could react, the club had smashed the crossbow and struck him in the chest. He was propelled backwards through the air, slamming into the trunk of a tree twenty feet away with a sickening thud. He fell to the ground in a crumpled heap.

Cross quickly raised his sword, but the giant swatted it away like it wasn't there. Leto watched in awe as Viggo seized the bandit leader by the neck and tossed him into the air. He flew in a perfect arc, brushing the underside of the forest canopy thirty feet up. His screams came to an abrupt halt when he struck the forest floor. His body shuddered for a moment, and became still.

'Are you alright?' the big man said.

Viggo looked down at him with deep concern. Leto took a moment, still reeling from another near-death experience.

'Sure … sure.'

'You don't look it,' Viggo said, unconvinced.

Leto picked up his sword again and winced as he stood. He hurt all over.

'Darcy, did she get away?' Leto said.

'She's safe,' the big man said.

The giant leaned down and scooped Leto up in his arms. The gentleness of the huge man surprised him. Viggo carried him deeper into the forest. He looked back once more at the crumpled bodies of the two bandits. The power and intensity of Viggo's attack had stunned him. Previously, he'd only been able to imagine the damage one of these giants could do. Viggo was one giant, an extra-large one to be sure, but still only one. He could dispatch a score of normal men in the blink of an eye. It sent chills through his body as he thought, the gods help anyone who goes up against a giant.

At the makeshift camp, Leto cried out in agony again as Little Gil poured a dark concoction into the deep wound in his left shoulder, having staunched the flow of blood after yanking the bolt out moments earlier.

'You said it wouldn't hurt,' Leto said, grimacing.

'Did I?' Little Gil said with a smile.

His eyes watered as the sharp pain reduced to an intense ache.

'The expectation of pain can often be worse than the pain itself,' Wulftan offered.

Leto begged to differ but said nothing.

'You got off lightly,' Little Gil said, now dressing the light sword cut on his arm. 'It could have been much worse from what I hear.'

He spoke the truth. He looked across to Darcy where Sunni tended to her wounds. Thankfully, she had escaped with only a few scratches and cuts. Leto could not have forgiven himself if she had been more seriously injured.

'I'm sorry, Darcy,' he said.

She looked up at him, distress in her eyes.

'Why did they chase me?' she said. 'I didn't do anything to them.'

'They were bad people,' Leto said.

'I should have stayed home,' she whimpered and looked away.

'Not all people in Avaleen are like that. Most are good and kind,' Leto said. 'I promise you.'

He nearly laughed at himself in disgust, offering another promise he may be unable to keep.

'He's right,' Rogar agreed. 'There are always a few that make things difficult for the rest of us.'

Leto was relieved his friend had voiced his support. He could see Darcy was upset and probably wouldn't listen to anything he'd say, but she had known Rogar all her life, so he hoped his words would have more sway with her. Leto didn't want Darcy to regret leaving her father and mother. He wanted her to be happy here, though this wasn't a good start.

'There you go. It'll be fine in a week or so,' Big Gil said. 'Unless you plan on getting shot again.'

Some of the other giants chuckled. Viggo did not.

'Thank you for saving me,' Leto said to the big commander. 'I should have listened to you. I'm sorry. It won't happen again.'

'I know,' Viggo said, turned and walked away.

What did that mean? Did the giant commander not believe him, or was it something else?

As much as Leto would have liked to rest, Viggo soon insisted they get moving. With all the commotion from the encounter with Cross, Leto wanted to be long gone before someone found the dead bodies, so he didn't argue. He had been recognised by Cross, so it was possible others may have as well. If word of his return reached the capitol, soldiers might be dispatched after him. He wasn't afraid for his own safety, not with his giant escort, but they didn't need the complication.

They headed deeper into the forest, but his tangle with Cross had taken more out of him than he'd thought, and he couldn't move as quickly as he had before.

'Any slower, and I'd be standing still,' Little Gil joked after a while.

Only Arve and Wulftan laughed, but even their mirth was subdued. Leto tried to walk faster, being careful not to stumble. They trudged through the trees for a while longer before Viggo called a halt. The big man said something to Sunni, who was leading the procession. She replied and called Big Gil over and said something to him as well. Their discussion ceased, and the three giants turned and approached Leto.

'Why have we stopped?' Leto said.

'You are injured,' Viggo said.

Why was Viggo stating the obvious?

'You need assistance,' the giant continued.

His shoulder was hurting, but it was bearable.

'I can manage it,' he said.

The giant commander sighed, seemingly uncomfortable with this exchange.

'What?' Leto said.

Big Gil stepped forward.

'You're too slow, so we will carry you,' he said.

So that was the real reason, not his relatively minor injury. He was walking slower than usual, but wanted to travel under his power. He didn't want to be carried.

'No, thank you. I'll be fine,' Leto said.

'I insist,' Viggo said.

Leto was surprised and bothered at the giant's attempt to stamp his authority over him. He was here to keep the other giants in line, not Leto. He could do what he pleased.

'What if I disagree?' Leto said.

'Didn't you promise to listen to my advice?' Viggo said.

He had, but the danger diminished, the further they got from the town.

'If the directions you gave us are good, Sunni says it will take four more days to reach our destination,' Viggo continued.

'At our current pace,' Big Gil said.

Four more days?

'We could get there by the day after tomorrow,' Sunni said. 'Earlier if we hurry.'

Leto glanced around. Everyone was looking at him. If only he had a horse. He felt a touch on his arm and turned. It was Darcy. Thankfully, her mood had lightened since the morning.

'It's not so bad,' she said with a smile.

Little Gil had carried Darcy on many occasions since leaving Kresor. Leto's first reaction was to castigate her and accuse her of being weak and lazy, but he bit back the retort. That wouldn't have been fair. She wasn't weak or lazy, and he was ashamed for even thinking it. He sighed. She was right. He softened his gaze and turned back to Viggo.

'Okay, but I don't want to be carried like a baby,' he said.

Viggo stared at Leto and shot Little Gil a questioning look. Little Gil thought for a few moments and nodded.

Within half an hour, the party was underway again, this time at a much more rapid pace. Darcy had taken up her usual position on Little Gil's shoulder, and Leto was now perched on Rogar's back. His feet hooked into loops on a rope, part of a simple harness hastily constructed by Little Gil. There was also a rope around his waist to keep him from falling backward, but at least he could retain some dignity. He gripped Rogar's shoulders to steady himself. Leto peered past his friend's head and admitted they made much better time. Even through the trees, they travelled at least five times faster than with Leto walking.

It wasn't long before they left the forest and a grassy plain opened before them. Leto grinned as he looked to the north and saw the Daylight Mountains. It was his first truly recognisable landmark since stepping back into Avaleen. This meant there would be an increased chance of encountering people. After the debacle in the town that morning, it was something Leto wanted to avoid as long as possible. He attracted Viggo's attention and told him as much.

'And there's only one road over the mountain, and that's through Kings Pass,' Leto said.

Viggo glanced to the west at the setting sun, and towards the mountains. 'We'll make camp at the foot of the range.'

Leto could see the mountain range in the distance. The base was way over the horizon and out of view. It was easily half a day's walk, and there were only a couple of hours of light left at most.

'Let's make up some time,' Viggo said.

'Finally,' Little Gil said with a grin.

'Hang on,' Rogar said. 'Tight.'

He tightened his grip on the ropes, wondering what was about to happen.

'Let me know if your injury gets too painful,' Rogar began following the others directly north at a slow walk.

Too painful from what? Darcy was now held down in Little Gil's arms, no longer perched high on his shoulder.

'Here we go,' Rogar said.

All the giants broke into a run. Leto almost lost his grip but managed to stay upright, though his shoulder protested with bolts of pain shooting up his arm and into his back. After the initial shock, he finally began to hold his balance, moving with the rhythm of the giant's slow-loping stride, and he felt exhilarated. Up so high, speeding across the plain as fast as a galloping horse, he found himself grinning like he had when he had first galloped on a horse as a young boy.

It was well before sundown when they arrived at the base of the mountains and set up camp under a rocky overhang. Darkness fell before the exhilaration from their race across the plain had worn off, but once it did, Leto felt exhausted. So much so, that soon after having a bite to eat and Big Gil tend to his shoulder, he retired to his bedroll. Not even the throbbing of his wound kept Leto from falling asleep within moments.

He was shaken awake just after dawn. Darcy handed him some hard cheese and dried meat. He sat up and looked at the simple food. He'd be glad when they reached Anchorage. His new friends wouldn't let him starve, but he looked forward to a real meal with gravy, fresh bread, and something sweet. Not thinking, he reached for it with his left hand and grimaced as the pain flared.

'Does it hurt?' Darcy said.

He could hardly move it. It was to be expected, but that didn't lessen the pain.

'I'll be fine,' he took the proffered food with his other hand.

'Sunni found a way through,' Darcy said. 'We'll be leaving as soon as you're able.'

Leto shouldn't have been surprised. Sunni was as good as any tracker he'd ever met. Darcy packed away his bedroll as he ate. After he'd finished, Little Gil took another look at his shoulder.

'A bit stiff today?'

Leto nodded.

'I don't know whether I'll be able to travel as fast as we did yesterday,' he said.

Rogar approached, already wearing the harness.

'Don't worry,' Big Gil said. 'It'll be a slow climb up the mountain. If you can hold on with one hand, Rogar will make sure you don't fall.'

'That's right,' Rogar said.

Part of Leto was glad he didn't have to walk and climb, though he still harboured some embarrassment at being carried. However, this small dent in his pride was extinguished once the small party began ascending the mountain. He could not have climbed it alone, but the giants scaled it with little effort. Leto just held on, and by noon, they had started descending into a deep ravine that split the northern side of the range.

Leto could see a smattering of trees and the desert beyond. To the west, he could now see the tallest spires of Shorehaven Keep. The familiarity of it felt good. The relatively close proximity to his destination caused him to stop and think again about what he would do when he arrived.

They made camp within a thin copse of trees, about a mile west of the foot of the mountain range where they had emerged.

'We'll arrive before sunset tomorrow,' Sunni said as everyone sat around the campfire.

'Assuming we don't have any more surprises,' Big Gil said with a smile.

'What will happen once we get there?' Rogar asked Leto.

He'd thought he could enter Anchorage and possibly even Shorehaven Keep undetected. However, his ideas all required stealth and Leto going in alone. He knew this would not go down well with Viggo and Rogar.

'I think the best way is for me to sneak in after dark,' Leto said. 'I know a way –'

'No,' Viggo said, interrupting him.

'But it's the best –' Leto said, but again, the Commander cut him off.

'No!'

'Why not?'

'What Viggo is trying to say,' Big Gil said, 'is that after what happened yesterday, we aren't letting you out of our sight.'

'I know Anchorage. I'll be safe.'

This wasn't entirely true. Any large city contained hidden dangers, but Leto was confident he could avoid them. After all, he had done it for years in Twin Falls, a much larger and more dangerous place than the port city.

'No!' Viggo repeated, forcefully.

He thought of offering to take Darcy but thought better of it.

'I can't very well take one of you with me.'

All the time he spoke, Viggo shook his head.

'I'm sure I'll be able to get into the keep undetected,' Leto continued.

'You'd only need one alert guard, and you'll end up with another arrow in you,' Sunni said, 'and you might not be so lucky next time.'

Leto was taken aback. Like Viggo, the giant tracker never said much, and that was the most she had ever spoken directly to him since the journey began.

'I'm going in by myself, and that's final,' Leto said, trying to be forceful. 'You can't stop me.'

'No!' Viggo said.

'No? Is that all you can say?'

Leto's frustration was building. He couldn't see how he would get into Shorehaven Keep in secret with one of these creatures behind him every step of the way. Even Leila, the smallest of the giants at ten feet tall, would not stay undetected for long.

'Leto,' Rogar said. 'I agree with Viggo and Sunni. You cannot go in alone.'

Leto looked up at his giant friend in surprise.

'I thought you were my friend?' Leto said.

'I am.'

'Fine!' Leto stood. 'You come up with a better plan. We may as well just –'

Leto stopped talking as an idea came to him. He mulled it over in his mind for a little while. It wasn't complicated, and if Viggo wouldn't let him sneak into Anchorage, then it was the only alternative.

'Leto,' Darcy said. 'Are you alright?'

He glanced at the young woman who had been sitting next to him.

'Leto?' she repeated.

'Err … yes, I'm fine,' he said.

He turned to Rogar and Viggo, a broad grin spreading across his face.

'I have another idea.'

13

OWEN

Owen's wife looked at him with a mixture of curiosity and disbelief.

'Do you think it's really his?' Addwyn said.

They sat at the table across from each other, having the morning meal. He'd been mulling it over since Alwen's initial message. He'd been sceptical of the Abbot's declaration and had said so to his wife. To accept it as the truth meant a mere handmaiden now carried the most important baby in Avaleen.

'Who else could it be?' said Addwyn. 'From what you've told me, she spent a lot of time with him before you left the capitol; by all accounts, they were very close.'

Owen sighed and nodded. He wasn't happy about it, but he had to resign himself to the fact that Dariah carried Leto's child.

'If Alwen believes it to be true, then it's true. This complicates things.'

'That's an understatement.'

Addwyn's exasperated manner reflected his thoughts on the matter.

'If Greythorpe gets wind of this, he'll try to kill that baby, either before or after it's born.'

'So, what do we do?'

'She'll be in grave danger if anyone even suspects that Leto's the father,' Owen said. 'There are too many eyes and ears in Twin Falls.'

As expected, Addwyn nodded her agreement.

'I'll draft another message to Alwen,' he added.

Later that day, Owen sat at the head of the long ironbark table in a room overlooking the bay. So far, all but three had arrived at Cliffs End, but he had been assured everyone had promised to attend. The full war council would begin tomorrow, but now he met only with his most senior advisors.

He looked around at the other men in the room. Owen couldn't question the loyalty of any of these experienced, battle-hardened commanders. His brothers, Penn and Dunmar sat to his right, and next to them, the Lord of Alder, Sir Lachlan Sulley. A staunch ally of the Redstones and the Blackwaters, he brought a formidable force and undivided loyalty to the table.

To Owen's left sat Jesper Holt, Commander of the Citadel Home Guard, and Sir Caden Angworth, a veteran of the War of Colours and one of his most experienced commanders. During the Eastern Uprising, Owen had interceded in a dispute involving Caden's son, Nico, and shortly afterwards, the Lord of Riverglen pledged the complete allegiance of his house to Owen.

At the other end of the table sat the Lord of Beaconwatch, Sir Guy Westhall. Like Caden Angworth, he had commanded alongside his father in the War of Colours. Time had not been kind to Sir Guy. Years of overindulgence made him unable to ride a horse. The big man now had to travel by carriage. Still, he had pledged soldiers, and his superior knowledge of tactics and strategy made him an invaluable ally.

Archer stood behind and to the right of Owen.

Regrettably, these men began protesting at Owen's lacklustre response to the impending war. No-one liked war, at least none at this table, and it always put people on edge.

'You do realise this puts us at a significant disadvantage?' Guy Westall said. 'Preparations will take much longer now the snow is here, and we have less time.'

Owen had expected the well-deserved criticism. He had screwed up, and now he and his allies may pay for it with their lives.

'What's done is done,' Penn said.

He could always depend on his brother to defend him, even though Penn had also chided him for his lack of action, as soon as he arrived at Cliffs End the day before.

'We have to deal with the current situation,' Penn continued, 'not one that may have eventuated.'

'That may be so,' Sir Lachlan Sulley said. 'But we want assurances that no more decisions will put us at a further disadvantage.'

'We can't have any more delays,' Sir Caden Angworth added.

'Owen is your liege lord,' Penn reminded them. 'He shouldn't have to give assurances.'

'But we –' Owen's raised hand stopped Sir Lachlan from completing his sentence.

Owen agreed with them, but despite their valid complaints, he could not appear weak. He looked hard at each man in turn as he spoke.

'Do you question my right to command?' Owen asked them.

'Not at all,' Dunmar Redstone said.

Owen's youngest brother had been silent until now.

'The loss of the King and his children shocked us all,' Dunmar continued. 'We just need to know that there aren't any more … extenuating circumstances which could affect our ability to organise our defences.'

He knew he had Dunmar's undying support, but he always impressed Owen with his subtler ways of showing it. He agreed with the other lords while speaking of their support for Owen. Thankfully, the three objecting lords nodded their agreement, though with varying levels of conviction.

'Good,' Owen said. 'Now we can get on with winning this war.'

He sat back in his chair and signalled Penn to update them on the preparations. As his brother spoke, Owen thought about the upcoming conflict. He could put just over two thousand men onto the battlefield, whilst Lord Regan would easily command over four thousand. The massacre at Hampstead Heath had galvanised some central and eastern lords against the Steward of Avaleen, but some neutral lords would ally themselves with Greythorpe out of fear.

Owen's attempts at spreading the truth that Regan had killed the King had proved fruitless. Greythorpe had Twin Falls firmly in his grip, with the Capitol Guard seeking out and quashing any hint of dissent. Even outside of the capitol, the effect of rumourmongering against the Steward had little effect.

'What of the eastern lords?' Guy Westall said.

'Pickney, Roper and Waters have pledged their support,' said Owen. 'They'll be marching before the next full moon.'

'And the others?' Lachlan Sulley spoke up. 'Surely they wouldn't side with Greythorpe.'

'I may be able to convince the Lords Rammon and Upperton, possibly Rokman and even the Lady Stockman,' Dunmar said. 'But it'd require a visit from me personally.'

'Do we have the time?' Caden Angworth said.

'More to the point,' Penn said, 'how many more soldiers would it give us?'

'I'd expect a hundred and fifty at most, maybe a score more if we're lucky,' Dunmar said.

Luck. Owen felt they would need a lot of it if they wanted to live to see the summer.

The Lord of Beaconwatch glanced at Owen. 'We'll need all we can get.'

'Dunmar,' Owen said. 'You'll leave tomorrow.'

His brother nodded.

Owen enquired about the central lords but received a similar answer to the one Dunmar had given about those in the east, and the news proved even worse for the west.

'I know of a dozen that have already sided with Greythorpe,' Lachlan Sulley said. 'Any of them could be in the path of an army marching south. They'd have already made a deal to avoid having their lands sacked.'

'Greythorpe doesn't give a shit about them,' Caden Angworth said. 'He'll take what he wants, and there's nothing they can do about it.'

'Why don't they fight with us?' Penn said. 'Most of them have no love for Lord Regan, that I know.'

'I spent nearly three weeks riding from castle to keep, garnering support,' Caden said.

'You didn't try hard enough,' Penn said.

Caden's face hardened, but the Lord of Riverglen continued before Owen could rebuke his brother.

'Do you know what most of them said to me. Do you?' Caden Angworth leaned forward in his chair and glared at Penn. 'They don't think we can win, that it's a lost cause.'

Owen sighed as Caden continued.

'They said they would rather have their lands picked clean by a passing friendly army, than fight one. At least they'd be alive afterwards.'

'Cowards, the lot of them!' Penn burst out.

Lachlan Sulley said, 'That's harsh judgment coming from one who lives –'

'Enough!' Owen barked, cutting off Sir Lachlan's censure of his brother.

He couldn't have his most trusted advisors squabbling at a time like this. Owen eyed each man around the table, finally settling on Guy Westhall.

'What do you think?' Owen said. 'Is this a lost cause?'

The Lord of Beaconwatch returned his gaze.

'It will be difficult,' Guy said. 'They'll outnumber us more than two to one, but our forces are better trained, and our commanders are more seasoned. If we're smart about it, we might just shock them.'

A shock? Owen had hoped for something more optimistic, but he knew the Lord of Beaconwatch wasn't one to embellish the truth.

'Greythorpe wants this war, we don't,' Sulley said. 'Let him come to us.'

'If we choose our battleground carefully,' Guy said, 'it will increase our chances markedly.'

Owen already knew this but hearing his commanders speaking with at least a hint of optimism gave him some semblance of hope.

They talked into the night, discussing everything from battle tactics to logistics and even worst-case scenarios. Owen finally returned to his apartments and found Addwyn awake, reading a text in front of the fire. She looked up as he entered the living room.

'You look tired,' she said.

'Long day.'

He fetched himself a goblet of wine and sat in the chair opposite his wife.

'How did it go?'

'As expected.'

'That bad?'

'Our chances of winning this war are slim,' he said, hating to admit it.

'So, our prospects have improved since this morning?'

Owen grinned at his wife's humour.

'Always finding a silver lining.'

'Someone needs to.'

Her veiled dig at his recent dark moods didn't go unnoticed. It had taken both an impassioned plea from his wife and the massacre at Forest Keep to finally drag him out of his despondency. Owen looked across at Addwyn. Her brother and his family had been brutally murdered only weeks ago, but she supported him, encouraged him, and offered her counsel. She hid her grief well.

'Their deaths will not go unanswered,' he said, 'no matter the outcome of this damn war.'

Vengeance did not make up a big part of Owen's psyche, and Addwyn would usually have scolded him for contemplating it, but her silence signalled her approval. Greythorpe had gotten away with far too much. Too many people and loved ones had died because of that man's lust for power.

Addwyn stood. 'Let me arrange a hot bath for you.'

He wanted to sleep, but maybe a soak in the tub would help. Tomorrow would be another long day.

'That would be wonderful.'

'If you behave, I may even wash your back.'

Her cheeky grin made him smile again as she entered their bed chamber. Despite the dire situation in which they found themselves, Owen still felt himself fortunate. He drained the cup of wine and went to the sideboard, grabbed the jug, and began pouring another.

A scream pierced the air, and Owen cursed as he spilled wine over himself and the floor but realised from where the cry originated … the bed chamber … Addwyn!

He dropped the jug and goblet and rushed to the bed chamber. The main door open and two guards rushed in, swords already drawn.

'My lord, no!' a guard called.

Owen ignored them and burst into the room.

Addwyn leaned against the bedpost nearest the door, hand on mouth, her chest heaving. He glanced around but could see nothing. Owen took her in his arms, and she buried her face in his chest,

'Addy,' Owen said. 'Addy, are you alright?'

He could feel her body shaking.

'Are you hurt?'

She shook her head, her face still leaning against him as the guards rushed into the room and took up a position near Owen and Addwyn.

'Amos, check the room,' one of the guards said.

Owen faced the guard who had given the order, Sergeant Alden Janz, the younger brother of Captain Archer Janz. The other, Amos Bailey, nodded and moved around the end of the bed.

'My lord,' Alden said. 'What happened?'

'I don't know.'

Addwyn removed her head from his chest and stood a little straighter.

'Addy, what has frightened you so?' Owen said.

'Sergeant,' the young guard said before Addwyn could answer.

Owen heard the unease in his voice and looked over towards the far side of the bed nearest the window. Sergeant Janz reached the other guard and squatted down.

'Is he dead?' Amos said.

'It looks that way,' said the Sergeant.

'Wait here,' Owen said.

He let go of his wife and stepped around the end of the bed. A man dressed in dark clothing lay face down in a pool of blood with a dagger protruding from the back of his neck.

‘Check the rest of the room,’ Sergeant Janz said. ‘Don’t forget the balcony.’

The young guard continued his search as Alden rolled the dead man over. The blood caked face held a look of confusion, most likely surprise at his impending death. It sent a chill down Owen’s spine. He turned as his wife came over and looked at the dead man. She no longer trembled, and her usual poise had returned.

‘Is this the man that was after you?’

He had eventually told Addwyn of the visit by Grim Baldonado, the deal Owen made with him, and the rogue assassin. That she had not been pleased proved to be an understatement.

‘Trust an assassin?’ she had said. ‘Are you serious?’

She demanded that his protection be doubled despite the Grim Shadows leader’s promise to protect him. He didn’t quite double it, but it had been notably increased.

‘I think so,’ he said.

The assassin lay dead at his feet, no longer a danger, but Owen still felt sick at the thought of what could have happened.

‘Thank the gods,’ she said.

Like him, Addwyn wasn’t overly religious, so to hear her thanking the gods showed the depth of her relief. He embraced his wife again, and she returned in kind.

‘I’ll be around for quite a while longer,’ he said. ‘Don’t you worry.’

‘You’d better be,’ Addwyn said, her face again buried in his chest.

‘My lord,’ Sergeant Janz said and held out a small scroll tied with a black ribbon. ‘It was stuffed in his tunic.’

Owen let go of Addwyn and took the parchment. He pulled the ribbon loose and unfurled the dirty yellow parchment. The message contained only a couple of lines and confirmed the identity of the corpse at his feet. It wasn’t signed but Owen knew the author.

The first promise has been kept.

The second to be fulfilled at your discretion.

14

DARIAH

The door opened without a knock, and her father entered. His heavy footsteps gave him away, unlike her mother, who moved like she walked on feathers. Dariah ignored him, staying curled up on the bed facing the wall. The door closed and she waited for the inevitable scolding.

Nothing.

'What?' she said, irritated.

He whispered something but she couldn't understand it. What did he want from her now? Hadn't he admonished her enough already?

She turned over to face him. 'Why can't you –'

Her father stood in the centre of the small room and looked at her, his cheeks wet from the tears.

'I'm sorry,' he sputtered.

Sorry for what? Her father never cried, except when her younger brother, Dirk, died. Had something happened to Robb? Mother?

'What's happened?' Dariah's anger shifted to dread.

What had he done?

'I'm so sorry.'

She swung her feet over the edge of the bed and stood. He had always favoured her brothers. Eventually, she'd left home in frustration and made her way to the capitol, and ultimately ended up in the employ of the Greythorpes. She opened her mouth to speak, but her father lurched forward and grabbed her shoulders.

'He told me everything. All about the Greythorpes, Lord Owen, what you did for the prince,' he said, embracing her tightly. 'I'm so proud of you.'

This wasn't her father's way. Dariah had not expected an apology but welcomed it all the same.

'I love you, baby girl,' he said, squeezing her tighter.

She wrapped her arms around him. He hadn't called her baby girl for years.

'I love you too, Papa.'

They stood there in silence. After a few moments she broke the embrace as a thought entered her mind … she had never told either of her parents about Lord Owen or the prince.

'Who told you?'

'The Abbot,' he said, wiping his eyes and nose on his sleeve and sniffing.

Her father hadn't been to the city for over two weeks, so how could he … and the significance of her father's words hit her.

'He's here?'

He nodded.

'And he wants to see you,' he said as he stepped back towards the door. 'You better not keep him waiting.'

Why would Abbot Alwen travel out here to see her? She couldn't be of use to him anymore. Her failure had guaranteed that.

'Did he say what he wanted?'

Her father nodded again.

'But it's best you hear it from him,' he said, almost whispering.

Her confusion turned to worry as she straightened her hair and glanced down at her clothes. She looked hideous, with her dress dirty and crumpled from her chores. Not like she used to look when she worked for Lady Greythorpe: regular baths, beautiful dresses, and servants to style her hair any way she wished.

Her father opened the door, and she hurried out of the room into the living area, which only housed a kitchen and a simple wooden table and chairs, where her mother and the Abbot now sat. The Abbot stood as she approached.

'Hello, Abbot Alwen,' she said and curtsied.

'Young Dariah,' he said with a smile. 'It's good to see you.'

He glanced down at her growing belly.

'You are positively glowing,' he added.

Most people wouldn't even notice the change in her, not yet anyway. She had always been skinny, so the extra pounds she had put on over the past few months would only be noticed by those who knew her well.

'Thank you,' she said, embarrassed. 'Are you well?'

'I can't complain,' he said with a grin. 'Who would listen, anyway?'

It was pleasing to see the old man despite the reminder of what she now thought of as her previous life.

'What brings you out here, Father?'

'Ill news, I fear,' he said, his smile disappearing. 'Please, sit.'

Dariah sat opposite her mother. She noted her concern as the Abbot sat at the end of the table across from her.

'What's wrong?' Dariah said, looking back to the Abbot.

'Rumours are circulating,' he said, 'about … your condition.'

She moved her hand to her stomach but said nothing.

'But they're just rumours,' her mother said. 'So, what if she's pregnant? It's not like she's a noble.'

Dariah winced. She had not yet divulged the identity of the father of her baby to her parents, not even to her mother. However, she suspected how the rumours had started. She had told only one other person, her Aunt Lowena.

After her flight from Riverview, Dariah ended up at her Uncle Leon and Aunt Lowena's home. She had been distraught, and whilst talking to her aunt, she had just blurted it out.

'Please don't tell anyone,' Dariah had pleaded. 'No-one can know.'

Her aunt had promised, but had nevertheless told her husband. Several weeks later, she had been working in her uncle's tavern despite feeling sick that morning.

‘Move your arse, girl!’ her Uncle Leon had shouted.

Dariah’s stomach turned, but she hurried to grab the next platter.

‘Drop anything else, and it comes out of your pay!’

Her uncle was a hard taskmaster, so she had not been surprised to hear that her cousin, Edmund, had left the family business last summer to make his fortune across the Dividing Sea. She also wanted to be as far away from here as possible.

‘Move it!’ her uncle had shouted.

Head down, Dariah rushed out of the kitchen. The exposure to the pungent smells of the tavern made the constant sickness even worse, but she needed the job. She couldn’t face going home to work in the fields with her parents and brother.

She reached between two patrons to place the food on the table.

‘Thanks, darlin’,’ one said, putting his hand on her buttock and squeezing.

With both hands still on the platter, she tried wriggling free of his grasp, but that seemed to encourage him.

‘Why don’t you stay here with me and my friend,’ he said, squeezing her left cheek hard.

She yelped and dropped the platter the last few inches. Thankfully, the food didn’t spill onto the table this time. He grabbed her waist and began pulling her towards him.

Not again, she thought.

‘I’d rather not,’ she said, slapping his hands away.

‘We’ll make it worth your while, a beauty like you.’

She turned in his grasp, his face now inches from her breasts, which felt like they would burst out of her dress at any moment. Her body had changed so much since fleeing Riverview, but she didn’t want to dip into her paltry savings to get new clothes.

‘Leave me alone, or I’ll –’

Dariah’s stomach lurched again, and without warning she heaved and vomited a stream of brown liquid into the man’s face. The man reeled, nearly falling from his chair.

‘You certainly have a way with the ladies,’ his friend said, bursting into laughter.

'You fucking bitch!' he spluttered as he hastily scraped the vomit from his eyes and mouth.

Other patrons laughed as he grabbed at Dariah, but she stumbled back out of reach. She could now see the man's face, with the contents of her stomach dripping down his cheeks and through his bushy beard. It made her want to throw up again, but she put a hand to her mouth, turned and ran back through the kitchen and out into the alleyway.

Why had she left Riverview, she wondered? She had a good life there, nice clothes, wanting for nothing. If Lady Greythorpe wanted to take others to her bed, Dariah had no right to object. She had contemplated returning but realised she couldn't now.

'Don't bother coming back,' her uncle yelled after her as she rushed out of the kitchen. 'I don't give a shit if you are Bern's daughter.'

'But she's family,' her aunt said. 'And she's going to have a baby.'

'Just because she fucked a prince doesn't give her the right to puke on my customers,' he railed at his wife. 'Take her back to your sister. She can be a burden on them, instead.'

'Leon!' her aunt had exclaimed.

Dariah leaned against the wall and burst into tears.

Eventually, her contrite Aunt Lowena came out and agreed to take her back home. Dariah retrieved her meagre possessions and convinced her aunt to take her to the Abbey first. There, Abbot Alwen met with her, and she told him everything, including that she was with child, and who the father may be.

'I am so sorry,' she had sobbed. 'I have let you down. I'm so ashamed.'

'What's done is done,' he had said, not appearing angry. 'Firstly, we'll get the sisters to examine you to ensure you're alright.'

She nodded her assent.

'Then let your Aunt Lowena take you home.'

Now, Abbot Alwen looked at Dariah across the table, his brow furrowed. 'They don't know?'

She lowered her gaze and shook her head. The Abbot's eyebrows rose in reply.

'What don't we know?' her father demanded.

Dariah glanced up at the Abbot, who tilted his head. He nodded and turned to her father, who had stepped closer to the table.

'The father of your daughter's baby,' the Abbot said, pausing momentarily. 'The father is Prince Leto.'

She watched the enormity of what her parents had just been told slowly wash over them. They both gave the Abbot a questioning look, who nodded his affirmation.

'The prince?' her mother said as she turned to Dariah.

Her father stared at her, his mouth agape. 'You and the prince … you … with the prince?'

She only nodded, not knowing what to say.

The Abbot faced her. 'You're in great danger, Dariah.'

Her father seemed to gather his senses. 'We're half a day from the capitol. How much danger could she possibly be in?' her father demanded as he moved towards the front door.

'Those that oppose the Blackwater rule have a long reach,' Abbot Alwen said. 'It has become too dangerous for her to remain here.'

'Leave?' Dariah said, incredulous. 'But I can't.'

She liked living here despite the initial treatment by her father.

'Excuse me,' her father said and opened the door. 'Sounds like we have more visitors. Probably men looking for work. I'll get rid of them and be back in a moment.'

The door closed behind him.

'Dariah, you know Lord Greythorpe better than most,' Abbot Alwen said. 'If he believes there's a possibility that these rumours have any truth, he will come looking for you, no matter where you are. He cannot risk the legitimate royal bloodline not being under his control.'

'Are you saying my baby girl could be killed?' her mother whimpered as the Abbot nodded his head.

'You need to leave today,' the abbot said. 'And I –'

A pained cry split the air, and everyone looked towards the door.

'What was that?' Dariah gasped. 'Was that Father?'

Her mother had risen and already headed for the door.

She yanked the door open. 'Bern!' she shrieked and rushed out, leaving the door ajar.

Dariah began to head outside, but a hand on her arm stopped her. The Abbot, still seated at the head of the table, gave Dariah a mournful look and stood.

'I fear I have arrived too late,' he said. 'I'm sorry.'

She tried to shrug off his hand, not comprehending his words. Her father needed her help.

'No!' the Abbot said. 'You must flee.'

He gestured to the back door. 'Now!'

'But Mama and Papa?' she pleaded.

'There's nothing you can do,' he began to pull her towards the rear of the cottage.

'I have to help them!'

The Abbot grabbed her shoulders firmly and turned her to face him.

'The fate of Avaleen is at stake,' he said with a conviction she had never heard from him before. 'We have to escape.'

Her mother's voice pierced the air. 'Leave him alone!'

Dariah glanced at the partially open front door and back at the Abbot. Tears had begun to flow, but she allowed herself to be led by the arm. She glanced back again towards the front door.

'You have to protect the baby,' he said, opening the back door.

Dariah glanced behind her one more time then nodded.

'Good girl,' the Abbot said and guided her outside.

She could see the forest beyond the fields, about half a mile away. It wouldn't take her long to get there, but Abbot Alwen was old. He couldn't keep up with her, even in her current condition.

'You go on ahead,' he said, patting her arm. 'Don't worry, I'll be right behind you.'

'Not so fast!'

Both Dariah and the Abbot turned towards the deep voice. Two soldiers had appeared from around the side of the house.

'Go!' the Abbot said, pushing her away, stepping between her and the soldiers.

'Get her!' the larger of the soldiers instructed.

Abbot Alwen strode towards them. 'Leave her alone!'

His voice had an unexpected edge, but the smaller soldier just shoved him aside and rushed at Dariah. She turned to run but knew it would be a wasted effort. She couldn't outrun him, even if she wasn't pregnant. She'd only taken a few steps when a rough hand grabbed her collar and yanked her to a stop.

She squealed as she stumbled backward, but the man's iron grip held her up, her collar beginning to choke her. She scrambled to take the weight on her feet as the soldier dragged her around towards the front of the house, not caring that she couldn't maintain her footing.

'Don't hurt her!' the Abbot pleaded. 'She's with child.'

'Then she should have kept her fucking legs closed,' said the soldier holding the Abbot.

Both soldiers erupted into laughter.

Eventually, they stopped, and Dariah could stand, but the soldier still held her collar.

A dozen mounted soldiers milled around the front of the house. She recognised the emblem on their armour, the Capitol Guard. Why would they be here? Two other men held her mother, one at each arm.

'You can't do that!' her mother cried. 'He's done nothing!'

Dariah's father lay face down in the dirt near the horses with a tall, armoured man with greying hair standing over him. She couldn't see her brother anywhere. Hopefully, Robb had escaped.

'I can do whatever I want,' he said and kicked her father in the side.

Her father moaned but did not move.

'And if someone gets in my way,' the tall man continued, 'they get punished.'

He kicked her father again, this time in the head.

'Noooo! Leave him … ' her mother's screams descended into gut-wrenching cries of anguish.

'Now tell me who owns that fucking wagon!' he demanded.

'It's mine,' Abbot Alwen said as a soldier pushed him beside Dariah.

The tall man turned to face them. Her blood ran cold, and she felt a constriction in her chest. Sir Baltair Drum, the Commander of the Capitol Guard, approached her with slow, deliberate strides.

'Ahhh,' he said. 'The spy.'

His words shocked Dariah out of her reverie, and her eyes flicked from her weeping mother to her prone father and back to Sir Baltair, now only a few steps away from her.

'Leave them alone,' she quivered. 'They haven't done anything wrong.'

The Commander of the Capitol Guard looked down at her.

'You're a criminal,' he said, 'and they were protecting you, so that makes them criminals too.'

'But –' she started, but Sir Baltair's huge, mailed hand gripped her throat, silencing her.

He lifted her slightly, stretching her neck, forcing her onto her toes.

'Don't interrupt me, slut!' he said, but let go of her neck with a slight shove, causing her to stumble backward.

'Be grateful I haven't killed them already,' the Commander sneered.

He began to walk around her, looking her up and down as she rubbed her neck. He stopped behind her and leaned in, his face near her ear.

'I honestly don't know what he saw in you,' he continued. 'You've got a pretty face, but you aren't my type. Maybe I'll get one of my men to try you out and give me his opinion.'

Dariah shuddered, hoping he wouldn't touch her again.

'Maybe they can all have a go,' he laughed. 'It's not like you can get pregnant again, is it? Especially if they –'

'You will do no such thing!' Abbot Alwen said.

'Aah, yes … the oldest Brother himself,' Sir Baltair mocked as he turned to face the Abbot. 'I'm glad you're here. Saved me a lot of work.'

'As a member of the Ruling Council, I demand it. '

'You can no longer demand anything,' the Commander interrupted. 'Lord Regan has finally kicked you off the Ruling Council.'

'But I'm still the Abbot of the Brotherhood of –'

'I don't give a flying fuck,' Sir Baltair said with a malicious smile.

The Abbot's body sagged at the Commander's words.

'I'll go with you,' Dariah said, trying not to cry. 'Just leave them alone. They've done nothing wrong.'

'As if you have a choice, girl,' Sir Baltair sneered.

'Look what we found, Commander,' came a voice from the direction of the barn.

Dariah turned towards the commotion and suppressed a cry. Two Capitol Guards dragged her brother between them, his face a bloody mess from fresh cuts. He could barely keep his head up. They released him, and Robb dropped to the ground a few feet from their father.

'He resisted, so we had to teach him a lesson,' one of the guards said with a smirk.

Her poor brother had sustained a beating.

Sir Baltair looked down at the unconscious body of the young man. 'Is that everyone?'

'Yes sir!' the second of the two guards said, nodding.

'Good,' Sir Baltair said and pointed to the guards nearest to Dariah. 'You two put the girl in the wagon.'

'Yes, Commander,' the smaller guard said, grabbing her arm.

'I'm sorry, Dariah,' the Abbot said. 'I have failed you.'

Guards manhandled her into the rear of the wagon.

'You will regret this, Commander,' Abbot Alwen said, but his voice wasn't as resolute as it had been.

'Consider yourself lucky to have lived this long, Father,' Sir Baltair spat the honorific. 'If it'd been up to me, you'd have been hanging from the main gate by your shrivelled old balls long ago.'

One of the guards hoisted Dariah into the wagon. He climbed up onto the driver's box and grabbed the reins and gave them a pull. The horses moved back a few steps, jostling Dariah. Her mother raised her head.

'My baby girl!' she cried out.

'Mama, I'll be alright,' Dariah said, barely able to get the words out. 'Look after Papa.'

Red with fear and sorrow, her mother glared at Sir Baltair.

'Don't you dare hurt her!' she screamed.

The Commander of the Capitol Guard chuckled and turned towards the wagon. 'Head back to the city. We'll catch up after we've had a little fun.'

'Please, Commander,' Dariah implored. 'Don't hurt them.'

'You should be more worried about yourself, girly,' he snarled and turned back to the driver. 'Go!'

The driver gave the reins a flick, and the wagon sprang forward with a start. Dariah gazed back at her family as tears flowed freely down her cheeks. The guards still restrained her mother, while her brother and father remained in the dirt, unmoving.

This may be the last time I ever see them again, Dariah thought as the wagon rolled away from her home and family.

15

LETO

Today, he would get answers to all his questions, Leto hoped.

Who had been ruling Avaleen in his absence? If his sister, still too young to rule in her own right, sat on the throne, who had been appointed Regent? Would Leto even want to replace her? He'd never really wanted to rule, so leaving her on the throne could be his way out. Darker thoughts followed. Had Lord Regan usurped the throne and taken the crown for himself, or had he manipulated Melina like he had tried to do with Leto? What had become of Lord Owen? Of course, this would all be dependent on the success of his plan.

Leto urged his mount back to a trot. The lumbering bay mare wasn't great but she responded well to his cues and didn't seem bothered by the giants. Big Gil had found the horse for him. He didn't say from where, and Leto didn't ask. He tried to appear nonchalant, but his stomach churned. He couldn't guess how people would react to this scheme.

The people of Anchorage stood and stared in utter disbelief or ran away in fear, some screaming. He couldn't blame them, recalling his reaction less than three moons ago. Of course, they weren't staring at or fleeing from him. Leto caught some looking at him, but most directed their attention to his escort. Rogar led the procession, with enormous, slow strides. Behind him marched Sunni and Big Gil, Little Gil and Leila, with Darcy again perched upon Little Gil's shoulder. Arve and Wulftan followed, with Viggo bringing up the rear.

Viggo had not been pleased with this approach when Leto had suggested it the night before.

'I don't approve,' the Commander said.

'I love it!' Little Gil laughed.

'It's dangerous,' Big Gil said, glaring at his namesake.

'I have to agree with Viggo,' Rogar said. 'Just walking through the front gate makes me a mite uncomfortable.'

'That's an understatement,' Sunni said.

Leto understood their reticence.

'I have to get into Shorehaven Keep to see my uncle, or this,' Leto said, spreading his arms wide to encompass the group, 'is all a waste of time. I may as well not have come home.'

'But Leto,' Rogar said. 'You cannot –'

Leto stopped his friend with a raised hand.

'Viggo won't let me sneak in by myself, and I can't get in undetected with one of you at my side, so it'll have to be the complete opposite,' Leto said. 'No hiding, no skulking around, and I'll have all of you to protect me.'

'How will your people react to us?' Leila said.

'Yes,' Big Gil said. 'I'm sure no-one has ever seen the likes of us before. Do you know what they'll do?'

'No, I don't,' Leto said. 'It's a risk, but what other choice do we have?'

No-one could give him an answer.

'We just have to appear as non-threatening as possible,' Leto continued.

He wasn't sure how eight giants could appear harmless to people less than a quarter their size.

Well, my giant friend, what do you think about that, Leto had thought as he looked to Viggo for his support. The giant's stern expression eventually dissolved into one of resignation.

'I don't like it,' Viggo said, 'but we will do as you suggested.'

Leto blinked in amazement, and the others displayed looks of mild disbelief, astonished that their commander had agreed to this crazy idea.

'But I'll need a horse,' Leto said, smiling. 'The future King of Avaleen can't be carried or made to walk.'

So far, so good, Leto thought as they came to the western gate of the keep's outer wall. He hadn't been recognised, and they hadn't been challenged. He pulled on the reins, and his mount came to a stop. They had closed the large timber and iron gate on them. No doubt, the City Watch had seen the strange group approaching. He couldn't blame them.

Guards lined the walls, and all had weapons ready but not yet aimed. Viggo had moved up to stand near Rogar, while the other members of his giant escort had formed a loose semi-circle around Leto, though Big Gil and Sunni faced outwards, watching their backs.

Leto found it odd that a crowd had assembled in the street behind them. The mob numbered over fifty, and more continued to join the throng, but they always kept about forty yards from Leto and his giant escort, venturing no closer.

'Stay calm,' Leto said to Viggo and Rogar. 'We'll be fine.'

'I am calm,' Viggo said.

'I hope they stay calm,' Big Gil jabbed his giant thumb at the men on the wall.

Leto looked back to the gate. He took a deep breath and sat up straighter in the saddle. Confidence and authority – that's what he hoped to project.

'Who is the gatekeeper here?' Leto said in a loud voice.

A few moments passed, and a voice came from the parapet above.

'I am.'

'Introduce yourself,' Leto said, 'or has the level of civility dropped sharply in the Borderlands while I've been away?'

'I am Sergeant Isaac Draper,' the man said, 'and who might you be stranger, calling my behaviour into question?'

Leto ignored the Gatekeeper's question for the moment.

'I have urgent business with the Lord of Shorehaven Keep,' Leto said. 'Open the gate and allow us to pass peacefully.'

'Hah!' Sergeant Draper said, his voice full of derision. 'I don't think so.'

'Who is your superior?' Leto said. 'I will speak to him instead.'

'That's not your business,' the Gatekeeper said. 'Now introduce yourself, or you and your … companions can leave.'

Leto had hoped to conceal his identity until he met his uncle or one of his cousins.

'If you insist,' Leto said. 'I am Prince Leto Blackwater, son of Caleb the slain King, heir to the throne and rightful ruler of Avaleen.'

A brief look of confusion appeared on the sergeant's face, and it hardened.

'You lie. Everyone knows the prince is dead,' said the Gatekeeper and turned to speak to the men beside him.

'I don't like this,' Viggo said.

Leto turned to reassure Viggo when the guards along the wall raised their weapons. He heard a shuffle of large feet behind him, sure the members of his escort had drawn their weapons, ready to defend him. Leto didn't want any bloodshed, particularly his own. To come all this way to be killed here would be absurd, to say the least.

'Sergeant!' Leto said with a conciliatory tone. 'Have your men lower their weapons. We aren't here to fight.'

'Then tell me who you really are and what business you have with my lord,' the Gatekeeper said.

'I am exactly who I said I am,' Leto said. 'Why would I lie about something like that? And my business with Lord Malachy is none of yours.'

'Stranger,' Sergeant Draper said. 'If you don't turn and leave right now, you will give me no choice.'

Leto sighed. Why so stubborn? Undoubtedly, the Gatekeeper recognised that the giants could scale the walls and tear his men apart in moments if they wanted.

'Sergeant Draper,' Leto said in a more diplomatic tone. 'I have no doubt your weapons could harm me, but they would only anger my friends, and neither of us would want that.'

'Don't threaten me,' the Gatekeeper said.

'Time to leave,' Viggo said. 'Now!'

Leto turned in his saddle.

'No! We can't leave,' he said.

Darcy no longer sat exposed upon Little Gil's shoulder but lay cradled in his arms. Leto's gaze moved back to the Gatekeeper and his raised arm.

'You are making a serious mistake, Sergeant.'

'You're the one making a mistake, a big one,' the Gatekeeper said. 'Now, do as your friend suggests and leave.'

The giants moved to surround Leto. He could see nothing except the legs and backs of his huge escorts.

'We're going,' Rogar said.

'No, No!' Leto said. 'I'm not going anywhere.'

Big Gil reached down to grab Leto, but he quickly slipped out of the saddle.

'Damn!' the giant said.

'Leto, no!' a worried Darcy shouted.

Leto dashed between Rogar's legs towards the gate. He couldn't turn back now.

'Aim!' Sergeant Draper shouted.

Rogar reached for Leto but only succeeded in knocking him off-balance, but that had been enough to cause him to stumble and fall. Viggo roared in exasperation as he crashed to the ground, sending up a small cloud of dust.

'On my mark!' the Gatekeeper said.

Leto lay sprawled face down in the middle of the street and thought of how close his plan had come to working. He hoped his friends would escape unharmed, especially Darcy. He should have ordered her to be returned to her father if anything happened to him.

He waited for the arrows to fly.

'Hold… hold!' a voice shouted from the wall. 'Weapons down, now. That's an order!'

No arrows came.

Leto lifted his head from the dirt. Moments later, the gate opened a crack and someone came out and approached him. From his prone position, he could only see his boots. They stopped ten feet short of where he lay.

'Seriously,' the man said with a laugh, 'how many lives do you have?'

Leto recognised the voice. He pushed himself up to a kneeling position and focused on his saviour. The familiar face of Sir Ewen looked down at him.

'More than I care to need,' Leto said as he stood and dusted himself off. 'It's good to see you again.'

He embraced his cousin.

'And why is it the last few times I've encountered you recently, you look like absolute shit?'

Leto grinned at Ewen. He could only imagine how he must look. Over two moons without any real grooming, he had rarely bathed, except for a few dips in the cold river.

'My choices of late have been less than ideal,' Leto said. 'But that's all going to change.'

'That's good to hear. My father will be pleased that you aren't dead, again.'

'We have a lot to discuss.'

'I don't doubt it,' Ewen looked past Leto. 'And you should introduce us to your unusual friends. They are friends, aren't they?'

Leto nodded and turned to face his escort. They all had their weapons out, still wary.

'Viggo, Rogar,' Leto said. 'It's alright. You can put your weapons away.'

The commander gave Leto a questioning look.

'Sir Ewen is my family,' Leto continued, 'he'd never harm me or those I count as friends.'

Viggo stared at Leto briefly before setting his gaze on Ewen. 'You're Prince Leto's kin?'

'Err … yes,' Ewen said.

'How?' Viggo said.

'How?' Ewen said, confused. 'Oh, his mother is my father's sister.'

Viggo's gaze flicked between Leto and Ewen and back again. Leto nodded to the big man, urging him to believe what they had said.

'Viggo?' Leto said after a few moments of silence.

Everyone seemed to be holding their breath, waiting for Viggo, who stared at the two men for a while longer.

'Put away your weapons,' Viggo said, turning to the others. 'He is safe here.'

The other giants complied, with sighs of relief from Leto and Ewen, the guards on the wall, and even the crowd gathered on the street.

'Are you sure? I don't see the resemblance,' Big Gil said.

Viggo nodded.

'If you say so,' Big Gil said. 'It's a good thing too. It wouldn't have been a fair fight anyway.'

'No, probably not,' Ewen said, looking up at Big Gil.

Leto knew his cousin had stopped a potential slaughter.

'Well then,' Ewen turned to Leto, 'my father will be most pleased to see you all. Open the gates!'

Leto approached the gates with Ewen at his side and Rogar and the other giants close behind. He glanced back after he'd passed through the gate. Most of the giants no longer brandished their weapons and seemed almost relaxed. Darcy again sat on Little Gil's shoulder, and she even flashed Leto a smile when he caught her eye, which he returned.

Only two giants still carried their weapons – Viggo his monstrous club and Big Gil his staff – though they both held them down by their sides. Leto looked back up towards Shorehaven Keep with profound relief.

They entered the Inner Ward, where Lord Malachy waited, accompanied by his wife, Corinna, Sir Gurney Jansen, Sir Peyton Holmguard and Sir Kit Hansen. Leto wondered why the Knight-Commander of the Noble Guard and his second-in-command weren't in the capitol, and why neither wore their cloaks.

Leto and his uncle gripped each other's forearms. The man usually wore a perpetual frown, but now he sported a wide grin.

'We'd given up hope,' Malachy said. 'But the gods have finally smiled upon us.'

'I'm glad to be here, Uncle,' Leto said.

Leto introduced the members of his giant escort, as well as Darcy. His uncle acknowledged each of them as he would any other important visitor. His Aunt Corinna kept her composure despite her obvious fear.

'What's been happening while I've been away,' Leto asked and glanced at Sir Peyton.

His uncle's smile faltered.

'Let's get inside,' he said. 'We have much to talk about.'

Leto couldn't agree more.

His uncle had wanted to adjourn to his private quarters, but Leto insisted that Rogar and Viggo be present for any initial discussions. They had saved his life, and he didn't want to dismiss them out of hand now that he had safely returned to Avaleen. Consequently, they met in the First Hall. Rogar easily made it through the doors without issue, but Viggo needed to crouch to enter the hall.

Leto sat in the middle of one side of a long table hastily erected in the centre of the hall. A nervous Darcy sat immediately to his left. She would have happily stayed with Little Gil and the others, but she needed to understand her situation by coming to Avaleen, and he also felt a high level of responsibility for her.

His Aunt Corinna sat next to Darcy, with his uncle at the head of the table. Across from Leto sat Ewen and Matteus, with Gurney Jansen and Sir Kit Hanson to his left. Rogar and Viggo took up positions at the other end of the table, seated cross-legged on the floor but still towering above everyone else in the room.

Sir Peyton Holmguard had taken the seat to Leto's right. The old knight looked tired, his face more drawn and haggard than he remembered. Ewen had mentioned the disbanding of the Noble Guard to Leto on their way up to the keep, so when Sir Peyton had explicitly asked to be near Leto, he had readily obliged.

Food and drink was brought, then the discussion started in earnest. Leto began to recount what had happened after he'd left Anchorage nearly five moons ago, sailing away from Avaleen, the deaths of Jacob and Jeremiah at the hands of Cedric Greythorpe, and his journey back to the capitol.

'We wondered what had happened to Jeremiah,' Malachy said solemnly. 'He was always reliable in sending reports when he was in the Diamond Isles; I was concerned when we hadn't heard anything.'

'There were rumours, but nothing that sounded remotely believable,' Ewen said.

'My condolences,' Leto said. 'He was a good man.'

'That he was,' his uncle said, lowering his gaze to his plate. 'That's not how a man like him should die.'

The Lord of Shorehaven Keep sighed deeply.

'I'll send word to Sir Ramin,' he continued. 'He should know what has become of his brother.'

Malachy looked up.

'And our condolences to you as well,' Malachy said.

Leto's face hardened. Talk of his father or his best friend still upset him. They both occupied his thoughts every day, and the hurt hadn't abated, but he had begun dealing with it.

He nodded to his uncle but said nothing in reply, and continued his story, detailing his escape from Twin Falls and the events at the Red Pass.

'I was foolish,' Leto said. 'But I got lucky. Rogar saved me from the river, and then Darcy and her family nursed me back to health. I wouldn't be here talking to you today if it weren't for them.'

He looked up at Rogar. 'I owe him my life.'

Leto recounted his meeting with Viggo and the other giants, his return to Avaleen and his most recent encounter with Cross.

'Finn will be pleased that bastard is finally dead,' Ewen said.

'So am I. I'm not sure I'd survive another confrontation with him,' Leto rubbed his injured shoulder.

'That's quite a tale,' Malachy said. 'You've been favoured by the gods.'

Leto snorted.

'With everything that's happened to me lately, I get the feeling the gods hate me,' he said.

Lord Malachy looked up to Viggo and Rogar. 'You have my thanks for bringing our prince home to us.'

The huge men nodded.

'And you, young lady,' Malachy said to Darcy. 'My thanks also go to you and your father and mother.'

Darcy looked at Leto nervously, and he nodded his encouragement.

'Thank you, my lord,' she said, giving him a brief smile. 'He was no trouble.'

'I'm sure he wasn't,' Malachy returned her smile and looked back to Leto. 'Do you know how many others survived the Dragon's Throat?'

'Uncle, I'm sure you have many questions regarding my journey, and I will endeavour to answer them, but before that, I have questions of my own.'

'All in good time,' Malachy said.

'I need to know now,' Leto demanded.

His uncle's smile disappeared.

'If you insist, Your Highness,' Malachy said, leaning forward, placing his elbows on the table and clasping his hands together in front of his chin.

'I do,' Leto said, his uncle's formal address not lost on him.

'We are in a delicate situation here at Shorehaven Keep,' Malachy began. 'There will be war in the south very soon, possibly before the next full moon.'

'With Greythorpe?' Leto said.

Lord Malachy nodded.

'And by all reports, it may not go well for Lord Owen and his allies.'

'How many soldiers have you sent?' Leto said.

Lord Malachy leaned back in his chair, dropping his gaze. The others shifted their gaze between him and his uncle.

'How many?' Leto repeated.

'None.'

That couldn't be right. The Blackwaters had no closer allies in the north than House Kirkwood. They were family.

'None?' Leto asked, incredulous. 'Why?'

Malachy took a sip of his wine.

'Explain, Uncle,' Leto continued. 'Tell me everything.'

Lord Malachy nodded and placed the goblet on the table.

'We were warned in no uncertain terms to stay out of the coming war, to stay neutral,' Malachy said. 'And I accepted it.'

'Warned, how?' Leto said.

'Lady Lennane Greythorpe came with a message from the Steward of Avaleen,' Malachy said.

'She was escorted by Regan's dog, Harrow,' Ewen said.

Leto's heart skipped several beats.

'They're here?' he said. 'You do know she planned to kill Melina?'

Malachy nodded.

'Lord Owen said as much,' his uncle said.

'But she's gone now,' Ewen said.

'You let her go?' Leto said, facing his cousin.

Leto wanted her arrested and thrown into the deepest cell he could find.

'We couldn't very well stop her from leaving,' Malachy said. 'She was on official business from the Steward. A position to which Greythorpe was elevated legally. We're isolated up here. Confining her would just be asking for Greythorpe to march on Anchorage.'

'He wouldn't dare,' Leto said.

'Your Highness, I think you underestimate his power and support within Avaleen,' Malachy said.

Everyone, including his father, seemed to have underestimated Regan Greythorpe's influence and ambition.

'What of Melina,' Leto said, turning to Sir Peyton Holmguard. 'Did you and Lord Owen get her away from Sisters End?'

'Sir Fergus did manage to spirit her out of Whitehall and into the Greenhavens,' Sir Peyton said.

Finally, some good news.

'That's great,' Leto said. 'Where is she now?'

Sir Peyton's face went ashen.

'Your Highness –' the Knight-Commander began, but Lord Malachy interrupted.

'I'll tell him,' his uncle said.

His Aunt Corinna had bowed her head, unable to meet his gaze. He turned back to his uncle, who glanced at the giants.

'I would prefer to discuss this in private,' he said.

'Whatever you have to say can be said in present company,' Leto said, feeling uneasy.

The Lord of Ships took a deep breath.

'There is no easy way to say this,' his uncle said and paused for a moment. 'Your sister is dead.'

The words hit Leto like a hammer. He started to object, his mouth opening to speak, but he paused. His uncle wouldn't say those words if it weren't true. He closed his mouth and lowered his gaze. Melina, his beautiful sister … dead?

'I am so sorry to give you –'

Leto held up his hand, and his uncle stopped speaking.

'How … how did she die?' Leto said, his words barely above a whisper.

'We should talk about this later,' Malachy said.

'I want to know now!' Leto barked.

His uncle moved uneasily in his seat.

'Harrow killed her, I believe,' Malachy said. 'I know not how.'

Leto's head shot up.

'What? He was here, and knowing what he did, you let him walk away?'

'We learned of the princess's fate less than a week ago,' Malachy said. 'He was long gone by then.'

'Surely you sent someone after them?'

'They boarded a ship to Amberfall,' Ewen said, 'Though I'm sure she and Harrow would have convinced the captain to make the deviation to Sunset Cove as soon as they cleared the bay.'

Damn it! He would never see his sister's smiling face ever again. As Leto felt the tears well in his eyes, he remembered something.

'Lord Owen said he sent a message to Hampstead Heath as well,' he said. 'Lord Gruffydd wouldn't have allowed any harm to come to Melina once she was in the Greenhavens, would he?'

'There's more you need to hear,' his uncle said.

More? What more could there be?

'What is it?' Leto said.

'Even before this war started, all was not well in the south,' Malachy said, his expression grave, and told him of the massacre at Hampstead Heath.

Leto slumped back in his chair. 'All of them … gone?'

'Old Griffen Greenwood and the Lady Riona were at Cliffs End, fortunately,' Malachy said, 'as was Gruffydd's daughter, Renata.'

Leto sat quietly for a few moments. He already hated the Greythorpes. Both his father and best friend had been savagely killed by them, and now his sister too. And House Greenwood had been all but wiped out.

'What has been done about it?' Leto said through gritted teeth.

'I expect Lord Owen has dispatched soldiers and supplies, but that's about it,' Ewen said.

'Has anyone been held to account?' Leto said, looking at his uncle. 'Have they been avenged?'

Malachy lowered his gaze, and Leto knew the answer. He stood as he felt his anger swell. The Greythorpes had run roughshod over Avaleen with impunity. How could that happen? They should be made to answer for what they'd done. Lord Regan and the rest of his traitorous house should be punished.

'Are you alright?' Darcy said.

He needed to think.

'Take me to my quarters,' Leto said. 'And not in the bowels of the keep like last time. I will no longer hide.'

'I'll take you,' Ewen said and stood.

'Arrange lodgings for my friends,' Leto said.

'They'll be looked after,' his uncle said.

Leto went to walk past Rogar, but the giant put out his huge arm. Leto stopped and looked up. Concern etched his friend's face.

'I'll be fine,' Leto said.

The giant laid his hand gently on his shoulder.

'I just need some time alone,' Leto said. 'We'll talk later.'

Rogar patted his shoulder.

'Who's in charge of guarding this place?' Viggo said as Leto followed Ewen from the First Hall.

'I am,' Gurney Jansen said.

'We need to speak,' Viggo said.

He couldn't be any safer here in Shorehaven, but Viggo continued to take his assignment from his chieftain very seriously.

Unlike on Leto's previous visit to Anchorage, this time his quarters befitted a prince of the realm; an apartment with a full suite of rooms. It included a living room, dressing room, two bedchambers and thankfully, windows and a balcony to the outside world. Leto went out and leaned on the balustrade, and looked out over the busy harbour. The boiling rage he felt earlier had settled to a simmer, but the anger persisted. He needed to decide what to do, but decisions made with anger are usually bad ones. Yet another piece of advice his father had imparted to him.

Despite the gravity of the situation, he smiled. Even though he had never wanted to be King and often ignored his father's guidance and lectures, he'd found himself repeating his words to himself more and more often. Leto missed his father and his beautiful little sister, his mother, brother and Jacob. He was alone, the last Blackwater. He closed his eyes and tried to picture the last time his whole family had been together, but he couldn't.

He went to the bed and lay down, buried his face in the pillow and screamed. It wasn't fair. He rolled onto his back and took a few deep breaths. Then he opened his eyes and wiped them with his sleeve. No more crying. He knew what he had to do and exactly where to start.

His Uncle Malachy looked at Leto in disbelief. 'You want to attack Greythorpe?'

This time, they sat at a small table in his uncle's solar with Sir Ewen, Sir Peyton Holmguard and Gurney Jansen.

'I want to hit him where it'll hurt the most,' Leto said.

Malachy didn't even try to mask his dismay.

'I want to attack Highland Keep,' Leto continued.

'And what good will that do?' Malachy asked.

'It'll show that he can be hurt,' Leto said, 'that we aren't afraid of him.'

'It's not that simple,' Malachy said.

'Why not?' Leto said. 'His army would probably be in the Shadowlands already.'

'True enough,' Malachy said, 'but what do we gain by capturing Highland Keep?'

'Gain? Wouldn't it be enough that he loses his home?' Leto said. 'It may even distract him from this war. That could only help Lord Owen.'

His uncle sighed.

'As I've said before, it doesn't look promising for our allies in the south. Owen has superior tacticians and soldiers with more experience, but I'm afraid he doesn't have enough of them.'

Had the situation deteriorated that far?

'And I know Regan Greythorpe,' his uncle continued. 'He won't be distracted. If he succeeds in the Shadowlands, he will come up here and wipe us from existence.'

Leto sagged back on his chair; his confidence flattened. He'd made all these plans but hadn't thought how to carry them out, and most damning of all, he hadn't considered the consequences of his actions. Hundreds of people would die for no good reason.

'We have to do something,' Leto said. 'We can't just sit here on our arses and let Greythorpe do whatever he pleases.'

'What would you have us do?' Malachy said.

He'd foolishly assumed his uncle would go along with his ideas, but he and his advisors had shot them down with reasoning against which Leto could not argue. The men around the table were all older, more experienced and considerably more knowledgeable than Leto.

'You don't need to know everything,' his father used to say. 'Decide what you want to do but leave it to those who know how.'

Leto's eyes settled on his Uncle Malachy.

'I want Greythorpe destroyed,' Leto said.

'Attacking Highland Keep is not how to do it,' Malachy said.

'Then what is?' Leto said.

'Your Highness,' Sir Peyton spoke for the first time. 'If Lord Regan is victorious in the south, then there is nothing we can do.'

'Then we have to ensure that he isn't,' Leto said.

'I've said the people of the Borderlands will be neutral,' Lord Malachy said.

Leto's face hardened.

'You made that promise, not me,' Leto said.

He hadn't wanted it to come to this, but he had no choice. Leto stood.

'Am I or am I not your liege lord?' Leto said with as much confidence as he could marshal.

He locked eyes with each man in turn.

‘Am I?’ he repeated, louder this time.

As he gave each man a stony glare, an awful thought came to him. What if they said no? His confidence wavered. He had never considered that they may not want him as their King. Again, his gaze settled on his uncle. If he didn’t pledge his support to Leto, he may as well have died at the Red Pass.

Lord Malachy’s grimace softened and turned into a smile. ‘You are definitely your father’s son.’

What did that mean? The older man stood and slowly walked around the table towards Leto. He met his uncle halfway and stopped.

‘Make him proud,’ Malachy added, and stepped forward and embraced Leto.

He couldn’t remember the last time his uncle had embraced anyone. It felt odd, but Leto returned the embrace, nevertheless.

His uncle stepped back and slowly went down on one knee, placing an elbow on the other and bowing his head. Leto fought to keep his composure at his uncle’s unexpected act. He would’ve settled for a simple nod in acceptance of his position. His uncle tilted his head up and looked directly into Leto’s eyes.

‘My liege, my King,’ he said and bowed his head again.

Leto didn’t know what to do or say, so he just nodded.

‘Thank you, Uncle,’ Leto eventually said, his voice soft.

The other three men had risen from their seats and come up behind Lord Malachy. They also went down on one knee and bowed their heads in unison.

‘My King,’ they all intoned.

Shivers ran up Leto’s spine, knowing he wouldn’t wake up and find it all a dream. He stood there looking at the four men who had declared him their King.

‘Get up,’ he said. ‘Please.’

The men began to rise. Ewen helped his father to stand and turned to Leto.

‘Well, cousin,’ he said with a broad grin, ‘or should I say, Your Grace?’

It sounded surreal to be addressed in such a way. ‘Your Grace’ had always been his father ever since he could remember.

'Umm ... I don't know,' he said uncertainly.

'You'll get used to it,' his uncle said.

Leto wasn't so sure, but he accepted the comments with a quick smile. Gurney Jansen held a grin almost as wide as Ewen's, but Sir Peyton seemed slightly apprehensive.

Then Leto gave his first command as King.

'I hereby reinstate the Noble Guard,' Leto said. 'Sir Peyton, will you accept the position as their Knight-Commander?'

At once, Sir Peyton went down on one knee again.

'You honour me,' he said. 'I accept.'

'Stand,' Leto said. 'How long will it take to assemble them?'

'Not long,' the Knight-Commander said, getting to his feet. 'Most of them have stayed in or around Anchorage.'

'Do it,' Leto said and turned to his uncle. 'How many mounted soldiers can you call on?'

'Around two hundred, no more than that,' he said.

That wasn't as many as Leto would have liked, but he nodded and said nothing.

'If given a couple of weeks, we could bring together another two hundred and fifty, but I'm assuming you'll want to move sooner than that?' Malachy added.

'Time is short, it seems,' Leto said. 'How soon could we leave?'

He would have liked to leave tomorrow, but even Leto knew assembling and equipping an army, albeit a small one, took time.

'Speed is paramount,' Ewen said. 'No wagons and minimal non-combatants. Everyone will ride. We can be ready to leave in three days, maybe two, if all goes well. We'll be there within a fortnight.'

Leto hadn't formally voiced where there would be. They just seemed to know.

'What of your new friends?' Malachy said.

Leto had been thinking about them and how they would react to his being King and his plans to help Lord Owen.

'I'll go and see them now,' he said.

'Let me take you,' Ewen said.

Leto went to follow Ewen out of his uncle's solar, but Sir Peyton took up a position ahead of him.

'I'd feel better knowing you had protection, even from an old man like me,' the Knight-Commander said and turned to Gurney Jansen. 'Commander, fetch Sir Kit for me. I cannot leave His Grace unprotected.'

'I'm safe here,' Leto said.

'From this moment forward, there will always be a Noble Guard at your side,' Sir Peyton said. 'Always.'

Leto stood with Ewen and his Uncle Malachy in one of the larger halls of Shorehaven Keep, where the giants had settled.

'I will look after her as if she were my own,' his uncle said, to Leto's relief.

He had broken the news to Darcy earlier, and she had been upset.

'How long will you be gone?' she had asked.

'I don't know,' he had replied. 'But until then, you need to stay here, where it's safe.

'What will I do?'

'You will need to learn about Avaleen and its history. The Kirkwoods are one of the oldest families in the realm. They will be good teachers.'

He had taken her hands in his. 'And when I return, I'll personally escort you to your family in the Greenhavens.'

She had seemed mollified at this offer. 'You promise?'

'I promise,' he had said with a reassuring smile.

Leto knew she would be well looked after.

'You have my thanks,' Leto said to his uncle and turned to his giant escort.

He had explained to them his plans to travel to the Shadowlands and the forthcoming war. They hadn't tried to dissuade him from his path but seemed slighted by Leto's words.

'I am forever in your debt, but I cannot ask you to follow me.'

'You would refuse our help?' Viggo said.

'No, no, but this isn't your fight.'

Leto had seen what one of these giants could do and had been hopeful they would accompany him, but he still had reservations.

'You and Big Gil are warriors, but what about the others? It will be perilous, even for someone your size,' he said, glancing at Leila.

Big Gil must have noticed because he stepped forward and put a hand on his smaller brethren's shoulder.

'We all know how to fight,' he said. 'And young Leila may be small, but she would give a good account of herself against any of us.'

'But she's the chieftain's –' Leto started but stopped as Leila stepped towards him, irritation showing on her face.

'My uncle would be ashamed if I didn't fight,' Leila said.

'I did not mean to offend,' Leto said, 'but this is different.'

'Don't worry about us,' Big Gil said.

The other giants nodded and murmured their agreement. Viggo stepped forward and went down on one knee.

'We are yours to command,' he said.

The others followed suit, kneeling before him and bowing their heads.

'You honour me,' he finally managed to say.

Leto stood there, amazed at the turnaround in his fortunes. Three days ago, he had nearly died, but three from now, he would be doing something no-one in the history of Avaleen had done. He would be riding to war – with giants.

16

REGAN

Regan Greythorpe shivered and cursed his impatience.

The cold air bit at his exposed skin. Winter should have broken, he thought as he pulled his cloak tighter and stood near the fire burning in the small hearth. He could have waited a few more weeks to bring his army south, but his spies had indicated that the preparations for war of Lord Owen and his allies had fallen woefully behind. As a result, Regan had assembled his army sooner, reckoning he could get the jump on his enemy, finish the war quickly, and return to the capitol before the next full moon.

However, his spies had not been entirely accurate, and the Redstone army had indeed been ready, easily rebuffing their initial attacks. Granted, he had not committed his entire army to battle, but they had still greatly outnumbered the enemy. His army had lost over two hundred soldiers, and if the reports could be believed, Redstone had suffered barely a score of casualties.

Regan had punished the leader of that failed attack. Sir Rafe Singer, his nephew by his older sister Murne, had been removed from command. He would not accept mediocrity from anyone, and had replaced Rafe with his younger brother Saul. Despite the losses of the first engagement, it had produced some valuable information; Redstone had a well-organised and well-disciplined army at his command.

He turned away from the hearth. Sparsely furnished, his tent contained only the necessities. Divided into two rooms, with the sleeping area at the rear, which had been curtained off with heavy drapes from the living area at the front, it could accommodate a small hearth and the large table that he now approached. It also doubled as the command tent, so the chairs had been all pushed to the side. He always stood for the meetings with his commanders.

He examined the map that covered over half the table. It showed the simplicity of this war, taking place in a single location with only two armies and only a few moving pieces.

It had now been a week since that first failed attack, and every night since, Regan's camp had been attacked, always from different directions. Despite the light casualties, the men were on edge. The attackers used flaming arrows, meaning that many soldiers had taken to sleeping out in the open, preferring to brave the cold rather than risk burning to death in their tents. Extra patrols had been ordered up to a mile from the camp's perimeter, but still the attacks came. The overcast skies made spotting these attackers nearly impossible.

Regan had also ordered night raids on the enemy camp, but nearly half his troops did not return. His Spymaster had assured him they had informers in the Redstone camp, but nothing useful had yet come from them. Regan had stopped short of threatening the man, but made it extremely clear he wanted results very soon.

Familiarity with the terrain had proved a distinct advantage to the enemy. Redstone may be winning that small part of the war, but it wouldn't save him. If what he suspected turned out to be accurate, in two days, Regan would be victorious, and he'd have Owen Redstone and his brothers executed. House Greythorpe had been very patient. Their revenge on the Blackwater kings and their allies would soon be complete.

'My lord,' a voice came from outside the tent.

'Yes?' Regan recognised it as one of his guards, who pulled the tent flap back and stepped in.

'They're here,' he said.

Regan nodded, and the soldier stepped back out and opened the tent flap wide. In came Whitman White, Walden Hardwinter, Godwin Greythorpe, Llewellyn Greythorpe and Saul Singer. On seeing these men, he realised again how much he missed the strategic skills of his brother. Aside from Regan, Steffan would have been the most experienced and skilled strategist, had he lived.

The loss of his brother significantly reduced the level of command experience. He now had to rely more on younger men such as Godwin and Llewellyn Greythorpe, and Saul Singer. He didn't get along especially well with his half-brothers. However, Godwin, the youngest of them, had shown some promise and proved to be the least insufferable.

It wasn't as crowded around the table as it had been. First of all, Rafe Singer had been banished, and most recently, Cedric had gone missing.

They'd been at the camp only three days before his son had requested to lead a scouting party. He had relented, but instructed the Scoutmaster to send his son's party away from the enemy camp. When Cedric found out, he quickly complained to Regan.

'You'll do what you're told. Count yourself lucky I'm letting you go at all.'

Regan didn't expect the war to last very long and had said as much to his son. Cedric had backed off, realising he might not get another chance to spend time outside the command tent. But three days ago, Cedric's scouting party had not returned from patrol. No bodies or signs of fighting could be found.

Cedric had been acquitting himself well as Regan's right hand. So well, he had begun thinking there may be no need to bypass his eldest son as his heir. Regan looked after himself and didn't plan on dying any time soon, but as with everything else, he liked to plan ahead. He didn't need this type of distraction, so he pushed the thoughts of his son out of his mind and looked at the men around the table.

'Are the war machines ready?' Regan asked.

'After that storm a few days ago, the road turned to mud, and it's taking a lot longer for them to get here than expected,' Whitman White said. 'They should arrive tomorrow; we'll require another two days to assemble them all.'

'You have two in total,' Regan glared at his most experienced commander.

Whitman didn't argue.

'My lord,' Waldin Hardwinter said, 'I don't see why we need these machines. On an open battlefield, they are as dangerous to our men as they are to the enemy and quite ineffective compared to two thousand cavalry.'

Regan's eyes shifted to his brother-by-law. Those under his command seemed to like him, but the man was stuck in the past. Being ten years older than Regan, he couldn't help but cling to some of the old ways.

'Really?' Regan said. 'Please refresh my memory, but I don't recall the last attack on the enemy camp being very effective. Neither was the one on the previous day or the day before that?'

'That's different,' Sir Waldin spluttered. 'We didn't have sufficient preparation and didn't commit enough soldiers.'

'That is your opinion?' Regan continued to glare at his brother-by-law.

'Err … yes,' Waldin eventually said.

'And you would be right,' Regan said, and eyed each man around the table. 'Therefore, from now on, we will ensure we have real plans, backup strategies, and all the resources available to carry them out. We will not go in waving our swords, as we've done so far, hoping the enemy will turn tail and run.'

The men in the room nodded and murmured their agreement.

'Redstone isn't scared of us,' Sir Llewellyn said.

'No, he's not,' Regan agreed. 'All the more reason not to attack on a whim, like we did when we arrived. That was stupid.'

The commanders remained silent at Regan's stinging words, no doubt noting the continued absence of Sir Rafe Singer and not wanting to be the next one to be banished.

'Shouldn't we attack with all of our army?' Godwin broke the silence. 'Attacking with half our force hasn't been working.'

'No,' Regan said. 'Not yet. We'll test them one last time with your and Sir Whitman's detachments. Lord Owen has chosen the field of battle well. It's not quite big enough for us to effectively utilise the entire force, unless we're organised. That will take more preparation.'

Godwin and Whitman's forces attacked the following morning just before dawn. They hurt Redstone and his allies – possibly the most successful attack in terms of casualties and damage inflicted – but didn't break them. The win had also come at the cost of another hundred and fifty deaths. Regan had surveyed the battlefield from afar and had eventually surmised their high losses weren't due to the ineptitude of his commanders, at least not this time.

It irked Regan to admit it, but the superiority of their enemy eclipsed them in every way except numbers. If Redstone had even close to an equal number of soldiers, Regan's army would be in serious trouble. He now had no choice but to send forth the bulk of his army, horses, men and machines, the whole lot, and overrun them.

'The day after tomorrow, we'll hit them with everything,' Regan told the commanders the following evening.

He had no doubt they'd be victorious. He would sustain a large number of casualties, but it couldn't be helped. Losing more men reflected badly on its commanders, so if his allies lost too many more, they may question the wisdom of this war and go home. They would forgive a high body count if the war ended quickly.

'Aside from Llewellyn's men, who will hold back to fill any potential failures in the line, we'll commit all forces to the battlefield at once,' Regan continued.

They discussed the specifics of the battle ahead, well into the night. By the end, everyone at the table appeared confident.

'We will crush Redstone once and for all,' Regan said.

'Good,' Godwin said. 'Let's get this over with. It's too damn cold here.'

Regan could not agree more, though he considered his own reasons somewhat less frivolous.

'My lord,' Sir Waldin said, his tone subdued. 'I'm in full agreement with Sir Godwin, and I'm sure I speak for us all when I say we're grateful for this impending victory.'

The old man paused.

'What?' Regan said.

'I hate to bring this up now, but I can't foresee a better time,' Waldin said. 'Some of the lords are asking whether you'll honour the agreement for a share in the spoils.'

Even in their short time in the Shadowlands, rumblings of dissatisfaction had reached Regan's ears. He knew that not everyone in his army served out of loyalty. Some fought through fear, some for political advancement, and, as with most large armies, some waged war for financial gain. Nothing treasonous had been said yet, but without a significant victory soon, he may have an outright revolt on his hands.

'Everyone will receive their fair share,' Regan said.

'I'll pass on your reassurances,' Waldin said.

The Shadowlands contained riches, and there would be plenty to go around. Despite that, Regan would ensure the houses that questioned his honour would earn their share by being in the vanguard.

'Please do,' Regan said.

His commanders turned to leave.

'Godwin, stay,' Regan said.

'Certainly, my lord,' he said.

After the others had left, Regan looked at his cousin.

'Has there been any word on Cedric?'

'No, my lord.'

'I want him found.'

'Of course, but the searches have failed to turn up anything, not even a stray horse. It's like the whole scouting party has disappeared into thin air.'

'Search further out,' Regan scowled. 'I want to know what happened to my son.'

'Yes, my Lord.'

'That is all.'

Godwin bowed his head, turned and left.

The next morning, Regan rose well before dawn. He stepped out of the tent and ordered the nearest guard to fetch his morning meal and have the fire in his tent stoked. The guard rushed off as Regan made his way to the nearby latrine. By the time Regan returned to his tent, the fire had been set, and he stood close to it, trying to banish the cold from his body.

As usual, the coming battle was constantly on his mind. The whereabouts of his son entered his thoughts again, but this morning, his mind also wandered to the fate of his wife. As expected, she'd sent him a message by raven that the Lord of Ships had acquiesced to his demand of neutrality. Knowing Malachy Kirkwood to be a greedy coward, Regan knew he wouldn't risk losing control of Anchorage, or the riches and power that came with it.

Regan had gone from Twin Falls before Lennane and Harrow returned to the capitol but had left strict instructions for Harrow to join him immediately upon his return. However, the latest communication from Sir Baltair noted that neither Lennane nor Harrow had been seen in the city.

Thinking of his wife reminded him that her former handmaiden had finally been caught. He'd yet to decide what to do with the pregnant little harlot. He could have her executed along with other bastards and wipe out the Blackwater line forever. That would be the simplest solution.

'My lord!' a shout interrupted Regan's contemplation.

He wasn't really in the mood to receive visitors, but he heard an urgency in his cousin's voice.

'Come,' Regan said.

A guard pulled the flap aside, and Godwin entered. He carried a large timber box in his arms and wore a grim expression on his face.

'What's this?' Regan looked at the box.

'It was found by one of our scouting parties about a mile south of the camp.'

'Found?'

'We were meant to find it, my Lord,' Godwin said.

Regan glanced at his cousin, his brow knitted.

'Why do you say that?'

'It was left out in the open, next to a banner.'

Regan took a closer look at the box in his cousin's arms. At about three feet long, it could hold several things. The fine-quality timber had images of horses and their riders carved into the sides and the lid. He gestured towards the table, and Godwin carefully placed the box on the edge nearest Regan.

'The banner, what was on it?'

Godwin reached into his tunic and pulled out a length of red material. Hesitating briefly, he spread the banner on top of the timber box and stepped back. Regan scowled at the black prancing horses spread across the cloth. Had the coward sent a peace offering? Amusing, if true, but Regan wanted the Redstones wiped from history once and for all.

'Did you open it?' Regan glanced at Godwin, who nodded.

'I wanted to make sure there were no dangerous surprises.'

Regan pulled the banner from the box and dropped it on the floor. He inspected the box, inserted his fingers into the grooves at either end of the lid, and lifted. It opened with barely a creak. Inside, two pieces of a broken sword rested on a cushion of red silk. Regan's face hardened as he recognised the weapon. It belonged to Cedric. He stared at the broken blade for a few moments, and pointed to a small leather bag loosely tied to the pommel.

'Did you check this as well?'

'Yes, my Lord.'

Regan removed the bag and loosened the thin leather ties. He peered into it and tipped it upside down, emptying the contents onto the blade. Out fell a fistful of red hair and a small scroll. He grabbed the lock of hair and stared at it. Regan had hoped that maybe Cedric had misplaced the sword, and this was Redstone's attempt to bluff him, but this hair could only be from his son's head. His mother had beautiful, rich red hair, which Cedric had inherited. Regan tossed the hair back onto the box and picked up the scroll. He unrolled it, read the message, and threw the scroll back into the open box in disgust.

'My lord?' Godwin said.

Regan ignored him. How could Cedric have been so stupid? He had been scouting in the area furthest from the enemy, but he still managed to get himself captured. He sighed and closed the box.

'Who else knows about this?' Regan said.

'Me, the Scoutmaster, and the scouting party,' Godwin said. 'But only I and the Scoutmaster know what's inside it … err … and now you, my lord.'

Everyone knew the scouting party had not been found, but he wanted to keep his son's capture a secret for as long as possible.

‘Let’s keep it that way,’ he said.

Redstone may have his son, but he refused to change his plans.

That afternoon, his commanders again stood around the table in Regan’s tent, analysing and discussing the plans for tomorrow morning’s assault on the enemy camp.

‘The war machines are ready to go,’ Sir Whitman White said. ‘They’ll be in place before dawn as planned.’

Regan nodded.

‘As long as it doesn’t rain overnight, of course,’ Whitman added.

‘Ensure your captains know what to do and when to do it,’ Regan said. ‘There’s limited room out there, so precise movements are paramount.’

His commanders all knew the plan, but he repeated it again so they knew exactly what he required of them and their soldiers, leaving no ambiguity whatsoever.

‘I don’t want our foot soldiers being trampled by our horses because they ignored a signal and took a wrong turn.’

‘So, we’re going ahead with the assault tomorrow?’ Godwin said.

‘What kind of stupid question is that?’ Waldin Hardwinter said.

Regan glared at his cousin. He knew why the question had been asked, but he had decided to keep the information about Cedric to himself. That Godwin had hinted at it in the presence of the others irritated him.

‘Yes,’ Regan said. ‘We will attack as planned.’

Godwin shuffled nervously and nodded.

As usual, Regan woke well before dawn and felt refreshed. Decisions had been made, and everything had been organised down to the smallest detail. Now, they would ride into battle and wipe Redstone from the face of the earth. He ate his morning meal with gusto, after which his squire helped him into his chainmail and armour.

His black-and-grey breastplate shone in the pre-dawn light as he exited the tent. He hadn’t worn full battle armour in a long time, but it still fitted him like a glove. His stallion waited, the reins held by one of the grooms.

As he approached his mount, he looked up at the clear skies. Excellent, perfect weather for battle.

Today would see the end of Owen and his ilk, and Regan could begin reaping the rewards in earnest. He went to lift his foot into the stirrup but paused. Godwin cantered up to his tent and brought his horse to a skidding halt. He dismounted and strode towards Regan, breathing heavily, his face flushed.

'My lord,' Godwin managed to say.

'What is it?' Regan said.

'They're gone.'

'Who's gone?'

Regan immediately assumed that the minor lords who had begun to give some trouble had up and left in the night. It wouldn't matter. The number would be small, and they'd pay for their cowardice later.

'Lord Owen's camp,' Godwin gasped. 'It's empty!'

17

DARIAH

Dariah awoke with a shriek.

The rat that had been chewing on her arm scuttled off into the depths of the cell. She pushed herself into a sitting position and rubbed at the stinging wound. She had begun to sleep sitting up, wedging herself into the corner of the cell so as not to fall over. But again, she had somehow tumbled onto her side, which made it easier to be bitten or stung by the rats and other small creatures that infested the dungeons. She never slept longer than a few hours anymore.

Dariah still could not fathom why she had been thrown into a cell. She carried the prince's baby and fully expected to be given a room like she had when she was a lady-in-waiting. She had been stunned when they dragged her into the depths of Riverview's dungeon. Soon after being shoved into the cell, the putrid, dank air had sickened Dariah so much that she vomited. The cell had no bed, bitter cold emanated from the dirt floor, and she had a small wooden bucket without a handle to use as a privy. The simple dress she wore had quickly become covered in grime.

The only light came from the small, barred window in the door to her cell. Terror struck Dariah, scared for herself and her unborn child. She had cried hopelessly for the first few days, not understanding why she had been left here, but now she had no more tears, too tired even to cry.

No-one had come to see her. She had been forgotten, and had no contact with anyone except the gaoler. A few days into her confinement, she desperately tried to charge past him when he placed her paltry daily meal in her cell. The disgusting little man had easily caught her and held her close, his rancid breath hot on her neck.

'If you're kind to Gunther, Gunther will be kind to you,' he had whispered in her ear, his hand groping at her breasts.

Dariah had screamed and kicked, thrashing about until he had let go and shoved her back into the cell, ripping her dress even more than it already had been.

'Keep away from me!' she shouted, trying to cover herself with the torn dress.

He laughed.

'You'll be wanting favours soon.' Gunther slammed the door shut and put his face up to the bars, his lecherous cackle making Dariah shudder. 'They all do.'

From that point on she had kept away from the door, only venturing close to retrieve her food once she could be sure the gaoler had moved away.

Someone pulled back the bolt of the cell door. Dariah looked up at the loud clang. The door opened, and she waited for the gaoler to enter. Someone in a uniform came in, a guard. The flickering light of his torch pushed the darkness back, and she squinted. Drawing her knees up to her exposed chest, she wrapped her arms around them.

She didn't know the torch bearer, but the one who followed him in, even by the faint torchlight, she recognised as the one who had beaten her father.

Poor Papa. She didn't even know if he still lived … or her brother. The image of her mother being restrained whilst her father and brother lay on the ground unconscious continued to haunt her. The anger began to well up inside her, and she grimaced.

'Well, aren't you a sight,' Sir Baltair said. 'No-one will want to bed you now. You make a slum whore look like a queen.'

He laughed heartily, but the other guard did not.

Sir Baltair stepped forward and squatted a few feet from Dariah. She pulled her legs closer.

'I've got good news for you,' he said with a crooked smile. 'You're leaving here very soon.'

Her eyes widened at the words.

'In a few days,' he added.

Finally, her prayers had been answered. Where would she be taken? She didn't care. It couldn't be worse than this place. She looked up at him, hopeful.

'By order of the Steward,' he continued, 'you're to be publicly executed so all the city can see.'

The Commander's smile broadened as Dariah struggled to understand his words.

'We both win,' he continued. 'You leave this disgusting place. I see your pretty neck stretched at the end of a rope, and the Blackwater line is finished.'

'What?' she said, shaking her head, not fully grasping what she'd heard.

'Yes,' Sir Baltair said, nodding with a nasty grin. 'Your prince is dead, his sister is dead, and soon you and his bastard child will be too.'

Leto … dead?

Her baby would die without ever drawing a breath. She would never see her own baby.

The thought ripped her soul apart. She started to sob, but no tears came.

'Noooo!' she cried, her throat afire, unable to breathe.

Sir Baltair stood, all semblance of humour gone.

'Traitorous bitch,' he spat.

'Commander, if I may make a suggestion,' the other guard said. 'No-one's going to be interested if you execute a grubby prostitute, which is what she looks like.'

'What do you mean?' Sir Baltair said.

'Lord Regan was quite specific. He wanted to make an example of her. If she were clean and well-dressed, like a noble, it would show that not even well-to-do citizens are not immune from the law.'

The Commander glanced at Dariah and sneered.

'She does look like a slum harpy,' he agreed. 'Get her cleaned up, then.'

'I'll see to it myself,' the guard said.

The man with the torch gave her a pained look and followed the Commander out of the cell. The door slammed shut, and Dariah let her head fall. She would die, and she could do nothing to prevent it.

What seemed like hours later, the cell door swung open, rousing Dariah from a daze. She hadn't moved, still in the corner with her head bowed. She didn't look up at the rustling of boots. Leave me alone, she thought bleakly.

'She'll be light as a feather,' someone said. 'I'll do it myself.'

'Yes, sir,' someone else said.

Someone wrapped a blanket around her and picked her up. No! Leave me alone, Dariah tried to struggle, but she had no strength. She tried to raise her head but couldn't, and it lolled back as they carried her out of the cell.

The light got brighter, and she squeezed her eyes shut. She felt warmth and a slight breeze on her face. She was outside. As quickly as it had come, the brightness of the sunlight disappeared, and she opened her eyes. They passed stone corridors, steps, and eventually entered a small room. Whoever carried her, laid her gently on a small bed.

She looked up at the man. The same guard who had held the torch when her death sentence had been pronounced, now pulled a blanket up to her chin.

'Rest here for a bit,' he said, his voice gentle. 'Someone will be along to help you get cleaned up, and then we'll get you some real food.'

She should be grateful or pleased, but she couldn't see the point. What difference would it make whether I'm dirty or clean, or if my stomach is full or rumbling from hunger?

He covered Dariah with another blanket, and she closed her eyes. She rolled onto her side and gently stroked the soft pillow; she felt warm for the first time since … she had no idea. She had lost all concept of time down in that dark cell. Not that it mattered, but the warmth dulled her senses, and despite the despair into which she had sunk, she fell into a deep sleep.

Dariah woke and her eyes flew open. She had been lying down. She sat up with a start and pulled her arms close, expecting to be bitten by a rat or some other vile creature.

'Good,' a soft voice said. 'You're awake.'

A few moments later she remembered where she was and turned her gaze towards the voice. The girl looked familiar.

'I'm Hannah. I've been told to help you bathe and dress,' she said. 'Then I'm to bring you some food.'

She approached the bed and held out her hand. Without thinking, Dariah grabbed it.

'I hope you had a restful sleep, ma'am,' Hannah said and helped her from the bed.

The blanket that covered her fell away, leaving her nearly naked in her tatters. She reached for it but stumbled. Only her grip on Hannah's hand stopped her from toppling over.

'It's alright, ma'am,' she said, letting go of Dariah's hand and grabbing a cloak from the nearby table. 'This will keep you warm and covered until we get to the bath.'

The cloak rubbed against her bare skin, but at least it kept out most of the cold. Dariah let the girl lead her from the room and down the corridor to another room, with a large wooden tub filled with water at its centre.

'It's not much, but it'll do the job,' the girl said.

Hannah removed the cloak, placed it on the back of a chair, and helped Dariah into the bath. She could have sat in it, but didn't want to immerse her whole body in the cool water, so she remained standing. The girl picked up a cloth and began to wash her. Dariah shivered as Hannah rubbed at her arms and body, apologising before washing her breasts and between her legs. Dariah didn't care. The serving girl helped her out of the tub and dried her off, but it did little to alleviate her shaking.

Hannah dressed Dariah in an underskirt, chemise, and a plain long-sleeved dress. She sat on the chair while Hannah worked on her hair, combing it as best she could. She barely felt the pulling when the comb encountered the many knots, but the shaking lessened as she warmed.

The girl led Dariah back to her room. The two guards outside her door ogled her as they entered the room. Had they been there before?

'I'll get your food now,' Hannah said and left Dariah sitting on the bed. 'I'll be back shortly.'

She sat unmoving, and was still in the same position when the girl returned with a plate of food – some stew, and a lump of bread.

'Here you go,' she said. 'It's not much, but it's better than what you've been having in … err … sorry, ma'am.'

Dariah reached out to Hannah.

'Thank you,' she said, her scratchy voice barely above a whisper. 'You've been very kind.'

'I'm sorry for what they've done to you,' she whispered. 'Jane said you were her favourite lady-in-waiting.'

Dariah remembered Jane. She wasn't that different to Hannah: young, innocent and eager to please. She reminded Dariah of herself at that age. How things change, she thought … from being a confidante of the most high-ranking woman in Avaleen to being unable to move without anything hurting, waiting for her own execution.

Hannah smiled as Dariah nodded in recognition. The girl opened the door and left. The door closed and the bolt slid into place with a loud clang. She nibbled at her food, not feeling hungry despite her lack of nourishment. She placed the tray on the ground and lay down on the bed.

Hours passed, and Dariah dozed, lapsing in and out of consciousness, until someone started shaking her awake.

'Dariah,' a familiar voice said. 'Wake up. It's time to go.'

It took her a few moments to consider what she'd heard. It's finally happening. She didn't realise she had slept so long, but it didn't matter. Nothing mattered any more.

'Dariah!' the voice sounded more urgent. 'Get up!'

She gradually opened her eyes and recognised the guard who had brought her out of the dungeon.

'Hurry! There isn't much time.'

Time for what? To execute her?

He grabbed her shoulders and brought his face close to hers.

'I can't help you if you don't help me,' he said.

Groggy, she pushed herself upright. On the floor near the open door lay the two guards, pools of blood seeping from their bodies through the doorway.

'What … what did you do?' Dariah said and looked back at the guard.

He held a thick cloak in one hand and offered his other to her. What had he done?

'Can you walk?'

She took a couple of breaths and nodded.

'Are you rescuing me?' she whispered.

A stupid question, Dariah knew, but she had to know.

'I'm taking you away from here,' he said, 'but you'll need to walk.'

'You promise?'

Another dumb question.

'Yes. Follow me and do as I say.'

She reached for his hand and, with his help, pushed herself to her feet. He put the cloak around her and pulled the hood over her head. Dariah followed him out of the room, stepping over the guards, careful to avoid the pooling blood.

So much blood.

Her mind cleared as she realised the consequences of what this man had done.

'Are they dead?'

He had killed for her.

'Yes, now stop asking questions and be quiet.'

Dariah complied and followed in silence. They wound their way through the castle, down narrow corridors and several flights of steep stairs. She slipped and stumbled several times, but the guard always caught her.

He opened yet another door and ushered her through. They had made it outside, and Dariah pulled the cloak tighter. The stench of manure assaulted her senses. She knew of only one kind of place in the castle grounds that smelled like this … the stables.

Her suspicion proved correct when he led her to the smaller of the two wooden structures.

'This was the Noble Guard stable,' he said. 'It's rarely used now.'

Dariah detected sadness in his voice as she followed him into the smaller building where a lone horse had been tethered to a rail, already saddled.

He stroked the neck of the large bay gelding and spoke some words too soft for Dariah to hear. He turned and beckoned her to approach, made a cup with his hands, and bent low. She placed her foot in his hands, and he hoisted her up into the saddle, steadying her until she nodded.

'We shouldn't go any faster than a walk,' he said as he pulled himself up behind her, pushed her forward a few inches and settled into the saddle. 'But hold onto the pommel, just in case.'

He reached around her and took the reins, his arms holding her.

'Your face is known around the castle, but it's getting dark, which is good for us,' he continued. 'Just keep your hood low.'

Dariah nodded.

He pulled on the reins, directing the horse towards the stable door, and walked them out. They went up a wide alley into the central courtyard, followed the paved road and through the southeast arch into the outer ring of the castle.

'Okay, here we go,' he said as they approached the East Gate.

Dariah glimpsed men standing at the gate on the ground and the barbican. She pulled the hood lower over her face.

She felt the Captain give a light tug on the reins, and the horse stopped gently.

'Evenin', Captain,' one of the Watchers said.

A captain in the Capitol Guard had rescued her?

'Rufus,' he acknowledged. 'Let me through. I have business in the city.'

'Certainly,' the Watcher said but did not move. 'Who have you got there?'

'None of your business,' the captain said.

'We have orders to note who comes and goes.'

'Well, you know me, and that's all you need.'

'Is that a woman?'

Dariah felt the captain's arms tense, and the silence extended for a few moments.

‘Of course, it’s a woman, fool!’ he said, his voice full of authority. ‘Do you think I’d rather spend my time with one of you lot?’

‘No, of course not, Captain,’ the Watcher bumbled, shaking his head and stepping back out of Dariah’s line of sight.

‘Good. Now open the gate, or I’ll make sure your next job is watching over the latrines!’

‘Open the gate,’ the Watcher barked.

The large timber and iron gate creaked as it opened.

‘I trust I’ll not have the same trouble when I return?’ the captain said as the horse started forward.

‘No, Captain,’ the Watcher said.

The Captain urged the horse through the gate before it had opened completely, and they entered the city.

‘Are we safe yet?’ Dariah whispered.

‘Not yet,’ the Captain said.

‘Where are you taking me?’

‘Far away from here.’

‘Where?’

‘I’ll explain later,’ he said. ‘First, we must get you out of the city before they discover you’re gone.’

Dariah wanted to know more, but she had no choice except to trust this man. This man, whom she only knew as Captain.

‘What’s your name, sir?’

‘I’m not a sir,’ he said.

‘Captain, then.’

‘After today, I won’t even be a captain.’

‘Then what do I call you?’

‘Call me Armen,’ he said.

‘Thank you, Armen,’ she said and laid a hand on his. ‘Thank you.’

They made their way through the city streets in silence. Armen kept them on the main thoroughfares, amongst the crowd of people walking, on horseback, and in carts. Every so often, Dariah glimpsed a Capitol Guard and tensed up. She knew the sight and sounds of the city, having been through this part of it many times, and despite the protection of the night, she remained fearful someone might recognise her.

‘Do we need to stay on the main streets?’ Dariah said.

‘A single horse in a crowd is less likely to be seen than one in an empty back alley,’ he said. ‘Safer, too.’

She supposed that made sense, but it didn’t ease her, knowing they remained in danger of discovery until they escaped the city.

‘It won’t be long now,’ he said.

They rode through the city streets for over an hour before Armen pulled on the reins and brought the horse to a stop.

‘What’s wrong?’ she whispered.

‘Nothing,’ he said. ‘We’re at the North Gate.’

Her heart raced.

‘Good evening, Deputy Chief Watcher,’ Armen said.

‘Captain,’ the Deputy Chief replied. ‘Where are you going at this time of night?’

‘Just a short trip out to the lagoon,’ Armen said, ‘with my lady-friend.’

‘Lady-friend, hey?’ the Watcher said. ‘Isn’t it a bit cold for swimming?’

‘Who said anything about swimming?’

The Watchers laughed at Armen’s joke.

‘Who is she?’

‘That’s my business,’ Armen said, ‘and it’s going to stay that way.’

‘Come on, Captain,’ the Watcher pleaded. ‘You know the rules.’

‘Yes, I know the rules. I made them, remember.’

‘If you could just pull back the hood, you’ll be on your way in a trice.’

Dariah’s grip on the pommel tightened.

‘It could be your wife or your daughter?’ Armen joked.

‘Hah! I doubt that,’ the Watcher said, amused. ‘The wife’s butt-ugly and twice your size, and I only have sons.’

For a moment, Dariah heard the feet shuffling in the dirt and the flap of the horse’s mane when it shook its head.

‘We just want to see her face,’ the Watcher broke the silence.

She felt Armen lean close to her ear.

‘Have you met Deputy Chief Watcher before?’ he whispered.

She racked her brain. She would recognise many of the Watchers, and some might recognise her. She had met the Chief Watcher but couldn’t recall ever meeting his deputy. She shook her head imperceptibly.

'Just look up at the flags on our right,' Armen whispered and straightened up.

'If you insist,' he said.

Armen pulled back the hood from her head. She shivered as her face was exposed to the cool breeze. She dared not look directly at the men around them, concentrating her eyes on the banners fluttering above the gate.

'Well?' Armen said, unable to hide his annoyance.

'A pretty one,' the Deputy Chief Watcher finally said. 'You should be showing her off, not hiding her.'

Armen pushed the hood back over her head.

'May we go now?'

'Yes, Captain,' the Deputy Chief Watcher said and signalled for the gate to be opened.

He approached Dariah and Armen and stood close, nearly touching the stirrup. 'If it's not too much trouble, could you do me a small favour?' he said, his voice quiet.

'What?'

'Chief Watcher Anders, he's not too healthy. He may not last the winter.'

The massive gate started to open with a loud creak and rattle of chains.

'Get to the point,' Armen said.

'If the city is ever in need of a new Chief Watcher, could you please think of me? As you have seen, I'm a good Watcher, enforcing the rules no matter the situation.'

Dariah felt Armen take a deep breath as the gate creaked opened. The torch-lined road beyond disappeared around to the right.

'Of course, Deputy Chief Watcher,' Armen said. 'When I return, I'll put in a good word for you when I next see the Commander.'

Several carts lined the road outside the gate, with more than a dozen people milling about, waiting to be admitted. She knew that after dark, no-one entered the city unless they produced the correct documents or travelled with a royal family member, as she had done not so long ago.

The memory of that wonderful day at Queens Falls with Prince Leto came to her mind. She would cherish that memory, but it saddened her knowing she would never see him again, and her baby would never know its father.

'Thank you, Captain,' the Watcher said and stepped back.

Armen urged his mount to a slow canter, and they headed out of the city towards the City Bridge.

They rode on in silence.

'How long before they discover I'm gone?' Dariah eventually asked.

Armen glanced back towards the city, now over a mile distant.

'They probably already have.'

'What?' she said, worried. 'Shouldn't we ride faster?'

'We're almost to the bridge,' he said, unconcerned. 'Once we cross, no-one can catch us.'

His calm manner eased her mind. She relaxed and leaned back into his arms. Dariah had no idea where they were going or what lay ahead of them, but her baby would live, which was all she cared about. A short time later they finally crossed the river and rode into the darkness, and safety.

18

OWEN

'Should we gag him?' Sir Caden suggested, looking to Owen.

Owen shook his head and looked down at Cedric Greythorpe. He stood on the causeway of Cliffs End's outer wall just above the main gate, his retinue of personal guards nearby. Dawn hadn't quite made it to the Shadowlands yet, but the torches provided more than enough light. Members of the Home Guard finished lashing Lord Regan's son to a large timber log on the stone floor. They stepped back, allowing Penn to step closer.

'Are you comfortable?' Owen's brother asked.

The commanders had wanted to truss him up with manacles, but Owen had insisted on ropes and chains. He wanted the son of Lord Regan Greythorpe to be alert for as long as possible.

'Now we'll see how much your daddy loves you,' Penn continued.

'He'll raze this city to the ground!' Cedric spat.

'Really?' Penn said. 'I think you should shut your mouth, you cowardly little prick.'

'Or what?' Cedric said. 'Or you'll kill me?'

'You aren't going to be that lucky,' Sir Caden said.

'You idiots have no idea what you're in for,' Cedric said, laughing. 'You're all going to die, and I hope I live to see it.'

'The only thing you'll see is a noose around your neck or a large rock heading towards you, and bam!' Penn said, smacking his fist into the open palm of his other hand. 'Either way, you're a dead man.'

Cedric ignored Penn and glared at Owen. 'Once this is over, I'll throw your corpse to the dogs and make sure my boys have their way with your daughters!'

'I've changed my mind,' Owen said, gritting his teeth. 'Gag him.'

Cedric struggled against his bonds. 'You bastards!'

One of the guards forced open Cedric's jaw, and another pushed a chunk of wood between his teeth and tied it tightly in place around the back of his head.

'Now, who's the idiot,' Penn said, laughing.

It had been a stroke of luck that delivered Cedric Greythorpe into Owen's hands. Dunmar had been delayed while canvasing their northern and eastern neighbours for support. The arrival of Greythorpe's army in the Shadowlands had caused him and his company to detour west around the north end of the Burned Range and to the south. After crossing the Last Bridge, they ran into a small Greythorpe patrol. They outnumbered the enemy fifteen to one, and it didn't take long to dispatch them. Two Greythorpe men attempted to flee but couldn't escape Dunmar's soldiers. To their surprise, one of them was Cedric Greythorpe. Dunmar hid the corpses of those killed and continued south with the two prisoners and all the enemy horses. They'd missed the initial skirmishes and arrived just in time for the retreat to Cliffs End.

The guards hauled on the ropes attached to the log, grunting with the effort. Cedric struggled hopelessly against his bonds as the solid timber log rose into the air until it nearly touched the top of the frame. They tied off the ropes and pulled the metal rings into place at either end of the log.

It had been Sir Guy Westall's suggestion to string Lord Regan's son up above the main gate of Cliffs End. Owen wasn't too keen on the idea, but the others fully supported it.

'Will putting his son in harm's way delay Greythorpe at all?' Dunmar had asked the previous evening.

'I doubt it,' Sir Caden Angworth said.

'Surely, it should give him some pause at least,' Dunmar said.

'The man has ice in his heart,' Penn said, shaking his head.

Owen agreed. Regan Greythorpe didn't care for anyone except himself, but Owen saw no downside in putting the tyrant's son on display. It may not stop Lord Regan, but it would be worth it if it caused his soldiers to hesitate. Some of them had to have a conscience.

'Enjoy the view,' Penn said.

Owen looked up at Cedric Greythorpe. He had stopped struggling.

'Keep him awake,' Sir Caden said to Jesper Holt.

'Yes, sir,' Jesper said.

'We want him to see his death coming,' Penn said.

The sun had finally risen above the Black Cliffs, and Owen headed towards his residence in the Citadel. Half a dozen guards now flanked him and had been a permanent fixture since the retreat, even though they couldn't protect him from a well-placed arrow or being struck by a projectile from one of Greythorpe's damn war machines.

Owen could easily wait out the coming summer safe behind the city walls, if they had only foot soldiers or cavalry. The winters in the Shadowlands had a reputation for being harsh, which would force any army to retreat north to the warmer climate. Unfortunately, this wasn't the case. However, he had a few war machines of his own, catapults and trebuchets set along the city walls. They'd give as good as they got, but the war would be over quickly one way or the other, so he had decided to send his family away.

Captain Janz approached and fell into step beside Owen.

'Is everything ready?' Owen asked him.

'Most of the luggage and supplies have been loaded, my Lord,' Archer said.

'Most?'

It should have all been done by now.

'Lady Addwyn has not yet finished packing her belongings. She's … not happy.'

This wasn't a revelation. His wife had flat-out refused to leave when he had first told her of his plans.

'I will not run away,' she'd said. 'I am not a coward!'

'You are not running away,' Owen said. 'I am sending my family, whom I love more than anything else, away where our enemies will not find them.'

He hesitated and gently took her hand.

'And if things go badly here, the children will need you all the more,' he added.

At the mention of the children, her face softened, but her determination did not.

'I will not leave you here to die!'

'You will,' he said, 'and you will make sure our children are safe.'

'But –'

Owen cut short her protest. 'If we're to defeat Greythorpe, I need to be able to think clearly. I cannot do that knowing you and the children are in harm's way.'

Eventually, she relented, but it seemed she would leave on her terms. Owen entered the main living room and found his children seated, with Cordelia and Trynt on one seat and Gwenda and Cathwynn on the other. All wore mournful looks.

'Are you all ready for your journey?' he tried to sound cheery.

The girls nodded slowly, without any excitement. Trynt just buried his head in his sister's lap. Owen sighed and continued into the bed chamber. Addwyn sat silently in front of the hearth.

'I will accompany you to the docks,' he said.

She didn't answer but rose and left the room. Owen sighed and followed her, escorting his family to the courtyard where the carriage waited to take them to the docks.

The trip took about an hour, the silence broken only by the occasional sob or sniffle from one of the children. As with their departure from the capitol after the death of the King, tears flowed freely.

'Children, say goodbye to your father,' Addwyn said as they stepped out of the carriage onto the main dock.

Owen embraced each of the twins in turn, told them he loved them and reassured them they would be home soon. He knelt and kissed Cathwynn on the forehead.

'Be a good girl for your mother,' he said.

He lifted his son and hugged him tightly.

'I don't want to go,' Trynt said through the sobs.

Owen set him down gently on the ground and squatted down so he could look into his son's eyes.

'You have to go,' Owen felt a lump in his throat. 'It's very important that you help Archer look after your mother and sisters. Can you do that for me?'

'Yes … yes, Father,' Trynt said, wiping his eyes.

'Good man. And don't forget, a Redstone never gives up.'

Trynt nodded as Owen stood and ruffled his hair.

Owen had assigned Captain Janz and twenty of his best soldiers, all now clothed in civilian garb, to protect his family on their voyage and, aside from Archer, they had already boarded the ship.

Owen embraced Addwyn, but a sense of foreboding descended over him, and he found he didn't want to let her go. He had been confident of getting out of the capitol alive, but he wasn't so assured this time, knowing there may be a chance he'd never see his wife again or his children grow up. He gripped her tighter.

'Don't die,' she whispered.

He wanted to promise her he wouldn't, but he couldn't bring himself to say the words.

'I love you,' he said, his voice cracking.

She broke the embrace and kissed him gently on the lips. 'I love you too.'

As she turned away, he glimpsed tears rolling down her cheeks. Without looking back, she herded the children up the gangplank and onto the ship. Owen watched his family disappear from view.

'I'll send word once it's safe,' he said after gathering his composure.

The day before he had told Archer to make plans for the possibility of never returning.

'Pick one of the destinations from those we discussed,' he said. 'Give Lady Addwyn the choice once you're underway.'

'It's been an honour serving you.'

They clasped each other's forearms.

'Goodbye, my friend.'

‘Good luck, my lord.’

Archer stepped back and bowed. Once he had boarded, the ship’s captain, a very experienced and loyal man named Osin Hulsman, began barking orders. As the gangplank withdrew from the dock, Owen cast his eyes about the ship and again noted the name on the bow: *Fortune’s Favour.* Prophetic, he hoped.

Owen remained on the pier until it had left the inner harbour, but neither his wife nor children reappeared on deck, so he returned to the Citadel. He missed them terribly already, but the thought that his family would be safe steadied him. He would need all his wits in the coming days.

That afternoon Greythorpe’s army appeared on the northern horizon. Owen’s scouts had been watching and reporting on the advancing army since their retreat to Cliffs End, so it was no surprise. Owen felt profound relief flood through him. He hated waiting, even if it was for a large army about to besiege his home. The enemy gathered well out of range of Owen’s war machines and set up camp.

At dusk, he convened the war council as he had for the past several weeks. They usually lasted well into the night, but he wasn’t in the mood for long, drawn-out discussions tonight. Everyone knew what they had to do.

‘Are we sending out raiding parties tonight?’ Penn said. ‘We’ll need to destroy those machines.’

‘They’ll be more alert now,’ Sir Guy Westall said.

‘We can’t just do nothing and wait for them to pound us to rubble,’ Penn said.

‘I didn’t say that,’ said Sir Guy. ‘We just need to be aware that they’ll be more on guard.’

The odds were stacked against them, but he wouldn’t make it easy for the enemy. The more of those machines they could destroy, the longer they would last, and the longer they lasted, the more chance Greythorpe’s army would turn on itself. Owen's spies had informed him that discontent within the enemy camp was growing.

Owen turned to Sir Caden Angworth. 'I want as many raids on Greythorpe's camp as we dare. Disrupt their camp preparations and destroy as many siege machines as possible.'

The Lord of Riverglen nodded.

Owen turned to the Home Guard Commander. 'And what of our machines?'

'Guards have already been doubled within the Citadel,' Jesper said, 'and tripled on the ones on the city wall. No-one is getting near them.'

'You don't have to be near one to set it on fire,' Sir Lachlan said.

'We have barrels of water and sand at each location,' Jesper said.

'Good,' Owen said.

Jesper Holt's thoroughness impressed him. He couldn't have given them a better chance of defending Cliffs End. If they survived this war, Owen would reward him handsomely.

'Now, unless there's anything new to discuss, I'd advise you all to get a decent rest tonight,' Owen said.

They mumbled and nodded their agreement, but Owen knew most would be up half the night. Strangely, some could sleep like a baby before a battle, while others couldn't sleep a wink. Owen belonged to the former, but only if he knew nothing else needed to be done.

He ended the meeting and went to his residence, ordering Coen to bring food and wine. He ate slowly, his mind flicking from one thing to another, from the war to his wife, from Greythorpe to his children.

'Wake me an hour before dawn,' he said to Coen after he finished eating.

'Certainly, my Lord,' his steward said.

Owen took the goblet and the jug of wine and retired to his bed chamber. He dropped into the chair beside the fire, the one Addwyn had sat in just before they left for the docks earlier that day. I'll miss you, my darling. He sighed and refilled his goblet. Placing the jug on the nearby table, Owen lifted the goblet to his lips, paused, and put the goblet back down. He'd wake up with a headache, and on the eve of battle, that's something he could do without.

He approached the bed, undressed and climbed under the covers. Thoughts of his family dogged him. Would they make it to safety? Where would Addwyn and Archer decide to go? If he died, would Addwyn remarry? Who would his daughters marry? Would his son grow up to be like him? Owen began to feel anxious, so instead, he turned his thoughts to all the good times he'd had with his wife and family. These pleasant memories accompanied him as he drifted off to sleep.

At dawn the following day, Owen entered his solar, receiving apathetic greetings from his brother Penn and Sir Caden Angworth. Penn looked tired, and the Lord of Riverglen sported a bleak expression.

'Good morning, my lord,' Caden Angworth said.

Owen sat behind his desk. 'The look on your face tells me otherwise.'

'Yes … well … we sent a dozen scouting and raiding parties last night,' Sir Caden paused.

'And?'

'One of the scouting parties reported success in locating and destroying three ballistae without any casualties, and another reported finding a single trebuchet but only managed to damage it before they were fought off by the enemy, who killed half of their number.'

The casualties were higher than usual, and a possible cause for concern, but four war machines out of action by two raids wasn't a bad result. Owen waited for the remainder of the successes and failures, but none seemed forthcoming.

'And?' Owen repeated.

Sir Caden swallow hard, and his face tightened even more.

'We don't know.'

'How can you not know?'

Owen's concern deepened.

'Eight of the raiding parties have not yet reported back, and only six men from the other two have returned.'

'Only twenty-one men?' Owen said, 'Out of how many?'

'One hundred and twenty,' Caden said after a pause.

The night raids had always been a risk, but having whole raiding parties disappear en masse after losing barely any on previous outings didn't add up. The soldiers sent out were some of the most experienced scouts in Avaleen. Their loss would be felt.

'It's like the enemy knew they were coming,' Owen said, and the realisation hit him.

'We have a spy,' Caden said, coming to the same conclusion.

Penn shook his head in disbelief.

'That would explain the monumental drop in successful raids,' his brother said. 'But if there are spies, why now and not while we were more vulnerable at Silver Glen?'

'Because the spy is here in the city,' Sir Caden said.

That made sense, but it didn't make Owen feel any better. This meant that the spy must be one of the soldiers left behind or a member of the Citadel Home Guard. He could think of no others that could learn about the raiding parties.

'Find Jesper,' Owen said to Sir Caden, 'and tell him what we've surmised. We need to find this spy before Greythorpe decides to attack.'

The Lord of Riverglen nodded and left the solar.

'I don't like this at all,' Owen said to his brother. 'This is the last thing we need right now.'

'I can't argue with that,' Penn said and sat opposite Owen.

They sat in silence. Even if they found this spy, there would be others, but how many? Two … five … a score of them, and all serving different masters, with Lord Regan Greythorpe being one of them. A sharp rap on the door interrupted Owen's contemplations. It opened a moment later, and Sir Caden Angworth, Jesper Holt and Dunmar came in.

'My lord,' said the Commander of the Citadel Guard and gave a quick bow.

'Sir Caden filled you in?' Owen said.

Jesper nodded. 'I had already begun looking into it and was on my way to see you when Sir Caden found me.'

'And?'

'We got the bastard,' Jesper said with some satisfaction.

Owen's initial jubilation gave way to wariness.

'So quickly?' Penn said, thinking along the same lines as Owen.

'We got lucky,' Jesper said. 'Late last night, one of the lieutenants noticed a guard had strayed from his assigned position. This sometimes happens; guards get slack or don't follow orders, so he scolded the man who rushed back to his post. He didn't think anything more until I voiced my suspicions this morning.'

The others in the room listened with rapt attention.

'As it happens, the guard was found loitering near where Sir Caden and the commanders of the raiding parties had gathered. He may have overheard their plans. I confronted him in the barracks, but he denied it. When I ordered him taken into custody, the fool panicked and tried to escape.'

'Good,' Penn rose from his chair. 'Take us to him. I want to question this traitor myself.'

Something about it didn't quite sit right with Owen, but he wanted to ask this spy a question or two of his own.

'I'm afraid that won't be possible,' Jesper said.

'Why not?' Penn made his displeasure known.

'He's dead, my Lord,' Jesper directed the revelation to Owen.

'How?' Penn said before Owen could react.

'Does it matter?' Dunmar said.

'I apologise, my lord,' the Commander said. 'We couldn't let him escape, but killing him wasn't our intention.'

Damn it all to hell!

'I doubt we would have gotten anything useful from him,' Dunmar said. 'What kind of spy attempts to escape after being accused on flimsy evidence at best?'

'An inexperienced one,' Sir Caden said.

'Or a stupid one,' Dunmar said.

'That's not the point,' Owen said. 'Stupid or not, I would've liked to question him.'

'I know,' Jesper said and lowered his eyes. 'It won't happen again. I've directed all guards to patrol in pairs and will continue the investigation.'

‘Good. After I’ve finished here, I’ll be down to inspect the city wall,’ Owen said and waved his hand dismissively at the Commander.

‘I’ll be waiting at the eastern tower, my lord,’ Jesper said.

When the door had closed behind the Commander, Owen looked at each of the remaining men in turn.

‘Is it just me, or did the discovery of this spy seem a little too convenient?’ Dunmar said.

‘You don’t suspect Jesper, do you?’ Owen said.

‘No, no,’ Dunmar said, ‘but I don’t believe this spy they found is the one who caused us so much pain last night, not directly anyway.’

‘I don’t either,’ Sir Caden said. ‘But I’ll keep an eye on Jesper anyway.’

‘Offer your assistance,’ Owen said. ‘He’s a smart man. I don’t want him to think we don’t trust him.’

Sir Caden nodded.

‘So, how’s our gift at the main gate?’ Owen said.

‘Still alive, if that’s what you mean,’ Sir Caden said. ‘He’s being fed and watered, though he’s not being very cooperative, cursing and spitting his food at the guards.’

‘Ungrateful prick,’ Penn said. ‘And he has such a nice view.’

Owen smiled.

‘You may go,’ he said. ‘I’ll be touring the city in an hour if any of you want to accompany me.’

Once the others had left, Owen leaned back and rubbed his eyes. This wasn’t a good start to the day, and it troubled him that he hadn’t received any word from the capitol either. After a while, he stood, went to his chambers, and ordered Coen to retrieve his battle armour, the set gifted to him by the King.

Owen sighed and thought of his friend. Well, we may see each other again sooner than expected.

Coen returned with a couple of servants carrying the chest that stored his armour. His steward assisted with unpacking and donning the armour. He needed to look his best, as noble as possible, and an inspiration to his soldiers. This armour would do all that and more. It could also inspire fear, especially when he wore the helm, but he’d only wear that when facing the enemy. He’d lost some weight since escaping from Twin Falls, and didn’t feel anywhere near fighting fit. Thankfully, most of the armour still fitted him, albeit with some straps lengthened more than they probably should be.

When he strode out to the inner bailey, Dunmar and Penn had already arrived, waiting with Owen's prized stallion and a dozen other horses for his escort. He'd just taken the proffered reins from the stable hand when Alden Janz, Archer's younger brother, cantered into the courtyard and brought his mount to a quick stop. He dismounted and approached the group, but his bodyguards intercepted him.

'My lord!' Alden cried.

'Let him through!' Owen ordered.

The guards parted, allowing the young man to pass.

'What is it?' Owen said.

'Ships have entered the harbour,' Alden said, breathing heavily. 'Warships.'

'Whose standard are they flying?' Penn said.

A small part of him had hoped Malachy had ignored the threats levelled at him by Lord Regan and had somehow dispatched the royal fleet.

'The Steward of Avaleen,' Alden said, confirming Owen's worst fears.

'How many?' Owen said.

'Eleven, but there may be more outside the harbour.'

A painful thought entered Owen's mind. Addwyn … did her ship escape? Had they run into this fleet of warships, or had Captain Hulsman evaded them? He tossed the reins back to the surprised stable hand. The inspection would have to wait. He had to see these ships for himself, but he also needed to see the main gate. The northwest tower would allow him to do both.

Abandoning the horses, they all rushed to the north wall. Arriving at the tower, Owen peered over the battlements across the harbour. He counted fifteen warships in the outer harbour.

'Will they attack?' Penn said.

They could quickly destroy the docks and the ships at anchor. The harbour had a few defences, but if the invading vessels stayed far enough out, the ballistae mounted on the walls overlooking the docks could not reach them.

'I don't think so,' Sir Caden said. 'They'll just stop anyone from getting out.'

'Or in,' Dunmar added.

The warships lined up across the outer harbour, effectively sealing Cliffs End from the sea. Now under siege on two fronts with no means of escape, Owen pondered his options. Civilians and merchants could depart if they pleased, if the invading forces let them, but Owen had no plans to leave. He would die here, or he would be victorious. There could be no other end.

A distant horn sounded, and Owen looked towards the main gate. The Greythorpe army had begun to move. Lord Regan wasn't wasting any time. Let's get this over with, he thought, no matter the outcome.

Then smoke began to rise from the city wall.

His machines were burning.

19

LETO

Leto stretched his arms out wide and winced.

His small army had crossed the Red Pass bridge and stopped for a brief rest and to water the horses, and he tried to rid himself of the tension that had built up over the past few days. He knew it wasn't just from spending thirteen days straight in the saddle. The closer they got to Silver Glen, the more the burden of command, and trepidation about the forthcoming battle, weighed on him.

They'd ridden hard but not foolishly so. Leto didn't see the point in exhausting the horses or pushing riders to their limits. Arriving in time to assist Lord Owen only to be too tired to fight, would be folly.

Leto gazed up at the cliffs, then down to the waterfall and the Dragon's Throat. It seemed like an age since he had been here, another life. He glanced up at Rogar and Viggo, who had joined Leto, Sir Ewen, Gurney Jansen, Sir Peyton Holmguard, and a small group of Noble Guard at the edge of the small stream, watering the horses.

'How're you travelling?' said Leto.

'Too slow,' Rogar said, grinning.

Leto smiled back, constantly surprised at the stamina of his giant friends. Unlike the soldiers of the Borderlands and their horses, they could run all day and never seemed to tire. Of course, at the speed the column of riders had been travelling, the giants had never exceeded a slow lope.

'Please feel free to go ahead and start without us,' Ewen said, echoing Leto's smile.

'Don't give him any ideas,' Rogar said, gesturing towards Viggo, who glanced at him without a trace of humour.

Leto had been pleased and relieved at how most of the soldiers now reacted to his giant friends. Some kept their distance, and a few were terrified of the huge beings, especially Viggo. However, many soldiers regularly interacted with them, some even offering to share their campfires. It warmed his heart.

'I'd prefer it if you stayed with us,' said Leto.

Rogar bowed, still smiling. 'Whatever you wish, Your Grace.'

He returned the empty goblet to Sir Declan, swapping it for the reins of his warhorse. Leto had refused the offer of a squire. However, after the first night on the road, the Knight-Commander had insisted, and Leto had begrudgingly accepted the young Noble Guard as his squire. To Leto's surprise, he appreciated the attention and assistance Sir Declan provided.

They led their horses away from the stream towards the road. The rain had washed away most of the infantry and horse tracks, but the well-trampled grass beside the road and deep wheel ruts remained.

'War machines?' Leto glanced at Gurney Jansen.

At his uncle's recommendation, Leto had made Gurney a Captain in this small army of the north, much to the man's surprise. The experienced leader of men, being Commander of the Guard at the Crossroads, had been one of the few who had seen combat in anything more than skirmishes with bandits, so Leto didn't object.

Gurney squatted near one of the larger grooves. 'Quite a few, from what I can tell.'

Several different sized furrows had been gouged into the earth, some wider and deeper than others.

'What kind?' said Leto.

'If I were to hazard a guess, I'd say ballistae and mangonels, though possibly these were made by trebuchets,' the Commander said, 'depending on whether or not they transported them in pieces.'

'Whatever they are, I bet there are enough of them to do quite a lot of damage,' Sir Ewen said.

'True,' agreed Sir Peyton, 'but don't ever discount the Lord of the Shadowlands. He's a shrewd tactician and wouldn't be intimidated by Regan Greythorpe and his machines, even outnumbered three to one.'

Leto winced. The odds weren't great despite Lord Owen's superior command skills.

'Let's go then,' said Leto, climbing into the saddle.

He wanted to try and improve those odds as soon as possible.

'Yes, Your Grace,' Gurney Jansen said, mounting his horse and riding away, barking orders as he went.

'We should be at Silver Glen by high sun tomorrow,' said Sir Peyton, glancing at Sir Ewen, who nodded his agreement and mounted his horse.

They could ride through the night, which they had done on several occasions throughout the journey southward. However, since passing into the Shadowlands, the decision had been made to travel during the day and not too long after dusk. They had to avoid riding into enemy patrols, and given their proximity to Silver Glen, they could accidentally ride into the enemy camp.

Several Borderlands soldiers rode up from the south and pulled up near Ewen and Leto. He recognised them as the scouting party led by Sergeant Verne Barly, a short, stocky man barely older than Sir Ewen. They were late in returning from their patrol.

'Where have you been?' Ewen said. 'You should've been back this morning!'

'I apologise, my lord,' Sergeant Barly panted, 'but they're not there anymore.'

'What?' Ewen said.

Sergeant Barly glanced at Gurney Jansen, who trotted beside them and halted.

'We scouted ahead as ordered,' the Sergeant returned his gaze to Ewen and Leto, 'but didn't come across a single enemy patrol.'

The sergeant's horse was lathered, and its nostrils flared. They must have ridden hard.

'I thought this unusual, so we went further south and made it to Silver Glen without resistance,' Sergeant Bay continued. 'We discovered a large, abandoned camp a mile east of the road. We then rode to the south end of the plain and found another abandoned camp. There was a battle, but we've missed it.'

'Has Lord Owen been defeated already?' said Leto.

'I doubt it,' Ewen said. 'He probably retreated to Cliffs End. My father said he had planned a siege, just in case.'

'If Greythorpe had been victorious, he'd still be there,' said Sir Peyton.

That made sense, though it meant they were still too far away to be of any use to Lord Owen.

'How long to Cliffs End?' said Leto.

'An extra day's ride,' Ewen said.

'And if we rode all night?' said Leto, figuring they would not run into the enemy's camp, at least not tonight.

'If we pushed the horses,' Gurney said, 'tomorrow night.'

'We should do it,' Ewen said. 'Ride through the night and all of tomorrow. We'll camp and send out the scouts to see where Greythorpe is encamped, then attack the following morning.'

Leto thought about this for a moment, and nodded. The decision had not been all that difficult, with part of him relieved at not having to go into battle tomorrow. Still, it just postponed the inevitable, and he itched for it to be all finished.

They rode, or in the case of Rogar and his brethren, walked or ran until dusk and on through the night. With the sparse cloud cover, the moon lit their way, allowing the column to travel faster than a slow walk. However, clearer skies also meant bitter cold during the night and well into the morning.

Despite his weariness, Leto refused to call a stop unless absolutely necessary. Sir Ewen looked as fatigued as he felt, though he had not suggested stopping. Strangely, Gurney Jansen and the Knight-Commander showed little signs of weariness. Maybe the extra lines on their older, grizzled faces masked their tiredness.

'What if we get there and it's all over and Greythorpe has won?' said Leto.

'I suppose we'll turn around and go home,' said Ewen, 'and hope they don't see us.'

Leto looked at his cousin with concern. Would he want to turn tail and run back home to the Borderlands? They hadn't discussed that possibility before, not in any detail anyway. Leto assumed they would reach Lord Owen before or during the battle. He hadn't necessarily expected to win, though he would prefer that outcome. His cousin broke into a wide grin.

'Don't fret,' Ewen said. 'We've made good time. I'm sure there'll still be a battle for us to join on the morrow.'

'Why the smile?' said Leto.

'I apologise, Your Grace,' Ewen's face still held a light grin. 'I find humour the best way to cope with the fear.'

Leto couldn't believe his cousin, possibly one of the finest soldiers in Avaleen, could be frightened.

'You're scared?' said Leto.

'Of course,' Ewen said. 'Aren't you?'

Leto didn't know how he felt. He had been a bit edgy the last day or so, but he certainly wasn't petrified, as his cousin purported to be. Maybe his tiredness overshadowed his fear. He just wanted to sleep, but he nodded.

'Being fearful is healthy,' said Ewen. 'Helps you live longer.'

They made camp beside a small brook in the woods a mile west of the road.

'No campfires,' Ewen said. 'We can't risk being seen by patrols.'

Even with the bitterly cold night, Gurney Jansen and Sir Peyton agreed. Reluctantly, he gave the order, and Leto joined the others outside his tent. Leto had slept under the stars since the journey began, the same as everyone else. Sir Peyton had offered to have the tent built every night, but Leto had refused. The Knight-Commander had not asked tonight, and the small tent had been hastily erected before Leto could object.

'It's only about fifty miles to Cliffs End,' said Gurney Jansen. 'And depending on what information the scouts bring back, we can expect to engage the enemy just after dawn.'

A specific time had now been set down for the attack. This meant that a day from now, Leto would either be dead or victorious. At least it would be over.

Suddenly, two memories came to the fore, neither of which he liked. One, when a prisoner in his own home, he had been up on the balustrade off his bed chamber looking down at the rocks below; the other, when he stood at the edge of a waterfall in the jungle beyond the Black Cliffs. It must be the tiredness, he thought. He didn't want to die, but he did want this war to end.

'I'm going to sleep,' said Leto abruptly and stood. 'Wake me an hour before dawn.'

'Sleep well, Your Grace,' Sir Peyton said.

Sir Declan rose, but Leto waved him down.

'I'll be fine,' he said and yawned.

Leto knew he would sleep like a log, even with the prospect of battle tomorrow. He approached the tent and paused. Leto had admonished the Knight-Commander for arranging the tent without asking.

'You need a proper rest, Your Grace,' Sir Peyton had explained. 'We have a big day tomorrow.'

'I'll sleep in it if you don't want to,' Sir Ewen had said with a smile, though Leto would bet his cousin wasn't entirely joking.

Smiling at the memory, he pulled the flap back and entered, seeing a cot covered in blankets. The standard soldier's tent consisted only of a single space, just big enough for a couple of bedrolls, but Leto was grateful for it tonight. He removed his armour and lay down on the cot. It wasn't overly comfortable, but far better than sleeping on the ground. Leto pulled the heavy blankets up around his chin and promptly went to sleep.

The following morning, Leto watched the smoke rise from the fires ravaging Cliffs End.

'Are we too late?'

Leto, Sir Ewen, Captain Gurney Jansen, Viggo and a cluster of the Noble Guard hid in trees north of the city, which overlooked the battlefield on the plateau below.

'No, Your Grace,' said Gurney Jansen. 'The scouts reported only the outer wall has been breached. There is still time.'

'Lord Owen will have the Citadel locked up tight,' said Ewen. 'But none of our spies we sent have yet to return, so there's no knowing the condition of his army.'

He followed the Commander's gaze as it moved from the city to the enemy camp barely a mile to the east. The camp seemed half-empty to Leto, but he could see men and war machines moving about.

'About two thousand, I think,' Gurney glanced up at Viggo. 'What do you think, Commander?'

The giant gazed intently at the enemy camp for a few moments.

'I concur,' said the big man. 'You have a good eye for one so close to the ground.'

Gurney chuckled and looked back towards the camp.

'Do we attack now?' said Leto.

'Lord Owen should have received our messages by now,' Ewen said, 'so we should give them more time to prepare.'

'We don't even know if the messengers got through,' said Leto.

'Some of them must have,' said Ewen.

'Even if they did succeed, there's no guarantee Lord Owen will be able to mount any sort of attack,' Gurney admitted.

'They only have to get Greythorpe's attention,' said Ewen.

'I would have thought they'd have it already,' said Leto. 'Unless he knows we're coming.'

'I doubt it,' said Gurney with confidence. 'Nothing I can see indicates he expects an attack from anywhere except the city.'

'Excellent,' Ewen said. 'We can't lose.'

'Do you realise we'll still be outnumbered at least six to one?' Leto said, his stomach churning at the thought.

'Does it matter?' said Ewen. 'We're not going to change our minds, are we?'

'I guess not.'

'With any luck, some of Greythorpe's allies will change theirs and either swap sides or retreat.'

'Just like that, they're going swap sides or run away from us?' Leto said, not believing his cousin.

Ewen grinned and held up a gloved fist. 'Don't worry, Your Grace. We have three things going for us.'

'Three?'

Ewen extended a finger. 'We have surprise on our side.'

True, Leto thought, but surprise would only last a short time.

His cousin extended a second finger.

'We have the King and true ruler of Avaleen riding with us. That must count for something. Many lords follow Greythorpe because he coerced and bullied them into it, and until now, there's been no-one else to challenge his authority. They'll flock to your banner.'

Leto wasn't sure if simply waving the banner of the King would be sufficient to sway the allegiance of those fighting for Greythorpe.

'What's the third?' said Leto.

Ewen extended his thumb and turned to face Viggo.

'Our gigantic friends here,' said Ewen. 'Even the smallest of them is worth twenty of us, and this one here, fifty.'

Ewen almost seemed excited about it.

'And I guarantee that none of them has ever seen a giant,' he continued. 'Do you know how scared they'll be when Viggo and his brethren are bearing down on them as fast as a horse, swinging those massive weapons?'

Leto remembered Viggo's attack on the bandits in the woods and the immense power he had at his disposal. It still gave him shivers just thinking about it.

'They will shit their breeches,' Ewen continued. 'Our new friends will strike fear into the hearts of even the bravest of their soldiers.'

Facing down one of the giants in battle would be frightening. Having eight of them charging at you would be bone-chilling. It would swing the odds in their favour, but Leto turned to Viggo.

'Are you certain you want to be part of this?' said Leto, genuinely concerned. 'As I've said before, this isn't your fight.'

The giant man's brow furrowed.

'My people do not abandon their friends,' Viggo said, seemingly offended at the question, 'especially in their hour of need.'

'I just had to ask one last time,' said Leto, relieved at the answer.

'I'm glad they're on our side,' Gurney said.

Ewen nodded his agreement. 'You got that right.'

'Then it's settled,' said Leto.

They all headed back through the woods. Preparations for battle had already begun when they exited the north-western edge of the trees and approached the column. Weapons had been checked, saddles tightened, armour tied.

'Mount up!' said Ewen. 'It's time we showed Greythorpe what the soldiers of the Borderlands are made of!'

The command was repeated several times down the line, and the soldiers began to mount their horses. They all knew the plan. It'd been discussed at length earlier that morning after the scouts had made their final reports. Leto's heart beat a little faster as he mounted his warhorse and put on his helm.

Ewen brought his horse to a halt next to Leto. 'Are you ready, Your Grace?'

Leto nodded, and two hundred fifty horses and eight giants entered the woods. Less than a quarter of an hour later, they left the woods and moved onto the plain. Leto stopped fifty yards past the eastern edge of the woods. The riders and giants formed into three groups: Sir Ewen would lead the left, Captain Gurney Jansen the right, and Leto the centre.

The mounted cavalries would be a hundred yards apart, separated by the giants, mainly to give the giant warriors more room to move and swing their massive weapons. Viggo had insisted that at least one of his brethren be close to Leto, so Big Gil and Rogar would be running close to the centre group.

'Ewen!' said Leto, turning in his saddle.

Ewen turned his horse and stopped beside Leto, his back to the battlefield. They clasped each other's forearms.

'Good luck,' said Leto.

He could see a grin through the small gap in Ewen's helm.

'Good luck to you too, cousin,' he said as their arms dropped back to their sides.

'Whatever happens today, you have my thanks.'

'Just do me one favour … don't die,' said Ewen. 'My father will have my head if I return, and you don't.'

'I'll do my best,' said Leto with a wry smile.

Ewen brought his arm to his chest and bowed his head.

'My King,' he said, and rode away towards his cavalry.

Leto swallowed at the genuine gesture and watched Ewen ride away. He lost sight of his cousin as Noble Guard formed up around him, careful not to stray in front of where Leto held his warhorse. The Knight-Commander had objected to Leto's decision to lead the charge.

'What sort of King doesn't lead their soldiers into battle?' Leto had said. 'I'm no coward.'

'I never said you were a coward,' Sir Peyton had said. 'My job is to protect you from your enemies and, if need be, from yourself.'

What in blazes did that mean?

'You're saying it's a bad idea?' said Leto, put out by Knight-Commander's comment.

'This whole situation is bad,' said Sir Peyton. 'You've only just returned to us. We cannot afford to lose another King.'

Leto understood the reasons for the Knight-Commander's objections but wouldn't change his mind.

'Sir Peyton, I will lead my army into battle, and that's final.'

The Knight-Commander had relented, but remained displeased.

Leto's heart beat faster, and his throat went dry. His warhorse pranced around on the spot like it knew they were about to go into battle. This was happening … really happening. For the first time, he would be charging into a real battle in a real war, leading over two hundred soldiers, possibly to their deaths. He took a few deep breaths to calm himself and swallowed, trying to coax some moisture into his mouth.

He pulled his sword from its scabbard and pointed it at the enemy. Glancing to his left, past Big Gil and Sunni, Ewen raised his sword in response, with Viggo and Leila on the far left.

Leto looked to his right. Rogar acknowledged Leto with a dip of his great head; Little Gil paced in a rough circle . Further on, Gurney Jansen indicated his cavalry's readiness with his sword held high. On the far right, Arve and Wulftan stood waiting for the signal.

The banners of House Blackwater snapped in the breeze as Leto glanced at Sir Declan on his left and Sir Peyton, who had taken up the position immediately to his right.

'Are you ready, Knight-Commander?' Leto said.

'Always, Your Grace,' the old soldier said with determination.

Leto lifted his sword high until it pointed at the cloudy grey sky. The horns sounded, their deep reverberation penetrating his entire body.

This was it.

'Avaleen!' he shouted, and brought his sword down, slicing the cold morning air.

A roar went up as the army of the Borderlands echoed Leto's shout. He urged his mount into a trot and then a canter. He leaned forward and kicked his horse into a gallop. He could hear the thunder of hundreds of hoofbeats around him.

It seemed only moments, and he had already covered more than half the distance from the trees.

Five hundred yards to go … four hundred yards.

At three hundred yards from the enemy lines, they could see the enemy had only just begun to move and organise their defences.

Two hundred yards … some of the Noble Guards begin to pull ahead of him.

One hundred yards … Leto was close enough to see the shock and confusion on the faces of the nearest enemy soldiers.

Fifty yards … forty … twenty …

They slammed into the enemy line, smashing aside their hastily organised vanguard like straw dolls. He kept riding, knocking over anyone unlucky to get in his way and hacking at those still standing with his sword. His speed slowly decreased until his mount could only walk. Leto swung his sword down on anyone who got close to him, but not long after, he stopped, unable to push through the surge of bodies.

The clanging of swords and screams of the dying filled the air as the battle raged around him. Members of the Noble Guard closed in around Leto, giving him a brief respite. Big Gil and the other giants swung their massive weapons, decimating the terrified soldiers of the Greythorpe army.

The enemy lines thinned out, and Leto pushed his mount forward again, following the Noble Guard further into the camp towards the command tent at its centre, their goal.

Without warning, Leto's mount stumbled and fell to its knees, sending Leto flying over the horse's head. He hit the ground with a thump, landing on his back. A stab of pain burst in his chest, and air rushed from his lungs.

The sounds of battle momentarily dulled as Leto lay still. The pain persisted as he desperately tried to inhale without success. He tried to rise, but his body would not obey. Panic began to set in. If he lay here much longer, the enemy may find him and skewer him without him being able to offer any resistance. That's not how he wanted to die. Where was his Noble Guard?

Suddenly, he could breathe and felt the air rush into his lungs as he inhaled. The first few breaths hurt, but the pain began to subside, and the sounds of battle returned. Leto scrambled to his feet and surveyed the area. Dead and injured soldiers and horses lay everywhere. By the gods! Most of the dead bodies around him belonged to Noble Guards, and a long iron shaft protruded out of the chest of the nearest horse. What the hell had happened?

His hand reached towards his scabbard, but his sword wasn't there. He turned, his eyes darting left and right. Finally, he saw it. The hilt poked out from under a dead Noble Guard. As Leto pulled it free, he looked up at the face of the dead body, wondering to which of his protectors it belonged. He recognised Sir Declan and shook his head. *Sorry, my friend.*

A noise close by caught his attention and Leto automatically spun to his left and ducked his head. The slash of a sword missed by mere inches. He realised he no longer wore his helm. He raised his sword to block another attack, which would have cleaved his skull in two if he had not deflected it. He parried another slash and backed away to give himself a bit more room. Despite nearly tumbling over a dead horse, the short respite allowed Leto to organise himself and take stock of his attacker. He wasn't a Greythorpe soldier, but the man, covered in blood with a fierce expression visible through an open-faced helm, continued his attack.

Leto easily pushed aside the next attack and countered with a glancing blow to his opponent's the head. The man cried out in pain but didn't back down., However, it gave Leto confidence to go on the offensive. He soon learned his assailant didn't have anywhere near the sword skills that Leto possessed, and within half a dozen strikes, he scored a fatal blow with a quick thrust into the gap just below the helm. Leto wrenched the sword free, and with a horrified realisation of his impending death, the man collapsed to the ground, blood flowing freely from his wound.

'Get down!'

Leto turned towards the shout and crouched, ready for another attack. Thirty yards from him, a bloodied Sir Kit Hanson ran at him, with the Knight-Commander and several other Noble Guards close behind.

'Get down!' Sir Kit shouted again, gesticulating to Leto's right.

He looked towards where the Captain of the Noble Guard pointed. The war machine about fifty yards to the east. The ballista wasn't like any Leto had seen. This one could fire up to a dozen smaller shafts at a time, and it had been aimed in his direction. Now he understood what had caused the carnage around him. As Leto watched the last bolt being loaded, a huge body blocked his view.

'Be still,' said Big Gil, crouching down and grabbing Leto, holding him to his enormous chest.

The giant turned his body, his back towards the war machine. It took a moment before Leto's mind grasped his intention.

'No … We have to get out of here!' Leto shouted.

'Too late,' Big Gil said, completely enveloping Leto in his arms, then crouched and bowed his head.

'No!'

'Everybody down!' Sir Kit roared.

An instant later, he heard a whistling noise and several dull thumps. Big Gil grunted and lurched forward onto his knees. His grip on Leto loosened, but he didn't let go, as screams of pain echoed in the distance, but Big Gil stayed down.

'Have you been harmed?' Big Gil's said, his voice strained.

'No,' said Leto. 'What about you?'

The giant said nothing.

'Big Gil!' said Leto. 'Are you hurt?'

A few more moments of silence passed.

'Yes,' he eventually said, his voice a raspy whisper.

Big Gil attempted to stand but toppled forward, slamming Leto into the ground hard. He found himself trapped under the slack body of Big Gil, his legs pinned from the hips. Face-down in the dirt, he couldn't see anything. He tried to turn over, without success.

'Gil, Gil!' he cried. 'Wake up!'

Leto tried to lever himself out , but Big Gil was too heavy.

'Don't die, damn you!'

Leto attempted to extricate himself again but failed. Try as he might, the giant's body would not move.

'Your Grace!' said a voice. 'Your Grace!'

He arched his back and glanced around as best he could. Yet again, he couldn't defend himself, and Leto didn't want to call out and draw any unwanted attention.

'Knight-Commander!' a nearby voice shouted. 'Over here.'

Moments later, a Noble Guard appeared by his side.

'Sir Taran?'

The guard nodded.

'Your Grace, are you injured?' said Sir Taran, his gaze constantly flicking about, looking for dangers.

'I can't move,' said Leto.

Sir Peyton appeared, flanked by two other Noble Guards.

'We'll have you out in a jiffy,' said Sir Peyton. 'Tremane, keep watch. Jaxen, Rickard, Jannis, get ready to push him off.'

The guards took up positions on either side of him.

'Is he dead?' said Leto, glancing back at the giant's body.

'I don't know, Your Grace,' said Sir Peyton. 'Give me your arms.'

Leto stretched out his arms, and the Knight-Commander grabbed them.

'Now!' said Sir Peyton.

The Noble Guards pushed at Big Gil's motionless body as Sir Peyton pulled on Leto's arms. They strained with effort, but the body barely moved. Two other soldiers arrived and joined in to help. Leto felt the pressure on his legs lighten, but he gasped in pain as Big Gil's body rolled back into place.

'Again!' shouted Sir Peyton, and they all pushed and pulled at the giant form but to no avail.

'Move,' a deep voice said, and except for the Knight-Commander and Sir Taran, the Noble Guards jumped back.

A towering figure appeared above Leto.

'Rogar,' said Leto, surprised and relieved to see his giant friend.

From his position on the ground, Rogar seemed much more imposing than usual, almost threatening.

'I'm glad to see you still live,' said Rogar before giving the body of Big Gil a sorrowful look.

'How is he?' said Leto.

'Are you ready, Knight-Commander?' said Rogar, ignoring Leto's question.

Sir Peyton nodded and grabbed one of Leto's arms. Sir Taran grabbed the other. Rogar bent down, slipped the fingers of both hands into Big Gil's belt, and gripped tightly. The big man pursed his lips and slowly lifted the limp body, and Leto felt the pressure on his legs disappear. The Knight-Commander and Sir Taran dragged Leto back several yards before they stopped and let go. Rogar gently lowered Big Gil back to the ground.

Leto sat up and attempted to stand, but his legs gave out. Sir Peyton put a hand on his shoulder and bent down and ran his hands over Leto's hips and legs.

'You're fortunate,' said the Knight-Commander. 'Nothing is broken. I'm sure the feeling will come back soon.'

'How soon?' Leto looked intently at the Knight-Commander.

'Not long.'

He sat up and could now see more of Big Gil. He sucked in a breath. Two steel shafts, each nearly five feet long and two inches wide, had embedded themselves in Big Gil's body. One had pierced his thigh, from which blood slowly seeped onto the already darkened sand. The other had passed through his hardened leather armour and lodged in his back.

Leto's heart sank. Even as he looked up at a mournful Rogar, he knew either of those wounds could have proved fatal. Agony bloomed in his lower body, and he cried out. It felt like being stuck with a thousand needles all at once.

'It'll pass,' Sir Peyton reassured him.

Leto gritted his teeth and waited. After a while, the agony receded, replaced by a deep throbbing. With help from Sir Taran and the Knight-Commander, he struggled to his feet. The pounding in his legs continued to lessen, and eventually, he could stand without assistance.

He stared at the enormous, lifeless body of Big Gil and the dead bodies from his small army. Such a waste, Leto thought as he took a step towards the body of Big Gil, but a hand on his arm stopped him.

'Your Grace, we need to get you to safety,' said Sir Peyton.

Leto nearly laughed. A safe place … in the middle of a battle?

'I'm not leaving the field,' Leto said. 'Rally our soldiers, and we'll advance as planned.'

He wanted to ensure Big Gil and the soldiers of the Borderlands had not died in vain.

'I don't want anyone else to die, but I can't just run away,' he said. 'You understand, don't you?'

Rogar stared at him in silence for a few moments. 'But I will not be leaving your side,' said Rogar with the utmost seriousness.

Leto nodded his acceptance; glad his giant friend would be so close.

'We will mourn Big Gil later,' Rogar added.

'Yes, we will,' said Leto with a heavy sigh.

It only then occurred to him that, apart from his encounter with the enemy soldier after falling from his horse, there had been no further attacks. Leto turned towards their destination. Gurney Jansen's cavalry and the giants from the right had come around and intercepted the enemy, protecting Leto and the Noble Guard. Only a score of the centre cavalry remained mounted and another forty on foot. Damn it! Nearly half of his soldiers had already been lost, but they had to keep going. Their target, Greythorpe's command tent, was less than three hundred yards away.

'Let's go,' Leto said to the Knight-Commander.

'To me!' shouted Sir Peyton, and the remaining Noble Guard formed around Leto and the Knight-Commander, but the number of dead soldiers and horses littering the ground hampered their efforts.

Leto picked up a small shield that lay near his feet and gave the signal to move. Led by those few that had managed to remain mounted, they moved forward at a run and soon enough had re-engaged the enemy. Even though more vulnerable on foot, Leto found it easier to use his sword and shield. However, he hardly needed to defend himself as Rogar's proximity caused enemy soldiers to give him a wide berth. Occasionally, if one found himself in Leto's immediate vicinity, he would be cut down by Rogar or the Noble Guard.

Unexpectedly, they broke through the enemy line, and soldiers bearing the sigil of House Greythorpe offered only token resistance. In short order, Leto stood less than fifty feet from the command tent, with the sound of fighting getting further and further away.

'Search the tent,' ordered Sir Peyton.

Sir Taran and two other Noble Guards approached and carefully entered the tent. Moments later, they reappeared.

'Empty, sir,' said Sir Taran.

Sir Ewen rode around from the opposite side of the tent. He dismounted and made his way towards Leto. His cousin exhibited all the signs of having been in a vicious battle, covered in dirt and his lower body splattered with blood, but he also sported a wide grin.

'We've done it!' he said.

'How?' said Leto, not quite believing his cousin. 'Are you sure?'

He didn't want to get his hopes up.

'His allies started deserting him as soon as they saw your banner on the field,' Ewen said, 'though I'm sure having Rogar and his friends helped convince them Lord Regan wasn't worth dying for.'

Leto had expected a long, drawn-out fight they probably wouldn't win, but it had lasted less than an hour – if what Ewen said was true.

'Some deserted and high-tailed it out of here, while others just dropped their weapons and surrendered,' Ewen continued. 'Some even swapped sides.'

'Who are these lords, and where are they now?' said Sir Peyton, sceptical.

'There are ten so far, but I only recognised four. Kasper Lange of Whisper Falls surrendered before we even engaged him; Piety Baird from Ravenwood is now commanding the troops of her father, Lord Giles. She swapped sides and made quite a mess of Waldin Hardwinter's troops before they retreated. Linas Barton of Timberland surrendered as well.'

'You said four,' Leto pointed out.

Ewen's grin widened.

'Rafe Singer,' he said, 'and all the minor lords loyal to House Singer, about three or four of them.'

This surprised Leto. The Singers had been allies of Greythorpe for years.

'That would account for nearly three hundred soldiers, maybe more,' said Sir Peyton, incredulous.

'Lord Regan must have really antagonised Rafe,' Ewen said.

'He wouldn't have done it alone,' said the Knight-Commander. 'Rafe may lead Singer's army, but Arthur still calls the shots. Greythorpe thinks Arthur is an idiot. The old devil must have been planning this for ages.'

Leto was about to accept they'd been victorious but looked towards Cliffs End.

'What about the city?' he said. 'There must be nearly a thousand still in there.'

'Our messengers did get through to Lord Owen,' said Ewen. 'Rafe Singer informed me they'd just received orders to send reinforcements into the city. They were about to leave when we attacked. Greythorpe's army is falling apart.'

At this, Leto smiled.

'I hope you're right,' said Leto. 'Take your cavalry and our new allies and clear the city.'

'Yes, Your Grace,' said Sir Ewen.

Leto looked up at Viggo.

'I don't want to take any chances. Would you, Rogar and Little Gil accompany Sir Ewen into the city?' said Leto. 'I think your presence will ensure our new allies won't be inclined to change their allegiance again.'

'Rogar will stay here,' said Viggo. 'Sunni will go with us.'

'And find Lord Regan,' said Sir Peyton. 'This war won't end until he's in custody.'

At the mention of Lord Regan, Ewen's grin disappeared.

'We want him alive,' the Knight-Commander added.

'I can't make any promises,' said Ewen.

'Alive, Sir Ewen,' said Leto.

Ewen bowed and headed back to his mount.

As his cousin rode off with the three giants close behind, Leto felt a pang of apprehension.

'Do you think Ewen can handle the defectors?' Leto said to Sir Peyton. 'Should I send some of Gurney's soldiers as well?'

'Sir Ewen is a good judge of character, like his father,' said the Knight-Commander. 'He'll know which lords to trust and which to be wary of.'

Sir Peyton's words reassured him. His soldiers tore down the banners of the House Greythorpe, and in their place, raised the black and gold of House Blackwater. Leto began to feel a sense of gratification the like of which he'd never experienced before.

Just after high sun, a messenger arrived from Sir Ewen, and Leto recognised him immediately.

'I hope you bring good tidings, Sir Finn,' said Leto as his cousin dismounted.

'I do, Your Grace,' said Finn, 'My brother asked me to say these words … The war is now over.'

'Tell us,' Leto said.

'Most of Lord Regan's army has surrendered or deserted,' said Finn. 'The rest were either killed or managed to retreat. A few tried to escape to the ships, but Ewen had already sent one of Rafe Singer's commanders out to parlay with Sir Gerard Podborn. He didn't need much convincing that siding with House Greythorpe was no longer worth his while.'

'And Lord Regan?' Leto said.

'We have him,' said Finn with a triumphant smile.

'Where is he now?' said Sir Peyton.

'In a citadel dungeon, Knight-Commander,' said Finn. 'Ewen thought it best he be surrounded by stone instead of a makeshift prison out here on the field.'

'And Lord Owen?' said Leto. 'Is he alive?'

'He is, Your Grace,' said Finn. 'Ewen will escort Lord Owen to see you soon.'

Only knowing that Owen was alive exceeded Leto's relief at Greythorpe's capture. A lump unexpectedly rose in his throat, but he swallowed it. At less than two miles to the gates of Cliffs End, Leto could be in the Darkmoor in no time. As King, he could go anywhere he wished in Avaleen any time he wanted, but he didn't want to enter the city of his friend uninvited.

'When he comes, I want the army formed up as one giant honour guard,' Leto said to the Knight-Commander, 'from here to the city gates.'

He wanted to honour his future father-by-law, which was the only way he could think of out here on the battlefield.

'Certainly, Your Grace,' said Sir Peyton.

20

LETO

It was mid-afternoon when Viggo, Sunni and Little Gil exited the city. Even a mile away, they could easily be seen. The King's army had already formed into two long lines, stretching from the command tent towards the city. It didn't reach the gates, but it would do. Leto stood and waited, flanked on three sides by his Noble Guard, the soldiers of the Borderlands and the remaining giants, Rogar, Arve, Wulftan and Leila. Soldiers from the Redstone army had joined the honour guard and those from his newly acquired allies, though Leto had ordered the Greythorpe defectors to stand in the lines furthest from the tent.

Finally, Leto could make out the horsemen. Fourteen mounted riders led the three giants into the large open area in front of the command tent bordered by the honour guard. He recognised some of them, particularly the two lead riders. Sir Ewen had cleaned himself up, but his armour still bore the marks of battle.

Leto smiled as he looked at the other lead rider. Lord Owen Redstone wore the most impressive battle armour Leto had ever seen. It had been a gift from Leto's father, and Owen wore it proudly, sitting tall and straight in the saddle. Behind them, he knew Owen's brothers, Dunmar and Penn, and Ewen's squire, Egon, who sported a wide grin. Some others had familiar faces, but he couldn't put names to them. The remaining six wore the livery of the Darkmoor Citadel Home Guard.

The group dismounted, and Owen approached Leto, stopped five feet away, and stared at him. He seemed older than Leto remembered, a little less weighty, and slightly more haggard. His face projected joy, sadness and confusion.

'Nothing to say?' Leto finally said with a smile, part mocking, part concern. 'That's not like you.'

'My … my apologies,' said Owen. 'My heart aches to see you alive, though I still cannot believe it.'

'Believe it, my friend,' said Leto, stepping forward and embracing the older man.

'But how?' said Owen as they broke the embrace, 'and … '

His voice trailed off as he looked up at Rogar and Leila, the giants nearest to Leto. He'd never seen Owen at such a loss for words.

'All in good time,' said Leto, glancing at the crowd around them.

Leto wanted nothing more than to talk privately with Owen, but this wasn't the place.

'Yes, of course,' said Owen, understanding. 'Now, before I introduce my companions, there is something I need to say and do.'

'Go ahead,' said Leto, his curiosity piqued.

'You saved us; for that, I will be eternally grateful,' said Owen. 'We of the Shadowlands will now be able to continue our lives in peace because of what you have done here today.'

'I had help,' said Leto. 'I didn't do it alone.'

'But they chose to follow you,' said Owen. 'They wouldn't have come on their own, but because of you, they came … and here we are.'

Leto stayed silent, not quite knowing how to respond.

'Your father would be very, very proud of you,' Owen's voice quavered. 'I am proud of you, and honoured to call you my King.'

Owen dropped to one knee and bowed his head. Moments later, Owen's companions and their bodyguards knelt as well. Leto couldn't hide his surprise as the soldiers of the Shadowlands followed their lord's example and knelt. Sir Ewen knelt as well, and before long, the whole army had dropped to one knee, leaving only the Noble Guard and the giants standing.

A wave of emotion enveloped him. It wasn't happiness, but he also didn't feel sad or angry. He felt the impulse to cry and had to swallow the rising lump in his throat. Leto wondered if his father had been honoured in this way and how he had felt.

He stepped forward, and as he helped Owen to his feet, Sir Ewen cheered.

'King Leto!' he shouted with glee.

Those in the immediate vicinity took up the cheer, getting louder and more enthusiastic. The cheering grew, as those further down the honour guard line picked it up. The lump in his throat grew, and his eyes became moist at the sound of the cheers.

'Leto! Leto! Leto!'

He finally raised his hand, and the roars of jubilation began to die down. He gazed around at his army. The few whose eyes he caught looked at him with anticipation. They expected him to say something. He had heard his father give several speeches over the years, and he remembered them being eloquent and inspirational, but Leto had no clue what to say.

'I am humbled,' he said, louder so those further away could hear, 'and I am honoured to be your King.'

Another loud cheer went up.

'That wasn't so bad, was it?' Owen whispered.

Leto smiled, unable to say anything more at this juncture.

'Will you stay at Darkmoor tonight, Your Grace?' said Owen after the cheers had died down again. He glanced up at Rogar. 'And your friends are invited as well.'

Happy with the change of subject, he turned to Owen. 'The Citadel survived the assault?'

'The city sustained quite a bit of damage, but the castle itself was largely untouched,' said Owen. 'Though if you didn't arrive when you did … '

'I'm just glad you're still alive.'

'Likewise.'

'Return to the Citadel,' instructed Leto. 'I'll be there after sundown. I have something else I need to attend to first.'

Leto had many questions for Lord Owen, but he'd made a promise he needed to keep. He turned and looked up at Rogar.

'Let's go,' said Leto, soberly.

The rocks had been stacked into a pile ten feet high, twenty feet long and ten feet wide. Leto took his place, one of honour, at the end of the structure, being the only member of the inner ring of mourners who wasn't a giant.

To Leto's left stood Rogar, Leila, and Little Gil, and to his right, Arve, Wulftan and Sunni. At the other end stood the towering Viggo. A large circle of Noble Guard and Borderland soldiers encircled them thirty yards further back.

The sun had just touched the ocean as a solemn Leto gazed at the grave of Big Gil. He still couldn't believe he was dead. He'd thought the giants indestructible, but in truth, they were flesh and blood, and could be hurt, and could die. Big Gil's brethren all had their eyes closed; some had their heads bowed. Leto shut his eyes as well.

In the distance, he could hear the muted sound of an encamped army, but moments later, A deep, low hum permeated the air. The volume gradually increased until he felt it reverberating through his whole body. The hum became louder. Leto sneaked a glance at the giants. They all had their eyes closed with their mouths slightly open. He closed his eyes again and let the sound flow through him.

It was oddly soothing.

Big Gil had not exactly been a close friend, but Leto had had the utmost respect for him. And he knew he wouldn't be alive without the big man's quick reactions and enormous sacrifice. Now Big Gil lay at rest, killed in a war not his own. He felt a tear trickle down his cheek. Leto remembered how he had felt when he thought he'd never return to Avaleen and would die without ever seeing home again. But he had returned to his homeland. Big Gil would never get the chance to go home again.

A heavy hand on his shoulder caused him to open his eyes, bringing him out of his reverie. The humming had ceased, and the giants began to move away from the stone-covered grave, the surrounding soldiers dispersing to make way. The hand belonged to Rogar.

'We can go now,' said the big man.

Leto nodded and wiped the tears away with his sleeve. He and Rogar turned and began walking away from the grave. They approached Little Gil and Viggo.

'I'm so sorry about Big Gil,' Leto said to them. 'He sacrificed himself for me.'

'He did his duty,' Viggo said, his tone unusually soft.

They had all sworn to their chieftain they would protect Leto, but still he felt responsible for the giant's death. Many soldiers had died today, but the loss of this one giant hit Leto especially hard.

'No-one should die so far from home,' said Leto. 'I am truly sorry.'

'He was like my own brother,' Little Gil's voice had a slight tremor. 'If anyone should feel ill towards you for his death, it is me.'

Leto looked up at Little Gil. There was no sign of animosity, just sadness.

'But I don't,' Little Gil continued. 'He was here because that's what he wanted. He hated village life. He was always badgering the Chief to –'

The anguish was evident on the big man's face. Thoughts of Jacob flashed through Leto's mind. He was like a brother to him as well. If Little Gil felt anything like he had after Jacob was killed, he was surprised the giant was even able to speak.

'He was a brave man,' Leto said as Wulftan and Arve joined them. 'One of the greatest warriors I have ever seen, and he should not be forgotten.'

'He won't be,' said Wulftan. 'Our people have very long memories.'

The other four giants nodded at Wulftan's words.

'I don't want the people of Avaleen to forget him either. I want to honour his sacrifice,' said Leto. 'I have decided that this area here, from now on, will be known as Big Gil's Rest.'

The giants looked down at Leto in surprise. Even the stern demeanour of Viggo had fallen. His heart skipped a beat.

'But … but only if you give your permission, of course,' Leto added. 'I hope I haven't caused offence.'

A moment of silence passed, and Rogar cleared his throat.

'Quite the contrary,' he said.

Leto looked at the giant, his brow furrowed.

'For our people, one's name is sacred,' continued Rogar. 'Only the greatest among us, like Kings, great chieftains or warriors that have performed great feats of bravery, are remembered long after we're gone.'

'And even more rarely is a tree grown or a shrine built and given a great one's name,' said Arve. 'For a piece of land to be named so … Big Gil's name will now live longer than our memories.'

'I'll tell Sunni,' Little Gil said.

He raised his bushy brow and started towards the two female giants.

'I hope she takes the news as it's meant,' said Rogar, glancing after Little Gil.

'Why wouldn't she?' Leto said with a hint of concern.

Little Gil approached Leila and Sunni. Leila looked up at Little Gil as he spoke. Sunni stayed gazing at the ground.

'Some can be prickly when honouring one's name,' said Rogar, 'especially one they care about deeply.'

Leto gave his friend another questioning look.

'Did you not know?' said Arve.

'I thought we all knew,' Wulftan said.

'Know what?'

'Big Gil and Sunni were going to share a hut on their return to the village,' said Rogar.

Leto looked back towards Little Gil, who had spread his arms wide, gesturing to the area around them. Sunni raised her head and spoke something to Little Gil. He nodded and she turned to face Leto. He couldn't tell if she was pleased or angered by the news.

Without warning Sunni started towards Leto, covering the distance quickly in long, purposeful strides, with Little Gil and Leila scrambling to follow. In moments, she stood before Leto, looking down at him with moist red eyes.

'Sunni?' Viggo said.

She stared down at Leto, trembling. He'd glimpsed Sunni in the battle earlier in the day. She could kill him with a single blow if she so chose.

'It wasn't his fault,' Viggo said, sharing Leto's thoughts.

Abruptly, the giant tracker went to her knees. Even on her knees, Sunni was still nearly twice his height. His Noble Guard drew their swords and began to advance from all directions. Leto raised his hands and shook his head. They halted but didn't release the grip on their swords.

Leto stiffened as Sunni bent over, encircled him in her monstrous arms, and lifted him off the ground, drawing him close, his head now in the crook of her neck. He forced himself to relax, something he found difficult, still unsure of her intentions. His body jerked. A few moments later, he felt it again and again, but it didn't hurt. He heard a whimper, and he realised: she was crying.

At first, Leto wondered what he should do or say, but he lifted his arms and put them around her large neck as best he could and patted her gently. He glanced up at Rogar, who nodded his approval. A short while later, Sunni broke the embrace and lowered Leto gently to the ground. Still kneeling, she looked down at him with reddened eyes and damp cheeks.

'You're a good man, Leto, King of the little ones,' she said through sniffles. 'I was afraid that the name of Big Gil would only live on in my heart and be forgotten once I die. Because of you, it will live on forever.'

Sunni's words heartened him, but Big Gil's death still weighed heavily on his conscience.

'I'm sorry,' said Leto. 'He died because –'

'No!' Sunni interrupted him. 'Don't be sorry he died. Be happy he lived and made a mark on our lives. I am sad but not sorry.'

The big man had made an impression on Leto. With the loved ones he had lost, Leto had always thought of what he missed and how his life would be less without them, making him even more despondent. Maybe he should be thinking about them in this way.

'I will,' said Leto.

At that, Sunni stood and strode towards Big Gil's grave; the Noble Guard quickly moved aside to allow her through.

'Will she be alright?' said Leto.

Viggo nodded. 'She is strong.'

‘Good,’ said Leto. ‘What will you do now that all of this is over?’

‘Our task is done,’ Viggo said. ‘We will return to our village.’

‘It’s been a privilege having you and your kin by my side,’ Leto said. ‘We could not have won the day without you.’

‘You are welcome,’ Viggo said. ‘I am not knowledgeable about these things, but I am certain you will make a good King.’

Leto felt his face flush. ‘Thank you. That means a lot. I will try my best, but only time will tell.’

‘Time always reveals the truth of things,’ Rogar said.

That it does, Leto thought, that it does.

‘I would most likely be dead and Avaleen under Greythorpe’s thumb if it weren’t for you. How can we ever repay you?’ Leto asked him.

‘No payment required,’ Viggo said.

‘Just don’t forget about us,’ Rogar added.

‘You will be long remembered in Avaleen, my friends,’ said Leto.

Both Viggo and Rogar nodded their approval. Despite being offered a warm place to stay, the giants chose to camp in a nearby copse of trees. Leto bid them goodbye with a promise to visit the following day.

Even though the evening meal wasn’t as sumptuous as Lord Owen would typically serve, it was a feast compared to what Leto and his men had been eating the past weeks. He wasn’t in the mood to celebrate the victory, so he insisted on something low-key with as few attendees as possible. Besides, Leto couldn’t celebrate until he could rid himself of the architect of his family’s destruction. He had been told by his father that revenge wasn’t very kingly, that like anger, it clouded your judgement, but right now, it was all he wanted.

‘The people need to see you,’ Sir Ewen had said.

‘They saw me when I rode in,’ said Leto, ‘and they’ll see me tomorrow.’

Leto found it hard to believe that a battle had been fought that morning. It seemed so long ago, almost surreal.

‘As you wish, Your Grace,’ Owen had said.

After they'd dined, Owen led Leto down into the dungeons of Darkmoor. As well as the usual contingent of Noble Guard, he was accompanied by Ewen, Lord Caden, Sir Peyton Holmguard and Jesper Holt. They entered a narrow passage lined with only a few sconced torches.

'Has he been behaving?' Jesper said to the guard as they approached the cell.

'Not a peep, sir,' the guard said.

'Not really a surprise,' said Owen with undisguised loathing.

Leto stared at the heavy timber and iron door and sighed heavily.

'You don't need to do this,' Owen said. 'I'll gladly tell him myself.'

'It's something I need to do,' said Leto. 'Open the door.'

Jesper nodded at one of the guards, who turned and unlocked the latch and drew back the huge bolts. The other guard drew his sword and grabbed a nearby torch from its sconce. The first guard pushed on the heavy door, which creaked loudly as it opened, breaking the deep silence of the dungeon. The second guard stepped into the cell, followed by the first, who had also drawn his weapon. Moments later, the first guard returned.

'It's safe to go in, sir,' the guard told Jesper. 'He's sitting in the back corner.'

At a nod from Sir Peyton, two Noble Guards drew their weapons and filed into the cell. The Knight-Commander quickly followed. The other guard returned to the passage with only his sword, which he promptly sheathed. Leto took another deep breath as Sir Peyton came out and nodded.

Leto entered the cell with Owen, Ewen, Sir Caden and Sir Penn Redstone close behind. He glanced around the cell. It was much larger than Leto had expected, about fifteen feet square. Light filled most of the room as two of the Noble Guard held torches in addition to the one that Sir Peyton had taken from the guard. Dirt and grime covered the walls and floor of the windowless cell. Leto had to suppress the urge to cover his nose at the air, even more oppressive than out in the passage, which smelled like shit and rotten food.

'Come to gloat, have you?'

Leto turned towards the voice and steadied himself.

Regan Greythorpe sat on the floor in the far corner, his back against the wall, wrists and ankles manacled. Streaks of dried blood and dirt now covered his finely tailored trousers and tunic, and he had a few cuts and bruises on his face and neck. One eye had swollen shut, but he still held his head up high as he spoke.

'You speak only when spoken to,' Sir Peyton warned.

'Or what?' Regan said.

Leto had been both excited and terrified about this moment: excited because justice would finally be served and bring him closer to the end of the saga that had begun with the murder of his father, but terrified because he now had the responsibility to dispense the justice.

'Let him be,' Leto said.

Regan turned his head to gaze upon Leto with his good eye.

'The prodigal son,' Regan spat.

The intense hatred projected in this simple phrase surprised Leto, but he didn't show it. He didn't care anymore and found he no longer feared the man. As a prisoner in his own home, Leto had acquiesced to Regan's demands because, at the time, he had custody of his sister. But she was now dead, murdered by Greythorpe's minion. At the thought of his sister, Leto felt the anger rise, but more words from his father entered his mind.

Compassion and forgiveness … one needed both; otherwise, you could easily become a tyrant, but it must be balanced with discipline and respect. Some thought his father too benevolent, too trusting. That was possible, Leto thought as he met Regan Greythorpe's glare, but now wasn't the time for compassion,

'You killed my father, the King,' said Leto without emotion. 'You held my sister hostage and threatened me with her safety if I didn't comply with your wishes. Your bodyguard murdered her, and after thinking me dead, you attempted to usurp the crown.'

'I was elected the Steward legally, unanimously,' said Regan, irritated.

'Then you started a civil war, all to satisfy your own greed and lust for power,' said Leto, ignoring him.

'I was already the legitimate ruler of Avaleen,' Regan raised his voice. 'I already had everything I needed, you idiot!'

'No!' Leto said, careful not to raise his own voice too much. 'The moment you killed my father, I was the legitimate leader of Avaleen, not you. But it matters not. I now rule, and I will pronounce the sentence for your crimes.'

'You?' Regan scoffed. 'You'll be just like your father and his ancestors. Spineless weaklings unable to control their own kingdom, the lot of them.'

'Shut your traitorous mouth!' Owen bellowed and stepped forward, raising his arm to strike. 'King Caleb was –'

Surprised at his calmness, Leto put a restraining hand on Owen's shoulder. Until a few moments ago, his anxiety had been growing at the thought of facing his greatest enemy, even if he did sit helpless in the corner of a dirty cell. But now, the man Leto hated most in the world had insulted him and his family, and he could not care less. Regan's words just washed over him, doing him no harm whatsoever.

'It's alright,' said Leto. 'He can no longer hurt us.'

Owen stepped back as Leto glared at his prisoner.

'Regan Greythorpe,' said Leto, his tone as formal as he could make it, 'you are hereby stripped of your rank as Knight Elder of Avaleen, as are your offspring and their descendants. All your lands, titles and business chattels are now the property of the crown.'

'You can't do that!' Regan said.

'Furthermore,' said Leto, ignoring his protest, 'for the crimes of treason and the murder of King Caleb, you will be hung by your neck until you are dead. The sentence will be carried out tomorrow at dawn.'

Regan Greythorpe's steely demeanour faltered briefly, but his cold, hard stare reasserted itself. However, it no longer had quite the same effect on Leto.

'Do you have anything to say?' said Leto.

Regan remained silent.

'Good,' Leto said and left the cell.

Now Leto sat near the hearth in the apartment assigned to him by Lord Owen. The apartment had five rooms. His father had stayed here on his last visit to Cliffs End several years ago. Leto held a goblet of wine, as did Owen, who sat opposite on a matching settee.

'I've sent for young Constance. She'll be anxious to see you,' Owen said. 'She should be back about mid-morning, after Greythorpe has been dealt with.'

Leto nodded, though his joy at seeing his cousin again was tempered with the knowledge that she was the last person to see Melina alive. They had a lot to talk about.

'We also have some other … delicate business to discuss,' Owen added.

'What delicate business would this be?'

'Tomorrow, Your Grace, when we both have clear heads. It's been a long day.'

Leto couldn't argue with that.

'Okay, tomorrow, then,' Leto said, sipping his wine. 'And stop calling me Your Grace.'

His father had put up with that honorific for fifteen years. Leto had been King less than a cycle of the moon, and already he wanted to vomit every time he heard it, but the thought made him smile.

'Your father despised it too,' said Owen.

Leto's smile disappeared. He had just been thinking the same thing and had found it amusing, but when Owen had vocalised it, Leto felt his throat constrict and his heart beat a little faster.

'I miss him,' said Leto.

And I miss Melina, and I miss Jacob. Tears welled unbidden, and he leaned forward, placing the half-empty cup on the side table.

'I miss him too,' said Owen. 'But I know he'd be exhilarated by what you've accomplished.'

This only upset Leto more, and the tears began to flow freely. Owen stood and placed a hand on Leto's shoulder. Without a thought, he turned his head and buried it into the stomach of his future father-by-law and sobbed, all the grief and hurt pouring out all at once.

Flanked by an extra-large retinue of Noble Guard, Leto rode out from the stables of Darkmoor Citadel into a cold winter's morning. The sun had not yet fully risen over the cliffs, and he could see his breath turn to mist in the chilly morning air. Lord Owen rode by his side, relaxed and in good humour. He had stayed with Leto until well after midnight. The past year's events had finally caught up with him and his emotions had risen to the surface and burst out like a waterfall. The older man could never replace his father, but he would be Leto's father-by-law and mentor, which would be more than enough.

Leto knew the Lord of Cliffs End hated the capitol, but he needed trustworthy people in key positions. Yes, he'd appoint Owen as Warden of the South, or something like that. The exact title, he would sort out later. In this way, Owen could split his time between the Shadowlands and still officially be available to Leto when required. It would also enable him to visit his daughter, who would be Queen, residing at Twin Falls with Leto.

He had expected one or both of Owen's brothers to accompany them, or at least one of the others who had ridden out to greet Leto yesterday afternoon, but neither of them had appeared as yet.

'They'll meet us there,' Owen had said after Leto queried this. 'It's just you and me.'

You, me, and twenty Noble Guards, together with a selection of Owen's bodyguards, Leto thought with amusement.

Even at this early hour, the city was a hive of activity. Leto had ordered the army to assist in the clean-up of Cliffs End and to work night and day until the rebuilding could commence. However, that only accounted for some of the activity. The closer they got to the northern gate, the more congested it became.

It seemed everyone wanted to get a good view of the execution. Most who lived in the highlands detested Regan Greythorpe and his family. Those feelings would have only intensified after the events in the Greenhavens and the war; now they all wanted to see their despised enemy finally get what he deserved. Leto couldn't blame them.

They rode out of the damaged main gate. Most of the rubble had been cleared, but it would take a long time for the gate to be fully repaired. Less than a hundred yards east of the road, the gallows came into view. Leto brought his horse to a stop, causing the whole column to come to a quick halt. He stared at the structure. Larger than he had expected, the platform itself had been built fifteen feet from the ground. A better view for the masses, he supposed.

'He deserves it, you know,' said Owen, edging his horse close to Leto's.

Leto sighed and nodded. 'Let's get this over with.'

Finally, we'll be able to get on with the rest of our lives. Leto signalled the Knight-Commander to continue and urged his mount forward. They left the road and began to head towards the platform through a wide gap in the crowd bordered by members of the Citadel Home Guard.

To Leto's right, an incomprehensible shout split the air. He scanned the crowd. Nothing. He turned back, but his eye caught movement atop the outer wall. Something whistled past his ear, as soldiers converged on the damaged gatehouse. Leto ducked and someone grunted in pain as several Noble Guards rode up beside him, shielding him from the wall.

'To ground!' Sir Peyton shouted. 'Get the King off that damn horse!'

Leto recoiled at a sting in his right arm then a horse whinnied, as if in pain. His eyes flicked to the battlements, but a Noble Guard dragged him out of the saddle, his horse blocking the wall from his sight. Chaos ensued as the crowd realised what had happened and began to panic, fleeing in all directions.

'Protect the King!' bellowed the Knight-Commander.

Leto could hardly see a thing, surrounded at close quarters as he now was by six Noble Guards.

'Get him!' someone shouted above the din.

Leto could do nothing but wait. Someone had tried to kill him, but strangely he wasn't scared, just surprised.

'Sir Peyton!' shouted Leto. 'I want him alive!'

He tried to push his way through. He needed to find the Knight-Commander, but the guards surrounding him wouldn't give way.

'Your Grace,' one of the guards said. 'Please stay down until we know it's safe.'

'Where's Sir Peyton?' yelled Leto.

Leto tried again to push between his guards. This time, they moved aside, only for his path to be blocked by the huge frame of the Knight-Commander.

'Your Grace,' said Sir Peyton, breathing heavily. 'Are you hurt?'

'I'm fine,' Leto snapped.

'Please remain here,' Sir Peyton pleaded. 'I'll find out what's going on.'

'Whoever it is, I want them alive,' Leto commanded.

'I'll try, Your Grace,' the Knight-Commander said. 'Just please remain here.'

Leto frowned at Sir Peyton.

'Alive, understand?' and nodded his assent.

The Knight-Commander disappeared, and the Noble Guards closed in again, though not quite as close as before.

'My lord!' someone exclaimed.

'No!' another screamed.

Leto whipped around towards the voice. Owen's mount stood still, its saddle empty. Under the animal's belly, on the opposite side, Lord Owen lay in the dirt, an arrow protruding from his neck. The Noble Guard moved aside as Leto rushed and knelt at Owen's shoulder.

'No, no!' screamed Leto, his face contorted with horror.

Blood covered Owen's face and neck, his still-open eyes glazed over, lifeless. Leto gently lifted the old man's head onto his lap. Why him? They had won the war. The killing was supposed to be over, and they should be moving on with their lives. Leto passed his hand over Owen's eyes, closing them.

This good man … this man who was to be his surrogate father, the man who would have been a grandfather to Leto's children, and the last link to his father, was gone.

Leto didn't know how long he knelt on the blood-soaked ground, but shouting brought him back to the present. Leto gently placed Owen's head back on the ground and stood. His friend's blood smeared his tunic and hands, but he ignored it.

Sergeant Alden Janz and a Noble Guard headed his way, dragging someone between them. The man knelt and his head flopped forward as if unconscious.

'Is he dead?' Sir Peyton said as they approached.

'No, Knight-Commander,' said Alden. 'Though we're lucky we arrived when we did.'

Leto moved up beside Sir Peyton, looked at the man, and froze.

Even through the dirt and blood, Leto recognised the red hair, and the fury grew as he stepped forward. He grabbed a fistful of hair and jerked the man's head back. The familiar face showed fresh cuts and a bloody right eye swollen shut. Blood seeped from the injuries. Leto almost laughed. He sported the same injuries as his traitorous father.

Leto hated only one person as much as he hated Regan Greythorpe – this man, the son of his father's killer, murderer of his best friend and now killer of his mentor.

'You bastard,' growled Leto. 'You incompetent piece of shit!'

He remembered how Cedric used to boast to anyone who would listen of his fighting ability and superior skill with the longbow.

'You missed!' Leto shouted into Cedric's face. 'You had your chance, and you fucking missed!'

'Your Grace,' someone said, but Leto ignored it.

'It was an easy shot, but you screwed it up!'

Cedric's good eye flicked towards Owen's body and back to Leto.

'But I still hurt you,' Cedric spluttered, and the edges of his mouth lifted to form a grotesque smile.

Leto whipped out his dagger and pressed it against Cedric's throat. A trickle of fresh blood began to run down his already blood-caked neck.

'I should cut your throat right now for what you've done.'

Cedric's smile faded, and he weakly spat at Leto.

'Do it! I don't fucking care.'

Leto's hand began to quaver, and the blade cut further into Cedric's neck.

'Your Grace!'

The Knight-Commander's voice penetrated Leto's anger. He pulled the dagger away but kept his grip on Cedric's hair. He took a few deep breaths and felt his rage wane. What was he doing? He glared at Cedric.

'You'll pay for your deeds soon enough,' Leto snarled at him, his rage not wholly gone. 'I promise you that.'

Leto let go of Cedric's hair, and his head fell forward.

'We'll return to the Citadel and get you cleaned up,' said a concerned Sir Peyton.

'No. We'll go ahead as planned,' said Leto, pointing at Cedric. 'And bring him with us.'

Leto didn't want to wait another day to rid himself of the Greythorpes.

'He and his father can have a family reunion,' continued Leto, 'at the end of a rope.'

'Good,' Ewen said.

Leto turned towards a commotion near Owen's body.

'Let me through, let me through!' a voice shouted.

Penn burst through the crowd and looked down at his brother.

'No, no, no … Owen!' he exclaimed. 'What the … what the fuck happened?'

Leto's anger gave way to sadness as he went to Penn, who now stood over his brother's body. Leto put his hand on Penn's shoulder.

'How did this happen?' Owen's brother demanded, glancing at Leto. 'Who did this?'

Leto's eyes automatically flicked towards Cedric Greythorpe, still kneeling between Sergeant Janz and the Noble Guard. Penn followed Leto's glance and his face filled with fury. He shrugged Leto's hand from his shoulder and strode towards Cedric Greythorpe.

'Sir Penn!' Leto said, but Owen's brother ignored him.

Penn shoved Cedric's head back and cursed. 'You?' He struck Cedric with a fist in the centre of his face.

'We should have killed you when we had the chance,' Penn roared and struck him again.

'Penn, stop!' Leto shouted.

Penn rained down punches on Cedric until two Noble Guards grabbed his arms. 'I'll fucking kill you!' As they tried to pull him back, Penn kneed Cedric in the head. 'You're a dead man!' Penn screamed as he managed a vicious kick to Cedric's groin before the guards dragged him out of reach.

Blood streamed down Cedric's face from his broken nose and newly inflicted cuts. He would be hurting, but Leto didn't care. The bastard deserved a little pain, considering the agony he had caused, but he didn't want him dead, just yet.

'Get him out of here, now!' Leto ordered.

Sergeant Janz and the Noble Guard dragged Cedric out of sight. Leto approached Penn, still held by the two Noble Guards.

'Penn!' Leto said, but Owen's brother seemed not to hear, fighting against his controllers as he stared after Cedric.

'He killed my brother,' Penn eventually said and stopped struggling.

'He will pay for it, I promise,' Leto said, surprised at how calm he was having ranted at Cedric only moments earlier. 'Let him go.'

Penn shrugged as the guards released him and turned back to his brother's body.

'Where's Dunmar?' Leto said.

'Umm … he's not coming,' Penn said after a few moments.

'Why not?'

'He isn't interested in witnessing an execution.'

'And you?'

'I'll be there,' Penn spat, his rage barely in check. 'I'd hang them myself if you give the word.'

'That will not be necessary,' Leto said and turned to the Captain of the Home Guard.

'Jesper, find Dunmar and tell him what's happened. He may change his mind.'

Jesper looked at him, his distress simmering below the surface and nodded.

'Take his … take him back to the Citadel,' Leto added, his voice cracking. 'Make sure he is treated well as due a man of his stature. We will honour him, I promise.'

Leto squatted down next to Owen's body. He could have learned so much from him. Now, he would have to go it alone. His thoughts turned to Lady Addwyn, and the deep grief she would suffer when she learned of her husband's death. Leto would find Owen's family and bring them back to Avaleen. He would still marry Cordelia, he thought, and they would have many children.

'Goodbye, my friend,' said Leto quietly and turned to Penn. 'Follow when you're ready.'

Leto felt his face tighten as he headed towards the gallows on foot. He could have postponed the executions, but he couldn't have either of them living in his world any longer.

Less than half an hour later, Leto sat on a throne-like chair at the centre of a hastily built stage giving a good view of the gallows. The two chairs to his left were vacant. One had been for Owen, and Sir Ewen had chosen to stand just to Leto's left. He glanced at the two chairs to his right. A fuming Sir Penn sat glaring at the platform, barely controlling his emotions. Despite Owen's death, Dunmar had decided not to attend the execution, but instead escorted his brother's body back to the Citadel.

Leto sat back and rubbed his forehead.

On the platform, each of the two executioners held a noose that trailed over the front edge and up to the hanging bar. The crowd of onlookers had reassembled after the failed attempt on Leto's life. The murmurings of the crowd grew as two Citadel Guards brought Regan Greythorpe, his hands manacled behind his back, around from the rear of the gallows.

Cedric wasn't with him. Leto had given two orders for the executions: to make them quick, and to keep Cedric and Regan separate until the hanging. Because of Regan Greythorpe, Leto had been robbed of the chance to farewell his father before he died, so why should Cedric be afforded the opportunity?

Gripped firmly by two guards, Regan stood a foot from the edge of the platform. His executioner placed the noose over Regan's neck and pulled it tight. Two more guards dragged a barely recognisable Cedric Greythorpe towards the gallows steps. Regan couldn't hide his astonishment as they carried Cedric up the stairs.

'Did you think I was dead?' muttered Cedric through swollen, bloody lips.

The guards propped him up next to his father. Several cheers emanated from the crowd as the other executioner placed a noose around Cedric's neck.

'What did you do?' Regan said.

'I … I tried to avenge you,' Cedric said, his earlier bravado now gone.

Regan shook his head in disgust.

The crowd grew rowdier, beginning to jeer and hurl curses at the condemned men.

'I tried,' pleaded Cedric. 'I really tr –'

'And you failed again,' said Regan, accentuating the last word. 'Incompetent fool.'

Cries of 'murderer' and 'traitor' filled the air.

'But … but … Father,' spluttered Cedric.

'You disappoint me,' said Regan. 'You've always disappointed me.'

If it had been anyone else, Leto may have felt pity.

'I tried,' Cedric snivelled.

Regan snorted.

Leto couldn't listen to any more of this. He stood. Regan and Cedric Greythorpe looked towards him, and the crowd fell silent. He knew they expected a speech or some kind of pronouncement, but Leto wouldn't waste any more time on them.

He faced the executioners and nodded once.

A collective gasp sounded from the crowd as Cedric was pushed from the platform a moment before his father. He dropped until the rope pulled taut, breaking his neck with a sickening crack. Regan tripped and tumbled from the platform nearly diving off the edge. His head stopped in mid-air, and his body swung forward with a snap. The fall didn't kill him, but his eyes bulged, and his body contorted as he swayed back and forth in a wide arc, nearly touching the dead body of his son. Regan fought for breath, his body convulsing in a vain attempt to escape the noose. For what seemed an age he swung back and forth, his struggles becoming less and less intense. Eventually, his body went limp. At that, the crowd cheered. A few even began to throw rocks and vegetables at the now swinging bodies.

'Leave them there for a day,' Leto said to Ewen as he stood. 'Then throw their bodies into the forest. Let the animals have them.'

He stepped off the dais and began to walk back towards the city gate.

It's over.

The Greythorpes were no more, and the remnants of their house would easily be cowed. The Whites would be dealt with, like any others who didn't bend the knee and swear fealty. In time, House Blackwater would become strong again, he promised himself.

Leto would return to Twin Falls, eventually. When he did, he would be unable to avoid the politics and intrigue of the court. He would be the centre of everything, and his life would never be his own. Leto may now be the King of Avaleen, but it didn't mean he had to like it. His lips curled up slightly at the thought.

He was just like his father.

EPILOGUE

Leto sat on the throne, gazing out over the hall, which was full to capacity.

For reasons unknown to Constance, she'd been given this place of honour at the front with a perfect view of the throne. She was the King's cousin, but still his uncle's illegitimate offspring.

Constance had been standing for hours, and her feet hurt. She wanted to remove her shoes and give them a good rub, but she didn't dare. She shuffled her feet, unsuccessfully trying to alleviate the ache. Instead, she concentrated on Hamlin White, her former lover of sorts and nephew of the disgraced lord, Rainer White. They had not coupled, but they had shared some intimate moments last summer before her whole world had come crashing down. In another life, she and Hamlin may have had a future.

Despite this, she worried for him. Constance had fond memories of the young man. Unbeknown to either his father or uncle, the handsome, kind young man had helped her, the princess and Sir Fergus with their ill-fated escape from Sisters End.

A wave of sadness washed over her at the thought of Mellie and Sir Fergus, both now dead. She struggled to push aside the grief and concentrate on the here and now. Hamlin had been brought before King Leto, and he stood at the foot of the dais alone, waiting.

'One usually bows before a king,' the King said, looking down at Hamlin.

He didn't raise his voice or sound angry, but Leto's words hit Hamlin like a club, and he immediately dropped to one knee and bowed his head.

'I … I apologise, Your Grace,' said Hamlin.

Constance looked up at the King. Leto sat on the small throne with an amused expression. She heard the terror in poor Hamlin's voice and couldn't see the humour in it. House White no longer existed. They had been stripped of their rank and their property taken. He now had nothing.

'You may stand,' said Leto.

The young man hastily obeyed, though he kept his head bowed, not daring to look at the King.

'I'll get right to the point,' said Leto. 'Your house is no more, and your father and uncle will not see the light of day again. Not because they refused to bend the knee, but because they do not deserve to.'

Hamlin fidgeted, shuffling his feet.

'At Cliffs End,' Leto continued, 'your father fought against me until the last and then managed to retreat and make his way back to Whitehall, where your uncle was still holding the daughter of Sir Penn Redstone against her will. To make matters worse, he wouldn't give her up until there was an army at his doorstep.'

Everyone waited silently to see what would happen next, but Constance found the King's attitude loathsome..

'I've been asking myself, what do we do with you?' Leto said, leaning back on this throne and smiling.

'I … I don't know, my lord … err … Your Grace,' Hamlin said.

'Well, I do,' said Leto.

The King glanced at Constance, which caught her by surprise, and she hoped he hadn't noticed her disapproving look.

'I will accept any punishment that you deem appropriate,' Hamlin said.

'I hope that what I have planned for you will not be construed as punishment,' said Leto, raising his brow.

Constance's heart stopped as Leto turned his head and stared straight at her. 'Though that will depend entirely on you, Cousin.'

'Me?' she squeaked.

'Yes, you,' the King continued to smile.

Surely, she wouldn't be expected to decide Hamlin's punishment. That would be too cruel, and Leto wasn't that type of person.

'I don't understand, Your Grace,' she said.

'You told me that Master Hamlin is honourable and kind, unlike the rest of his family,' said Leto. 'Those were your words, were they not?'

'I did … they were,' she replied.

'And you also told me you were quite … fond of him.'

She felt her cheeks redden. Constance remembered their bittersweet reunion at Cliffs End after the war had ended. He'd questioned her about her experiences at Whitehall, including how Lord Rainer and his family had treated her and Melina. She had answered honestly and knew her responses did not paint a good picture of the White family, except when she spoke of Hamlin. Her glowing defence of him seemed to catch Leto's interest, and he had queried her further on the subject. Eventually, she confessed her love for him and her decision not to pursue him; that he deserved someone better than her.

'Yes, Your Grace,' she said and nodded.

'Do you still feel this way?' said Leto.

She glanced at Hamlin, who now gazed at her, puzzled.

'Yes, Your Grace,' she said, standing a little straighter.

Leto turned his gaze back to the young man. 'Do you still hold feelings for my cousin?'

Hamlin glanced at the King.

'Very much so, Your Grace,' Hamlin said, looking at Constance.

She felt a tingling sensation in the pit of her stomach, surprised at Hamlin's words. With the punishments dealt out to his family, she would've expected him to despise her. She wondered what Leto hoped to gain by questioning her this way. He'd already referred to her as his cousin, and then these strange questions, and in such a public forum.

'Excellent,' Leto said, and looked towards the doors. 'Bring them in!'

The large oak doors to the Hall of Law creaked open. Everyone in the hall turned to see the new arrivals. Constance tried unsuccessfully to see over the throng of people between her and the doors, and the murmuring started.

Leto pointed to a spot to his right. 'Hamlin, stand there.'

The young White did as ordered. As he did so, he snuck a peak at Constance; he seemed as bewildered as she, and her confusion turned to shock as her brother and mother came to a halt before the dais.

Egon gave a bow and her mother a low curtsy.

'Your Grace,' they said in unison.

She had not seen Egon in over three years. He would now be seventeen. He'd grown nearly a foot since, now a strapping young man who towered over their mother, not the skinny little boy she remembered. Their mother also stood straight and proud next to her son. Constance could not see her face, but a few wisps of white streaked her otherwise dark hair.

'Premila, Egon, it's good to see you both,' said Leto. 'Thank you for coming at such short notice.'

'It was no trouble, Your Grace,' said Egon, in a much deeper voice than Constance remembered.

Leto nodded, then beckoned to Constance. 'Come and stand by your brother,' his tone a little more serious now.

At the mention of her name, Egon and her mother turned towards Constance. Still in shock at seeing her family, it took her a few moments to realise what had been said.

'Connie!' Egon exclaimed.

Constance had to stop herself from running over and embracing them both.

'Hello, Egon,' she said as she approached them. 'Mother, it's good to see you.'

'Constance,' her mother said quietly, returning her smile.

Constance faced the King, who stood to address the crowd.

'Family is very important to me, as it should be to anyone. Unfortunately, I have lost most of mine,' he said, a tinge of sadness in his voice. 'However, before me stand two who have the blood of my family running through their veins. Through no fault of their own, they were judged as outsiders.'

Constance suppressed a frown. She did not enjoy having her illegitimacy so publicly highlighted. Having it shouted out by the King made it even more humiliating.

'Egon has squired for Sir Ewen Kirkwood for the past three years. He performed above his station in the recent war and will make a fine knight when he comes of age,' said Leto.

Egon, a knight? The King lowered his gaze and looked directly at her.

'And Constance,' said the King, 'who served my sister to the end with the utmost devotion and courage, as brave as any knight.'

Constance flushed with embarrassment and pleasure.

'Egon, Constance, please kneel,' continued Leto.

She knelt without question, as did her brother.

'When you rise, you will be of the royal house with all the associated rights and responsibilities,' said the King.

Constance heard muted gasps from the crowd and had to stifle one of her own.

'Furthermore, anyone who does not treat you with the respect due to a member of the royal house,' Leto's voice had hardened, 'will answer to me.'

Constance could feel her heart begin to beat faster. She waited to wake up from this dream and find herself alone in the servants' quarters, waiting to be summoned by her new master.

'Constance Blackwater, Egon Blackwater, rise,' Leto commanded, though his tone had softened.

Constance needed to take a few deep breaths to calm herself before she stood. Leto beamed, his smile wide. A few members of the crowd cheered and clapped. Moments later, a few more joined in, and even more, until it seemed everyone in the hall celebrated their ascension. Whether their applause was approval of the King's decision, or mere politeness, Constance didn't care. She and her brother were no longer bastards.

She turned to Egon, who still wore a look of disbelief while her mother cried tears of happiness. Constance knew her mother had always been disappointed that Lydall had never formally adopted them. Now everything had changed.

'Premila, I hope you approve of your children's new name,' Leto said. 'I mean no disrespect to yours.'

Constance and her mother both faced the King.

'You do them a great honour, Your Grace,' she said through her tears.

'Good, good,' said Leto. 'Now, Hamlin White.'

In the excitement of her new standing, Constance had completely forgotten that Hamlin still waited to hear his fate.

'In short,' the King continued, 'you will not be punished for the transgressions of your family. You are free to go.'

Constance squealed with delight, then remembered where she was, and looked at Hamlin, grinning. He smiled back. Leto had made the right decision. Hamlin did not deserve the same fate as his father.

A loud crack reverberated around the hall as Sir Ramin struck the stone floor with the Staff of Law.

'The King's court is at an end,' said the Master of Law.

The doors opened, and everyone began to file out. Constance started to shepherd her mother and brother out but stopped at the voice of the King.

'Not you, Connie,' said Leto. 'Egon, Premila, please stay.'

Leto looked towards Hamlin, who stood there unsure of what to do now.

'And you too,' the King added.

Constance and her family resumed their previous positions and waited. Everyone else filed out of the hall except a few of the Noble Guard. The door closed behind the Master of Law, and Leto stepped down from the dais and stood before Constance and her family. He embraced each of them in turn.

'Thank you, Your Grace,' her mother said. 'You've made a mother very happy.'

'It was my pleasure,' Leto said and stepped back. 'However, I'm not going to allow you to swan around being idle members of the court, gossiping and having tea and cake every day. You'll have responsibilities.'

'Of course,' said Constance.

Egon echoed her acceptance with a nod. She would work hard. Indeed, there wasn't a job in the palace that she couldn't do or learn.

'Egon,' said Leto, facing her brother. 'I have an important undertaking for Sir Ewen, and you will, of course, accompany him. On your return, if he advises me that you have performed well and are deserving, when you come of age, you will become Sir Egon Blackwater, Knight of Avaleen, after which you'll return to the capitol and serve me personally.'

Her brother stood unmoving, speechless. Moments passed before he dropped to one knee and bowed his head.

'You are most generous, Your Grace,' said Egon. 'I won't disappoint you.'

Constance knew he would make their mother proud. The King turned to her and she recalled his words that Hamlin's punishment would depend on her. But Leto had set him free.

'Connie,' said the King. 'My plans for you are a bit … grander than those of your brother. You will have greater responsibilities by far, but I'm sure you'll be up to the challenge.'

What position could he possibly have in mind for her that would be described as grand?

'You'll stay with me here at Riverview until next summer,' Leto continued. 'You will oversee the royal apartments. All the stewards, guards and whoever else it takes to manage them, will report to you. You'll also attend me when I host the King's court and entertain special visitors. It will be good experience for you.'

Experience for what exactly? She didn't consider running the royal apartments to be grand, though attending the King during the court could be interesting.

Don't be silly, she thought. You're already sounding like a stuck-up noble. Be grateful you don't have to clean any more chamber pots or sew any more ripped dresses.

'You will then leave Riverview and take up residence at Sisters End as the Lady of Whitehall.'

'The what?' the words came out of Constance's mouth before she could stop them.

'The Lady of Whitehall,' Leto repeated. 'Sisters End will be yours.'

'But … but, they hate me. And it'd be worse now since you … ' her voice trailed off.

She was aghast, the idea absurd in the extreme. They hated her, and she hated them, and she had only recently had her sixteenth name day. Why would the King make her the Lady of Whitehall?

'Possibly,' Leto admitted, 'But what if you had someone with you who knew the people, someone they were familiar with, someone you trusted?'

The King glanced at Hamlin, who nervously watched on. Constance looked across to Hamlin. Yes, he knew Sisters End better than anyone.

'Hamlin,' Leto said. 'You have my permission to court Lady Constance if she is agreeable.'

Court me?

'Thank you, Your Grace,' Hamlin dipped his head.

The King turned back to Constance. 'Connie, if you decide to marry, be it Hamlin or some other lucky fellow, you will keep the name of your house. Your children will be Blackwaters. You will never have to answer to anyone except me. You will be a Blackwater until you die. Do you understand?'

'I do,' said Constance, still trying to process everything that had just happened.

'Good,' said Leto. 'That is the only condition I will place on your marriage.'

She couldn't help herself. Constance stepped forward and hugged Leto, holding him tight.

'You are most generous,' she said, breaking the embrace. 'I cannot thank you enough.'

Leto just smiled.

'Now go and see the royal Steward,' he instructed. 'He'll show you to your new quarters within the royal apartments and assign you your staff. Take Master White with you and organise whatever accommodation you think is appropriate for him outside the royal apartments.'

Constance felt giddy. She had been elevated to royalty, gifted an entire estate, and had permission to marry whom she pleased. She beckoned to Hamlin. He approached her timidly, stealing glances at the King.

Constance turned and stopped. She looked at Egon and her mother. She hadn't seen them for so long and wanted to talk to them.

'You'll see them later at the evening meal,' Leto said. 'We all have a lot to talk about.'

Constance grinned and urged Hamlin beside her. They started towards the doors but stopped at the sound of the King's voice.

'There is one more thing,' Leto said. 'Another condition on your marriage.'

Constance stiffened, and her smile faltered. She knew this had all been too good to be true.

'At your wedding,' Leto continued. 'I will escort the bride to the altar.'

Leto's stern guise immediately transformed into another wide grin.

'Of course, Your Grace,' she curtsied, her smile returning. 'I wouldn't want it any other way.'

The King casually waved them off, and she and Hamlin left the hall and began the walk across the crowded courtyard. People were looking at them with either furtive glances or a blatant stare.

She leaned closer to Hamlin. 'They're looking at us.'

'No,' he said, beaming. 'They're looking at you.'

She didn't want to admit it, but he could be right. She also realised they had not had to dodge and walk around others. People moved aside for her. Some had even greeted her as My Lady or Lady Constance with a slight curtsy or bow of the head. Lady Constance … Sir Fergus would have been so happy for her. She felt a touch of sadness with that thought but held her smile as Hamlin continued.

'And why shouldn't they? You're the most beautiful and eligible woman in Avaleen.'

'I'm not eligible. I've already got you,' Constance said. She stopped and faced him. 'Don't I?'

'Only if you want a man with no house, no lands and no prospects,' he said, embarrassed.

'When I was a nobody, you wanted me.'

Constance reached out and took his hand, and they continued across the courtyard.

The afternoon sun shone through the tall windows onto the smooth marble floor of the sitting room. A man sat back in a plush chair and gazed through the window, a little boy perched on his lap, playing with a toy wooden boat.

'Grappa?' the boy said, continuing to play.

Kenan Mellek looked down at his grandson. He proved quite intelligent, not yet four years old, but he could converse better than a child twice his age.

'Yes, Jabran?' he said.

'Can I see Papa again?'

The question tugged at Kenan's heart.

'No.'

'Is he still sick?'

'No, he's not sick anymore.'

Jabran stopped playing and turned to Kenan, confusion on his little face. He looked just like his father had at his age. Kenan lifted the boy off his lap to the floor, stood, and held out his hand. Jabran reached up and grasped it without question. He was a good boy.

'Let's walk in the garden,' he said, 'before it gets too hot.'

Kenan's voice was of someone happy and at peace with the world, but inside, he seethed with rage.

Lars had been so full of life. He'd had a shrewd mind for business but had a headstrong attitude and an unhealthy adventurous streak. If Kenan hadn't given his son command of a ship, he would've gone elsewhere to get what he wanted. As such, he had been the youngest captain in Kenan Mellek's large merchant fleet.

Lars had performed better than Kenan ever expected; he couldn't have been prouder of his son. But just as the winter winds began to blow, the *Silver Robin* had docked at Amberfall with Lars racked by fever. He had two badly broken legs and was barely clinging to life. Kenan arranged for the best healers in the Diamond Isles to attend his son, but they couldn't save his legs, both amputated above the knee.

His son hovered between life and death for over a month. He fought the pain and infections, and for a time, it seemed he would recover, that he would see his son grow up and his newborn daughter for the first time. But three days ago, he had contracted yet another fever and died before the sun had risen the following day. Kenan still found it difficult to comprehend that his only son was gone. At least he no longer suffered.

Kenan had questioned every sailor, ship's captain and merchant who did business with Avaleen, discovering that a red-headed man named Greythorpe had ordered the attack on his son. He recognised the name, a rich and influential house in Avaleen. Some sailors had also heard someone being referred to as Highness and Prince.

It wasn't much to go on, but countries had gone to war with less evidence. Kenan was an important man and knew people of power, even more power than he himself or those minor lords across the Dividing Sea.

His son would be avenged.

THE END

Acknowledgements

The Empty Throne was written at the same time as *The Wooden Crown*; therefore, I would be remiss not to thank the same people as I did for my first novel. So, again, I thank my family and friends for their enormous encouragement and support. The biggest thank you goes out to my wife, Linda, without whom I could not have completed this crazy endeavour.

Matthew West, thanks for instilling in me that showing is far superior to telling. My writing is so much better for it.

And of course, a huge shoutout to Gracie, Jess and Lauren, who let me know that my story was actually good enough.

About the Author

Paul grew up in country Western Australia, devouring historical fiction, science fiction and fantasy books and movies from an early age. In adulthood, his love of these genres led him to turn his hand to writing his own science fiction/adventure screenplay. Following that, he wrote a short screenplay about a man coping with the onset of Alzheimer's, a topic close to his heart.

A national writing competition inspired Paul to try something slightly different, writing a single scene for a novel. Encouraged, he kept on writing, and *The Blackwater Chronicles* was born.

Paul lives in Perth with his wife, Linda.

www.ingramcontent.com/pod-product-compliance
Lightning Source LLC
Chambersburg PA
CBHW050555190726
48283CB00007B/2151